A Bride for the King

L.J. Dare

ISBN 978-1-912768-06-6

Published 2018

Published by Black Velvet Seductions Publishing

Dedication

To my Dad, Maurice, who gave me the greatest gift a father can give his daughter - to believe in herself. And to my Mom, Mary Hoefer, who taught me to persevere through life's challenges. Thank you both for your wisdom and encouragement. You are greatly missed.

Chapter One

Barovia -1859

Belle lingered at the rain splashed windows, her arms hugging her churning stomach. Although the summer downpour obscured the view of the quaint seaside village below, she could see the vague reflections in the window pane of the three men striding into the inn's private sitting room behind her. She glanced over her shoulder at her twin, nodded once and returned to peer at their reflections in the glass. She narrowed her fuzzy gaze as her sister walked toward the three British Naval Officers.

"Let me make sure I understand you correctly," Rita said, her mocking tone sending a trickle of trepidation through Belle as her sister addressed the Captain who had accompanied them ashore. "You are telling Her Royal Highness that you're not only abandoning her in a foreign port but you are also leaving her without British protection?"

"Your Ladyship, 'tis not our intention-" the Captain began.

"Are you saying we haven't accurately assessed the situation?" her sister inserted as she swept forward and halted with a swish of her skirts before the officer, her arms held akimbo.

"Excuse me for a moment while I verify something," the Captain said as he turned to confer with the other two men.

"By all means," Rita said giving a dismissive wave then she began to tap the toe of her slipper impatiently on the amber varnished wooden floor.

Belle noted her own tight smile reflected in the glass. Leave it to Rita to dive right into the crux of their problem. She sobered, afraid that her unguarded expression might be seen and reveal their ruse. Leaning forward, she studied the images of the three men whispering fiercely in the room behind her. She frowned. Granted, the men had escorted them from the ship, through the churning Ionian Sea to the quay and then up through the narrow, winding cobblestoned streets in an antiquated coach pulled by four mismatched nags to the Black Swan Inn. But really, Admiral Birkhead had assured her that his men would remain with them until their brother and King Stefan arrived. Obviously, that wasn't the case now and the plan had changed.

"Your Ladyship," Captain Waverly, wheezed, "'tis not so much that we're deserting you, 'tis..."

Belle took a deep breath. Time for her to go to work. Lifting the train of her bottle-green velvet riding habit, she straightened her spine and turned to survey the room. "Gentlemen," she announced to gain everyone's attention. "We do understand the untenable position you have been placed in," she said choosing her words carefully. "And we do deeply and humbly appreciate your valuable assistance."

"Oh! Thank you, Your Highness," Captain Waverly said, bowing his graying head at her, "for not only your kindness but also your patience and understanding. If King Stefan's troops weren't already stationed around the inn then we would gladly remain until His Royal Highness personally arrives. However, with his troops positioned around the perimeter, our orders from the Admiralty Fleet were to see you settled then return, post haste to our ship. We're to sail with the tide."

Belle nodded and glanced at her mirror image still tapping her foot. One thing for certain, life hadn't been dull growing up with such a mercurial older twin. Belle had never been able to predict what her surly sister would do next. "I am sure His Majesty and our brother will be here soon," she said, pride keeping her from arguing with the senior officer. "Therefore, we will remain sequestered here until they arrive."

"That would be advisable, Your Highness," Captain Waverly nodded and then opened his mouth as if he would like to say more but closed it as if he'd had a sudden change of heart.

Wise man, Belle thought as she glanced at the other two naval officers. Were they as cavalier about deserting them as the Captain? She narrowed her gaze wishing she had been able to wear her spectacles. It appeared that young Mr. Ainsley shuffled his hat from one hand to the other while Mr. Trumble looked everywhere but at them. She nodded. Rita had been right all along. There would be no help from the British Navy or from its officers. They were strictly on their own, abandoned in a foreign country.

Belle straightened. "Thank you, Gentlemen." Raising her chin, she took a resolute breath. Since she had assumed the role of the future

Queen of Barovia for her twin for a few days then she would act like one. "And since your services are no longer available, we bid you adieu."

The naval officers looked at each other then bowed quickly. "Thank you, Your Royal Highness," Captain Waverly said in a rush as he began to back out of the room. "And may we be so bold as to wish you every happiness in your marriage?"

Belle froze at the innocuous reminder then managed to unthaw enough to issue a hasty, "Thank you." She forced her lips to part in a stiff smile as she flicked her hand in dismissal. Quickly, the men removed themselves from her presence. As they shuffled out of the room, she glanced at her sister who had suddenly turned away. Belle frowned as she noted Rita's shaking shoulders. She bit her lower lip, hoping Rita's mirth wouldn't give away their game. She remained in her regal stance until one of the King's guard finally closed the private sitting room door, then she collapsed in the nearest chair. "Oh, my! Rita, how will you ever do this?"

A giggle met her question. "You were rather impressive, Belle," her sister said then swirled, her claret riding skirt belling away from her ankles. "Perhaps you were the one destined to be Queen."

Surprise along with a sense of relief washed over Belle. She'd passed her first test as the soon-to-be-Queen Rita. "Oh, don't talk nonsense," Belle scoffed. "Need I remind you, that being the eldest, you were the one who married King Stefan by proxy this morning aboard ship, and not I?"

"And how do you know that I didn't ... sign that document as Isabelle Marguerita Mary Elizabeth?" her sister asked, archly.

Suddenly, Belle felt lightheaded. Had Rita signed her name? The question had every muscle in her body turning to mush. Thank goodness she was sitting down otherwise she would've ended up in a heap on the floor at the frightening thought. "Rita," she gasped. Gripping the arms of the chair, she started to rise. "You didn't!"

Although a half smile curled the corners of Rita's mouth, her hazel eyes narrowed coldly. Sweeping her hands behind her chignon, she brushed a strand of ginger colored hair from her face. "Now, Belle, don't be tedious. Would I do that to you?"

Belle settled back into the chair. Her sister had played a variety of self-serving games before. She knew it was best if she remained calm. "I hope not but I distinctly recall that you, Marguerita Isabelle Mary

Elizabeth, vowed never to follow another dictate from either our brother or Queen Victoria after we left England. So, what's changed?"

"I didn't realize you were so eager to comply with our brother's arrangement for you to marry that old codger Umberford with his passel of brats once you return to England."

Belle inhaled sharply then decided she wouldn't give Rita the satisfaction of knowing how much the mere mention of Umberford's name made her skin shrivel on her bones. She shook her head and smoothed the material of her riding skirt over her knees. "You know I'm not the least bit happy with Edward's scheme."

"Oh!" Rita exclaimed. "Now, don't get your corset in such a twist. You'll get all flushed about the collar and we'll both be in trouble," she added in a rush. "I was simply being facetious." She pivoted then seemed to hesitate. "That's why I suggested you pose as me so I could have the time to adapt to my role."

Her pleading tone hung suspended for a moment in the silent room.

Finally, Belle nodded. Of course, she understood. Truth to tell, it was bad enough that their brother was forcing her to marry Umberford. But, for Rita to be used as a political pawn to regain their grandfather's lost estates in Barovia was an abomination of the worst order. She turned away gripping her hands in frustration. For her sister to be forced to facilitate their brother's greed and give up the man she loved was intolerable. No one should have to endure that kind of pain, especially not Rita. She had already sacrificed so much. Belle turned, suddenly chilled by her own selfishness for not being more empathetic. After all, she had never been in love like Rita was. "I'm sorry," she said. "I know none of this has been easy for you. Have you heard anything at all from Tony?" she asked, gently.

"Nothing," Rita whispered, her voice cracking. Hurrying across to the fireplace, she braced her forearm against the mantle. "But then I didn't expect to," she said. Pivoting, her twin faced her squarely. "Major Anthony Winston is gone. He accepted a post in India." She straightened, her jaw jutting forward. "When he found out that I was to marry King Stefan of Barovia, he told me that we had to set aside our love and not only obey Edward but our Queen as well."

Rita's words seemed to vibrate throughout the room. Belle hugged herself hoping to ward off the pain her sister's words caused. For one person to have such power over so many was frightening. She paused at the rebellious thought, suddenly realizing that perhaps Rita's championship of America's right to declare their independence from Great Britain had merit. She nodded, re-affirming her agreement with Rita to switch identities until her twin could come to grips with her life-altering situation and accept the fact she was to be the Queen of Barovia.

"And that being the reality," Rita added as she moved toward her, "we'll stick to my plan of you waiting to switch places with me until after I've met King Stefan." She raised her hand, halting Belle's further comments. "And if I decide that I can like him, then we'll return to our own identities and I will marry him in the Barovian Ceremony that has been scheduled three days from now. Agreed?"

"B-but," Belle felt obligated to say. "You agreed to this marriage. There is no way out but for you to become King Stefan's wife."

"Let me remind you that I never agreed to anything."

"Then why did you go along as if accepting it?" Belle asked as a fluttering sensation clenched her stomach. Her sister released a dramatic sigh then swirled with a dramatic flair to face her.

"That's just it," Rita said. "Like you, I've had no say in the matter. Everyone, including you, just assumed my compliance. So," she said, crossing her arms over her chest, "you're as much at fault as Edward. That's why I need your help."

Belle took a deep, pained breath. "I know," she sighed as a wave of guilt washed over her. "And I did promise that," she added. For truth to tell she'd been relieved that Rita had been chosen to be Queen instead of her. That is, until she'd met Umberford. She shivered and rose from the brocade padded chair. "All right," she said as she began to pace. "I promised I would help and I will. When I say I will do something, I do it. No, matter the consequences."

"That's what I love best about you," Rita said, latching onto her wrist. Belle found herself halting as her twin tugged her into a tight embrace. "You are the only one who truly understands me," she said. "Remember when we first switched places at age twelve and you went to Brighton for me?"

Belle nodded, caught in her sister's tight hug. "I was terrified the whole time that either our Aunt Ellie or Her Majesty would discover I was an impostor," she confessed as she returned her sister's hug.

"But that didn't happen, did it?" Rita said as she pulled away. "We are so alike that no one ever notices our differences." Turning, her sister faced the oval mirror above the fireplace. "You act and react exactly like me. We mirror each other. That is why I'm inherently confident that you will always react as I would. So there's nothing to worry about, is there?" she asked as she pivoted.

"I hope I can live up to your expectations," Belle murmured. She moved away to gaze out the balcony windows as a heavy weight settled in her chest. Rita was wrong. In many ways they were the complete opposites. The problem was that Rita had never taken the time to discover those differences.

Peering through the rain-streaked French doors leading onto the balcony, Belle searched the desolate inlet below for the HMS Sea Hawk. The British Man-of-War that had brought them to Barovia. A bleak sense of desperation swept through her as she searched the horizon for a tiny dot, hoping for one last glimpse of the British Man-of-War and a bit of the familiar. Finding nothing, she gulped back her dismay.

Straightening, she took a deep breath, forcing back her rising tide of uneasiness. Now wasn't the time to fall apart. For once again, circumstances demanded that she hold the tattered pieces of both their lives together. She took another deep breath and blinked back the tears welling inside. In a fortnight she and Rita would be separated. She to live in England and Rita to reign as Queen of Barovia. If what she'd learned about Umberford's strict dictates were true, then she and her sister would never see each other again. No matter what their brother had promised, Belle knew this would be their last time together. She had only this one last chance to make things right for her twin. She had to do all she could for Rita. She would have no more chances to correct the mistakes she'd made in the past regarding her sister.

Belle choked back the panic threatening to swamp her as she thought of their uncertain futures apart. She took a slow, steady breath. She knew from past experience that it did no good worrying about tomorrow. She couldn't change the past and the future was too ambiguous to predict. To do that she would need a crystal ball. She gulped at the thought. She'd watched their aunt dabble in the black arts. The arcane had led to nothing but disappointment and heartache for Aunt Ellie.

Slowly, she turned away from the balcony doors. She might as well face the inevitable. She had been abandoned in a foreign country with her sister, their aunt, and two lady's maids dependent upon her. All they had was each other. That being the case it would have to be enough until Edward arrived with King Stefan.

A frantic scratching sounded at the connecting door, followed by a yelp.

"There's Muffy," Rita said. "Aunt Ellie must be up from her nap."

The door swung open and a white ball of fur tumbled into the room followed by their petite blonde-haired aunt. The small dog raced around Aunt Ellie's floor-length mauve skirts, yipping shrilly preventing the middle-aged woman from moving further into the room.

Belle looked on in amusement as Rita scooped the small yelping dog up into her arms. The smile dropped from her lips as Belle realized that their ruse was about to be undone by a ball of fluff, Aunt Ellie's most recent addition to their entourage.

Hastily crossing the room as the dog licked joyously at Rita's face, Belle held out her arms. "Give him to me."

"Oh, Muffy," Aunt Ellie exclaimed. "Imagine that! Now you like her Ladyship just as much as you do her Royal Highness."

Rita arched her eyebrow. "You sure?" she whispered, pausing to deposit the wiggling canine into Belle's waiting arms.

Belle nodded, wishing their aunt hadn't turned so formal in her use of titles. Especially now that they had changed identities. But then her aunt had lived with them for nearly eight years and never seemed to be able to tell the two girls apart. So, surely she would be able to remember who her aunt was addressing?

"Definitely," she nodded then narrowed her gaze on the oversized rat as Rita handed the dog over to her. The dog squirmed then let out a high-pitched howl as Belle fought to hold onto its squirming, wiggling body. Maybe this hadn't been such a good idea after all, she decided.

"Oh, you bad boy," their aunt scolded as she quickly lifted her pet from Belle's arms. "I am so sorry Your Highness," she said. "I do not know what has gotten into Muffy?"

Belle knew exactly what was wrong with the dog but instead chose to say. "Oh, don't worry, I've heard that all males are fickle." She smiled to soften her words.

"Not just males," Rita said, her tone hard. "I've also known a few females that fit into that category."

"True," Belle acknowledged as she waved her hand for Rita to ring for tea.

"My Muffy has always been so good." Aunt Ellie's voice trembled as she looked soulfully up at Belle. "I just don't know what has gotten into him."

Belle laid her arm across their aunt's shoulders and directed her toward the armchair positioned near the fireplace. "Don't fret, my dear. Tea will be here soon."

"But, Muffy..."

"Is fine," Belle inserted. "Like humans, some animals don't travel well. It was a rough crossing for us all."

"Oh my, yes and especially for you, Your Highness," Aunt Ellie said. "I am so glad to see you have regained the bloom in your cheeks."

Surreptitiously, Belle glanced at Rita who still looked a bit pale.

"I'm told that the idea of marriage does that to one," Rita quipped as she crossed to the fireplace. "Aunt Ellie, allow me to take Muffy for you. He'll be better off with one of the maids while we have our tea."

"Good idea," Belle said as the sitting room door opened and Agatha, her lady's maid, wheeled in the tea tray. "Let's all sit and have a relaxing cup while we wait," she invited.

"Right, might as well make ourselves comfortable," Rita agreed with an awry twist to her lips. "Who knows how long we'll be forced to kick up our heels here," she added as she handed the dog over to the maid.

Without a thought, Belle crossed to the tea trolley and selected a teacup. "Aunt Ellie, would you-"

"Oh, no, Your Highness," Aunt Ellie popped up out of her chair as if she'd sat on a hot coal. Adjusting her pink-fringed paisley shawl, she hurried across the room. "Please, Your Highness, allow me to do the honor," she said, hastily snatching the cup from Belle's fingers before she could object.

Sphynx-like, Belle stared at the petite woman for a moment. Then she glanced over at her twin, her heart hammering in her chest. Had she unknowingly given away their game?

Rita's small shrug indicated that she had no answer and that only time would tell.

"Very well," Belle muttered as she allowed Aunt Ellie to proceed. Resuming her seat, she watched their aunt turn and set the cup on a saucer. "I really wish we could drop the 'Your Highness' bit though," she added.

"Oh, no, Your Highness," Aunt Ellie said as she glanced over her bony shoulder then turned back to pour the tea. Belle noted a blush stained her aunt's porcelain face as she crossed the room. "I couldn't possibly agree to that," she said, offering her the cup filled with Oolong tea. "You must become comfortable with hearing your new title."

"I suppose you are correct," Belle sighed then added, "Thank you," as she accepted the fragrant brew. When she took a sip, a tingling sensation floated across her tongue. Gracious! That wasn't Oolong. She frowned as she swallowed then noticed that their aunt had returned to the tea cart. What new brand had Aunt Ellie forced them into trying this time?

"Would you like a cup?" Aunt Ellie asked, twisting the black band of her cuff back into place before raising an empty cup and waving it at Rita.

"With or without what you just slipped into her Highness' cup?" Rita asked.

Belle choked as she went to swallow another sip. Her eyes began to water.

"Oh, dear!" their aunt squeaked. "You weren't supposed to see that."

Finally getting the tea down, Belle wiped at the tears streaming down her face and then managed to gasp. "See what?"

She heard Rita's cold chuckle. "I suspect you are drinking one of Aunt Ellie's offensive potions," her twin said. "But, by now we both realize that while they may taste awful," she shrugged. "They are innocuous."

"O-oh!" Aunt Ellie exclaimed then her shoulders drooped. "I know that I ought to be offended by your words but ... you've only stated the truth. I am a complete failure when it comes to casting spells." She signed, a doleful expression sweeping across her countenance.

"Um-m," Belle said clearing her throat. "So, what exactly did you put in this?" she asked as a tingling spread down her throat and into her chest. She coughed then managed to gasp out. "Should I be worried?"

"Oh dear! Do you feel ill, Your Highness?" Aunt Ellie asked. A deep frown drew her thinning brows together as she began twisting her lace hankie this way and that.

Belle shook her head, her eyes beginning to water again. "Not necessarily... ill, just...strange."

"Oh!" Aunt Ellie gasped. A delightful giggle erupting as a grin spread across her wrinkle-free face. She clapped her hands. "Imagine that! It's working! It's really working."

Belle coughed again then pinched her throat to prevent the sneeze tickling the back of her nose from spewing forth.

"What makes you say that?" Rita asked as she handed Belle a lace hanky.

"I have been practicing," Aunt Ellie said, proudly, her thin lips stretching into a wide smile.

"But, what exactly did you put in my tea?" Belle asked again as she mopped at her streaming eyes.

Aunt Ellie dipped her silver-streaked blonde head, then fingered the coral brooch she wore pinned at the neck of her dress for a moment. "A-a few of my very special herbs," she said, shyly.

"From our herb garden?" Belle asked, trying to decide if she should be alarmed by the strange aftertaste.

"That ... and a few other things I found," Aunt Ellie said, nodding vigorously. The movement caused the braids coiled at the back of her head to sway precariously.

"Like eye of toad?" Belle mumbled.

"Oh no, my dear," Aunt Ellie trilled, shaking her head briskly. "Love potions never use toads, or frogs, or lizards, especially not when dealing with royalty, Your Highness."

"A l-love potion?" Belle stammered. "Why on earth do you think I need one of those?"

"Well," Aunt Ellie seemed to hesitate then peered up at her as she extracted two pins from her hair and tucked them back into her coil. "Because I wasn't sure that the spell I put on your brooch would work. I thought... I had better mix you a special potion as well."

"Oh-h-h," Belle sighed, swallowing back the lump that had suddenly formed in her throat. "And the reason you felt it necessary to go to such lengths was–"

"Your Highness," Aunt Ellie said, leaning towards Belle and grasping her hand. "For the past eight years you and your sister have been the light of my life. I want only the very best for you. I want you...to be...happy."

Tears welled up in Belle. "And you think one of your potions will do the trick?" she asked, softly, wanting to remember this overwhelming moment of love pouring out to her for the rest of her life. Knowing that someone wanted the very best for her would have to be enough to sustain her through the dark years she served as Umberford's wife.

"Oh, yes, Your Highness, I know it will."

Belle flipped her hand to clasped Aunt Ellie's in her own. She knew the dear lady had loved and still mourned her husband. "And you really believe that love is necessary in a Marriage of State?"

"Oh, my dear child," Aunt Ellie said, softly. "Not only is it necessary but it is essential if the marriage is to succeed."

Belle peered into the kind blue eyes, so wise in courtly protocol yet naïve in so many of the ways of the world. "And you think your potion will help me attain happiness?" she asked as she remembered the blackened kitchen walls she'd help scrub down more times than not after one of Aunt Ellie's potions had gone awry.

"Oh, yes, Your Highness, it is my fondest wish for you."

Belle hated to disappoint the woman who had been a loving surrogate mother to them. She lifted her cup from where she had set it on the small table beside her. She stared into the cup for a moment then swirled the contents. Raising it to her lips, she tipped it and swallowed the remaining contents in one gulp. Gently, placing the bone china cup back on its saucer, she bravely met her aunt's expectant gaze. "Then may all your wishes come true."

The poignant moment was lost when Rita hurriedly clapped her hands. "Brava, Your Highness, brava!"

Belle wrinkled her brow and eyed her sister warily. She only hoped her bravado hadn't landed her in more trouble than what she was in already.

***

Prince Nikolai Orsini Garaini, otherwise known as 'Niko', slapped his black leather riding gloves against his gray breeches then frowned. Blast! The situation wasn't good by any stretch of the imagination. Although his men had secured the perimeter of the Black Swan Inn, the life of their future Queen was in jeopardy. "And you say the rebels have cut off all access by road into the village?"

"Yes, Your Highness," Colonel Cyrek Domokos handed him the spyglass and pointed to the main road leading into Saranda. "There is a main force waiting by the bridge down there."

"How many?" Niko asked as he swung the scope and adjusted the knob to focus on the road running east from the village of Saranda to the town of Suri Kalter over the mountains.

"About three dozen."

"Have they pitched tents?" Niko asked as he turned the glass to the south.

"No," Cyrek assured him. "Evidently they don't think they're going to be there that long."

"Good," Niko said knowing if his enemy was entrenched it would be more difficult to roust them out. "And the south road?"

"It's guarded by a small force," Cyrek replied.

"So, we're up against a contingency of about fifty-four rebels?" he asked then wondered if the rebels were there simply to attack another village or if they had been informed that their future Queen had come ashore. If that was the case, then their presence meant that they were there to harm the Lady with the aim of striking a crippling blow to the country.

"Could be more," Cyrek said, slowly.

Niko heard the caution threaded through his friend's words. "And the village itself?" he asked, pivoting in that direction, knowing stealth had always been the best option when creating a plan.

"We're not sure, Your Highness," Cyrek said. "The villagers are believed to be loyal to the Crown. However, there could be rebels planted in every house or none at all."

Niko nodded. In these uncertain times, his first priority was to keep Her Ladyship safe and to effectively extract her from harm's way. "Has there been any unusual movement seen inside the village?"

"Nothing out of the ordinary," Cyrek said. "As you ordered, our men have filtered into the village over the past two days. Some dressed as fishermen, others as itinerant peasants and a few appear as tradesmen. They are positioned both inside the inn and stationed around it."

"Good," he said then frowned. If there had been any way he could've delayed the Lady's arrival until after he'd found out with certainty that someone was supplying information to the rebels then he would've. But Stefan needed this marriage pronto to stabilize their country. "And the Lady?"

"She and her entourage arrived minutes ago while you were making your way up here."

Niko nodded then hesitated. "How large a group?"

"Nearest I can tell," Cyrek said, "there's a middle-aged chaperone, two lady's maids, and another female."

"Likely her personal secretary," Niko guessed, pleased she had kept the number of attendants to the maximum his cousin had requested.

But that by no means solved his problem of how to extract her from a village surrounded by rebels. Slowly, he began to pace the small ridge above the main road as he considered the solution. Halting, he waved his officers waiting for instructions over as he bent and drew a squiggly line in the dirt. "While I had planned on bringing her Ladyship into the Bay of Vlore," he said, pointing to the make-shift position. "With the storm and the Austrian-Hungarian blockade in the Strait of Otranto, I had no other choice but to move our rendezvous point to Saranda since it's the only port deep enough to handle a British Man of War." He drew a circle. "Now, we have the task of removing Cousin Stefan's bride from the threat of the Yugoslavian rebels blocking all our exits from the town." He straightened and stared at his friend. "Stefan hasn't been King long enough to gain the full backing of all of our countrymen. If the rebels can stop Stefan's marriage, our very existence is in jeopardy."

Cyrek nodded. "Because without this marriage, we have no link to Queen Victoria and England's might. And without that military power behind us-"

"Greece, Yugoslavia, and Austria-Hungary will invade, claim our land as their own and we will become a bloody battlefield caught between the three countries," Niko said. "Our defenses cannot withstand the collective invasion of all three nations at once," he admitted then took a deep breath. "Therefore to prevent that, here's my plan." Hastily, he began drawing in the dirt. "We'll leave you, Major Kelso and your rifle troop here to pin down the rebels at the bridge," he said pointing at the position he'd drawn. "Captain Bjorni, we will send you and a squad of your men to the south to hunt down the rebels along the road," he said moving his index finger over to that position. "Major Hondros, you are to maintain your orders to fire at will upon anyone threatening the safety of her Ladyship." He swept his gaze over his cadre of officers. "As for me, I'll circle around to the village of Vorshi. Procure Stefan's yacht and sail back here. Since we've masked the ship's markings and it appears as an ordinary fishing vessel, we'll anchor off the promontory. A skiff will bring me ashore. I'll then make my way up through the village and proceed on to the inn."

"And at the inn?" Cyrek asked as his bushy eyebrows drew together.

"I'll convince her Ladyship that she must accompany me out by boat," he said then straightened. "Any questions?" he asked as he swept his gaze over his men.

With a shake of their heads, they responded, "No, Sir."

Niko nodded then continued. "Once you have quietly rounded up the rebels, you and Major Hondros will escort Her Ladyship's entourage to Ksamilli. The following morning, you will proceed to Berat where we'll meet you outside the city in the field across from the public market."

"Yes, Your Highness," Cyrek snapped him a salute. "Rest assured the men guarding our future Queen will protect her with their very lives."

"I know," he said, returning the salute. The men in his command were seasoned veterans who had served together, like he and Cyrek had, for over ten years. With men like these, what inevitably went wrong was halted before it became a problem.

Chapter Two

Belle frowned as she took a deep breath of fresh night air wafting through the partially opened balcony door. The rain had stopped a short time ago but still there was no sign of either King Stefan or their brother. She worried her bottom lip. Had the men been unavoidably detained by weather? Or had the King had a change of heart?

A ray of hope filled Belle for a moment then dimmed as wisps of uncertainty surged through her once again. If the King had changed his mind then would Rita be free to follow her heart and marry Tony? But how would Edward handle that setback in his quest to regain the family's inheritance?

The thought of their brother brought a renewed wave of trembling, the like of which had seized Belle earlier in the day when she'd first agreed to impersonate her sister. If Edward discovered they'd switched places, Belle knew she would be promptly shipped back to England and hastily married to Umberford, something she definitely didn't want. She grasped the doorframe, realizing that now wasn't the time to go all weak in the knees with suppositions. She had to remain strong… to bravely forge ahead and see things through for her twin. She owed Rita too much to do anything else.

Her sister's strong gardenia scent closed around her and Belle turned to note her twin wore a light blue lace peignoir as she entered the sitting room and went to bank the fire.

"You coming to bed soon?" Rita asked as she replaced the fire screen and turned to face her.

"I'm really not that tired," Belle replied, managing to conceal her yawn as she dipped her head and waved a hand at the open book of Aristotle's Greek Philosophy setting atop a table beside where she sat. She'd abandoned the book earlier because she'd been too worried about their brother's nonappearance at the inn. She stared at the table where her reading glasses lay atop her book. Then she rubbed the bridge of her nose as she decided to remain silent with her concerns about their brother's continued absence. Rita had enough to worry about becoming Queen. She didn't need her misgivings added to the mix. "I plan on reading for a while yet," she said lifting her chin.

"Surely, you're not still having those old nightmares are you?" Rita asked as she wiped her hands on a cleaning cloth and tucked it out of sight on the mantle.

Belle shook her head, not about to tell her sister the truth about something she should've outgrown long ago. Lifting her spectacles, she placed them on her nose. Then opened the book to her marked place, she gathered it up in her hands. "Piffle," she forced herself to say. "Haven't had one of those in years."

"Really?" Rita asked crossing toward her and rapping her knuckles on the spine of the book. "If I was reading that drivel, I would've been asleep long ago."

Belle felt her lips curve upwards. "Obviously, you hold a vast disdain for my choice in reading material," she said as she waved it teasingly under her sister's nose. "Therefore, I won't bother to offer you anything to read."

"What an ungrateful wretch you are!" Rita said as she placed the back of her hand dramatically against her forehead. "Oh, and that's all the thanks I get for everything I've done for you?"

Belle laughed enjoying Rita's playful mood. "All right, I won't be such an ingrate," she said then smiled as she held her hands up as if in surrender. "I relent. You may borrow my copy of Culpepper's Complete Herbal."

"Ooh, goody!" Rita said clapping her hands, "your kindness overwhelms me." Belle watched as a sly smile danced across her twin's face. "But thanks, I'll pass on that. However, if you were to offer me a Minerva novel then I would gladly stay up all night and read."

Belle chuckled at her twin's teasing remark. For unlike her, Rita had never been ridiculed for being a bluestocking. Her sister had too much zest for living to ever be considered serious-minded. Belle sighed, wishing she could be more spontaneous like her sister. "How well I remember those nights," she said as a sudden breathlessness forced her to turn back to the balcony. They had been so carefree those days before their parents....

"If you're worried about meeting the King, then don't be," Rita said, quietly.

The potency of Rita's scent and the swish of her night robe gliding across the floor forced Belle into opening her eyes. She studied Rita's reflection in the glass pane.

"We'll wear our matching blue habits tomorrow," Rita said as she stopped beside her. "If I like him, I won't have my sneezing fit. You can pass the brooch to me and I'll put it in my pocket. When he asks about it, I'll put it on. Then things will be as Edward and Queen Victoria have decreed."

Belle touched the diamond and sapphire brooch pinned on her spencer. King Stefan had sent it to Rita as an engagement gift. "But, what if... you don't... like him? What then?"

"I'll need a day or two more to resign myself to the idea of marrying him... again. This time with all the pomp and spectacle necessary in a royal wedding," Rita said. "The extra time will allow me to settle into that mindset and then things will go back to normal."

Belle nodded, uncomfortable with the idea they would be cutting it extremely close in switching back. She was forced to admit that she seriously doubted things would ever be normal for either one of them again. Taking a deep breath, she pasted a smile on her lips and moved toward the fireplace. "So, you really do intend on switching back and marrying the King?"

"Of course I do," Rita gave a small laugh as if that settled everything. "I just need a day or two to get into my role."

Belle exhaled a whoosh of air and straightened. "Then it's off to bed for you. After all, we can't have our future Queen looking all pale and sickly when she meets her new husband for the first time." Looping her arm through Rita's, she walked her toward the bedchamber door.

"That reminder is bound to keep me tossing all night," Rita mumbled, slipping her arm free. "Maybe, I should snatch that book from you after all."

"Don't you dare," Belle chuckled as she opened the bedchamber door. "I'm not about to share my most cherished tome with you, even if you promise me the moon." She leaned toward Rita. "Besides, how else am I to ever fall asleep myself without my book?"

"You do know what they say about plans?" Rita said, her tone silky as she swept into the dimly lit bed chamber.

Belle frowned as a frisson of uncertainty slid through her. "You mean, that they often go astray?"

"Always, sweet sister," Rita chuckled as she turned to face her. "You can count on it."

Belle felt her breath hitch in her throat. Then with a shake of her head, she gave Rita a quick hug. "Night," she called softly before closing the door, surprised that for once she'd gotten the last word with her twin.

She smiled then sobered as she made her way back toward the chair positioned near the fireplace. A tightness squeezed her chest. She would miss Rita when she returned to England. But leave she must. Edward had arranged for her to marry his good friend, the Duke of Umberford. She was to be a mother to his five children. Although she felt ill-equipped to take on that role, did she really have any other choice? After all, family had always come first for her. Especially after she had been the cause of their parents' deaths.

A heaviness settled in her chest as she stared into the dying flames. No matter what she did, she knew it would never be enough to counteract the part she'd played in their deaths. Fearing the black hole threatening to engulf her at the thought of her selfishness, she hurried toward the balcony. Slipping through the doors, she crossed to the railing and gripped it. Then tilting her head back, she accepted the fact that while she might not be able to change the past, she could learn from it.

She gazed at the star-filled sky, studying the outline of the quarter moon. Taking a deep breath, she inhaled the fresh air mingled with a hint of wisteria and citrus. Somehow, somewhere she needed to reconcile with the past and make peace with her soul. She sighed at the improbability of that as she peered into the vast heavens. Then she noted the rain had stopped. The moisture had nourished the parched earth. And she realized an expectant sense of waiting filled her as she brushed her hand along the balcony's wet rail. Lifting her wet hand, she curled it into a tight fist. There were so many things she regretted in her life. Things she had failed to do, things she yet wanted to accomplish.

She closed her eyes as she thought of the list of wishes she'd written as a twelve-year-old. She'd read that list every night for the past seven years, knowing if she could only stand firm then she would find a way to make it up to her siblings for her failures. That is, she had until she and Rita had been summoned to Windsor this past Eastertide. She clenched her jaw as she recalled the audience with the Queen. After their royal appearance, all of her dreams had vanished like smoke. She had come to understand that she wasn't the master of her own fate. In fact, she realized she had never been a master but merely her brother's puppet.

She hardened her jaw at the thought. She hadn't asked for anything outlandish in her life. Why couldn't she travel to the places she'd read about? Or meet and marry a man she'd fallen in love with? Or have the opportunity to fulfill the burning need pulsing inside her to help those in need?

Opening her eyes, Belle swiped at the lone tear trickling down her cheek. She stared down at her tightly balled fists resting on the rail. She wanted to tilt back her head and howl out her frustrations at the quarter-moon but knew she wouldn't. For she was sure to wake everyone. And then she would have to explain her actions. Taking a steadying breath, she began counting the wet stones glistening in the moonlight in the street below, hoping to regain her composure. She balled her fists, not about to give further credence to her self-pity. She would find a way to fulfill her dreams she vowed. Scanning the lane leading into the village, she lifted her gaze to study the small hamlet.

The double-storied structures cast their long dark shadows over the rain-slick cobblestones below. A movement caught her attention. Narrowing her gaze, she rubbed the bridge of her nose, wishing she had kept her glasses on so she could observe the furtive black shape slipping from doorway to doorway in the village below. She frowned then shrugged as the figure edged up the hill toward the inn. She wondered about the furtive figure's purpose. Perhaps he was an example of what Aunt Ellie termed a 'bumblebee'. A man who flitted from woman to woman gathering nectar but never permanently settling down with any one woman. When she had been younger she had thought it was the woman's fault a man acted like that but lately she'd changed her mind as gossip had reached her about her own brother's amorous reputation.

Belle frowned as the dark figure disappeared from sight, the shadows seeming to swallow him whole. She waited for a few more moments but when nothing stirred, she backed into the sitting room and closed the balcony doors.

Moving to the fireplace, she glanced back at the door then sighed. Whatever the man was up to, it was no concern of hers. Unlike a woman, a man had the right to be out and about at any time of the day or night, doing whatever he wanted. She took a quick breath and sighed. She wondered what it must feel like to have that kind of freedom.

***

Niko pulled his hat over his ears. Settling into the doorway of the stables below the Black Swan Inn, he waited for Cyrek to join him. All he had to do was cross the courtyard, scale the wall to the balcony where his cousin's bride-to-be had conveniently left a light on in the sitting room. Then he had to convince her the threat she faced was deadly. And that she needed to leave with him in the dead of night, board the royal yacht and sail up the coast and disembark in the secured area. Realizing the probability of her cooperation ran slim to none, he took a deep breath. Although he hated subterfuge, not only her life and that of her entourage but also the lives of his men depended upon secrecy. Therefore, though he might want to stride up to the door of the inn, demand entrance, and state that he had come to rescue his cousin's bride, he knew he had to suppress that straightforward inclination and stick to the furtive plan.

He glanced at the garments he'd worn while in the field with his men. Along with his cape, his serviceable plain trousers tucked into his Hessians showed the mud spots he'd brushed away. And somewhere in his travels today he'd lost the button that closed the high standing collar of his coat. To him, there was nothing about his scruffy attire that made him appear the least bit 'princely'. But others might not agree with him he realized as he studied the muted embroidered insignia sewn on the cuff of his coat.

"Having second thoughts about that coat?" Cyrek asked as he joined him in the doorway. "If so, we can exchange garments. Though small, that Royal emblem sewn on your cuff could cause a problem. My clothing will draw less attention."

Niko nodded, knowing his second in command was right. The dangers he faced while getting her ladyship to Berat then safely slipping her into the palace would be enough of a challenge. He needed to pay extra attention to details in order to conceal their identities. "To ensure we travel incognito," he said quietly. "Let's do this."

"More than that, consider your own safety, Your Highness," Cyrek whispered. "Appearing as an ordinary citizen will not only grant you anonymity but safety as well."

Niko paused for a moment then smiled wryly as he removed his cape. "You mean, I'm also to forget shaving and add a bit of grime as we travel?"

"It's a suggestion. It would keep you both safe from the rebels who want to prevent the royal marriage," Cyrek said, slowly pulling off his cape.

Niko nodded. "Your idea has merit. However, how do you think

Her Ladyship will feel when she discovers I've lied to her about who I am?" he asked as he began to unbutton his coat. "I had hoped I might be friends with my cousin's wife."

"Introduce yourself as Colonel Orsini," Cyrek said. "Tell her that you've been sent to see to her safety, which in fact is what you've been sent to do. Just don't mention your connection to the King. If she doesn't know who you are, then she can't reveal your identity."

"Good point," Niko said shrugging out of his coat, "but will the half-truth be plausible enough for her to accompany me without arousing her suspicion?"

"I don't see why not," Cyrek replied removing his short coat. "You are in fact, Colonel Nikolai Orsini. You did earn your rank defending the country." He held out his plain coat and cape. "Besides, it's been my experience that people seldom question what is presented to them as fact."

Niko nodded. "You might be right," he said as they exchanged garments. "If I'm to be the Colonel then you, my friend, are now the Prince, Supreme Military Commander of Barovian Forces," he said as he began to thread his arms through the borrowed coat sleeves. "Our country's defense now rests in your capable hands."

Cyrek bowed then straightened. "I'll defend the Crown with my very life," he pledged, his hand over his heart.

"I know and I commend you for the noble service you are about to render," Niko said as he donned Cyrek's cape and gave him a mock bow. He grinned as Cyrek returned the gesture.

"I'll see you in two days," Cyrek said. "And if you're not at our rendezvous point, I'll come looking for you."

"I would expect nothing less," Niko said then darted across the open courtyard to the walled area behind the inn. As friends, their motto had always been, 'Leave none behind'.

Scaling the wall, he moved along the ledge at the top until he reached the wisteria covered trellis. Climbing to the second floor, he swung his leg over the balcony and hoisted himself over. Straightening, he peered through the glass pane at the profile of the woman sitting in an armchair before the fire. Although the winged chair blocked most of his view, he noticed that graceful long fingers held a heavy book. He frowned. Was his future Queen a bluestocking? Then he felt his mouth twitch into a grin. Stefan would have his hands full with a learned woman who liked to do more than sew samplers.

He swept his eyes past her ivory complexion enhanced by high cheekbones. The hints of auburn threaded through her chestnut colored hair that was bound in a chignon caught his gaze. Personally, he preferred women with long flowing raven locks, but then he knew the Council wasn't as discriminating. He stared at the woman then paused. Red hair usually denoted a fiery nature and although he liked a woman with grit, he couldn't abide a bossy, opinionated one. So, what exactly would his future Queen be like? Would she blow hot because of her hair color ... or cold because of her position?

She must've felt his perusal because she turned and placed her spectacles on the small table positioned by the chair. Then she glanced toward the balcony. Her mouth popped open as she spied him through the glass. Her book slid to the floor as she sprang from the chair and backed toward the banked fireplace.

Mobilized into action, Niko flung the door open and strolled into the room as the beauty grabbed an andiron from the fireplace and waved it at him.

"You'll be extremely sorry if you come any closer," the fragile beauty said in a high-pitched voice.

Quickly, Niko swept her a regal bow and straightened. "My Lady, I had no intention of frightening you," he said then flashed her a smile. "Colonel Niko Orsini at your service," he added as he clicked his heels together and bowed again.

"C-Colonel," she stammered her voice but a whisper. "W-what brings you to my chamber at this time of night?"

Her free hand grasped the brooch she wore at her neck. The same brooch he knew his cousin had sent her. Then her hand dropped to join the one she'd wrapped around her make-shift club. Keeping a sizeable distance between him and her weapon, he nearly laughed aloud at her bravado. Although petite, she was made of sterner stuff than he'd imagined. "His Majesty sent me to rescue you from the rebel forces camped outside the village," he said. "If we hurry, we can be away before they realize we've fled."

"R-rebels?" she gasped, her full lips revealing even white teeth.

"That's right," he began then paused as he noticed her high cheekbones had suddenly paled. "Surely you knew?"

"N-not about rebels," she whispered.

"Then pray be seated," he invited gesturing toward the brocade chair in front of the fireplace. Even though he knew they didn't have a lot of time, if his explanation convinced her that it was safe to go with him, then the time wouldn't be wasted. "I will be brief, Your Ladyship," he said then paused as he watched her shiver. "Would you like for me to restart the fire?" he asked although he hoped that she would refuse.

"No," she squeaked. She shook her head then propped the andiron against the side of her chair. "That won't be necessary." She waved her petite hand as if inviting him to proceed. "Just tell me about the rebels."

"As you wish," he bowed in acceptance, grateful to see she'd not only regained some of the color in her petal soft cheeks but had set aside her weapon. He took a few steps away then pivoted. There was no easy way to start so he figured he might as well jump right in. He took a bracing breath. "As you have probably surmised, the rebels are being held off by the King's troops surrounding the inn." He paused…at least he hoped she realized that fact.

"But I haven't heard a single shot fired," she said, her brow delicately furrowed in apparent disbelief.

"That's because they haven't attacked us yet," he replied, quickly.

"What are they waiting for?"

Pleased that she grasped the peril of their situation, Niko squared his shoulders. "We believe that they either do not know you have arrived or they're waiting to trap you here with His Highness."

"You think they're here because of me?" she gasped, her hazel eyes almost too large for her delicate face.

Niko hesitated not sure telling her the full extent of the situation was wise but then he shrugged. She deserved to know the whole truth. Or at least as much of the truth as he was willing to give, came the unbidden thought. He gave an imperceptible nod. "They're here to stop your marriage. If they can do that, the chances are Barovia will lose the support of the British Government and King Stefan will be deposed."

"Is this country so fragile that it depends upon me to prop it up?" she asked with a frown.

"It's not necessarily… fragile," he hedged. "I would say we're more in a state of… transition."

"Why?" She asked, shaking her head. "Why transition?"

He stared at the petite woman in front of him, amazed that he was having such a political discussion with her. Most women he knew would've fainted at the very thought of being surrounded by rebels but instead, this one sat challenging him for answers. "The rebels maintain that King Otto of Greece is the rightful Sovereign of Barovia but Austria-Hungary claims Emperor Francis Joseph is Supreme Ruler. Yugoslavia declares King Obrenovic is the King here. While the Church of Rome, the Elder Council, and the late King himself all proclaimed Prince Stefan Garaini is the rightful King," he said.

"What do the people say?" she asked as he watched her thick lashes sweep down across her high cheekbones.

Niko took a deep breath. "Most support King Stefan but-"

"Those who do not, have become rebels," she finished for him.

"Not all," he hedged, "some haven't made up their minds yet."

"And these rebels have guns," she mused.

"And dynamite," he added.

She nodded. "And they want me gone."

"They do want you gone," he agreed.

"Okay," she said rising and beginning to pace in front of the fireplace. "If I accompany you, what happens to my people left behind here at the inn?" She halted in mid-stride and swung around to face him. "I won't abandon them to danger," she paused, straightening her regal shoulders, "just because you think I need to decamp for my safety."

"Your Ladyship," he bowed, "surely you do not believe that King Stefan would desert anyone in such danger? Especially not, when he is rounding up all the rebels at dawn," he added.

"Oh!" she whispered. She glanced at the floor then raised her eyes to his. Her hazel eyes reminded him of a trusting doe. "Although I have never met His Highness, I would hope that he would always protect those in his care."

"That he does," Niko assured her, "with his very life."

"Good," she nodded, seemingly satisfied with his explanation of the situation. "But if he's coming at dawn, why must I go with you?"

"He wants you safely away from the action," Niko replied.

"I don't like splitting away from my entourage," she said again. "Are you sure my people will be safe?"

"Most assuredly," he replied.

"What does King Stefan wish for me to do?"

Niko paused, surprised by her willingness to comply. Maybe the Elderly Council had known a thing or two when they had selected her to be their Queen. "The King wishes you to accompany me to the quay, where we'll board his royal yacht, and sail along the coast to Vorshi where we will rejoin him and your entourage tomorrow evening."

"And you think embarking tonight will be of benefit?" she asked, her slender white neck bowed.

"Most certainly," he nodded.

"I see." Straightening, she clasped her white-knuckled hands in front of her. "And if I do this, will it save my retainers from traveling over the rough sea?"

"Most assuredly," he nodded. "They will travel by coach in the lap of luxury to our rendezvous point."

She nodded and turned to him. "How do I know you are really the King's man?"

"Open the door and ask your guards to step into the room," he said.

She crossed to the door. As she opened it the two Royal Guards snapped to attention. "Gentlemen," she said as they turned to her. "Do you know if this man is truly Colonel Nikolai Orsini?"

"Yes, ma'am," they said in unison without a moment's hesitation.

"And if he wants me to leave with him do you think those are the King's orders?"

"Yes, ma'am," they replied together.

"As you were," she said, "and thank you," she added before she closed the door. Turning back, she raised her chin. "Then I will accompany you." Stepping to the side, she moved toward the bedchamber door. "Now, if you will excuse me, I'll prepare a valise."

Niko placed a firm hand on her arm, knowing he couldn't permit her to delay any longer. "Your Ladyship," he said then realized his mistake in touching her when he felt her quiver beneath his palm. Promptly, he withdrew his hand. "My Lady," he said, his voice dropping to a hoarse whisper as he stepped away from her. He swallowed back his surprise at the unexpected jolt of heat he'd felt when he'd touched her. "I beg your forgiveness but we have no time for you to pack anything. If we're to sail by midnight we must leave immediately. All you'll need will be provided for you aboard the royal yacht."

"I see," she said slowly then turned her face away. "Then I do suppose there is no further reason for the delay."

"None," he said breathing a sigh of relief as he clicked his heels together one more time.

Lifting the train of her riding habit, Niko watched her place her hat on her head, tuck her gloves into her skirt pocket and loop the thin gauze trailing veil around her wrist. Crossing to the balcony, he watched her step to the rail, hoist her leg over, turn and lower herself over the railing. Suddenly, she disappeared from sight. He blinked in surprise. The last thing he'd seen was the gamin smile spread across her luscious lips, the animation of her character enchanting him.

About to call out 'a lady always exits through a door', Niko resisted the impulse and hurried to the balcony. He grinned as he climbed down the trellis and caught up with her as she began crossing the flat, narrow strip at the top of the wall. Amazement filled him as he realized his future Queen had a strength at odds with the slenderness of her body. A strength that didn't in anyway lessen her femininity.

He grinned then called softly as he observed her approaching the drop-down point. "Please wait," he called then observed her hesitation. The moon bathed her delicate features in a soft glow. One finely arched brow hovered in question as she peered at him from over her shoulder.

Leaping to the cobblestone path below, he reached up and slipped his hands around her trim waist. "Now, Your Ladyship," he said, lifting her from the wall in a smooth, downward motion. Her soft curves seemed to mold to the contours of his body as he lowered her down his torso. Surprise coursed through him as his eyes came level with hers and he realized how much his future Queen had charmed him.

Belle swallowed down the tight knot stuck in her throat as she noted her trembling limbs seemed to cling to the Colonel's muscular frame, her body tingling from the contact. "You may put me down now," she managed undecided if her reaction to him was the result of being unexpectedly lifted from the wall and then being held close to his masculine body or if extreme fatigue had set in and scrambled her wits. She took a shallow breath, her heart hammering foolishly. "I-I hope I'm not too heavy for you," she said, playfully peeking up at him through her lashes like she'd seen her sister, Rita do when she'd been flirting with Tony.

"Never," he said, softly as his mint-scented breath swept across her heated cheeks. Her pulse kicked up a notch as she traced the line of his smiling lips with her eyes. Taking a deep breath she closed her eyes as she inhaled the tantalizing essence of his masculine scent filtering through his citrus cologne.

Her eyes sprang open at the realization. A chill ran down her spine and she came back to reality as she was set on her feet. She gasped. What was she thinking? She was supposed to be the future Queen of his country. Rita was a promised woman. No matter what she might personally feel, she couldn't act on the instant attraction she'd felt for the Colonel. She had to put others' needs before her own. "Um-m," she said, clearing her throat as she felt heat burn her cheeks. "Thank you, Colonel, but you can release me now."

Belle watched as his lips curled as if he was on the edge of laughter. Then he seemed to hesitate. "My pleasure, Your Ladyship," he murmured, finally withdrawing his hands from her waist.

"Thank you for your assistance," she muttered forcing herself to move away from the rugged, vital power of the man. Regal-like, she tugged down her spencer to hide her trembling fingers in her riding skirt. If she didn't get a grip on herself, she would likely give away Rita's game. The thought caused her to stand ramrod straight. She tried to peek at the Colonel but knew she wasn't ready to gaze into his cobalt blue eyes again. Truth to tell, she wasn't sure she would ever be ready to face the Colonel again. One thing was for certain, Rita would have been furious with this cocky, confident man for touching her without her expressed permission.

"Anytime," she heard the Colonel mumble, softly.

She gulped down her hesitation and turned. Gathering the train of her riding habit, she straightened like she knew Rita would when she was faced with a situation like this. Although for the life of her, Belle couldn't understand why Rita didn't like men who took command of a situation?

"We best be on our way," he said, his voice just above a whisper.

She nodded, unable to glance any higher than his chin as embarrassment swept through her.

"Come, stay close," he said as he turned away. As he set off down the road, she watched his powerful well-muscled body move in an easy grace across the wet stones.

Then quickly realizing her folly, she took a deep breath and hurried after him. She had wished for an adventure and now she had one. So why did she suddenly feel as if her entire world had been turned upside down?

Chapter Three

The soft slap of waves against the shoreline was all Niko heard as he stared through the darkness into the patches of moonlight shimmering on the water.

He didn't need to turn to know that Her Ladyship stood nearby. The pleasant scent of vanilla floated on the gentle breeze, awakening his senses. He shook his head to clear them. He couldn't think of her in that alluring way. She was Stefan's future wife. He'd sworn allegiance to defend and protect his country. He wouldn't cross the line. He gazed at her standing serenely in the moonlight. Thank goodness she seemed to have plenty of courage for in the coming days and weeks ahead of her, she would need it.

An owl hooted in the darkness and he smiled. Cupping his hands, he answered the call. As expected, after a few moments, a small skiff rowed around the promontory and came into view. "This way," he directed. "We'll go down to meet the boatswain."

"Are you sure this isn't a trap?" she asked as she joined him.

He gave her a sideways glance. She looked ethereal in the moonlight. While he preferred women with more earthy curves, the Council had chosen well. He stared at her noting her fragility and wondered whether she would be able to keep up with the grueling pace he needed to set tomorrow if they were to be at the rendezvous point tomorrow evening? He frowned at the thought then motioned for her to follow him. "Hasn't it been safe thus far?" he asked as they trudged toward the waterline to wait for the skiff.

"It has," she said as she stopped. Then she hoisted her skirt up to her knees. Deftly catching the train of her riding skirt, she pulled it between her legs and neatly tucked the material into her waistband. "All right," she said, dusting her hands off by brushing them together, "I'm ready."

Caught off guard by her impetuous action, Niko stared at her for a moment. "Um-m," he said, clearing his throat. "Very resourceful, although it isn't necessary. The future Queen of Barovia needs not only to be a lady by birth but also by action as well."

"Why?" she asked, her tone making it clear that she wasn't impressed with him. She glanced up at him through her thick lashes.

Suddenly, his collar seemed far too tight. "Because a lady-" he began, then stopped to clear his throat again as he began to realize that perhaps discretion was the better part of valor.

"I've found," she interjected. "That being a lady means not being a simpering fool." Turning, she squarely faced him. "In other words, I'm not about to let either my heavy skirt or any other part of my attire drag me down into a watery grave."

"Your Ladyship," he said giving her a quick bow, knowing he'd best gentle his tone. "The King would never forgive me if I allowed that to happen." Then sweeping her up into the circle of his arms, he felt her slender body stiffen as he settled her against his chest. Gazing down at her flushed countenance, he noted the lace at her throat had parted to reveal the soft shadow at the base of her throat. Her softness heated his palms as he carried her snugly against his body. He frowned, surprised at how right she felt in his arms. "If you don't wish to visit Davy Jones Locker then I suggest you place your arms around my neck," he said as he waded into the water.

Stiffly, she pushed her upper body away from the Colonel's massive chest. Squeezing her eyes closed, Belle blocked out the sight of his firm, sensual lips. A brief shiver rippled through her and she sucked in her breath, denying the attraction she felt for him. She bit her bottom lip. She was supposed to be Rita, the future Queen. She had to think of the Colonel as her subject she told herself, firmly.

Her eyes popped open at the thought. She stared at the Colonel's generous mouth, then lifted her gaze to his aquiline nose. Drops of moisture clung to his forehead and she realized suddenly that the Colonel had waded further into the water. Water that would have been well above her knees if she dared to admit it. As his grip tightened, she turned her head away. She took a quick breath afraid she'd studied his chiseled, square chin much too long. She paused at the thought then realized that there was no way she would ever consider the Colonel a 'mere subject'. Her mind simply wouldn't accept that concept.

Suddenly a large wave splashed them. She gasped as cold water soaked her bodice and a brisk breeze swept over them. A chill raised bumps on her arms as the cold settled over her chest. She shivered as the frigid wind swirled around them then caught sight of a lantern bobbing inside a boat a few yards ahead of them. Quickly, she lifted her eyes back to the Colonel as she wondered what he would do.

Niko cleared his throat as he tightened his hold on her ladyship. "Ahoy there," he called. "Colonel Orsini here," he added as they waded toward the small rowboat.

"Higgins here, Sir," the young sailor returned as he rowed alongside them. "May I help you, Sir?"

"I can manage," Niko replied then realized that he'd responded as if he'd been ungrateful for the offer of assistance.

"Gracious," Her Ladyship said with a snap in her tone. "Just get me inside the boat before you drown me and then you can debate the merits of–"

"It's a skiff, Ma'am," Niko corrected as he set her on the rough plank used as a seat.

"Thank you for that correction, Colonel," she said as she sat up. "It's ever so helpful to know that interesting bit of information."

Niko took several slow breaths. If he didn't guard his tongue he would be in trouble with his cousin he reminded himself as he watched her adjust her skirt primly over her knees. "Thank you for your so generous assistance but from here on, I will take care of myself," she added with a definitive nod of her head.

He clamped his jaw closed as a hot flash of irritation spread through him. "Good," he managed to say as Higgins steadied the skiff while he hoisted himself inside. He'd just ruined a perfectly good pair of Hessians to keep her high and dry and that was his thanks? Women! Who could figure them out? Grabbing the nearest oar, he reached for the other one. At the moment, strenuous activity was exactly what he needed to keep him from saying or doing something he would regret.

"Sir, please, allow me to row," Higgins interjected.

"Thank you, but I've got it," Niko nodded toward the lantern with a taut jerk of his head. "However, if you'll grab the lantern you can guide us toward the Queen B."

"Aye, aye, Sir," Higgins replied, snapping a salute.

"The Queen B?" she asked.

"Named after King Stefan's late mother," he replied tersely as he glanced over at her.

Belle nodded, woodenly. She hated feeling this out of control but she couldn't seem to stop the shivering. Attempting to ignore the discomfort of her chilled body, she took a deep breath and filled her lungs with the cold, salty air. One thing for certain, it felt wonderful to be back on the water again. At their estate, Tony had taught her that sailing meant freedom. On the water, she had been free to be the mistress of her own universe. She smiled at the memory as the skiff rode the swell of the waves then dipped.

She closed her eyes. In spite of the chill of the air, she enjoyed the rising and falling motion of the boat. Without a doubt, Rita would've hated this adventure just as she would've loathed the Colonel ordering her about. Belle opened her eyes at the realization. She stared at the man sitting across from her. He had burst into her life less than an hour ago and already he had changed it.

Truth to tell, she wasn't sure she even liked him. Although she had been immediately attracted to him, she knew it wasn't fair to judge a man only by his looks because character mattered more.

"Ahead, Sir," Higgins called over his shoulder, "is the stern."

Shouts began to fill the air as she watched the Colonel with Higgins' help, pull alongside the bobbing yacht.

"Ahoy, there," the Colonel shouted, "Lower Jacob's Ladder. Passengers coming aboard."

Higgins swung the lantern upward as a knotted rope ladder cascaded over the side from above.

Belle clenched her jaw. There was absolutely no way she would allow the Colonel to carry her up that. As Higgins grabbed the bottom of the ladder, she stood. "I'll do this," she challenged as she glanced first at the Colonel then at Higgins who quickly averted his face.

"Yes, My Lady. Just place your foot in here," Higgins instructed as he lifted the lantern to show her the gap in the rope. "Reach above and pull yourself up," he said. "Someone topside will assist you."

Belle nodded then took a deep breath. Calmly she placed her foot as directed and began the methodically reaching, pulling, and then placing her feet as instructed. As the muscles in her arms pulled tight with the strain of lifting her body and fighting against both the swaying ladder and the wind tossed waves, a tired, numb lethargy set in. It took a few minutes for her to realize that her palms burned from the sting of the rope and she was forced to admit to herself that it was a lot harder to accomplish than what she had first thought. Shifting her thoughts away from her pain, she chanced a look downward then wished she hadn't.

Directly beneath her, the Colonel held the bottom of the ladder. Standing with his head tilted back and his feet spread apart, he braced himself against the tossing waves as he watched her every move.

Suddenly everything seemed to move at once. Belle gulped back her moan as nausea rose in her throat. No wonder Rita hated boats. Raising her eyes back to the next section of ladder, she heard a deep chuckle from above and then a quick shout of "Stow it."

Glancing upward, she focused on the pair of lanterns swaying dizzily above her. Then shifting her gaze she spied four men of varying heights, age, and ethnicities peering down at her.

"Don't just stand there," the Colonel shouted from below. "Assist Her Ladyship."

Eager hands shot downward.

"'ere, Ma'am, give me your 'and," a short, balding sailor said in an unusually gruff voice.

"Blimey, take mine," a thin, graying sailor called out in a raspy voice.

Belle grabbed the nearest hand. Strong, beefy fingers wrapped securely around her wrist. Releasing her other hand from its death grip on the rope, she reached up as a smooth, steel-like brown hand latched onto her other wrist. Suspended for a moment above the rolling sea, Belle felt a scream bubble up from the back of her throat. She gasped at the panic rising within her as she was summarily lifted up and over the side rail and set safely on the wooden deck.

As soon as her feet touched the deck, the crew members released her. But pounded by wind and tossing waves, the boat suddenly pitched downward. Belle gasped then grabbed for the nearest crew member to keep herself from sliding and falling overboard. Relief rushed through her when a strong hand grabbed her and she realized she'd been saved from a watery grave. Taking a quick breath of gratitude, she began grabbing and shaking everyone's hand. "Thank you, oh, thank you all so very much," she gushed as relief rushed through her at finally being safe. "I really appreciate all of your help."

"Glad to be of 'elp," a balding sailor lisped.

"Aye, me pleasure," a gruff voice added.

"Anytime," came the spontaneous replies from the men hovering around her.

Belle nodded then felt heat rush into her cheeks as she realized what an undignified sight she was presenting to the men. Not only had she revealed the curve of her calf but she now faced the quandary of whether she should leave her skirt tucked into her waistband and suffer the ignominy of flaunting convention or whether she should appear crass and remove the material tucked at her waist. Deciding discretion was the better part of valor, she released the material from her waistband. Shaking out the folds of her green velvet riding skirt, she fluffed the jabot at her neck then glanced up to find the Colonel's broad back shielding her movements from the sailors' view.

"Her Ladyship thanks you for your assistance," the Colonel said, his voice raspy. "Now, please return to your duties, men."

"Aye, aye, Sir," came a chorus of replies as the men scurried off.

The once crowded deck was suddenly empty but for the two of them. Belle licked her dry lips and peered up at the Colonel. Thankful the moonlight hidden behind the clouds concealed the extent of her embarrassment, which quickly turned to annoyance as she realized the Colonel looked ready to berate her for her foolishness.

"And now, Your Ladyship," the Colonel began, turning toward her.

She stiffened her spine. There was no way she would allow him to ride roughshod over her anymore. Rita would never allow such a thing to happen. "This had better not be another lesson in deportment," she snapped as she placed her balled fists at her waist. "Because if that is your intent, let me inform you that I am never, ever rude. I've been taught to treat everyone I meet with respect. That includes sailors in King Stefan's Navy right down to the lowliest match girl I might pass on the street."

"You're telling me this because-," the Colonel asked.

"I'm exhausted and would like to retire for what is left of the night and-"

"You're in no way willing to be lectured by me," the Colonel finished for her then grinned.

She raised her chin. "That's correct," she replied as her lips firmed. Darn the man! He'd taken the wind right out of her sails. She felt her shoulders slump. No wonder the man was a Colonel, he seldom missed a beat.

"Then Your Ladyship, please follow me," he invited with a bow. "I will escort you to your quarters below deck."

Belle clamped her jaw tight. Aggravating man, did nothing ever surprise him? Following him across the deck, she waited while he took the lead down the companionway.

"Your quarters are here," the Colonel said, opening the door at the end of the corridor.

Belle gasped at the royal blue and gold palatial hangings then closed her jaw with a snap. What else was she to expect? After all, she was supposed to be marrying a King.

"King Stefan hopes this will meet with your approval," the Colonel said with another bow.

"It's beautiful," she whispered overcome with awe. "I never dreamed I would find anything like this." She stared at the shimmering gold silk and royal blue velvet bed hangings. The golden candelabras dotting the room cast a warm, inviting amber glow. A crystal decanter with stemware set atop a snowy white linen-covered table in the center. She turned toward the Colonel as she felt a smile curl her lips upward then paused as she watched the Colonel's eyes widen as if in surprise.

"Then may I ask what it is that you did expect?" he asked.

She shook her head then met his steady gaze. "I expected ... nothing."

"Nothing?" he asked. "Do you think Barovia so barbaric that we lack all refinement and taste?"

"Oh, no," she gasped. Impulsively, she seized one of his iron fists. "It is nothing like that at all," she said, ignoring the warm, pulsing current leaping between them. "I don't know how much of my background you know, but opulence such as this isn't an everyday occurrence for those of us who live on a country estate, not even if we are a Duke's sister."

The Colonel nodded. "Years ago," he said. "A tutor of mine explained the difference between luxury and necessity. He said that only someone who had everything ... then lost it, could fully understand."

She searched his countenance for a hint of mockery. Finding none, she released her hold on him. "Why is it that one never fully realizes the worth of what one has until after they've lost it?" An overwhelming sense of grief for the death of her parents swept over her. Turning aside, she surreptitiously brushed the hot tears away, refusing to allow anyone to see her weakness. Lifting her head, she glanced at him hoping he would reveal more of his true nature. Only then could she be certain that her decision to place her life in his hands had been the right one.

Niko took a slow, deep breath. Her bravery and tears were nearly his undoing. He knew few women who when faced with the prospect of a rebel attack would have reacted as courageously as she had. A knot twisted in his stomach. "Sometimes the answer to those rhetorical questions can only be found in our future," he said. Then resisting the impulse to comfort her, he gave her a hasty bow. "And now, I will wish you a pleasant evening, My Lady," he added as he stepped out into the corridor.

"Good night," she replied. Her soft voice seemed to call him to linger for a few more moments in the room. Niko shook his head as he closed the door. He could neither allow her bravery or the attraction he felt humming between them to distract him from his mission. She was his future Queen and soon to be his cousin's wife. And although her nature called to him like a magnet attracted to metal, he had to resist. For he knew if he didn't, the consequences would be devastating not only for his country but for his cousin.

Belle looked around the opulent room and then slowly crossed to extinguish all but three of the candles. She moved to the bed, pressed her palm into the plush feather mattress and knew she would never be able to sleep there. Turning, she ran her fingers down the cool silk. Nostalgia swamped her and she gulped back her moan. Sometimes in her private moments her memories of life with her parents simply overwhelmed her and then she allowed the tears to flow. Only after she'd had a good cry could she mop at her eyes, gulp down the sorrow and go on with life, carrying the lump of grief hidden inside her chest.

She straightened as resentment seeped into the crevices of her mind. She didn't want to feel this sad or this filled with anguish and regret again. And she most definitely didn't want to hide from life anymore. She wanted to embrace what life had to offer her, just like Rita did.

Taking a bracing breath, she crossed to the chair sitting beside the bed. Lowering herself into the ornate brocade chair, she leaned back then slowly straightened as she realized that in the past few hours posing as Rita, she'd felt more alive than she had ever felt before. Quickly, she stood and began to pace. But had this change come about because she had assumed Rita's identity ... because she'd met the Colonel or ... because she'd become embroiled in an exciting adventure?

Pivoting, she began to pace in the opposite direction. She had to admit that the Colonel disturbed her in every imaginable way. Around him, she felt more assured, more aware of herself as a female. She became an entirely different person. And not someone she recognized she thought with a frown. Somehow, she was more spontaneous ... more daring. She halted. What spell of enchantment had he cast over her?

Suddenly, the closed-in confinement of the room made it impossible for her to breathe. Hurrying to the door, she pushed it open and took a quick breath. As the briny draft swirled around her from the open hatch, she made her unsteady way toward the steep steps that lead up to the deck. Only when she was standing on deck would she be freed from the thoughts threatening her peace of mind and firm resolve.

As she stepped onto the deck, a stiff breeze whipped her hair from its chignon. She grabbed a handful of it at the nape of her neck. Then clutching at her skirt with her free hand, she moved to the side of the bulkhead out of the wind afraid that her skirts would balloon over her head.

Then catching a deep gulp of sea air, she turned. Surprise jolted through her as she stared up at the Colonel silhouetted against the bright moon, his hands steady on the wheel. Her eyes froze on his long, lean form as the vessel cut through the rolling water. Standing tall, his body balanced perfectly on sturdy Viking legs, the wind ruffled through his black hair.

She studied the powerful set of shoulders that had held her so safe and secure. She licked her suddenly dry lips as his white shirt billowed out at the open neck. With sleeves rolled to above his elbows, he appeared as if one with the ship, devilishly handsome, his profile dark against the moonlight. Belle took a deep, steadying breath and turned away, hoping to disappear back into the companionway before he realized that she had been standing there gaping at him.

"I thought you were exhausted," his rich baritone voice said a few feet behind her.

She paused as heat flushed her face. Gathering her courage, she turned and noticed that a sailor had taken the Colonel's place at the helm. Dipping her head, she licked her dry lips. "I-I found that I couldn't sleep," she said, quietly.

"And why is that?" he asked as he came to stand beside her at the rail, his profile rugged and somber. "Guilty conscience?"

Belle gripped the rail as a cold wind swept around her. Surely, the man couldn't know about the switch? She peeked up at his rugged profile then squared her shoulders. Although she had to forge ahead with the ruse, she was also determined to be herself. Shifting her gaze to the rolling sea, she took a quick breath. "Earlier, I lied when I said that I was never rude." She cleared her throat to steady her voice. "In fact, I've been nothing but rude and ... willful since we've met. And for that, I owe you my deepest apology."

She heard only the waves crashing against the yacht for a few moments then curious, she turned toward the Colonel and watched him shake his head. "If anyone should apologize," he said, his voice suddenly husky, "it should be me."

She frowned as she noted her head only reached the level of his shoulder. "Why would you say that?" she asked as she tilted her chin up hoping to catch a glimmer of what he really thought.

Niko took a deep, steadying breath. Then balling his fist to keep his index finger from tracing along her tempting jaw, he cleared his suddenly dry throat. "Since meeting you, I've found myself saying and doing the most unexpected things," he murmured, his eyes silently following the gentle line of her full-bottomed lip. He watched as she blinked rapidly then became fascinated by the smile pulling her lips upward to reveal a dimple in her right cheek.

"Me, too," she whispered. "And that's what I find so confusing ... so strange." She seemed to realize what she'd unwittingly revealed for she dipped her head once again. "That's probably why I couldn't sleep," she added then gave a small laugh as if the jest was on her.

Niko nodded, realizing that while his Cousin's bride-to-be might not have been Stefan's choice, she was a woman of rare honesty and beauty. The same admirable traits he hoped to someday find in the woman he called 'wife'.

But what did her honesty and candor say about him? He shifted his gaze to the churning sea. While he hadn't exactly lied, he hadn't been entirely honest with her either.

He glanced at her and noticed an air of vulnerability clung to her as if she hadn't experienced much of life. He frowned as he realized that she reminded him of the newborn litter of pups he'd once come across in the royal stables. His uncle, King Rinaldo, had explained that the pups were like loyal subjects, each one needing to be cared for. He straightened at the thought. "What else did you learn living in the country?" he asked, diverting the deep sense of loss he always felt when remembering his uncle and his unexpected death.

"You mean besides climbing out windows and repelling down walls?" she asked as she offered him a small, mischievous smile.

"So that's where your experience comes from?" he asked unable to prevent a smile from lifting his spirits.

"Yes," a secretive smile softened her lips, "along with sewing, cleaning, and cooking."

His eyebrows shot up in surprise. "Cooking?"

"Well," she chuckled. "That is what the staff in the kitchens were kind enough to call it. Although after one week I was released from duty and told never to return."

"Was the food that dreadful?" he asked then chuckled.

She grinned. "Personally, I always thought the staff was divided between courtesy and self-preservation."

"And self-preservation won when faced with the prospects of confronting the Grim Reaper at the table."

"Absolutely," she laughed.

He glanced away realizing that this was the first time he had actually heard her laugh. He liked the lilting sound of her spontaneity. He also liked the way her lips turned up at the corners revealing her dimple again.

Casually, he turned and rested his forearm on the rail, facing her. Most women at this juncture in their acquaintance would either be batting their lashes at him, sidling closer, or putting their hand on his arm or his chest. He smiled. Those were not the actions of his future Queen. He studied her for a moment then nodded as he wondered if she even knew how to flirt. He felt his smile widen. Maybe he ought to teach her how to use her womanly wiles so she could capture and hold his Cousin Stefan's attention.

"Recently, I finished reading Blanc's L'Organisation du Travail," she said, her brow creased as if in thought.

He stared at her for a moment, surprised that she was not only cognizant of the book but was able to read it in French. "To each according to his needs, from each according to his abilities?" he finally managed to say.

She took a quick step back, her hazel eyes widening in surprise. "I must say, I am stymied," she said.

"Why?" he asked, "because you didn't think we read such tomes in

Barovia?"

She shook her head. "I thought we had moved beyond those assumptions," she whispered, her soft voice filled with hurt.

A frisson of guilt flashed through him for his pettiness. "You are correct," he said with a bow.

"Thank you," she said, her quiet voice a reminder that he'd best tread carefully with the young woman. His eyes searched her face as moonlight flooded the area they stood in. Attempting to capture this moment in his memory, he suddenly realized that he wanted more than a memory. He wanted to reach out ... to touch her and see if she was as real as she appeared. All he needed was a simple finger stroke down her jawline ... to taste those perfectly bowed lips beneath his and-

Abruptly, he turned away from the rail, denying the temptation standing before him. To continue along that line of thinking was not only foolish but bordered on treason. "And your point in mentioning Blanc is?" he managed to ask. Refusing to act on the desire coursing through him, he placed his hands behind his back and firmly grasped his wrists.

"Add his philosophy to that of Samuel Smiles-," she said, her voice filled with enthusiasm as she moved toward him.

"The man who wrote the recently published Self-Help?" he inserted to test if she had read the book.

A smile curved her lips upward. "Yes," she said, "the manual on how to manage life."

"And?" he asked, easing away from her. He glanced at her as he leaned over the rail as if he was about to check on something along the side of the yacht.

"And, you have an excellent idea on how to conduct your life," she said just before she let out a squeak as a wave lifted over the bow and water swept onto the deck.

"Ah," he murmured. Straightening, he braced his feet as the ship plunged downward. "If only life were as simple as reading a book."

"So, why isn't it?" she challenged. Grasping the rail, she moved along it toward him.

He smiled at her naiveté. "Because a horse always throws a shoe at the most inopportune time," he returned with a grin.

"In other words," she nodded as she stopped a few feet from him. "Things happen no matter how much we prepare and hope otherwise?"

"I prefer to think of it as…something always comes along to challenge me," he corrected.

He watched as she tilted her chin upward and eyed him.

"And you like challenges?"

"Indeed I do," he admitted as he studied the outline of her full bottom lip. "And now, Your Ladyship," he said knowing he was dangerously close to over-stepping the boundaries he'd set for himself. "My watch is over and it's time to retire."

She dipped her head. "Thank you for your kind words of wisdom," she said. "But I'm going to remain up here for a few more minutes before I go below."

Unable to decide if he was relieved he wouldn't have to fight off the temptation she presented when he escorted her back to her quarters or if he was disappointed that he wouldn't have the opportunity to overcome the challenge she presented, he clicked his heels together and bowed. "Very well, My Lady, until tomorrow," he said taking a step back.

Belle watched the Colonel move away. "Yes…tomorrow," she uttered as he pivoted and rapidly strode across the deck to disappear down the companionway. Trembling, she stepped back and leaned against the bulkhead, confused by her conflicting emotions. On one hand, she felt a heated connection to him. She frowned as a cold wind swept over her. She hugged herself, hoping to recapture some warmth. And although she'd learned tonight they shared an affinity for reading the same books she realized she was repelled by the cold, remote barrier the Colonel erected around himself. She felt her frown deepen. When questioned, why did the Colonel clam up revealing so very little about himself? Was it because he was an intensely private person or was it because he had something to hide? She nibbled on her lower lip. And while she knew that most women would find his remoteness a definite challenge, she wasn't one of them. Besides, she had a role to fulfill. Honor demanded that she use the Colonel's detachment as a catalysis to prevent any further attachment on her part.

While she'd never encountered a man as attractive as the Colonel, he was a huge threat to her peace of mind. Not only did he have the ability to listen intently to everything she said but he had a gentleness that was at odds with his physical strength. Experiencing his attentiveness had been a heady experience for her. It had made her feel…treasured. She sighed at the thought. Then paused as she recognized the cold, disquieting urge of restlessness slithering through her. The temptation to defy her brother and refuse to marry Umberford swelled beyond a soft whisper to bedevil her fully. She straightened as a warm feeling of rightness coursed through her. Not since her parents' deaths had she felt so sure in which direction her future lay. Nor so determined to cut the ties binding her to her brother.

She inhaled, sharply at the honesty of her realization. But what could she be thinking? She shouldn't feel tempted, especially not by a man she'd only known for a few hours. She was playing the role of someone engaged to another man. She frowned. That frivolous behavior belonged to Rita... not her. She was the stable one...the ever practical one. Her feet had to remain firmly planted on terra firma. Unlike Rita who with her overactive imagination...wove impossible dreams in the fluffy white clouds floating above her head.

Belle took a deep breath and straightened. She truly hoped that by impersonating her twin, she had given Rita time to come to the realization that she had to marry King Stefan. She fervently prayed that by impersonating her sister she'd not made things more difficult than they already were.

She shook her head wondering what her sister would think when she awoke in the morning and found her gone. Would Rita be proud of her for deciding not to raise the alarm and disappearing with the Colonel? Or would she be furious with her for doing the unexpected?

All of a sudden a yawn overtook her and she realized she couldn't stand at the rail all night. Even if she couldn't sleep in that soft, plush bed, she could pull the blankets from the bed, pile them on the floor and made a bed fit for a Queen's imposter. She smiled at the thought. After all, that's exactly what she was...an imposter.

Turning, she made her way back to her quarters, softly humming a ditty she'd heard the sailors singing earlier. She'd taken care of tonight. Now all she had to do was make it through to tomorrow evening. She slowed as she began to worry her lower lip. But what was she to do when she met up with her twin tomorrow if Rita refused to switch places?

Chapter Four

Niko bounded out of bed and grabbed his trousers as he remembered the woman he was to keep an eye on. Although he'd stood the midnight watch and it had taken him a long time to get to sleep, he felt renewed. He grinned as he pulled on his trousers. So, all right, if he was honest, he would admit that he actually liked his future Queen. Her courage... and her honesty were attractive traits that boded well for the country. But from now on, he needed to remember to think of her only as 'his Queen'. And to accomplish that, he needed to maintain a respectful distance and do nothing to jeopardize Stefan's future with her.

He frowned as he lifted his white linen shirt from the back of the chair he'd draped it over the night before. How then was he to curb her impetuousness he wondered as he threaded his arms through the sleeves? He could almost guarantee that at least twice a day she would do something spontaneous. He combed his fingers through his hair then began to button his shirt. So, how did one go about containing a-

A tap came at the door, interrupting his thought. "Enter," he called as he tucked his shirt into his trousers.

"You sound pleased, Your Highness," Briggs, his valet, said as he swung the door open. Sidling through the doorway carrying a tray with coffee, a plate of pastries and one piled with slices of cheese, ham, and strawberries, he paused as he cautiously maneuvered the tray through the narrow aperture.

Niko waited to respond to the man's inquiry until he had successfully entered the room. Then he casually waved him toward the nightstand. "Today, I'm the 'Colonel'," he said then grinned as he finished buttoning his shirt. He enjoyed playing this daily game of 'who am I' with his valet.

"And so, today you will be spared laying out all the regalia," he added for he knew how much Briggs fussed over everything royal. Catching a whiff of the aroma of rich dark roasted beans, he stopped to enjoy the moment. It was one of the few pleasures he allowed himself every morning.

"Right you are Your...ah, Colonel," Briggs said as he set the tray down and poured a steaming cup of coffee. Turning, Briggs held the cup out to him. "Captain Russo said I was to tell you Her Ladyship's already up. He also said he would keep her busy if you wanted to slip into your quarters and shave."

Niko nodded as he accepted the cup then paused. It had been his observation with new recruits that the more impetuous a person, the more they attempted to find ways to alleviate their restless boredom. "I hope she's hasn't decided to assist in the galley," he added before taking a sip of the thick, black brew. He closed his eyes to savor the enjoyment.

"Why would a future Queen do that, Your High-Colonel?" Briggs asked.

Niko opened his eyes to notice a frown furrowed Briggs' high forehead. "Just an observation I made last night." He halted in the act of lifting his cup and inhaled sharply. 'We could have a problem if her cooking is as bad as she claims," he said, finishing his coffee. "Our entire crew could be down with a bad case of indigestion."

"Mercy," Briggs gasped. "Then it's a good thing Cook declined her assistance for it sounds as if the lady is most unusual."

Niko nodded as he handed the empty cup to his manservant. "Therefore, I need you to keep an eye on Her Ladyship and help her avoid any disasters until I can join her," he said as he exited the Captain's quarters he'd slept in the night before. Striding down the corridor to his own room, he entered and halted, surprised to see the room appeared as if it had never been used. He frowned. How long had Her Ladyship remained on deck last night? Moving toward the pristinely made bed, he stopped to skim his hand lightly over the cool, royal blue silk.

Hadn't he just resolved not to become more involved with her? His duty was to keep her safe. What she did otherwise was no concern of his. She could come and go as she deemed appropriate. Grabbing his shaving gear from beneath the sink and his clean clothing from the trunk at the end of the bed, he returned to the Captain's quarters. After bathing, shaving, and dressing, he ambled down the corridor toward the galley. He paused as he heard a distinct groan coming from within. He clenched his jaw tight. If his crew was complaining about the food, they would pay dearly for embarrassing their future Queen with their antics.

Stopping at the doorway, he took a deep breath and relaxed as he peeked into the galley. She stood with her back to him, and he noticed her thick chestnut hair was tied with a green velvet ribbon at the nape of her white neck. Her hair hung in a graceful tail that followed the curve in her slender back. He watched as she turned toward Dubroc, a young cabin boy who could often be found atop the crow's nest. He shook his head then grinned and he wondered what mischief the boy had gotten into. As he watched to see how Her Ladyship would handle the situation, he noted her high cheekbones carried a delicate flush. Her flush reminded him of the rare blush petals of the Lediz Flower that only bloomed in the early spring, high in the mountain meadows above Berat.

"Now, I know this is going to hurt a bit," he heard her say, her gentle voice pulling him quietly into the room. Entering, he scanned the room and noticed there was no one in there but Her Ladyship, his cabin boy, and Heims, the cook. Relaxing, he remained near the entrance.

"Please do try to stay out of the Crow's Nest during the next storm," she admonished as she wrapped a bandage around the boy's wrist.

"Aye, aye, Your Ladyship," Dubroc replied and snapped a mock salute.

"Good," she chuckled, returning his gesture. "Now, see that you do."

"Yes, Ma'am," the young boy said, hopping off the stool he'd been sitting on. Then reaching over, he swiped a biscuit off the cooling rack and scurried toward the door.

Niko stepped out of his way marveling at the ease Her Ladyship had exhibited with the youngster.

Belle watched the young boy hurry away then noticed the Colonel push away from the jamb. Briefly, she wondered how long he'd been standing there but shrugged as it was really no concern of hers. Nonchalantly lifting a strip of unused lint, she began rolling it.

"If you think this will slow him down," the Colonel said as he entered the galley, "you would be wrong."

"I would be very surprised if it did," she grinned. Rising, she put the salve and bandages back into the basket then returned it to the cook. "Thank you."

"My pleasure," the cook replied, accepting the basket from her.

"We will be docking soon," the Colonel said. "If there is anything you would like to gather for this short jaunt, please do so."

"Oh," she said, "thank you for the consideration. But is there anything I can do for you in preparation?"

The Colonel seemed to pause then nodded. "If you will oversee the packing of a food basket, I'll take care of everything else."

"As long as I'm not expected to cook it, then we'll be in fine shape," Belle said then noted the smile lifting the corners of the Colonel's mouth. Realizing that she'd become fascinated by how the Colonel's lips turned up at the corners, she shifted her gaze to watch the cook remove a batch of biscuits from a pan.

"Any special requests?" the cook asked.

"Surprise me," the Colonel said, snagging a biscuit from the cooling rack and cradling it in his hands.

Belle smiled. Boys would be boys...no matter their age.

"That I can do," the cook laughed.

"But no squid," the Colonel admonished.

"Right," the cook replied as he held up a hand as if in surrender.

Belle chuckled at the by-play. She like the easy manner the Colonel exhibited with the man.

"You would not think it funny if you were the one who developed a rash from eating it," the Colonel replied.

"Did the rash burn and you found yourself unable to breathe?" she asked as she leaned toward him. "Or was it merely red and irritating?'

"I had itchy dots everywhere," the Colonel said before he bit into his biscuit.

"Ah-h," she exclaimed. "And were you quarantined?" she asked then watched him shake his head.

"King Stefan's physician gave me some salve and a concoction to drink," he said then seemed to shudder. "At least after three days, the redness had disappeared."

"Really," Belle said, moving toward him. "Do you remember any of the ingredients that were used in the drink?"

The Colonel flashed her a wry grin. "I wasn't that interested in finding out why it tasted so vile."

"Um-m-m," she nodded. "To be effective, most concoctions are." She paused then brightened. "Do you think it would be possible for me to meet this physician?" she asked, eagerly. "I can then ask him first-hand what he used."

"I am sure you will," the Colonel nodded. "He is, after all, the King's personal physician."

"Oh!" she gasped. Belle felt her face flush as she suddenly realized that she had been so caught up in her quest for medicinal knowledge that she had forgotten the most important element of all. She was no longer 'Belle the herbalist' but 'Belle the impostor'. Suddenly breathless, she took a deep breath and softly cleared her throat. Had she tipped her hand? "H-how long will we be traveling today?" she asked to change the subject.

"Barring any unforeseen complications," the Colonel replied, "we should arrive in Berat before nightfall."

Belle exhaled in relief. "And so a small food hamper will be sufficient?"

"More than," he replied. "And now, if you will excuse me, I must be off. Please join me on deck as soon as you are ready."

"Of course," she mumbled as he executed a bow and moved toward the door as if nothing had happened between them last night. As if they hadn't exchanged confidences. She watched him step into the corridor, enjoying the way his broad shoulders tapered to a slim waist and the way his long and lean legs strained against the fabric of his trousers. Turning, she found a large grin spreading across the cook's weathered face. She felt her face flush at having been caught admiring the Colonel.

"Forgive my outspokenness, Your Ladyship," the cook said. "But you do understand the Colonel's haste in getting to Berat, don't you?"

"Not really," she forced herself to say. She wasn't sure if she really wanted to know but she did feel compelled to find out for Rita's sake.

"Once the King makes up his mind, no one changes it," the cook said, placing sliced ham, a small loaf of bread, a flask, a brick of cheese and four apples inside the basket.

"He's that inflexible?" she asked. If so, that wouldn't bode well for a marriage between the mercurial and free-spirited Rita and a man set in having his own dictatorial way.

The cook shook his head. "A King must be decisive," he said closing the lid on the hamper. "People's lives depend upon him."

"But surely people realize that all those decisions...can't be in everyone's best interests," she said, slowly.

"Perhaps not," the cook said, "but being right all the time is a difficult thing for a man to achieve...and whether he be King...or a Colonel, admitting when he is wrong can be a challenge."

Belle nodded. Rita was like that. She never wanted to acknowledge when she made a mistake or a wrong decision. "Do you think it is any easier for a woman to admit that she's wrong?"

The cook shrugged. "Should be."

The word, why hovered on her tongue because she knew that wasn't the case at all. She felt a frown furrow her brow. So, maybe men and women weren't all that different in the way they thought about things. She straightened and flashed him a smile. "Personally, I think it's too nice a morning for such a deep philosophical thought," she said neatly side-stepping a confrontation, something she knew she did more than she liked. But for now, she needed to play nice. Someday she would learn to stand up and defend her position without worrying about the other person's feelings...but not today. She took a deep breath vowing then and there that someday she wouldn't be so accommodating or so conciliatory. She would take a much-needed stand and assert herself, especially when dealing with Rita.

"The hamper is ready," the cook said. "I'll call someone to carry it for you."

"Phooey," Belle said firmly, deciding that now might be the perfect time to begin asserting herself. "That's not necessary." Lifting the basket off the counter, she gave the cook one of her best smiles.

"But, Your Ladyship-" the cook began.

"I am perfectly capable of carrying one small basket," she said. "But, thank you for all of your help."

The cook bowed then straightened. "My pleasure, Your Ladyship, anytime."

Belle gave him a small wave then moved through the companionway up to the deck. The first thing she noticed was the sun highlighting the sheer limestone cliffs in its bright light. The next, was the Colonel issuing orders as if he had been born to command

She paused, noting he stood head and shoulders above the crew. She bit her bottom lip. Did a man like the Colonel inherently know how to command or had he gained the knowledge through experience? She narrowed her gaze as she watched him. Had he ever suffered from indecision...or regretted any decisions he'd made?

Belle set the hamper beneath the awning near the bulkhead and moved to the rail. A mild breeze skimmed across the sails and she leaned over, mesmerized by the yacht slicing through the clear aquamarine water. If life was as simple as them cutting through the water then maybe she would know what to do if Rita refused to accept King Stefan as her husband.

"Fascinating isn't it," the Colonel asked from behind her.

She straightened shaking off her melancholy and forced her lips into a smile. How could anyone be gloomy on such a glorious day? "It is," she agreed as she turned to find him but a heartbeat away, holding out her riding jacket and her hat with her gloves laying inside the crown of it. When she lifted her gaze, his smile stole her breath away. Then she gulped as the pit of her stomach did a strange flip.

"I took the liberty of sending Dubroc to your cabin for your things," he said, his breath feathering along her cheek as he held her jacket open to her.

"T-thank you," she managed as she threaded her arms through the sleeves and tugged it down to her waist. She fumbled with the buttons for a moment before she could force her fingers to work. Hesitantly, she raised her gaze to stare at the hat and trailing veil the Colonel still held. She bit her bottom lip. She hated the current fashion preferring to go hatless, but taking a quick breath, she tucked her gloves inside the pocket of her riding skirt, placed the hat on her head and wrapped the thin green gauze around her wrist.

"Dubroc will bring the hamper," the Colonel said as the yacht changed course and headed toward a small bay. "We'll row to land then travel overland to Berat," the Colonel said gesturing toward a narrow band of white sand jutting out into the water.

Belle squinted through the sunlight following his gesture. A man stood holding the reins of two horses. Ice trickled through her veins as she spied the two riderless steeds. Fear tightened her throat as she realized that she would be expected to ride one of those beasts. She clamped her jaw shut, swallowing back her oath of dismay. There was no way that her limited riding skills would ever be enough to survive a trek through the steep mountains rising beyond the shoreline. Squeezing her eyes closed, she nearly groaned aloud. Darn, why couldn't Rita have been the sailor and she the horsewoman in the family?

She peeked over at the Colonel. His square jaw told her that there was no sense pleading or trying to cajole him. He would never leave her behind. Straightening, she took a deep breath and then reached behind to catch the train of her riding habit. The Colonel's steel-banded hand grasped her forearm, stopping further movement. The heat from his palm both surprised and dismayed her. She raised her eyes. Eyes of cobalt blue met hers. Inherently she knew that if she gazed into those eyes long enough she would confess all her sins and be lost. Stoically, she arched her brow as if she had a question.

"It won't be necessary to depart using the ladder," the Colonel said, "I've had the lift basket brought out for you."

"B-basket?" she stammered, shaken by his hand continuing to rest on her forearm.

Lifting his hand away, he swept it toward the area of the mid-ship. There beside the rail sat a large woven basket rigged with a series of ropes. "Come," he said, taking a step in that direction.

The rumble of heavy chains and the splash of the anchor hitting the water greeted them as they moved toward the center of the yacht. A dinghy disappeared over the rail as they arrived at the lift.

Belle watched the Colonel tuck the food hamper beneath a narrow plank that served as a seat inside the woven contraption. Her stomach churned as she stepped forward and peeked inside the canvas-lined conveyance. She bit her bottom lip to stop her chin from trembling. Stepping back, she felt a boulder lodge in her throat as the Colonel reached inside and released a latch. Ice crusted her veins as a small door opened and he motioned her forward.

"I w-would rather use the l-ladder," she managed to say, grateful that they hadn't offered the use of the thing the night before. She clenched her jaw as she eyed it in trepidation. She no longer placed any trust in man-made devices. Not when the memory of their traveling coach lurching off the road, tumbling down the steep ravine and coming to rest in the icy water still haunted her. Slowly, backing away, she shook her head.

"My Lady, you will be perfectly safe as long as you don't move around in the lift," the Colonel said holding out his palm to her.

Belle tightened her jaw. Then glancing up at the Colonel, she realized that no matter what her objections might be, his narrow-eyed glint said she would be using the apparatus.

"Surely, you're not about to turn coward on me?" the Colonel asked. "Those aren't the actions of the lady who bravely left the village with me a few hours ago."

She dipped her head. He was right. She no longer was herself but was masquerading as Rita. And Rita always ran where angels feared to tread. Straightening at the thought, she took a deep breath. Then, taking a few steps forward, she stepped inside. She felt her throat tighten and her heart begin to pound as she sat gingerly on the makeshift bench.

Closing the door, the Colonel latched it. "Sit very still," he cautioned. "You will be lowered in increments down to the skiff. I will meet you at the bottom to assist you."

Belle nodded and watched the Colonel disappear over the side. Anxiety clouded her vision as the basket lifted. She gripped the sides of the swinging basket, frantically biting her lip. Then the basket swung over the rail and dangled for a moment. She let out a squeak as it began to lower in a series of scary jerks. She squeezed her eyes closed anticipating the worst as the flimsy contraption rocked and lurched downward. She huddled in fear waiting to be dumped into the cold sea.

"I've got her," she heard the Colonel call.

Quickly opening her eyes, she blinked several times to clear her vision as the top of the Colonel's head came into view. She took a deep breath thankful when his strong grip stopped the swaying contraption. Straightening, she peered over the side. The basket hovered about a foot above the bobbing skiff. As the Colonel reached inside and unlatched the door, Belle sat perfectly still, afraid to breathe.

"Stay low in the basket. Don't make any sudden moves," the Colonel instructed. "There's no rush. Wait until you regain your balance."

Although her nerves hummed and jumped to be free of the device, Belle forced herself to rise slowly. Suddenly, the basket swayed as a wave tossed the small boat about. Frantically, she reached for the Colonel.

"That's right," he said as he placed his palms on each side of her waist. "Now, brace your hands on my shoulders."

Re-assured by his gentle, deep tone, she planted her trembling hands on his broad shoulders now encased in a plain dark cape. She lifted her gaze. This close, his dark hair gleamed bluish-black in the sunlight. A swath of wavy hair fell casually on his forehead and as she studied him a feeling of calm flowed through her and she relaxed.

"You're safe, Your Ladyship," he said, his voice quiet. "Soon you'll be riding across the steppes with the wind at your back."

Riding?

She dipped her head as fear rushed through her. How was she to tell him she couldn't ride when Rita was such a proficient rider? She trembled at the thought. "T-thank you for your a-s-sis-tance," she stammered as he lowered her until her feet touched the bottom of the boat. His hands remained a second longer as she sat.

She watched as he reached back into the basket and lifted out the food hamper. "There seems to be no place for this," he said holding up the food basket. "If you would hold it that would help."

Grateful to have something to grasp onto, she took it and hugged it to her chest. Right now, she had no idea which was worse, dangling in a scary lift basket or being jostled on the back of a horse she would never be able to control.

She licked her suddenly parched lips. No matter the personal hardship, she had to face this next challenge like Rita would.

She raised her gaze to the Colonel's broad shoulders. His powerful well-muscled body moved with an easy grace as he removed both his cape and coat. Then he sat and lifted the oars. Setting the skiff skimming with ease across the water, his muscles rippled under his white shirt. She raised her gaze to study him. Her fingers itched to sketch the strong planes of his face bronzed by the wind and sun. Fascinated by the sensuality of his classical features, a memory of a portrait painted by an Old Master surfaced. Like the artist's rendering, the Colonel exuded the essence of honor and trustworthiness, traits that sent her pulses throbbing every time she looked at him. Which at this point, she cautioned herself, was way too often for her peace of mind. She straightened as she realized she had to nip her admiration for the Colonel in the bud if she was to safeguard their ruse.

Belle inhaled sharply as an icy shard of fear slid through her. Stiffly, she returned his smile, not about to panic at the horse problem waiting for her on shore. She shivered as she reminded herself that she had to meet each obstacle as it happened and not anticipate what might occur. She hardened her jaw as she admitted to herself that prolepsis had always been her downfall.

Narrowing her gaze, she freed one hand from its death grip on the hamper and lifted it to shield her eyes from the harsh glare of the sun shimmering on the water. Realizing persistence was one of the keys she needed to utilize if she was to discover something to foster disdain of the Colonel, she squared her shoulders. "I've done most of the talking since we've met," she said, offering him a conciliatory smile. "Now, it's your turn to reciprocate."

Her request seemed to hover in the air between them. Although the Colonel arched his brow, he continued to stroke the oars through the water. She stared at him waiting, her patience beginning to wane. After what seemed like forever, he finally said. "What would you like to know?"

Momentarily surprised that he had actually responded, she licked her dry lips. "D-did you always want a military career?"

"Always," he said. Then as if the topic was closed, he leaned into the oars and sent the skiff shooting across the water.

"Uh-h," she grunted. Not about to allow the Colonel's antics to stop her from further inquiries, she swallowed back her spurt of annoyance. "What first attracted you to the military?"

"Horses."

Belle frowned. The Colonel's brief answers were beginning to irritate her. She took a quick breath then paused as she brushed the tendrils of hair escaping from her bound hair off her face. Although horses were the one topic she did not want to discuss, if discussing them would help dissolve her fascination with the Colonel then so be it. "At what age did you first learn to ride?" She asked quickly in order to give herself time to formulate the next question. Suddenly, she paused as a frisson of excitement hummed through her. Did the Colonel's hesitancy in answering her questions indicate there was some personal secret he was afraid he would inadvertently reveal?

"Six," he said, unexpectedly as she watched his gaze dart away.

She felt her jaw drop open. Quickly, she snapped it closed and frowned. Perhaps if she changed her tactics she would discover the reason he didn't want to answer her questions. She brightened.

"Is there anything else that you would like to know?" he asked, grinning at her.

Belle returned his smile as an imp of mischief coursed through her. Not only would she change her tactics but she would also change the topic. "Yes," she said, firmly. "How well do you know King Stefan?"

Unexpectedly, he stopped rowing and penned the wooden oars against his abdomen, allowing the skiff to ride the waves. "Define the word, 'well'."

Belle frowned as agitation shot through her. The Colonel toyed with her like a cat teasing a canary. "It means, do you recognize him by sight?" she asked, her jaw tightening at his provocation.

He nodded as a wide grin spread across his face. His smile so big that she could nearly count all his teeth.

She took a deep breath, hoping to contain her vexation. "What is he like?"

"Like?" he asked, lifting the oars and beginning to row again.

"Ush-s," she muttered through clenched teeth. Although she wanted to scream out her frustration, she took a quick breath. There was no way she would allow him to alter her course. "You know," she said, "as in, what are his interests? His likes and dislikes-"

"Ah-h," he said as if the heavens had opened up and he'd seen a shaft of divine light. "You are not interested in his appearance?"

Belle stared at the Colonel for a moment as a red hue of anger flared within her. Was the man being obstinate or merely using his distorted view of women to avoid answering her? "Neither a description...or a picture gives one the essence...nor the measure...of a man," she finally managed to say.

The Colonel's brow furrowed. "You want to know what he is like?" he asked.

She nodded at his incredulous tone, proud she had surprised him. By asking the Colonel his opinion on his monarch she hoped to gain an insight into what the Colonel really through and felt about his King.

"The thing is," he said slowly, "very few people see the man behind the crown."

She rubbed at her tired eyes then squinted at him. It was times like this that she needed her spectacles. She needed to see if the intent resonating in the Colonel's voice matched his facial expression. "Then you do know the man," she replied, relieved she was finally discovering a crack in the Colonel's façade. "What is important is who he is...what he believes...how he acts. The crown is simply his position. And although I know many believe the crown defines him...it isn't who he is" she added.

"Then what do you want to know about the man?" the Colonel asked. Skepticism resonating in his voice made her wonder if he knew the King at all.

She smiled. "Everything."

"Then be specific," he said.

Belle took a deep breath. One of Rita's mantras had been 'in for a penny, in for a pound'. She straightened, reminding herself that she was now Rita and his answer was important to their safety. She wouldn't act the 'frivolous Rita.' She had to find a half-way measure and be 'Belle' in order to guard her sister from harm. She raised her gaze to meet his. "What other reasons do the rebels have for wanting to prevent this marriage?"

"You already know the Emperor and two neighboring Kings want the throne for their own use. Mainly for gold and silver. However, I believe the Serbian Rebels are jealous of the prosperity and freedoms the citizens of Barovia enjoy. While the rebels have sided with our neighbors against us, they have their own agenda."

She glanced toward shore. Noticing they were a few feet from the shoreline, she tightened her hold on the hamper she hugged to her chest. "And what is that?"

"A discussion for another time." He grinned. "It's time to disembark onto the beach."

She nearly groaned aloud as she turned to see a man wade out into the ankle-deep water. The Colonel was right. She needed to shelve her questions and wait until later to dig around and find the crack in his façade. Her breath hitched as she realized she could no longer put off dealing with the inevitable. A few feet away, a horse waited for her. She shivered at the thought.

"Morning, Sir, Ma'am," the gray-haired man said, doffing his cap. Then he latched onto the rope looped over the bow of the skiff. "Sit tight and I'll have you to shore in no time," he added. Tossing the free end of the rope over his shoulder, he hauled them through the water toward the beach.

As the skiff scraped the bottom, the Colonel jumped out and helped haul the skiff up onto the narrow, sandy beach.

Belle stood, accepting the hand the Colonel offered. She ignored the tingling that raced up her arm as she stepped out of the skiff. If she was to halt her growing attachment to the Colonel then it was in her best interest to think of him as 'a stranger'. Turning, she watched the Colonel retrieve the hamper from the skiff then felt her breath catch as he walked toward the horses tied to a large piece of driftwood. Frigid fingers of dread slithered over her and she found it difficult to swallow as she stared at the Colonel who was rubbing the horses' muzzles. Slowly, she backed away as he leaned forward and whispered to them.

There was only one way a horse would allow her to mount it and ride. And that was if she were to bribe it. Fishing two apples from the bottom of the hamper, she gulped back her fear. Hesitantly, she forced herself to approach the horses.

"Say hello to Moonlight," the Colonel said as he brought a dappled gray horse around to meet her.

The horse was huge and the same color as the horses that had pulled her parents' coach the day they had died. Belle trembled at the recollection as she accepted the reins. She was nearly pulled off her feet as the horse jerked its head upward. Instinctively she tugged downward on the reins. As the horse lowered its head, she cautiously offered the apple by placing it on her open palm. As Moonlight took the apple, she tried to remember all of Rita's instructions about horses. "You're such a beauty," she cooed, her voice sounding stilted to her own ears as she mimicked Rita's first lesson. Lesson two had been to gently stroke the side of the horse's neck. She looked at her quivering fingers and reached toward the horse's neck. Unexpectedly, the horse tossed its head in her direction. "Oh!" she exclaimed as her palm landed near the horse's mouth. Horse slobber coated her palm. "E-ew," she gasped as she wiped the slobber and bits of apple on her skirt. She couldn't believe that Rita actually liked touching the beasts. Gritting her teeth, she forced herself to make a soothing "m-m-m" sound in her throat replicating the noise Rita made whenever she groomed her mare. Belle's nerves tightened at the idea of even touching the horse again as her stomach somersaulted in her throat.

"I see that you are getting acquainted with Moonlight," the Colonel said as he moved around the horses, inspecting their fetlocks and shoes.

She twisted around to watch. "Is everything all right?" she asked. Personally, she hoped something was terribly wrong and they would have to walk to Berat. She brightened. If that was the case, then she wouldn't have to get on the beast.

"Fine," he said, straightening. "Ready?" he asked as he stepped toward her and cupped his hands.

She stared at his hands, her heart in her mouth. She bit her lower lip then swallowed back the denial hovering on the tip of her tongue. "About as ready as facing a firing squad," she finally mumbled as she placed her left foot in his palm and found herself being tossed upward. Grabbing the fixed head of the lady's side-saddle, she looped her right leg over the top pommel and smoothed her skirts. Suddenly the horse side-stepped and she let out a squeak. Frantically, she wrapped both hands around the fixed head afraid she was about to be tossed to the ground like the last time she'd been on a horse. Her heart thundered in her chest as she realized that she still sat atop the animal. She felt a gasp rise in her throat. Attempting to gain control of the panic rising within her, she lowered her gaze to calm herself then noted the sandy ground looked too far away. She swallowed back her gasp of dismay as a set of Hessians stepped into view.

Lifting her head, she discovered the Colonel standing near, holding the reins out to her. Dread seized her. If there was any way she could avoid this, she would. Suddenly, darkness clouded her vision, but fear forced her to shake her dizziness away. She had to ride this horse because she was Rita and there was no other option available to her. Squaring her shoulders, she shivered as she accepted the reins. Gingerly holding them across her cupped palm, she bit her bottom lip. Hadn't Rita told her that once you knew how to ride, it's a skill you never forgot? She felt a frown furrow her brow. So, maybe riding to Berat wouldn't be that difficult as long as she could stay in the saddle and the horses walked all the way to the palace.

Chapter Five

Niko bit the inside of his cheeks as he watched Her Ladyship study the reins as if she had no idea what she was to do with them. Hoping to offer encouragement, he nodded. "You look born to the saddle." Then he realized him saying so, didn't make it true. He took a step back. The longer she stared at the reins, the more convinced he became that not only was she a beginner but her inexperience would slow them down and might prevent them from making their rendezvous point that evening. He clenched his jaw understanding that his irritation wouldn't help the situation. Stepping closer to the mare, he adjusted the stirrup leather hoping to give Her Ladyship time to regain her plucky backbone.

"Um-m,' she said, softly clearing her throat. "You do know that looks can be deceiving."

Swiftly, he raised his gaze to meet hers then realized her bravado didn't measure up to her pale features. "So I've been told," he said. Turning, he lifted into his saddle atop the Lipizzaner gelding. Then he felt compelled to ask, "Have you ridden much?" as she continued to stare at the reins.

She shook her head. "Not lately," she said, her voice an octave higher than he'd heard before.

"Lately meaning what?" he asked. Dread beginning to tighten his gut as he guided his horse toward hers.

"Um-m...nine years."

"Ah-h-h," he said then forced a smile passed his clenched teeth. Although what he really wanted to do was cuss, he swallowed the oath and nodded in resignation. "Then we'll take it easy until you grow accustomed to Moonlight." He leaned toward her. "Meanwhile, hook that part of the lower pommel over your left thigh," he said, pointing to it. "It will help stabilize you during the ride." He waited until she complied with his direction then lifting his own reins, he straightened. "Would you like for me to lead you until you're comfortable?"

"Yes, please," she said quickly tossing the reins back to him. "And thank you," she murmured, clutching the fixed head with both hands.

Catching the reins, Niko took a resolute breath then guided the horses into a slow amble as they crossed the sand. Turning in his saddle to check on her, he noted her eyes were closed as she clung to the fixed head with both hands wrapped around it. Squaring his shoulders, he turned back and expelled a deep breath unable to decide if riding up the steep narrow path cut into the face of the cliff with her eyes closed was good or bad.

It was good if she was afraid of heights but bad if her horse stumbled. And spying the white knuckles of her hands grasping the fixed head, he knew that the next part of their journey was going to be a challenge for both of them. For her...the lack of skills, for him...a test of his patience. But they needed to get to Berat as quickly as possible. The longer they delayed, the more likely it became that they would encounter rebels roaming the countryside.

Gaining the top of the cliff, he glanced over his shoulder to check on Her Ladyship. He let out a sigh of relief as he noted her eyes were open and she seemed to be surveying the area around them. "This way," he said, guiding them along a boulder-strewn path. Spotting a meadow in the distance, he glanced back at his passenger. A frown marred her forehead. "We need to pick up the pace when we get there," he said as he gestured toward the meadow then looked back at her. Noting her wordless nod, he turned forward realizing that for her, fear of falling from a horse might prove to be an insurmountable barrier to conquer.

Although Belle would've liked to have resumed their conversation from earlier in the skiff, she was too afraid to shift her focus from the swaying beast. They broke into a jog as they reached the meadow resting below the mountains rising high in the background. She gasped as she tightened her hold hoping to stay in the saddle but her hands began to cramp in pain. Her breath seized in her lungs. As numbness tingled through her hands, her grip relaxed. She realized suddenly that she wasn't going to be able to hang on any longer. Fear rushed through her as a scream tightened her throat. But unexpectedly, Moonlight slowed to a walk as the Colonel dropped back to ride beside her. Relief pounded in her chest. About to ask how he'd known what was happening to her, she paused as his large hand came over hers.

"Focus," the Colonel said as a dizzying light-headedness washed over her. "You...will not...fall," he added. "I won't allow it."

She blinked up at him in disbelief, shocked by his words. He wouldn't allow it?

Really? Did he think he had that much power?

She gasped at his audacity then straightened her spine. The Colonel was right. She wasn't about to fall off the beast, not when it meant such an ignominious defeat to her pride. "I am perfectly able to do this myself," she said then hoped the Colonel hadn't heard the shakiness in her voice.

"Then do it," he said, a frown deepening his brow. Lifting his hand away, he slapped the reins into her hand. "Try to keep up." With that he took off, walking his horse toward a road that meandered in the distance.

Belle gritted her teeth. Then mimicking the Colonel, she clucked at the horse, tapped its side with her heel and jiggled the reins. The horse took off at a slow walk after the Colonel. As she bumped along, she fervently hoped that while holding a rein in each hand as the Colonel had yet alternately resting one hand at a time on the pommel that her fingers wouldn't become numb again. Raising her gaze to check on the location of the Colonel, she spied him a few feet ahead, looking back at her. As she watched, his frown disappeared and his shoulders seemed to lose their stiffness. Satisfaction skated through her. She must be doing something right. For why else would he relax?

She paused then hunched her shoulders, not about to let over-confidence gain control. Past experience had taught her that she made too many mistakes when she allowed that to happen. Leaning forward toward the horse's neck, she knew that all she could hope for was to stay atop and believe that her misery would soon end.

In what seemed to Belle to be forever, but she knew was only minutes, she came to the road where the Colonel had stopped to wait for her. Pulling back on the reins she slowed the horse and waited for it to stop. An effervescent bubble of joy lifted her chest and she realized that what hadn't killed her had made her stronger. She had placed her trust in the Colonel and both he and Moonlight had kept her safe.

"Great job," the Colonel said as he turned in the saddle to look at her. "I think you have proven you can handle the reins now," he said as he moved his horse so that it stood next to hers. "You might want to try to relax and flow with the movement of your horse."

"Thanks," she said then frowned as he reached over and adjusted the reins in both of her hands. Not about to question the Colonel's expertise, she clamped her jaw. Then she narrowed her gaze, mimicking the Colonel's actions as he steered his horse along the road.

They rode until the sun was directly overhead, the Colonel leading the way until he slowed and waited for her to come alongside.

"Not bad for a beginner," he said as she joined him.

"Thanks," she managed, though she seriously doubted she would ever be able to walk or want to sit ever again.

"We will ride until we either come across a stream or are forced to take shelter from the rainstorm gathering in the distance behind us," he said. Then pointing to the food hamper attached to his saddle, he added. "Either way we'll stop and eat."

Belle clutched the reins and nodded. She took a quick glance behind her then gulped back her exclamation as she spied the pearl gray clouds accumulating in the sky behind them. She'd been so busy staying on the horse that she noticed nothing else. Swallowing back her groan, she gritted her teeth. Hopefully, the shower would veer off and miss them. She shifted her attention back to the horse and slowly arched her back. Pain shot all the way up her spine to the base of her skull then raced back down to her toes. She took a quick breath at the sharp, shooting pain.

"A quarter mile ahead is a copse of trees," the Colonel said pointing forward. "Maybe we'd best stop there for a short break."

Not about to object, Belle gave a quick nod. "Good idea," she managed to get out through clenched teeth as the Colonel lengthened the space between them.

She stared at the grove of trees in the distance. Only a little bit longer, she promised herself. Then she bit her bottom lip as she recognized the lie she'd just told. Who was she kidding? She had hours yet to ride and even then her torture wouldn't end. While she might not be sitting atop a horse, she would still have to deal with the pain and discomfort of unused muscles for days. She took a bracing breath. Ah, the sacrifices she made for her twin.

She focused on the mountain glade. She could almost feel the cooling breeze whispering through the trees offering a respite from the hot sun beating down on them. Moistening her dry lips with her tongue in anticipation for what awaited her, she grimaced as she tasted the film of dirt coating her lips. Although she cringed at the idea, the dirt would have to remain on her mouth. It didn't take but a second to decide that the first thing she would do when she was on solid ground was to scrub it off. Then she'd take a long, cold drink of water. Clenching her jaw, she continued toward the wooded area.

Finally arriving, Belle closed her eyes as Moonlight came to a stop. She paused then slumped in the saddle, grateful to be free from the stress of holding herself so stiff and upright. The silence surrounding them was a moment of heaven. Then she noticed that a slight breeze rustled the tree leaves overhead and that nearby, water bubbled over stones. She smiled. It was just as she had imagined. She took a deep, satisfying breath, cherishing the rare moment of quiet contemplation. For with Rita as a sibling, these moments were usually few and far between. She straightened as she recalled hearing that a Queen never slumped her shoulders.

"Has My Lady fallen asleep?" she heard the Colonel ask softly, "or is she playing opossum?"

Reluctantly, Belle opened her eyes then frowned down at the man. After what seemed like hours of riding in the heat and the dust stirred from the horses' hooves, the Colonel looked fresh as a mountain daisy. Although she wanted to groan aloud, she realized it would take too much effort. "I'm not asleep," she managed to grumble through her parched lips. "I was just enjoying the moment."

"You might enjoy it more if your feet were planted solidly on the ground," he said, placing his hands on each side of her waist.

Belle took a bracing breath and then sighed. "Can't dispute the logic of that," she said, placing her stiff fingers on his shoulders.

Lowered to her feet, she took a deep breath, preparing to step away from him. But pain shot up the backs of her legs and she clutched at his strong forearms as her knees began to buckle. "Oh-h-h!" she gasped as her eyes darted up to meet his. "I-I think the earth just tilted on its axis."

"Well, it's not every day that I get to rescue a damsel in distress," he murmured as his breath feathered across her cheek.

She froze for a moment then straightened. "Well, don't let it go to your head," she said quickly lifting her hands from his forearms. Roughly, she cleared her throat and looked away. "I'm fine now," she added as the sound of her rushing blood thundered in her ears. What had possessed her to clutch at the Colonel so? She was supposed to be repelling him. She darted a swift glance at him.

"And if you weren't fine, you wouldn't allow yourself to acknowledge it," he said, his gentle observation halting her movement as he took a step back from her.

Although she frowned at his keen discernment, honesty propelled her to admit, "Probably not...but h-how did you know?"

He smiled. "It's that stiff British upper lip you have," he said as he looped the reins over his palm and gave them a tug. "That and your bravado," he added as he began leading the horses further into the trees.

"Great!" she muttered as she walked alongside him. "Add that to I can't seem to say no to anyone and it's sure to land me in a boatload of... trouble," she mumbled then touched her upper lip.

Um-m, stiff? Well, maybe.

She watched as the Colonel disappeared around the bend in the path then smiled as she hurried after him. She liked the idea that the Colonel thought her brave and independent. A bubble of joy lifted her chest as she realized that being Rita brought unexpected results. And by continuing in her sister's persona for a few hours more, who knew what she might do or be like?

Encouraged by the thought, she followed the Colonel toward the sound of rushing water. As they neared, the trees thinned to reveal a large clear pool beneath a waterfall. Belle smiled then hurried toward the fallen log jutting out into the water.

Hot from the heat of the day and itchy from the dust stirred up by the horse's hooves, Belle quickly removed her hat and set it on top of the log. Then unbuttoning her spencer, she peeled it off her perspiring body. Folding her jacket, she placed it next to her hat. Unfastening the top two buttons at the neck of her blouse, she extracted her lace handkerchief from the pocket of her riding skirt and shook it out. Bending toward the pool, she plunged the kerchief into the snow-melted water. Wringing out the excess, she inhaled sharply as she scrubbed the dirt from her lips and then dabbed at her hot face. Closing her eyes, she sighed as the moisture cooled her skin. If she could only plunge into the clear pool, she would be one happy traveler. But disappointment coursed through her as she realized that wasn't possible. A Queen would never act so precipitously.

"Didn't sleep much last night?" The Colonel asked from somewhere close by.

Her eyes popped open as she jumped, startled by his nearness. She hated the fact that he seemed to make a habit of catching her unaware. Then nonchalantly dipping her kerchief into the water again, she wrung it out and placed it on the back of her neck. "No," she said as she stood. She turned and observed that the Colonel stood a few feet away. He must've been just as hot and uncomfortable as she'd been for he'd removed his cape and frock coat and now stood in his shirt, the sleeves rolled up to his elbows.

She raised her gaze to note that he seemed to be staring at her. Quickly she averted her gaze and looked out over the water. Swiftly she reminded herself that the dangerous attraction she held for the Colonel was not only perilous to her peace of mind but to Rita's future as well. She glanced at him again. Although she couldn't deny that his nearness kindled a spreading warmth within her, she knew for sure that she could never do anything but keep a respectful distance.

She clamped her jaw attempting to halt the dizzying currents racing through her. Although she might feel weak, she wasn't powerless. She would resist the pull of his magnetism she told herself. Like a sleepwalker, she stepped to the side. Her ankle banged against the log. A log she realized that she had forgotten was there. She yelped in pain as she lost her balance. "Oh!" she gasped as she began to topple over.

"My Lady," the Colonel said, catching her in his arms. "Are you hurt?"

Belle's palm lay flat against the Colonel's solid, warm chest. If he only knew, she thought then snatched her hand back from his body. Wiggling free of his hold, she lowered herself to the fallen log then shook her head feeling like the fraud she was. "I-I'm fine," she stammered as she retrieved her kerchief from where the lace had snagged on the tree's bark. Dipping her kerchief back into the water, she wrung it out and dabbed at her face until the heat of embarrassment had cooled and her pulse had slowed.

Finally, lifting it away from her face, she hesitated then bit back the urge to confess her perfidy to him. She knew she couldn't. It wasn't her secret to keep. Only Rita could release her from her vow of silence. And her sister wouldn't do that until they met up again later that evening. If she revealed that they had switched places, it would not only embarrass Queen Victoria and England but also King Stefan and Barovia. And no matter how honorable their motives had been at the beginning, in the end, Rita would lose the King's trust and respect not only as his wife but as his Queen. Therefore, she owed it to Rita to safeguard their secret.

Thunder rumbled close-by and Belle raised her gaze to the darkening sky. "Doesn't look like we'll be having that lunch anytime soon," she said as she picked up her hat and spencer from the log.

"We need to get out from under the trees and away from the water," the Colonel said as he grabbed her wrist and tugged her toward the horses.

"Why is that?" she asked, hurrying to keep up with him.

"According to a scientific journal article I recently read," he replied as they arrived at the horses. "One should never stand under a tree or be near water during a storm." Quickly, he took a rolled blanket from behind his saddle. Untying the bundle, he handed her a sailor's slicker. "Here, wear this, it will keep you dry."

"But, what about you?" she asked as she threaded her arms through her spencer and then pulled the slicker over her head.

"Mine's right here," he said as he shook it out and tugged it over his head. Rolling his cape back into the blanket, he secured it behind his saddle. "Ready?" he asked as he threaded his fingers together to serve as a foothold for her to mount.

Belle stared at his cupped palms. Although she had proven to herself that she could remain atop the horse that didn't mean that she wanted to get back on the beast. She bit her bottom lip then hardened her resolve as she reminded herself she had no choice but to mount up. "As long as you know where it is that we're going," she said, slapping her hat on her head.

"Always," he said as he tossed her into the saddle. "But for now, we're headed up into the mountains toward a cave I know."

She glanced at the jagged mountains in the background. The jostling and jolting would add more pain to her already sore body. But resigned to what had to be done, she forced back her groan of protest. "Lead the way,' she invited as she watched him swing up into his horse. A few raindrops plopped onto the brim of her hat. She tilted her head back and then wished she hadn't as the rain dropped through the leaves and splashed on her face.

"Give me your reins," the Colonel demanded.

Quickly, she tossed him her reins then grasped the fixed head of her saddle.

"Hang on," he called. "We need to canter." Pelted by rain, they took off at the faster pace as they crossed the thirsty earth. But soon, they had to slow to a jog as the ground became a slippery quagmire. Eventually, they slowed the horses to a walk as they wound their way through a series of twists and turns up the mountain toward the cave in the continuing rain.

Finally, dismounting at the cave's entrance, Niko swiftly lifted Her Ladyship from her horse. No matter how many times he assisted her, a rush of satisfaction always coursed through him when he touched her. It was good to be needed, he told himself. Not about to acknowledge any other emotion that might invade his consciousness, he turned and led the horses inside the cave. Then sighed in relief at being out of the rain pelting the area outside.

Slowly, he surveyed the area inside. While he'd never before had to rely on the space for shelter, at least the cave was wide enough to keep not only them dry but also their horses. "This will do nicely," he said, hoping he sounded more optimistic than he felt. Glancing at Her Ladyship, he noticed her hunched shoulders and realized that she had to be just as cold and miserable as him. "This should at least keep us dry and safe".

"Are we still in danger from the rebels?" she asked, whirling around in a circle as if expecting a rebel to leap out at them from behind the boulders dotting the inside of the cave.

He bit the inside of his cheek to keep from laughing. "We haven't been followed, if that is what you're asking," he said, careful not to indicate by word or action that he wasn't about to let his guard down and relax,

"Oh," she said, "that's good to know."

Hearing the relief filtering through her words, he decided he'd best add a word of caution. "However," he said, loosening the cinch and removing the side-saddle from her horse. "It doesn't mean that we're out of the woods, yet." He watched as her soft lips formed a perfect "o". Unable to look at her without wanting to give her a hug of reassurance, he pivoted and began to rub down the mare. He frowned. So, whose idea had it been for him to escort his Cousin's bride to the rendezvous point...his or Stefan's?

"Here, let me do that," she said, coming alongside him.

He gazed at the petite woman who would soon be his Queen. While she might appear fragile, she had demonstrated that she was more resilient than she looked. And unlike most females, she hadn't once complained. He chewed on his bottom lip, unsure if Stefan would appreciate a woman like Belle. "Very well," he said finally passing the blanket to her. Her help would make his tasks easier to complete and they would give her something to do while they waited for the storm to pass. "Ever done this before?"

She shook her head.

"Here, like this," he said as he placed his hands over hers. As a flash of heat arched between them, her small hand seemed to tremble beneath his. Ignoring the warming sensation, he showed her how to rub down the horse then quickly broke contact. His heart hammered in his chest as he took a small step back, careful not to touch her again. She had been chosen to be his cousin's wife. She was his future Queen, he reminded himself as he turned away. Loosening the cinch, he removed the saddle that contained his firearm and placed it next to hers. Then keeping his back to her, he rubbed his horse down.

A wary silence permeated the small space as they worked in tandem to complete their tasks. When finished, he draped the blanket over a rock and looped his horse's reins around a jagged rock nearby.

Stepping aside, he noticed Her Ladyship had followed his example by draping her blanket over a similar rock. After watching her loop her reins over the rock atop his, he moved to the entrance of the cave and stared out into the torrential downpour. Thank goodness they had made it in time and had avoided a total dousing he thought as the rain hammered the area outside. He frowned as he realized this delay meant that they likely wouldn't make today's rendezvous point or tomorrow's either.

"I know us getting caught in this rain storm will delay our trip," she said as if she could read his mind. "But how long do you think we'll have to wait here before we can resume our journey?" she asked joining him at the entrance.

"It will be a while," he said. Turning to study her, he wondered if she would be more comfortable if he invited her to use a less formal means of address. "Might I suggest you call me Niko instead of addressing me as Colonel?"

She seemed to hesitate for a moment as if considering his request then nodded.

"And you?" he asked. "What do your friends call you?"

"Belle," she said, softly. "Shortened from Isabelle because I've never been fond of the name, Marguerita." She dipped her head.

"Belle," he repeated. He let it roll softly off his tongue. The name suited her much better than Marguerita.

Unsure how long the storm would last, Niko glanced at the circle of stones and shook his head. Without dry wood, they wouldn't be lighting a fire nor would they be warm or dry anytime soon. Bending and removing the topmost blanket he'd tied on the back of his saddle, he removed his slicker and draped it over the pommel. Shaking out the spare blanket, he spread it over a small portion of the cave floor. Retrieving their canteens of water and food basket, he set them atop the blanket then gestured toward their mock picnic. "May I invite you to join me, Belle?" he asked, liking her name more each time he used it.

"T-thank you, Col—"

"Niko," he corrected with a quick smile.

"Niko," she repeated, softly. His name on her lips jingled in unison with the horses shaking their heads. A loud rumbling started outside the cave and the ground began to tremble inside.

Jerking their heads up, the horses tugged at their reins secured to the jagged rock. Swiftly, he ran to quiet them then watched helplessly as rocks and mud slid into the cave's entrance. Taking a deep breath, he prayed that nothing bigger would fall and block their only way out.

"What is happening?" she asked as she came to stand beside him, her eyes too large for her pale face.

He released his spent air with a 'whoosh'. "It's a landslide," he said matter-of-factly. "We often have them out here in the mountains during our rainy season."

She nodded. "Are we safe inside here?" she asked, her palm stroking the mare's neck.

"Safe enough," he said knowing there wasn't anything they could do but wait until the rumbling stopped. He found himself crossing his fingers, once again hoping that nothing too large fell and blocked their exit.

When the rumbling finally stopped, he walked to the entrance and peered out. Most of the debris had landed off to the side, near the trail they'd used to travel up to the cave. He took a deep breath then released it, thankful for small favors. But that by no means meant that they were free from further disasters.

With the horses now quieted, he turned back to their makeshift picnic. "I think we had better eat," he said studying her surreptitiously.

Belle nodded, surprised that anyone could be hungry after such a scare. But settling herself once more on the blanket, she accepted the flask of water he handed her. Lifting the open container to her lips, she took a deep swallow, grateful to finally quench her thirst.

"Thank you," she said, offering the container back to him. He handed her a biscuit with a slice of ham wedged in between. Accepting it, she shivered as the cold, damp mountain air swirled around her ankles. As the icy air settled on her damp clothing, it seeped through the fibers and came to rest on her skin below. She shivered again, her jaw dancing uncontrollably. Suddenly, she found Niko wrapping a blanket around her upper torso, his warm hands seeming to linger on her shoulders.

"T-thank you," she stuttered, raising her gaze to meet his. Something shifted again between them. But what? Her mind raced with possibilities but the only safe conclusion she arrived at was that he was afraid she'd become ill and then he would have a sick woman on his hands.

"There's something I would like to know," Niko said as she felt him remove his hands from her shoulders.

"A-and what is that?" she asked, hoping that she didn't cause too much of a fiasco by answering him.

"How did the Elderly Council happen to select you to marry the King?"

She inhaled deeply. Out of everything he could've asked, she hadn't thought this would be it. A lightness invaded her spirit as she relaxed. "Years ago my grandfather was the Barovian Ambassador assigned to Italy," she began. "That's where my father met my mother."

"I see," Niko said, glancing away from her. "So when the Council began searching for a suitable bride for King Stefan, someone must've remembered that one of their former ambassadors had a daughter who had married a British Lord?"

She shook her head. "I think it had more to do with my brother enlisting the aid of Queen Victoria. She, in turn, petitioned your Council of Elders requesting that they grant him our grandfather's estate here."

A grin settled on his lips. "And the rest is, as they say, history?"

"As to that," she said, suddenly overcome by an unnatural stillness as she studied the outcrop of rocks surrounding the entrance, "I think it rather depends upon King Stefan, don't you?"

"How so?" he asked as she watched his brow form an arch.

"Well," she hedged, "he might find me...quite unsuitable."

"Unsuitable?" he asked, disbelief darkening his tone. "How so?"

"Um-m," she hesitated. Then finding her courage she said. "He might think my nose is too long...or my teeth not straight enough or... my eyes too large for my face," she said naming all the faults she had found daily in her mirror.

"Or," Niko said, "He just might find a petite beauty that has the courage of a lioness and is as honest and straight as an arrow."

Belle froze at his words. "Y-you think I'm courageous?" she asked, choosing to acknowledge his first compliment rather than the honesty bit.

He gave a crisp nod. "Not many women would do what you've done when faced with obstacles like rebels and a surly escort," he said.

"You're not always surly," she inserted, flashing him a grin. "But, I could add...stubborn and opinionated to the list."

"You are indeed a brave woman," he said, a half grin curling his lips upward. "There are very few who have the courage to list my faults face-to-face."

"Why is that?' she asked delighted to have tapped into Niko's sense of humor, "because of your rank?"

Niko paused as unease shifted in him. Had he somehow alerted her that he was more than a Colonel? That he was, in fact, concealing his position as Prince, heir apparent to the throne? Swallowing back his need to fidget, he held himself still as if hiding from a nearby stalker. Then without further movement, he lifted his eyes and asked. "You mean because of my military rank?"

He watched her give a nonchalant shrug. "What else is there?"

What else indeed, he wanted to ask but instead opted to discover if her suspicions had been aroused. "Perhaps you're asking if I also hold a title," he said then feigned a chuckle.

"And why would I do that?" she asked fidgeting with the edge of the blanket.

Relieved to hear no proof of suspicion, he shook his head. Then paused to wonder if he had been fooled by her. Had he seen any sign that she measured the people she met by the position they held in society? He eyed her for a moment then realized she hadn't thus far but decided to further test her mettle. "Because you are a woman," he said.

"Meaning?" she asked, her eyes narrowing to slits.

Although he knew he was wading into deeper water, he felt an obligation that went far beyond Stefan being his King and cousin. Stefan was also his best friend and he had vowed to his uncle that as long as he breathed the air of Barovia, he would guard Stefan's life and that included not only his physical self but his emotional well-being. Not one to back down when he wanted to know something, he took a quick gup of air and said. "That you like to have the final word."

Her eyes seemed to widen as if she'd just realized something. "Do you think the King will like that?"

Surprise held him immobile for a moment as it dawned on him that Belle was just as uneasy about her future with Stefan as Stefan was about his future with her. He studied her pale countenance for a moment. She had to be scared. She'd been forced to travel to a foreign land, been surrounded by rebels and strangers and was now expected to marry a man she'd never met. She had to be quaking inside her half-boots. And yet, as he studied her, the only weakness he'd observed was an occasional hesitation, a trembling hand, and a sporadic paleness that swept across her cheekbones. He laid his palm over her hand resting near him on the blanket. "If you ever need a friend, someone to talk to, promise that you'll come to me."

"Niko," she began. "I'm not sure I-"

He knew first-hand how fake and cruel the court could be. "Please, Belle...promise me."

As tears pooled in her eyes, he suddenly felt as if someone had punched him in the gut. Opening his mouth to apologize for making her cry, she beat him to the punch.

"All right, I-I promise," she said as she pulled a wispy kerchief from her pocket and dabbed at her eyes. "And...thank you for your kind offer."

Now feeling like the biggest brute, he extracted his own kerchief from the inside of his jacket. At the rate she was dabbing, her wispy little square would soon become ineffective. "It was never my intention to upset you. Rather I had hoped only to give you reassurance," he added as he offered it to her.

She waved his goodwill away as she continued to dab her eyes.

About to replace his kerchief inside his jacket, he paused, thankful she had refused his offer of it. He suddenly realized that he'd just offered her the kerchief his mother had embroidered with the colorful insignia of the Royal House of Garaini. Hoping she hadn't seen it, he quickly tucked it inside his jacket. Then deciding to give both of them time to regain their composure, he turned aside.

Patting the now secure kerchief inside his jacket, he took a quick breath. And to calm himself he thought of his parents. A warm flow of nostalgia rolled through him as he remembered the laughter and the tender moments they had shared when his father returned home after spending a long day training troops. Because of their loving example, the one thing he'd come to understand was that he didn't want a Marriage of State like that of his aunt and uncle.

He wanted something more. He needed a wife who was not only a companion but a best friend. Someone he could share his entire life with like the marriage his parents had once had.

He shook his head then sighed at the improbability of it all. His uncle had once told him that if he had taken the time to get to know his bride then their arranged marriage might've been different. But after his aunt had revealed to him that while she had never wanted the responsibilities of being a Queen, she had wanted the glamour and prestige, he knew there was no way the marriage could've been any different than the armed, distrustful camp it had become.

He glanced at Belle. So, what did she want? "What will you do as our future Queen?" he asked, his voice sounding loud even to him.

She turned, surprise widening her eyes. "Do?" she asked.

"Yes, that is, after you've settled in and...discovered King Stefan isn't quite the ogre he's been painted in the press."

"I-I don't know," she said, hesitantly. "Is he an ogre?"

"Definitely not," Niko denied, heartedly. The last thing he needed was a bride who debunked on her wedding day because of something he'd said or done. "But, let's not digress," he chided, mildly. "What would you like to do as Queen?"

She gaped at him for a moment, then said. "I-I think I would like to get to know the people first and then assess their needs before I make any grandiose plans to help them."

"Help them?" he queried as relief swept through him.

"You know," she said, waving her hand, "as in if they need more schools...or hospitals...or things like that," she said beginning to pull at the threads in the corner of the blanket.

"Then you aim to assist the King not only in your official duties but you want to be a real helpmate to him?" he asked, stunned yet pleased with her answer.

A blush stole across her cheeks. "I would hope to be his friend," she said, simply.

"Ah, a confidant," he added, quickly.

"His...assistant," she clarified.

"And a lover," he said testing her resolve.

"L-lover?" she stammered, her tone registering her shock.

A bright blush deepened her face to a bright red glow. Instantly, he wished his words unsaid. "Forgive me. I had no right to mention something as private as that."

She shook her head. "No, it must be faced," she said and then glanced up at him. "I will do my duty. I will be whatever the...King...needs me to be." Her stoic words seemed to fill the void in the cave.

Niko nodded. He had his answer but why didn't it bring him any satisfaction? Rising, he gazed curiously down at Belle for a moment then walked to the mouth of the cave.

She studied Niko's profile etched in the gray light and sighed. Strong...honest...and amiable were the words that immediately came to mind when she looked at him. Which was quite often...too often she cautioned herself. She sighed, again. If only...

Belle paused as she realized she not only trusted and admired Niko but she liked him...really liked him and that hadn't changed no matter what she seemed to do to the contrary. Her heart pounded in her ears and her breath hitched in her chest. And should he discover the ruse she'd perpetrated against his King and his country then she would forever lose his trust and goodwill. Her throat tightened at the devastating thought. Swallowing back her groan of dismay, she traced the black threaded border running around the outside of an insignia stitched on the navy colored blanket. Her fingers stilled on the insignia of an eagle in flight with a laurel wreath clasped in its beak. She bent her head to get a closer look and saw the bird carried a shield in its talons.

She darted a glance at Niko to find him staring out into the rain. When her gaze returned to study the insignia, a chill of recognition flowed over her as she realized that she'd seen the same design on the lid of the box that Rita had received from King Stefan. The box had contained Rita's bride gift, the sapphire and diamond brooch she now wore. She shivered as she placed her palm over the brooch, thankful she hadn't lost it and it was still pinned there.

"The rain appears to be lessening," Niko said as she raised her gaze to see that he'd turned toward her.

"Does that mean we'll be leaving here soon?" she asked, hoping he hadn't heard the uncertainty quivering in her voice. Quickly, she gathered the flask and spare apple and returned them to the basket.

"It's too dangerous for us to ride out of here in the dark and then travel all the way down the mountain," he said, lowering himself to the blanket once again. "This isn't what I had intended but we'll have to stay here until morning."

Belle shrugged. She'd learned to trust her gut but now that she'd seen the insignia, unease began to nibble at her.

While there might be unpleasant ramifications for spending the night unchaperoned with a man, after recognizing that insignia, she had more important things to consider. Like...was Niko really who he claimed to be...or had he lied?

Chapter Six

Niko moved to his saddle. Unrolling the bundle he'd carried strapped to the back of his horse, he shook out a dark cape which had been wrapped inside. "Might as well try and get some sleep," he said as he noticed Belle bite her lip as if trying to reach a decision.

He watched her abruptly turn away. "I'll take the first watch," she said. "I'll wake you when the moon moves to that point over there," she added as she pointed to a jagged mountain peak resting at the two o'clock position off in the distance.

"I don't imagine I can talk you out of that, can I?" he asked, hoping to lighten whatever concern that had suddenly caused her to frown.

She shook her head. "Definitely not! I pull my own weight," she added as she stalked toward the mouth of the cave.

"Of course," he muttered wondering what had happened to cause her to go from a congenial companion to a surly one. "I will move the blanket so you can sit with your back braced against the rock wall," he said. Then suiting actions to words, he repositioned the blanket near the entrance. Sweeping his hand in the direction of the blanket, he added. "Your blanket awaits, My Lady."

"Thank you," she said, a definite snap ringing in her voice. Then sitting on the blanket, she waved her hand in the direction of the horses. "You'll need to rest," she said. "I'll wake you when it's your turn at watch."

"See that you do," he said, surmising she could very well use that stubborn determination he'd seen her demonstrate and forget to wake him. He hesitated then felt his brow furrow. "If you should find yourself nodding off, wake me."

He watched her shoulders stiffen. "That won't be necessary," she retorted, her eyes narrowing to slits. "When I say I'll do something, I do it. No matter what I must do."

"I've spent enough time with you to know the truth when I hear it," he said, realizing he wasn't gaining any ground with her. Then deciding he would give chivalry one last try, he shook out his cape then swirled it over her shoulders. It didn't even have time to settle before she shrugged it off.

"You will need this if you plan to get any sleep at all," she said gathering his cape up off the blanket and offering it back to him.

Niko felt his jaw harden as he accepted his cape back from her. What bee had flown into her bonnet he wondered as he settled himself a short distance away from the two horses? He stared at her for a moment before she turned away to face the entrance. "Good night, Belle," he called as he rested his head on his saddle.

Belle felt as if a knife had plunged into her chest as his low vibrant voice strummed the strings of her heart into a fierce fandango of mistrust. Somehow during the last twenty-four hours, she had changed, not because she was impersonating Rita but because she had blended their personalities. And the amazing thing was that she had become stronger...more self-assured...and more confident in her ability to be strong and see the ruse through. She chewed on her lower lip. But now she faced her biggest challenge yet. What was she to do if she discovered Niko had lied about everything?

A yawn caught her unaware and she straightened. She had to remain awake for she refused to take the chance that she would have another nightmare like the one she'd had two nights ago on board the British man-of-war. She had to remain awake...stay calm...and be vigilant. She glanced over at Niko lying on his side, facing away from her. Had she allowed her suspicions to get the better of her because she needed a solid reason to deny the fascination she felt toward him? She traced her fingers over the emblem once again. Who did the blanket belong to? Niko...or someone else? Or was she making a mountain out of a molehill?

Drawing her knees up to her chest, she lifted her gaze to study the night sky. What was she going to do now that she no longer fully trusted him? She yawned then shook her head, hoping to clear away her sleepiness. She had to remain awake, she cautioned herself. If not, the dream would come and... She stiffened, momentarily stymied. Why hadn't she been visited by the nightmare last night while on board the royal yacht?

Her mind whirled in bewilderment. Did it have anything to do with Niko or...the fact that she'd been so caught up in the windstorm and her impersonation of Rita that total exhaustion had claimed her last night?

She gazed longingly at the midnight sky then watched the moon move closer to the jagged peak as her mind reeled in confusion. Pensively, she looked out into the darkness as the clouds scuttled in front of the moon blocking its light. Rita believed in love at first sight. That being the case, had she unknowingly assumed more of Rita's personality than she'd intended? She sighed, knowing that she'd always been able to come up with more questions than answers regarding life.

"I thought you were to wake me when the moon moved over the peak," she heard Niko say from behind her.

Instantly, she became more alert. Embarrassed to have been caught wool-gathering, she peered up at the moon. Then she noticed it had moved beyond the point where she was to have awakened him. "How did you do that?" she asked to hide her confusion. "How did you know it was time to wake?"

"When you're a soldier you learn to sleep when and where you can," he said simply.

His words seemed to have a ring of truth about them. So, maybe he hadn't lied about that. But to test him further, she asked. "But how did you do it? How did you wake yourself? Or," she paused to reconsider, "were you playing opossum?"

"Ah, My Lady," he chuckled, "suddenly you are wanting to know all of my secrets?"

"That would be beneficial," she said as she leaned back to stare at him.

Niko felt that fierce, cold stare rush through him all the way to his toes. He eyed her for a moment as he wondered what he had said or done to cause her mistrust. Deciding he had best discover the cause, he gave her a nod, playing along. "Nothing opossum about me," he grinned. "But if you want to know my scientific method for waking, you will have to learn to trust me," he said as he lifted the food basket and carried it toward where she sat on the blanket.

"Promises, promises," he heard her say as she moved to the far corner of the blanket into the shadow created by moonlight.

He took a slow breath, inhaling her light vanilla scent as the moon dipped beyond the peak.

"All right," she said. "What's your secret?"

"You go right for the heart, don't you?" he asked as he sat the hamper near her.

"I've been told that's a family trait," she quipped as she opened the lid.

"Good to know," he said then nearly groaned aloud as he found her scooting closer to him. This close, it became hard to fight the attraction.

"And the secret?" she prodded.

"You are intent on extracting the truth from me, are you not?" he teased, gently.

"Think of it as...not so much an extraction but...rather as instruction," she replied, her tone light.

Much too unsettled by their repartee, he moved away. He knew he couldn't cross the line he had so painstakingly created. As with Stefan, who was his cousin and his King, he was her trusted colonel, her friend, and her confidant. He could be nothing more.

He paused as a thought streaked across his consciousness, but you're not her subject nor her cousin yet. "Um-m, yes, instruction," he said, hoping to gain a few more minutes to regain his composure. "Well then, close your eyes," he said then waited until she did so. "Now answer me this, what time would you like to rise?"

She opened her eyes. "What time would you like to leave?"

"Daylight," he murmured.

"Then first light it is," she said.

"Good. Now close your eyes." He waited until she did so. "Now, tell yourself you want to wake at first light."

"What?" she exclaimed as her eyes popped open in surprise. "That's it?" she said, her voice rising an octave. "That's all there is to your sci-en-tif-ic secret?"

"That's all there is to it," he grinned.

"I think you are a fraud."

He shivered at how near she came to the truth. "But you haven't tried my method yet, so how do you know?"

He heard her take a deep breath. "Unfortunately, you are right," she mumbled. "Now, what is it I have to do?"

He grinned. "Close your eyes and take three deep breathes." He watched her thick lashes flutter down to rest on her cheeks. He heard her breathe in and then slowly release the air trapped in her lungs with a 'whoosh'.

"Now, quietly tell yourself you want to wake at first light," he directed. "Take slow breaths and think about nothing. Let your mind go blank," he said then waited until she yawned. Turning to face away from him, she tucked her hand under her cheek and settled the blanket over her shoulders. He sat perfectly still until he could tell that she'd fallen asleep as her breathing deepened.

He'd never felt such a tremendous affinity to...or such joy from being with a stranger as he had with her, he realized as he tugged the slipping blanket back over her shoulder. For a woman like this, he would gladly give up his life.

He rested his chin on his knee as he inhaled the scented vanilla shampoo she used. She had surprised him from the moment he'd first laid eyes on her. And she continued to do so by the minute. Months ago he hadn't given a single thought about who Stefan's bride might be for he, like Stefan, had no say in the matter. He had simply resigned himself to what was to be. But now, the only one that mattered to him was Belle. What she wanted...and what he could do to make her happy.

In many ways, she was a contradiction. He'd never met anyone quite like her. She was impetuous...yet cautious, brave yet shy, trusting yet wary. Moving to sit next to her, he covered the both of them with the extra blanket. She was his to protect and care for...to honor and to guard. Guard, as in keep her safe from all possible harm...including himself, he cautioned himself as he tilted his head back to rest it against the weathered rock. Glancing down at her, he watched her sleep. He'd never once considered that a woman like her existed in the real world. Most royals like him never let themselves dream of what could never be. Marriage was always a matter of state. Of putting the nation's needs first and denying the personal ones. He frowned as he peered at her then wondered what his best friend, Cyrek would think about his thoughts and feelings regarding Belle.

***

Belle opened one eye as she came awake her ear pressed against a rhythmic thud. She took a slow breath as she opened her other eye to find Niko grinning down at her. She blinked her sleep filled eyes and started to sit up only to find she had wound her arms around Niko's waist and he had done the same to her.

She felt heat flush her face. Oh dear, what had she been thinking? Not only had she slept in the same space with a man but she had clung to him in her sleep. Slowly, she pulled away and sat up. Immediately, she noticed both the loss of his warmth and his smile.

"G-good morning," she managed to get passed her stiff lips. She straightened, her sore muscles protesting as she shifted to view the cave's entrance. Surprise left her stunned for a moment before she turned to him. "It worked, your method of waking actually worked."

He smiled that lazy smile that tied such terrible knots in her stomach. "It's first light," he said, his voice rumbling through her.

"So it is," she observed then clambered up to busy herself. After combing her fingers through her hair and binding it with a hair ribbon at the nape of her neck, she turned to find him holding a canteen.

"Here," he said, offering her the water flask. "Have a drink."

She nodded. Shyly accepting the canteen, she took a swallow. The cold water bathed her tinder dry throat. "Thanks," she said as she awkwardly handed it back to him. "Now, what can I do to help?"

He lifted his saddle. "If you will fold the blankets and secure the flask and basket, I will saddle the horses."

She nodded, as anxious to leave the cave as Niko seemed to be. In record time they had accomplished their tasks.

Niko grabbed the reins, then paused. "Ready to go?'

Belle gave the cave one last glance then nodded.

"We'll walk a way down the mountain until it's safe for us to mount up and ride," he said, waving her forward to join him.

Taking it slow, they moved single file down the muddy slope. They passed boulders that had fallen in their pathway leaving gaping holes where the land had slid away, forcing them to go slowly until eventually, they reached the base of the mountain. Then mounting up, they rode back through the damp, foggy air to the copse of trees. Stopping, Niko looped his reins over a branch and went around to lift Belle off. "You're mighty quiet this morning," he said as he retrieved two apples and the water flask from the hamper.

"I didn't want to distract you with my chatter," she said accepting the flask and the apple from him.

"I appreciate that," he said then quickly ate his breakfast.

Moving back to the horses, he untied the reins from the branch. Turning he paused as he spied a group of men riding slowly down the road from the vicinity they had come from yesterday. By their colorful wear, Niko guessed they were members of a band of Gypsies. But if they weren't, he'd best be ready to protect Belle. He reached for his firearm and felt her place her hand on his forearm.

"That might not be necessary," she whispered. He paused as she continued. "There appears to be women and children traveling with them."

As she finished, he heard a series of oinks and barks that were followed by laughter. He grinned as relief spread through him. "Apparently there are also dogs, goats, pigs, and chickens," he added as a caravan came into view. One after the other, carts covered in canvas as colorful as a rainbow rounded the bend. Quickly, he tucked his firearm into the waist of his trousers at his side. He flipped his jacket over it knowing it would take him but a split second to reach across his body and withdraw it.

Stepping away from his saddlebags, he offered his arm to her. "Follow my lead," he said as she looped her arm through his. Then side-by-side they led their horses out of the woods to meet the men.

Chapter Seven

"Hello," Niko called.

The band of men halted at the sound of his voice. Several men dropped back to walk with the women and children strolling beside the carts. Fully emerging from the copse of trees, he escorted Belle down the road as if they were out for a morning stroll.

A man looking to be in his mid-thirties broke away from the group and ambled forward, his hand outstretched as the caravan slowed to a stop. "Welcome, friend."

"Thank you," Niko said, shaking the man's hand.

"You are a brave man to be out here alone with your lady," the man said as he doffed his hat toward Belle.

"Brave?" Niko asked, hoping his feigned innocence sounded authentic. "How so?"

The man shook his curly dark head. "Three days ago rebels rode through our camp traveling south toward Ksamilli. Then yesterday, we came across their encampment on the road to Saranda."

"And you think the rebels will return, heading northward this time?" Niko asked beginning to wonder if he had erred in thinking they might avoid the rebels this far north.

"Should they do so," the man said, "then you and your lady shouldn't be out on the road alone."

"Are you offering us safe passage with you?" Niko asked as a niggling of suspicion slithered through him. From all appearances, he had thought that the group was a band of gypsies. Had he been wrong?

"That we are," the man said, "for no one should have to contend with that bunch of misfits on their own. By the way, I'm Rikard, the King of the Mimseco Tribe," he added then he whirled around. His short cape flared out in a circle, revealing the revolver tucked into the band of his pants. When he stopped, he doffed his hat and straightened. "I've always found there is strength in numbers even if we are only a band of lowly gypsies."

"And I'm Niko Orsini," he said, bowing politely to the man.

"Orsini?" Rikard asked, scratching his chin. "Of the Berat Orsini branch?"

Niko paused. Since the War of 1852, his uncle had granted all Gypsies' a safe haven in Barovia. From personal dealings with them, he had found them to be not only loyal and honest but hardworking and trust-worthy as well. People, he had been happy to welcome into their country. Deeming there was something trustworthy about Rikard, he said. "The one and the same. But I would appreciate it if only you and I share that information."

"Ah, yes, I see what you mean," Rikard nodded. "And this must be?"

Niko frowned as he watched a surprised look cross Rikard's swarthy features.

"I'm Belle," she said extending her gloved palm, ready to shake the man's hand.

Bowing from the waist, Rikard lifted her hand and unexpectedly touched her knuckles to his forehead. "Ma'am, your secret is safe with me," he said as he released her hand and took two steps backward.

Niko inhaled sharply. Had Belle's likeness already been painted on banners and displayed throughout the country? He felt his muscles tense at the thought as he gazed at her.

Belle glanced at Niko, unsure of what had just transpired between him and the gypsy. Then deciding to err on the side of courtesy, she managed to whisper, "Thank you." She took a step back as she wondered if the gypsy King had somehow recognized her as the future Queen of Barovia. A shiver of unease coursed through her as she wondered about the ramifications of the thought.

She watched as Niko and the gypsy King took a few steps away then put their heads together. She fiddled with the gauze tail attached to the band of her hat, then tossed it to the side when the two men returned to her.

"We will be traveling with Rikard and his people for a while," Niko said with a nod. "It isn't safe for us to be alone."

Not about to be left in the dark regarding the true situation, she cleared her throat softly then asked, "Because of the rebels?"

She watched Niko's eyes widen. "Amongst other things," he said. "And that is why you will be riding concealed in the back of a wagon."

"Come," Rikard said motioning to her. "We must get you settled in Etel's wagon." Walking the short distance back to the line of carts, they stopped at the second wagon. She watched Rikard pivot toward her. "Let me introduce you to Etel," he said, "you will riding with her."

Belle studied the elderly lady sitting on the seat in the front of the wagon with a young boy of about twelve who held the reins. She dipped her head in greeting.

"This is Etel, my grandmother," Rikard said proudly, "and my son, Tass."

"Would your grandmother happen to speak either French or Italian?" Belle asked quietly so as not to embarrass the woman if she spoke neither.

"Both," he said, pride ringing in his voice. "However, her Italian is more proficient."

Belle nodded then greeted the elderly woman in Italian. "Good morning, my name is Belle and thank you for offering me a ride," she said, thankful her mother had insisted she learn both Italian and French.

Etel smiled a gap-toothed grin. "Good morning, little one, best hop in the back so we can get on our way."

"Thank you," Belle said then hurried around to the back. As Niko opened the small door for her, he placed his hand on her arm, halting her. "It's been my experience with tribes like this that the men and women don't mix. But you can trust these people. They are loyal subjects to the crown," he said. "And if you need anything I'll be out in front with Rikard."

Belle nodded then scrambled into the back. As she did so, she looked around. The wooden cart was covered with canvas and appeared to be a rolling home on wheels. Black bottom pots and pans hung down from the arched beamed construction with the thick outer canvas attached to it. Multi-colored patchwork quilts, secured to the ribbing of the cart, hung above two benches. A narrow aisle divided the center of the cart. Spotting a three-legged stool at the front, she headed for the open flap where Tass and Etel sat on the driver's bench. Grabbing the stool, she centered it behind the two in front of her.

"Your name is like your voice," Etel said, her elderly voice but a whispered croak.

"Heavens!" Belle exclaimed. "I hope I'm not that loud."

She heard Tass chuckle "No, my lady, grandmother means your voice is like a musical chime singing in the wind."

"I bet you say that to all the pretty girls," Belle said then grinned.

"No, you're the first," he said as he glanced back over his shoulder and winked at her.

"Best keep your eyes on the road, young man," his grandmother admonished. "For around the next bend-" Etel stopped mid-sentence, grabbed the boy's hands, pulled on the reins and gave a twittering whistle. "Quick, My Lady, pass me the man's hat and cloak from the shelf across from you," she said as she flipped the partition separating the driver's box from the living space closed "Now, change out of that fancy riding getup you're wearing into the skirt and blouse on the ledge hanging above you. Rebels are coming."

Belle grabbed the man's items and shoved them through the gap she'd created in the partition. She had just passed the items to Etel when Niko came striding back toward the wagon. "Stay out of sight," he ordered as he removed his cape and jacket and handed them to Etel. Then swiftly, he donned the peasant gear. Stepping away, he turned and limped back toward Rikard at the head of the caravan.

Aghast, Belle stared at him. What had they seen that she hadn't, she wondered then frowned as she studied the men walking at the front of the group.

"Hurry," Etel said. "The rebels have wounded with them. We're going to need every hand we have. Now, change into the skirt and blouse laying on the shelf above you. Take one of those scarves and tie it over your hair, remove your stockings but put your shoes back on. Find the green jar in the basket near the back door. Rub the liquid over any part of your skin not covered by your clothing," Etel finished as she handed Niko's garments to her.

Tossing his clothing under the bed, Belle began to undress. "Don't come out until I tell you to," the elderly woman croaked as she twitched the covering over the opening behind the wagon seat.

Enclosed in the tomb-like structure, Belled hurriedly changed into the multi-colored peasant skirt and blouse. Then rolling her riding outfit into a ball, she hid it under the other bed.

Straightening, she wrapped a green paisley scarf around her head to hide her hair, removed her stockings and then tucked her feet back into her shoes. Standing, she grabbed for the shelf ledge to steady herself as she felt the cart slow then she noticed that her hands were trembling. Her heart began to race in her chest as she realized fear of the unknown was beginning to slow her movements. Forcing herself toward the basket containing the green jar, she bent and retrieved it. Then making her way back to the narrow bed, she sat and unstopped the jar. Sniffing, she inhaled the crisp scent of mint with an undertone of marigold. Frowning, she dipped her fingers into the jelly-like substance. Then shrugging, she began slathering her arms with the substance. She felt her eyes widen as her skin began to darken to a golden brown. No one would ever believe that she came from the cold northern country of Britain. After rubbing it on her face, ears, back of her neck, shoulders and legs and feet, she grabbed a shawl and tossed it around her shoulders to conceal any skin she hadn't been able to reach.

Too anxious to remain seated, she made her way to the front. Leaning forward, she gently grabbed both sides of the partition and created a slit she could peek through over the heads of Etel and Tass. Suddenly, she spied a motley assortment of men stumble into sight. She clutched at the curtains as she heard a man shout, "Halt."

"How did you know–," she began to whisper through the slit.

"Later," Etel mumbled as Belle felt the cart roll to a stop. She bit her bottom lip as she realized only a space of several feet separated the two groups. She hoped it was enough to keep the caravan safe.

"Good day to you, I'm Rikard," the Gypsy King said as he went to meet them. "May we offer you food and medical assistance for your wounded? Or burial for your dead?"

Belle inhaled sharply at the word, 'dead' then squinted into the sun to search for Niko.

Niko lowered his eyes as if in deference to Rikard's wise judgment. Then surreptitiously lifting his gaze, he quickly scanned and counted the number of rebels. He was quick to note that everyone, including their leader, had sustained an injury. That meant they must've lost at least a dozen or so men to his forces.

"Prince Jorge advised us to leave the dead where they fell," the spokesman for the group said.

Niko felt as if he'd been struck with a streak of lightning. Prince Jorge...his uncle? His father's younger brother was the force leading the rebels? His mind seemed to freeze in disbelief. No, it's not true. He wanted to shout as a lightheadedness settled over him. While he knew his uncle was a wastrel and spent the majority of his time with like-minded people, he found it difficult to believe his uncle was guilty of treason...or that he was actively plotting the collapse of their country. He shook his head rejecting the treacherous idea then paused as a niggling of doubt filtered through him. Two months ago Stefan had mentioned that he had refused their uncle's request for a substantial increase in his monthly funds. Their uncle had threatened dire consequences in response. He tightened his jaw, swallowing back an oath. Recently, he had discovered that his uncle was deep in gambling debt. He felt his breath hitch in his chest as he realized the ramifications of his uncle's perfidy. An icy chill seized him as he surfaced from his dismay and heard the rebel leader say, "He also told us that if we could find your band that you would be of assistance."

Numbly, he studied the man who seemed to be in charge. By his dark, bushy beard and soiled clothing, Niko knew the man was a paid mercenary probably hired by his uncle from somewhere in the Slavic Empire. He stiffened as the reality of what he'd heard pelted him like the smell of eggs rotting in the summer's heat. Anger rolled through him. If his uncle was behind all the unrest in the country then not only was his uncle responsible for the chaos rampaging through the towns and villages but also for the kidnappings and extortion demands, the robbery of wealthy merchants and the killing of innocent civilians caught in the crossfire.

His breath seemed to seize in his chest at the enormity of his uncle's crimes. And if his uncle was anywhere near, that meant by rescuing Belle from the Black Swan, he had not only placed her in a deadly position but also his men and the gypsies. As he balled his fists, he felt his veins crust with ice.

"We'll set up camp over there by the big rocks," Rikard directed as he motioned for his band to drive their wagons in a circle near the rocks.

"I'll have my men gather wood and water," the ruffian leader said as he joined Rikard and Niko. "I'm grateful I've found you," he added in a gravelly tone.

Niko realizing he could no longer remain passive, lowered his tone an octave to disguise his voice and asked, "What happened to your men?" He wondered what other transgression his uncle was planning to spring on them.

"Encountered the King's forces outside of Saranda and as you can see being the small band that we are, we suffered heavy losses and casualties."

Niko frowned. Hoping to conceal the rush of satisfaction that flowed through him, he turned aside in feigned concern to survey the rebels.

"Is that something that need concern us," Rikard asked as he glanced toward Niko. "By the way, this is my cousin, Kolai," he said introducing Niko to the mercenary.

"Call me Gus," the ruffian said, scratching his beard. "Think your women can wash my clothes?"

"I imagine all of our wives will be busy tending to your wounded," Niko replied as he glanced toward Rikard.

"And serving the midday meal," Rikard added as he began clearing a place for a fire in the middle of the camp.

'I'll gather the pots for the water," Niko volunteered quickly. Knowing he had to warn Belle of the dire circumstances they found themselves in, he turned. Slowly limping toward where Belle was hiding in Etel's wagon, he pondered how much he should reveal to her.

"What's wrong with him?" he heard Gus ask.

"Born that way," Rikard said as Niko opened the back gate that served as a door to the wagon.

The rest of the conversation was lost as he entered and placed his finger over Belle's lips then shook his head. Leaning close, he whispered. "I need to tell you a few things. These are the rebels I warned you about back at the inn."

"Do you think those we left behind are safe?"

A sour taste filled his mouth. Although Niko didn't want to lie to her, he knew it wasn't safe for him to reveal the truth. "I've roughly counted over a dozen wounded," he hedged, hoping his officers had thoroughly routed the rebels yet suffered no casualties. Then not about to add to her worry, he added. "I would say your entourage is safely on their way to Berat."

Belle nodded then frowned. "What happened to your leg?"

"I was afraid they might recognize me," he said, "so that's why I'm limping."

"And," she said, her brows furrowing into a frown.

"Call me 'Kolai,'" he said. "Just remember to drop off the 'Nik' and you'll have it."

"All right," she nodded then continued to stare at him. "And?"

"And by the way, you're my wife," he said then quickly placed his palm over her mouth to prevent her gasp from becoming an outraged exclamation.

"I-I'm-m your-" she mumbled into his palm.

"Wife," he said, finishing the sentence for her. Then withdrawing his hand from her mouth, he added, "for the time being until the rebels have left the area."

"I see," Belle said. He heard the undertone of her uncertainty filtering through her whisper. "That's something no one should joke about," she said, her frown deepening.

He nodded, at this point in time, he wasn't about to get into an argument with her. "But it's safer for you if the rebels believe that," he said.

"You're concerned about my reputation?" she asked.

He paused. If his uncle was commanding the rebel forces, they had much more to worry about than reputation. He stared at her for a moment. "I'm only doing my job...I'm protecting you."

She nodded and stepped away from him. Turning, she sidled past him.

He grasped her shoulders, then noticed that his hands met her silky flesh. He gaped at her for a moment. "What do you think you're doing dressed like this?" he asked as he took his first good look at her gypsy outfit.

Saints Above! She was breath-taking! Her sun-kissed arms and shoulders glowed with a sheen of satin. His eyes swept downward to view her hiked skirt that revealed her delicately trimmed ankles.

Mother of Mercy! He couldn't let the rebels see her for they would surely molest her.

Gathering the pots, she glanced up at him. "Well, are you going to stand there or are you going to help?"

He shook away his disturbing thoughts. "Depends if you're going to be an obedient wife or a shrew?" he riposted, knowing he had to disarm the situation.

"What would you prefer I be?" she asked, simply.

"Out of sight," he mumbled, staring at her.

She shook her head. "That can't happen," she said assembling various supplies on the table. "The women are going to need all the help they can get to take care of the wounded."

Hoping to dissuade her from helping, he asked, "Do you even know what you're doing?"

"Have you ever cleaned a wound?" she countered, placing her balled fists at her waist.

"A few," he admitted.

"Well, so have I," she said, then asked. "Have you ever stitched together flesh?"

"Can't say that I have," he said, cringing at the remembered pain that had felt like a thousand sharp needles piercing his skin.

"I have," she said, "along with caring for a fever, purging a stomach from poison, wrapping an ulcerated foot and draining a deep wound. What of you?"

"All right," he said, raising his hands in the air as if in surrender. "You've convinced me. So, what can I do to help?" he asked, knowing he had to remain beside her for her own protection.

She grinned as she handed him a pot. "Haul water."

"Already assigned," he said offering the pot back to her. Then lifting the long vest-like unbleached muslin garment from the hook by the back door, he held it out to her. Hoping to convince her to put it on so as not to call undue attention to herself, he said, "If you are to help with the wounded like the rest of the women, you need to wear this to keep your clothing clean."

She frowned as she set the pot aside and straightened. "The women are wearing this?"

He nodded as he shook the garment open. He knew it was a gypsy custom for the younger women to hide beneath the long muslin garments when strangers were present. "All except Etel and the other elderly women." He held his breath for a moment then released it in relief as she slipped her arms through the garment.

He watched her gather the front of the garment together and button it down the front. As she lifted her chin, he noted a gamine grin settle on her lips. "I've decided you can keep the fires supplied with firewood," she said as she reached for the handle on the back door.

"Also already assigned." He nodded as he felt a grin lift the corners of his mouth. Not only did the garment conceal the gypsy attire she wore but also her ankles as well. He smiled, beginning to enjoy her frowning countenance.

Suddenly, he noted she brightened. He unfolded his arms and straightened warily. "Then it looks as if you'll be my supply runner," she said flashing him a grin.

"And what does that entail?" Niko asked, hoping it had nothing to do with emptying or scrubbing out the camp's piss pots.

"You gather and keep me supplied with everything I need."

Although he wanted to groan aloud, he realized that he would at least be able to monitor her movements. "Then that's what I'll do," he said then hesitated. "Although I would rather stay near enough to protect you."

"We all do what must be done," she said as she piled his arms full of pots and pans. Then lifting the gauze they would need for wound care from the shelf, she exited the wagon.

Niko paused on the steps and surveyed the scene which now appeared to be a well-organized triage area. Toward the tree line, a medical area had been established with the rebels building their own fire. A lean-to of sorts had been constructed of four long branches stuck in the ground and a fifth branch serving as a center pole was lashed at the top. Blankets covered the perimeter of the structure serving as a dispensary. A line had formed. Men on make-shift crutches, others lying on the ground or propped against the base of the trees waited to receive medical care.

He watched as Belle headed toward the wounded but changed directions as Etel summoned her.

Anxious to get started, Belle hurried over to Etel. "What would you like me to do?"

Etel seemed to stare at her for a moment before she asked. "Can you care for the seriously wounded?"

"As long as you have whiskey, I can," Belle replied, firmly.

Turning, Etel shouted. "Bring the keg."

At that, Tass scurried away from the main campfire and into the back of their wagon. A few minutes later he emerged with a small jug tucked under one arm. Grinning, he hurried over and set it down in front of his grandmother then he took a step back and smiled.

"Well, must I tell you everything," the old woman asked as she made a shooing gesture with her hands. "Get a cup. Belle looks mighty thirsty."

The other women working with the injured began to chuckle. Realizing the joke was on her, Belle joined in knowing that it would undoubtedly be a long day.

By midafternoon they had tended all the wounded and had eaten a late meal. Most of the rebels napped, leaving the women free to pursue their own chores.

"Come, child," Etel said as she patted the log beside where she sat near her wagon. She lifted a short piece of board and set it on her lap then dug into her multicolored skirt of reds, blues, and yellows and withdrew a small bundle. Reverently, unwrapping the royal blue velvet material, she revealed a deck of cards. "You're new to the camp and must have your fortune told," she said as she rapped the deck of cards three times with her bony knuckles and began to shuffle the deck.

Belle stared at the cards. Suddenly not only afraid of what they might reveal but also afraid if she didn't comply with Etel's request that she would create problems for her and Niko.

She glanced over at Niko sitting amongst the men. He raised his head, glanced at her then nodded as if she'd voiced her concerns aloud. Taking a deep breath for courage, she asked. "What would you like for me to do?"

"Do?" Etel parroted as she blew on the cards then shuffled and fanned them. She spread them out in a line then lifted the topmost card from the deck. "I don't-" she paused for a moment, her eyes growing round as if in surprise. "My cards are picky about who touches them but they seem to call out to you. They want you to select them."

A tightness settled in Belle's chest as she watched Etel fan the deck out face down on her make-shift table. As Belle started to reach toward the cards, she quickly dropped her hand back into her lap as a sinking sensation settled in her stomach. She knew from Aunt Ellie's ventures into the arcane that tarot cards seldom lied. Surreptitiously, she placed her other hand over her crossed fingers resting in her lap. "H-how should I do this?"

"Without touching them, you will choose three cards by slowly moving your hand over the deck," Etel instructed. "When you feel an energy, a warmth, tap the table above the card and I will place it on the numbered outline drawn on my table."

Belle nodded and raised her left palm. Slowly, she began moving her hand above each card. Suddenly she gasped as heat tingled in her palm. "Wait," she said as disbelief flooded through her. Slowly, she tapped the index finger of her other hand on the table indicating the card. Then immediately, she moved her palm over to the next card then stared at Etel. Her heart thundered in her ears as she realized the significance of the heat that she'd felt. This reading wasn't anything like Aunt Ellie had claimed a tarot reading should be. A shiver of fear coursed through her. Not only was this reading different but there was something extraordinary about it. She trembled at the thought then straightened unwilling to accept what her mind was attempting to tell her.

Disbelieving what she'd felt, she forced her hand to reverse back to the selected card and once again felt the tingle. "This one," she said. This time she allowed Etel to remove the card and place it in the first spot marked on the lap table then continuing on through the deck she felt the warm tingle two more times then stopped although there were still more cards left.

"The cards want you to continue and select one more," Etel said, "but this time you will pick up the card you've selected and place it yourself in the final remaining space."

"I-I'm to touch the card?" Belle asked as a frisson of fear coursed through her. She knew that if she actually touched the cards, her fear would pass from her to the deck. Aunt Ellie had been adamant about telling them that no one was to touch her cards. That if they did, the cards would absorb the person's energy that had touched them. And that energy would be revealed in the reading. Afterward, the cards couldn't be used again until they went through a purification ritual. She felt her fingers tremble as she tried to swallow back her panic. But could the cards pick up her perfidy simply from her sitting near them?

"Strange as it may seem," the old woman said, "the cards talk to me and I always follow their directions."

Belle nodded, her tongue frozen to the roof of her mouth as she forced herself to continue as instructed. Dread seemed to build and slow her movement. It wasn't until she had gotten to the very last of the deck that she once again felt the heat. She cringed in fright as she carefully lifted the card from the table.

"Now, place it here," Etel said with a grin.

Belle dropped the card in the spot indicated. Then sat back and grasped her trembling digits as she studied the card placement which resembled a basic four-point compass rose.

"The first card you selected is the card of your past," Etel said as she turned it over.

Belle squinted at the horse and cart painted on the card as stunned disbelief rushed through her. "I don't understand?" she whispered hoarsely, her heart thundering in her chest. "How can this be?"

"Then the chariot is significant to you?" Etel asked.

Belle wet her suddenly dry lips. She had lived through that freezing winter day wedged under the seat as the coach had slid across the icy road, tumbled into the ravine and crashed at the bottom. It had killed both of her parents. And yet she had survived. But she had discovered that surviving had been the easy part, suffering through the anguish and guilt had become nearly impossible.

"The past will continue to haunt you until you make peace with it," Etel said as she leaned forward, her voice but a whisper.

All Belle could do was nod, too stunned to think of anything to say. How could anyone ever find peace after living through something like that? Certainly not her, she didn't deserve it. She straightened as Etel tapped the second card.

"This card represents the present," Etel said as she lifted a card with a tower painted on it and placed it face up. "The one who looks like you will bring you much pain."

Belle felt her heart skip a beat. She inhaled sharply then froze in trepidation. The cards had discovered her lie. She shook away the numb feeling then quickly bit her lip, not about to discuss the present time with anyone. "A-and the future?" she stammered hurriedly, hoping to skip onto the next card.

Etel flipped over the third card at the topmost position on her board then smiled. "Ah," she sighed. "The Lovers. When this card appears, it means you have found happiness and love."

Belle swallowed back her of exclamation of denial. Was she supposed to find love and happiness with Umberford? "W-wait a minute," she stammered. "Please repeat...what you said."

Etel's grin widened. "Surprised you didn't I?" She cackled then sobered. "Like this reading, the unexpected happens. The card indicates that you have already found love."

"Did you say found?" Belled asked then frowned. "As in, I've...already discovered it?"

"Ah, child, why so surprised? That man of yours worships the ground you walk on, how could you not love him in return?" Etel asked with a shrug.

Niko loved her? The thought caused her to nearly swallow her tongue in surprise until she realized that of course he did. He thought of her as his Queen. She paused at the thought. But, how could she tell if a man loved a woman for herself or because of her position?

Belle turned her attention toward where Niko sat with the other men. Granted she would admit to herself that she found him extremely attractive and that she cared about his well-being. But regardless of those facts, she was still deceiving him and would continue to do so for as long as she was playing the role of Rita. So, as far as she was concerned, there was nothing but friendship between them.

"Would you care to turn over your last card?" Etel asked. "It is your advice card."

Just what she needed, more advice Belle decided as she resolutely flipped the final card over. She inhaled sharply as she stared at the Grim Reaper.

"Ah, the death card," Etel said then frowned at Belle. "This is important in that it means the end of something. A relationship, an untenable situation you might find yourself in. It doesn't mean you'll physically die. It means that whatever is troubling you will end and something new will take its place." Etel studied the cards for a moment then lifted her gaze. Belle shivered at the intensity of Etel's concentration, hoping the woman couldn't read minds as well as she did Tarot. "The cards are telling me three things," Etel said, a frown wrinkling her brow. "The first is to defend yourself. Stand up. Be firm about what you want and what you believe in. The second is...your destiny is in your own hands. Follow your heart. And the third is to let no one take away from you...that which you desire most. You must shake off the old and embrace what is new."

"That's a lot to remember," Belle mumbled relieved to actually hear words that she could consider as encouragement.

"Think about it," Etel advised. "But remember, first you must make peace with your past."

"How do I do that?" Belle asked as she squinted at the cards wondering if they contained the hidden answer.

"Forgive yourself," Etel responded, sagely.

"But...how do I do that?" Belle asked then clenched her jaw as irritation surged through her.

"Um-m," Etel said looking around. "See that boulder over there," she said pointing her bony finger beyond the campfire to the large rock.

Belle stared at the massive boulder then felt her jaw drop open. "I can't possibly move that," she began.

"Of course not," Etel said then chuckled. "You are to walk around it three times this afternoon, three times this evening and three more times tomorrow morning. While walking, you are to chant, 'I forgive myself for all I've done'. And you will be forgiven."

"Surely it can't be as simple as that?" Belle asked, clearly hearing her disbelief filtering through into her tone.

"Forgiveness can be as simple or as difficult as we make it," Etel said. Then gathering the cards, she rapped them three times with her knuckles and covered them with the velvet cloth.

Belle realized she had a lot to consider. And the least of it was whether she was brave enough to circle the rock while chanting the forgiveness phrase. She swallowed back her trepidation then stood. "Thank you," she whispered as she eyed the massive boulder then shifted her gaze to Niko.

Niko had almost called across the campfire to Belle as she had glanced in his direction when Etel had pulled out her tarot cards. Personally, although he didn't believe in the arcane he did believe in following the protocol he'd been raised with. The set of guidelines dictated 'when one was a guest, one always complied with the host's request' even if it meant something one was allergic to...like squid. He grimaced then watched Belle and Etel as they huddled over the cards. Belle would make a most excellent Queen he thought and if—

"Don't you agree 'Kolai'?" he heard Rikard ask.

Niko swung his gaze back to the Elders sitting around the campfire. Feeling a bit foolish for being inattentive, he leaned forward. "About what?" He asked as nonchalantly as he could.

"In order for you to stay the night, we have a policy that all couples spending the night in our encampment must go through a rite of initiation," Rikard said.

"All?" Niko asked then made a point of peering at the rebels loitering around the camp. "Don't suppose you would grant a special dispensation for extraordinary circumstances?"

Rikard shook his head as the elders chuckled. "No one violates our rules and lives to tell of it," he said, simply.

"And...this initiation ceremony...consists of?" Niko countered, suddenly wary of the grinning men around him.

"It's simple," Rikard said. "We tie a scarf around the couple's hands after making a small cut on the inside of each of their wrists."

Niko felt his brow furrow. "Sounds more like an ancient marriage rite my grandfather once described."

"Some have used it as such," Rikard said with a nod. "But in your case, this will be used strictly for your lady's protection."

About to object Niko noticed Belle disappearing behind the large rock across from the campfire. Didn't she realize it wasn't safe to disappear out of sight? Quickly, he excused himself and hurried after her. As he neared the rock, he heard her mumbling.

"I forgive myself for all I've done. I forgive myself..." she repeated in a sing-song voice.

"Belle," he called softly so as not to startle her. "It's not safe for you to be out here alone."

"I know," she said, her voice muffled from the other side of the rock. "I am being careful."

"So, what are you doing?" he asked as he rounded the large boulder and caught sight of her ready to disappear around to the front side of the rock.

He watched her turn back toward him. "I'm doing what Etel told me to do," she said placing her hands on her hips.

"And that is?"

He watched her lift her hands into the air as if giving up. "I'm forgiving myself," she said, simply.

"Ah," he said, "this has to do with the tarot reading?"

She nodded then turned away.

"May I join you?" he asked.

He watched Belle stop for a moment. Then she shook her head. "You'll only get dizzy."

He swallowed back a laugh. "How many times must you circle the rock?" he asked as he approached her.

"Three times now, three more times this evening and then three times tomorrow morning," she said, her tone uncertain as her eyebrows squished together.

Niko scratched at his jaw to hide his smile. He liked the fact that Belle seemed to be embracing the gypsy culture. Though they had both donned the peasant attire and he was growing a beard and limping... it still remained his job to keep her safe. And to do that, he needed to walk with her. "I think I can last that long."

She stared at him for a moment then shrugged. "All right," she said as she started circling the rock again repeating the mantra Etel had given her.

He slowed his limping gait to accommodate her smaller steps.

Scanning the perimeter of the camp he realized they had gained the attention of the elders and a few of the rebels. Something they didn't need if they were to keep their identities secret. "Is this the last time around for this afternoon?" he asked hoping it was.

"It is until this evening," Belle said as she came to a stop. She smiled up at him. "I thank you for that escort. If there's anything I can do to assist you, please let me return the favor," she said as she took a step back.

"As to that," Niko said, gently grasping her wrist and preventing her from moving away. "There is a small matter regarding us spending the night here."

"Surely, they're not throwing us out?" she gasped.

"No, it's not that," Niko said hurriedly then paused to feign a chuckle. "They're initiating us into their tribe."

A huge smile blossomed across her lips. "Really? I'm going to belong to a band of gypsies?"

"That you are. We both are," he said in a whoosh, grateful that he had cleared that hurdle so easily. He would use his uncle's belief that the gypsies were his allies. If they maintained a low profile and remained with the band until Berat then they might reach the safety of the palace.

"This is so-o-o exciting!" she said with a big smile.

Her enthusiastic reaction brought Niko to a halt. He had never seen her so animated. He studied her for a moment and realized that something seemed a bit off. It was almost as if she was an entirely different person. As if he was seeing her for the first time. "How can you have forgotten that soon everyone in this country will be your subjects?" he asked.

Her shoulders seemed to slump like a blacksmith's bellows deprived of air. "Ah, yes...my people," she muttered, then shaking her head, she turned and walked toward Etel's wagon.

Niko scratched his itchy jaw again. What had he said to have caused such a reaction?

Chapter Eight

"Come," Etel said as she opened the door and poked her head inside. "One of the wounded men is worsening."

Belle put aside the shirt she was mending and stood. "I was afraid that would happen," she murmured as she joined Etel outside the wagon.

"Hush, child," Etel warned then looked around cautiously as she picked up an empty pot and rag. "You must be very careful in what you say and do. Your words and actions could reveal you are not one of us."

"Niko said that after our eventide meal that we were to be initiated into your tribe," Belle said, quietly. "That will make us members of your band."

"Who told your friend that was happening?" Etel asked.

"Rikard," Belle said as they skirted the camp's perimeter to enter the area where the rebels lay recuperating from their wounds.

"We'd best not speak of this until later," Etel advised as she swiftly dipped her pot into the swift-flowing stream beside their camp.

Belle frowned, glanced at Etel and swallowed back her questions. If Etel thought she should wait, then she would.

"This is the one who's developed a fever," Etel said as she set the pot of water on the ground beside the perspiring soldier. She handed the cloth to Belle. "Will you cool his flesh while I make him some willow bark tea?"

"Of course," Belle replied as she knelt beside the restless moaning man. Dipping the cloth into the cold mountain water, she wrung it out and placed it on the young man's forehead. He could not have been but a year older than her, she surmised. As she began to withdraw her hand, the man grabbed her wrist.

"No," he moaned, tightening his hold. "Can't do."

"It's all right," she whispered, trying to soothe the agitated man. "I'm just going to rinse it and put it right back on your forehead."

As she started to draw away, the man opened his blue glassy eyes and stared up at her.

"Get… the… Prince," he uttered, slowly.

"Get the Prince?" she asked. Was the man delirious? There was no Prince here. "Who do you mean?"

"Jorge," the man rasped. "Must tell him that—"

"Perhaps if you told me what you wanted to say then I could find him and relate your message to him," she said, hoping to placate his feverish mutterings.

"Can't," the man rasped. "Tell…only… him."

"But which man is he?" she asked, feverishly looking around. "How will I be able to find him?"

"In Berat," the man said, tiredly.

"You're in no shape to be traveling there," she said, placing the cloth back on his forehead. "I don't know why you think you are."

"Have…to…"

"To what?" she inserted, feeling fear bubble up within her.

"Hondros," the man managed to mumble just before his head slumped to the side.

Hoping to revive him, Belle frantically dipped the cloth back into the water, wrung it out and quickly laid it back across the man's forehead.

What did the man expect her to do? Walk to Berat? And who was Prince Jorge? And exactly what did he mean by 'Hondros'?

Belle glanced up to observe Etel winding her way through the wounded, carrying the cup of medicine. How would Rita be able to send young men off to die in war when she couldn't even resolve herself to be Queen?

She inhaled sharply. And what was she to do if Rita decided that she wouldn't marry King Stefan? She froze.

What if Rita refused to revert back to herself?

Belle took a shaky breath at the disquieting thought. She'd best not get the cart before the horse. She'd best wait until she'd rejoined her sister in Berat before worrying about what she'd do if—

"Here's his tea," Etel said, thrusting the cup at Belle. "Try to get as much down him as you can."

"Do you think a spoon would work better?" Belle asked.

"It might," Etel said as she waved her grandson over then sent him to the wagon.

Running back with the spoon, Tass handed it to his grandmother. "Rikard said that Belle needs to return to the wagon," he said.

"Why?" Etel asked.

"Her man wants her there," he said, simply.

Her man?

Belle tightened her jaw and hid her balled fists. Although not about to reveal the game she and Niko played, she did feel her ire rise to be so summarily summoned. Turning away, she took several deep breaths. Finally calmer, she turned back. "And exactly what is it my man needs me to do?"

"Sister," Tass said, "If you don't know then I'm not telling you."

"Now, none of that," Etel said as she swatted at her grandson. "Get you gone. You've caused enough mischief for one day."

"Ah, Grams, I—",

"Enough, I say," Etel retorted. "I don't wanna hear it. Go." She turned, her hands on her hips. "As for you," she said, pointing her bony finger at Belle. "You heard Tass. Get to the wagon."

"But, I—"

"It makes no sense balking like this," Etel shook her knobby knuckles at her. "When a man says, 'come', we come. When a man says 'go', we go. Does no good railing against kismet. There's no changing it. That's the way it is."

Belle sighed. Although she wanted to rail against fate, she realized that Etel was right. This was one battle she wasn't going to win.

"Walk straight across camp," Etel said as she dipped a cup into the water bucket then straightened. "You'll be safe if you don't stop for anything."

Belle nodded, not about to draw any more attention to herself than she had. She didn't want to endanger herself or Niko nor did she want to sit through another lecture from him. She stared at the rebels gathered around the main campfire sitting amongst the tribe members. Then glancing neither to the left or the right, she crossed to Etel's wagon as if on a mission. Once at the back door, she slumped to the wooden step and took a deep, steadying breath.

"You sulking?" Niko asked as he joined her at the back stoop.

"No," she whispered, attempting to quiet her jangled nerves. One thing was for certain, she could never be a real Queen, not with everyone constantly watching her every move. Rita of course, would love the attention and would make a wonderful Queen. She glanced up at Niko. "Why do you ask?"

"You looked like a ten-year-old marching off to face your governess. Why the attitude?"

Belle stared up at him for a moment. Why did he have to prod and probe every little thing? Didn't he realize that he made people angry or was that his purpose? She shook her head, not about to explain either her insecurities or her guilt to him. "Perhaps I wasn't finished with my task?" She said, hoping to change the topic of their conversation.

"That's a prevarication," he said, leaning toward her. His warm breath brushed the curve of her cheek. "Why lie when it's more honorable to tell the truth?"

She scooted to the side, not about to give into his intimidating tactics. "Perhaps it's because men like you can't handle the truth," she said, hoping her taunt would find its mark.

Squatting on his haunches, he grabbed the sides of the stoop, effectively trapping her within his arms. "And the truth is?" he asked, balancing on the balls of his feet.

"I don't like being summoned in that manner," she said as she quickly placed her hands flat against his chest and gave him a hard shove. She sprang to her feet as he went sprawling on his backside in the dirt. "Now, please remember that-"

"And that would be?" he asked then laughed as he picked himself up off the ground.

"You are not an eastern potentiate," she sputtered as she placed her hands on her hips. "And I am not your—"

"Concubine," he finished for her as he dusted himself off.

"That's not at all what I had planned on saying," she said. "Had you given me the opportunity I would have said—"

"Wife?" he supplied then grinned as he took a step toward her.

"Slave," she corrected as she held her hand up.

A stunned expression settled on his face and he halted. "You believe a wife is a man's slave?"

"In many societies, yes," she said dropping her hand to ball her fingers into a fist. She had read too many books and talked to too many married women not to know the truth.

"Not here in Barovia," he said, straightening.

She shivered as she felt his eyes sweep over her. "What's so different about here?" she asked as she searched his somber face for any sign of provocation.

"Everyone is free."

"To do what?" she asked, not about to take his word for something that was this important to her sister. Both England and Barovia were ruled by a monarchy. And in most cases, one's life was at the whim of the ruler. That didn't constitute freedom as she'd learned to her dismay.

"King Stefan governs with benevolence. And we treat each other with dignity and respect."

"And," she prompted, knowing there was more to this than what he was telling her.

"We care for our families."

"Then you are married?" she asked then bit her bottom lip as she waited for the answer to the question she should've asked days ago.

"Not at the present moment," he said then grinned.

She studied his grinning countenance and wished she could wipe the smile from his face. "Sounds as if you intend to be shortly."

Niko stepped closer, not about to let her get away from him a second time. "That all depends," he said. He knew they had to settle this discord between them now because Rikard and the council were waiting for them. Gently, he lifted one of her wrists.

"On what?" she squeaked as he tugged on her wrist.

"On our induction into the tribe," he said dipping his head to inhale the scent of her vanilla fragrance. It reminded him of the special cakes his mother used to make for him.

"If you fear that I will do something to jeopardize this country or the marriage of King Stefan, then think again," she said, attempting to wrest her arm from his grasp.

"I didn't say that you would," he said, releasing her. "But, it's not safe for either of us to leave this camp while the rebels remain here. Therefore, it's imperative we comply with all of Rikard's orders."

"And what orders are those?" she asked as a frown wrinkled her forehead.

"To participate in the tribal ceremony," he said matter-of-factly.

"And the ceremony?" She asked, her eyes narrowed to slits.

"It will only take a few minutes," he said to reassure her, "and is guaranteed to keep you safe this evening."

"And what of the morning?" she asked.

"We can go around the rock three times together, chanting, 'I absolve the association'," he said then hoped his grin relieved her from her anxiety.

"That's not funny," she snapped then hesitated for a moment. "But that might not be a bad idea." She met his gaze then nodded slowly. "All right, I'll do it."

Niko took a quick breath then held out his arm to her, not about to give her an opportunity to reconsider. "We'll slip behind the wagon and meet Rikard and the Council near the rain barrel for the ceremony."

"Now?" she asked as he heard the sound of an owl hoot nearby. "We have to do this now?"

"No time like the present." He shrugged then felt himself tense as he raised his eyes to study the tree branches above him.

"It's obvious the word 'procrastination' isn't part of your vocabulary," she mumbled.

He lowered his gaze then assisted her as they rounded a boulder sitting in their path. "Naw," he countered, allowing a teasing note to warm his voice. "That's a lesson every junior officer learns to his detriment."

"I see," she frowned, doubt flowing through her tone.

"Important matters," he said, leading her away from camp toward the stream where Rikard had parked his wagon. "Should never be delayed." He paused as an owl hooted again. He slowed and scanned the trees.

"That's a good lesson to learn," Belle said as the moon slipped over the mountains and bathed them in silvery light. Ahead of them, three elderly men and Rikard stood waiting in front of the flickering campfire. An owl repeated its hoot and this time he located the bird perched on a branch above the campsite.

He took a deep breath, relieved the sound was real and not merely an imitation made by one of his scouts as a signal.

Rikard motioned them forward then stooped near his campfire to hold a small knife over the flame.

"This is where it gets a little tricky," Niko said, peering down at her to judge her squeamishness. "In order to do this according to Mimseco Custom, we both need to have our inner wrists scored. Then we will be joined together by tying a purple scarf around our hands. Any problem with that?"

"If it doesn't bother you, then it won't me," she said with a lift to her shoulders.

It was all over in a matter of seconds. Niko accepted the goblet of wine from Rikard and waited for Belle to take hers.

"Are you sure this is customary?" She asked as she raised her wine in a salute.

"Probably more so than either of us realize," he mumbled as he touched the rim of his goblet to hers. "Now, we are to loop arms. You are to drink from my cup and I am to drink from yours."

"I thought only the Vikings did things like this?" she whispered as she peered at him for a moment and then touched her sinfully beautiful mouth to the edge of his goblet.

Like coals raked over a spent fire, heat curled through him. Surprised by the unwanted sensation, he tipped his goblet for her to take a sip. As she did so, he cleared his throat. "Viking Raiders traded goods in various ports in the Mediterranean," he said then found himself focusing on her nearness.

She was such an enigma. One moment he found himself non-pulsed by her knowledge and the next, fascinated by her artless naiveté. He studied her as the light of the pale moon caressed her alabaster face. A tightness settled in his chest as he beheld her trusting nature. He hoped that he could continue to live up to the trust she'd placed in him. She believed him to be an honorable man. He took a deep breath. But as the tip of her tongue dipped out to capture a last taste of wine glistening on her lips, he felt his resolve slip. He inhaled sharply then froze as he recognized that her uninhibited spontaneity was part of his weakness. Straightening at the thought, he clenched his jaw. He was stronger than this. He could resist her siren's call. He had defeated fiercer opponents than this temptation. Not only was he the Commander-in-Chief of all Barovian Forces but he was also a Prince of the Realm. Squaring his shoulders, he nodded in resolution.

But then he heard her moan softly as delight curved her lips upward. He swallowed back his own groan with difficulty. How could the sound of her simple joy tease and taunt him so? He stared at her for a moment then realized it wasn't the fact of her drinking the wine that he found so irresistible, it was her unabashed enjoyment of the experience. And that was why he found her so fascinating...and so hard to resist no matter how much he fought his inclinations. He froze at the thought. What was the matter with him? He could never give in to his urge to touch her. She belonged to his cousin. She would soon be his Queen. He hardened his jaw, denying the attraction.

Tilting her goblet up toward his mouth, he took a gulp, seeking the sour tang of the lemons used in the fruited ambrosia. Swallowing, he lifted the goblet to take another sip then paused. It almost tasted as if the wine had something more than grapes and citrus in it. He swung his gaze toward Rikard then watched as the Gypsy King raised his cup in a friendly salute.

In the past, he had learned not to take things at face value. There always seemed to be layers beneath the surface one must peel back, like an onion, in order to get to the heart and the truth of the matter. He released his arm entwined with hers. "And now we are to toast the Elders," he whispered. Holding his own cup aloft, he lowered it and took a deep sniff. He could detect nothing unusual with the smell of his drink. He felt his brow furrow as he wondered why Rikard and the Elders felt it necessary to get them drunk. Not about to alert anyone to his suspicions but deciding caution was the better part of valor, he placed his mouth on the edge of the goblet and took in enough of the drink to wet his lips. He dipped his head in confusion. Had he been wrong? Both drinks tasted identical. He straightened, his mind racing as he searched for an answer before he said. "I do believe we've had enough."

"Not F-fair," she said, slurring her words as a happy smile curled her lips upward. "I t-thought we were t-to t-toast each other...c-cheers," she said. Tilting her head back, she raised her cup high above her head.

"I think we've both had more than plenty," Niko said, swiping the goblet from her hand thus preventing her from consuming more of the potent brew. Setting both cups on an overturned water barrel, he turned back to her.

"B-but I wasn't f-finished-"

"We are now," he said as he threaded his arm through hers.

"N-not like t-this," she said. Yanking her arm away, she jerked her wrist upward. Their wrist tied together with the purple scarf shot upward. "Oh," she exclaimed as she waved their bound wrists around. "I-I need to l-look a-at t-this."

"I think you s-should let me do that," he said then realized he was beginning to slur his own words. He turned to berate the Elders but noticed only Rikard remained. His vision seemed to waver. From the way he was feeling, he knew for sure the wine had been doctored. But had he somehow missed the fact that this was all part of the initiation ceremony? He shook his head to clear his vision then felt as if he was walking across a lisping vessel as he peered down at Belle.

"Oh-h, I d-don't...f-feel s-so...g-good." She said as he noted her face carried a grayish tint. "E-everything's sp-in-ning."

"There's only one cure for how you f-feel and that's s-sleep," he said, pulling on the scarf to get her to move. When that didn't work, he settled his arm across her shoulders. Then leaning toward her, he placed one foot in front of the other and partially lifted her. Hoping he could get them safely to the wagon, he began to move. As they swayed and stumbled toward Rikard, frustration seized him. He knew he no longer had the ability to act and reason on his own. He only hoped that by placing his trust in the Gypsies, he hadn't made a deadly mistake. A bolt of anger flashed through him. As he came near the man, he growled. "As f-for you, l-let us hope that you honor t-the Gypsy C-code of hos-pi-tal-ity. And w-we'll be discussing t-this in the m-morning."

"Don't think you have to hurry to wake on my account," Rikard said. "We won't be breaking camp until after our uninvited guests have left."

"Think that w-will h-help you?" Niko asked. He shook his head, hoping to clear the cobwebs away.

"No, but the herbs Etel placed in your wine should keep you out of harm's way," Rikard said.

"Oh," Niko said as he hugged Belle to his side. The way he was feeling he'd sleep for days. He stared at Rikard trying to decide if he should thank the man for his care or slap him senseless because he was no longer in control of their safety.

No matter what, with the rebels in camp, he could neither challenge the Gypsy King nor threaten him. They needed his protection. What was done...was done. He could take no further action, his hands were tied. He blinked at the realization and lifted his bound wrist. "I won't f-forget t-this," he promised as he slowed to a stop.

"I never supposed you would," Rikard said. Striking a match, the man lit his pipe. After taking a puff, he removed it from his mouth and waved it toward Etel's wagon. "Hadn't you best take her to bed before she falls over-"

"Since t-this is your h-handiwork," Niko began, feeling as if he had just run to the top of Majae Jezerces with a full pack of rations strapped to his back. "Then the l-least you could do is h-help."

"I did," Rikard said. "By drinking Etel's sleeping compound, you should get a peaceful night's sleep," he added then gestured toward their bound wrists. "But, I think you will still find those knots in the scarf a challenge in the morning."

Niko shook his head, hoping to stay alert enough to make sense of what Rikard was saying. "H-how s-so?"

Rikard tipped his head back and blew out three rings of smoke. They floated into the air, hovered for a moment then disappeared. "The thing of it is ... it's not so much about the knots as it is the material. Besides the unusual color, you will find it has some peculiar qualities. But then, I hear you are a man who likes both a challenge and a puzzle."

"I wouldn't b-believe everything I h-hear," Niko stammered. Then lifting Belle up on her toes, he maneuvered them toward Etel's wagon. The closer they came to the wagon, the tighter her arm seem to become around his waist.

"Sleep well," he heard Rikard call.

Niko bit his lip to keep from issuing a pithy retort. It wouldn't do any good. It was...what it was. No use berating fate. Truth to tell, he expected he would get no sleep at all until he freed them from the knotted scarf.

He stifled a yawn as they entered the wagon. The lantern suspended from the beam above them arced its light giving him glimpses of the narrow bunks on each side of the aisle

Settling a sleeping Belle on the bunk, he covered her with a thick quilt. He turned but the short length of the scarf binding them together prevented him from moving to the other bunk. He peered longingly at the empty bunk, knowing he wasn't going to be able to fight his weariness much longer. Feeling as if his knees were made of pork jelly, he blew out the lantern and lowered himself to sit on the floor. His gaze strayed to the bunk and the pillow and quilt folded on top of it. Using his last bit of energy, he lifted his untethered hand and snagged the pillow and quilt off the empty bunk. Placing the pillow on the floor, he sighed and pulled the quilt over him.

***

Belle opened her eyes and stared at the roof of the cold, silent coach. She shivered, unable to move any part of her body. Her arm ached so bad that she let out a moan. "Momma," she whispered then noted that her breath created a puff of white like a cloud riding high in the summer's sky. She frowned at the thought. She tried to turn her head but discovered she couldn't because she was tucked so tightly between the back of the upside down seat and a large grey object.

She narrowed her gaze on the grey heavy wool. Papa's cloak was made of material like that. "Papa," she called, softly. Her breath hitched in her throat as pain throbbed throughout her body. Where were Momma and Papa that they would leave her alone like this?

She blinked away her tears. Why hadn't Momma and Papa answered?

"There's a young'n in there," she heard a gruff voice say. "Best we get to mov'n them bodies out."

Belle ran her tongue over her cold, chapped lips. "Papa?"

"Need to hurry," the gruff voice said. "Best send for the preacher and the doc."

Belle frowned. Why would she need to see the preacher?

She opened her mouth to ask but then stopped. Her eyes widened as she stared at the back of the gray mass floating above her. The grey cloak familiar yet shredded and drenched with large spots of brownish-red. As the lump lifted, a single black polished Hessian boot came into view and its gold tassel swayed with the movement. She lifted her gaze to watch then suddenly realized the man was missing his other knee and the lower half of his leg and foot.

"Papa," she managed to scream.

***

Niko bolted upright out of his sleep at the deep guttural sound. Then he sat shaking in the dark for a moment from the sudden wake. It seemed as if he had but closed his eyes moments ago. Then realizing the agonized sound had come from Belle, he forced his listless body to his knees and bent toward her thrashing, mumbling form. "Sh-sh-sh," he whispered as he dropped his palm over her mouth. "Y-you're s-safe," he managed to mutter as he leaned closer. Then slowly realizing that it was going to take more than the comfort of his words to calm her, he crawled over her and wedged himself on his side between her and the wall. "N-no har-m-m will c-come," he added, his words slurred as he gathered her quivering form loosely into his arms. If only he didn't feel as if he was made of jellied eel he might be able to help her more.

She moaned as if in pain and he heard her draw in a deep, shaky breath. He shook his head hoping to clear away the cobwebs of lethargy the wine had spun inside his brain. Then he felt himself tense as a cold panic flowed through him and he realized that she was about to scream.

"No-o-o," he whispered, the fierce word sounding hoarse to his ears. Cognizant enough to realize that if he allowed the scream she was gathering in her lungs to be heard, she would wake the entire camp, he plopped his hand over her mouth. She began to thrash violently, her groan of anguish rising loudly in her throat. "I'm-m-m h-here whiff you," he whispered slowly as he wrapped his tongue around the words. He hoped the effort he'd taken with his soothing tone would disrupt not only her fractious dream that had seized her but would also help him in casting off his mantle of listlessness. "Y-you are not-t -lone B-belle," he stammered as he pulled her closer to his chest.

She seemed to quiet for a moment as she turned toward him. But then a groan erupted from deep within her and her body stiffened. He frowned. It didn't seem normal for her not to wake. As the fog of his memory cleared a bit, he remembered that shortly after his father's death, his mother had been afflicted with the same aftermath. He had woke numerous time to her screams. The physician had advised him to call her name as he rushed into her room. He had been assured that upon hearing her name, she would awake from the nightmare. And surprisingly, she had. He felt his frown deepen as he drew Belle into a hug.

So why then hadn't Belle awakened?

He shook his head that seemed to be clearing from the herbs that had been mixed in their wine. Maybe she needed a stronger stimulus to climb out of her drugged nightmare. He felt the muscles of his chest tighten as he placed his hands on her shoulders. "Sh-sh-sh, Belle," he said, gently shaking her as he attempted to bring her out of the dream that had disturbed their sleep.

"You are s-safe, nothing will h-hurt you h-here," he added as he noticed his speech pattern had adjusted almost to normal. She seemed to relax for a moment then he heard her short, breathy pants. Drawing her back close to him, he felt her chest expand as she gathered her breath into her throat. Desperate to snap her out of her nightmare, he realized there was but one way to stop the scream gathering in her throat. Dipping his head, he planted his mouth on hers.

Having effectively silenced her scream, he lifted his mouth. Stunned by his impulsive action, he froze then felt his lips soften. But as he heard the rumbling of another moan rising within her, he placed his lips gently over hers and swallowed her breathy moan. Then on their own volition, his lips brushed across her petal smooth lips. Tasting the residue of the wine remaining on her lips he recalled that she had consumed significantly more of the drugged wine then he had. And that being the case-

He jerked away at the realization that he had crossed the line. By touching his lips to hers, in her inebriated condition, he had taken her purity and innocence. Not only had he compromised that virtue but he'd also lost his own honor and self-respect. Ice crusted in his veins and he shivered at the ramifications of his action. Bowing his head, he waited for the feeling of additional condemnation to assault him. But when that didn't happen, he frowned in disbelief. Then attempting to understand the crux of his problem, he thought of the wine they had consumed. Had the doctored wine freed them from their inhibitions and made them both a little crazy? Feeling that explanation too trite and easy to use, he rubbed at his bristly jaw. Or perhaps their forced togetherness had caused a measure of uncalled for intimacy to develop between them. And in turn, the freedom generated by the wine had allowed them to drop their guard? He shook his head, casting his supposition aside. One thing he knew for sure, he'd used the most expedient way he could to quiet her. And it had worked.

She moaned again but this time the sound rolled from deep within her. A sound, not of pain but of pleasure.

He gulped at the acknowledgment. "Belle, are you awake?" he asked as he surmised that he was playing with fire by remaining on the bunk beside her.

"Um-m. m-maybe-e," she sighed, her words slurring. Then turning away, her breathing became deep as if she slept.

Finally freed from the effects of the drug, he knew how easily it was to miscalculate and find oneself consumed by the fire of passion. Even one deep in sleep was bound to remember figments of what had happened the night before. Even if only in a dream.

Deciding not to pull the tail of fate again, he removed himself from her bunk and returned to his make-shift bed in the aisle. He hadn't any more than settled in the deep darkness on the floor before she began mumbling. Rising, he returned to lie on his side atop the quilt next to her on the bed, hoping once more to quiet and calm her. After all, wasn't it more important to keep them safe through the dark hours of the night than it was to worry about his improper actions and the improprieties he'd already breached?

Chapter Nine

Belle snuggled deeper into the counterpane, seeking its warmth. She frowned as she became aware of a steady thumping sound close-by. "Oh-h," she breathed as pain shot from the base of her skull to the center of her forehead. Not about to open her eyes and aggravate the rat-a-tat rhythm pounding in her head, she took a slow, shallow breath.

She felt as dreadful now as she had the morning she'd been pulled from the overturned coach nine years...seven months and...twenty-seven days ago. She froze at the thought. Her eyes springing open. A heavyweight suddenly pressed upon her chest making it difficult for her to breathe. Sweet Angels! Had she had another one of those harrowing, horrible night dreams about-

"Good morning." The sound of Niko's mellow baritone voice skidded across her consciousness rousing her from the nightmare haunting her memory.

She blew the errant strands of hair that had slipped from the ribbon away from her face hoping it would give her a few extra moments to compose herself. Then raising a tentative gaze, she paused as a flush of heat surged through her. Saints above, Niko's sleepy-eyed stare not only curled her toes but her lashes as well as she noticed he lay fully clothed beside her atop the bed. Annoyed by her sudden flash of disappointment that he hadn't taken off a single stitch of clothing, she attempted to swallow back her own self-disgust as his gaze slid downward to rest on where her hands clutched the quilt to her chest. "M-morning," she managed to get past her stiff lips. Whether it was good or not remained to be seen.

"Are you feeling better this morning?" he asked as she watched his eyes dart up to her face.

The blue flame smoldering in the depths of his cobalt eyes startled her. She pressed her shoulders into the straw ticking of the mattress, knowing she couldn't respond to the heat of his gaze. "A-as opposed to what?" she managed to ask.

"Last night?"

A tight ball of dread plunged into the pit of her stomach. Sweet angels! What had she done? Her breath hitched in her chest as she wondered if she had revealed the ruse she and Rita played. "W-what happened last night?" she forced herself to ask.

"Don't you remember?" His eyes seemed to harden as if he didn't believe her.

Although Belle knew she shouldn't pursue this line of questioning, she also knew for Rita's sake she had to continue. "You almost sound hopeful that I don't remember," she said as a fuzzy recollection surfaced of the two of them standing together at a campfire. As she stared at him waiting for his response, suspicion slithered through her. "Why is that?"

"I wouldn't want to embarrass you by mentioning we shared a certain goblet of wine together," he said, a teasing grin crinkling the corners of his mouth.

Belle snapped her mouth closed and swallowed down the 'what else happened?' that hovered on the tip of her tongue. Whatever she'd done or not done, there was only one way to interpret Niko's tone and that was that she'd made a complete fool of herself. "Um-m," she said, clearing her throat as waves of distress rolled over her. This was worse than horrible...it very well could be a fatal blow to Rita's reputation as Queen. She squeezed her eyes closed, hoping to clear her fuzzy memory.

Then determined to ascertain exactly what it was that she had done, she snapped her eyes open and asked. "And we...linked arms and drank a toast."

She watched as a smile stretched the corners of his mouth upward. Belle knew from the teasing gleam in his eyes that he was enjoying himself. And that she was going to have to dig and prod him for every bit of information she needed. She took a quick breath and held it, waiting for his answer. Finally, he nodded and said. "That we did."

'Not good' she wanted to shout but refrained as she released her spent air with a whoosh. Then realizing that the only way to find out what had happened last night was to give tit for tat, she squared her shoulders. "The Tribal Elders were also there witnessing the event," she said, proud that she had at least remembered that much.

"There...meaning, where?" he asked as he flashed her a wide smile that did nothing but make her more determined than ever to beat him.

"At the camp," she said, then clenched her jaw. As annoying as she found Niko at times, she knew she had to persevere if she was to discover if she could salvage a portion of Rita's reputation as Barovia's future Queen. At this point, she could only fully recall a knife scoring her wrist, feeling light-headed, linking her arms and taking a deep drink. From there, things became muddled. And she wasn't sure if they had actually happened or if they were merely figments of her imagination. Wanting to leave no doubt in Niko's mind that she remembered some of the things that had happened, she said, "We walked to Rikard's campsite." Then hearing him chuckle, she shot him a suspicious glance, feeling as if she'd missed something. "What did I do or...say that makes you so hesitant to answer?" she finally asked.

Niko shrugged his shoulders. "Nothing," he said, "but maybe you had best look at your wrist."

If he thought he could distract her from asking her questions then he could think again. "And?"

A chill feathered its way down her spine as she pulled her hands out from under the quilt. The morning light filtering through the separated sections of canvas serving as a curtain across the front of the wagon created just enough light for her to see her hands. The first thing she noticed was the purple scarf knotted at her wrist. "Ah," she said. "I see we are still tethered to each other," she added as she raised her gaze to meet his. "I thought that you were going to separate us."

"Before you get your bloomers in a twist, you had best notice the incision," he said as he reached over and moved the silky scarf down her arm to reveal a small red mark on the inside of her right wrist.

A sick feeling of trepidation settled in her stomach. She bit down on her bottom lip. One of the few things she clearly remembered was the flick of the blade scoring the inside of her wrist. Then things had become a bit jumbled. She'd felt weak-kneed, light-headed and thirsty. She'd taken several deep drinks from the cup she'd held, hoping to alleviate both her thirst and her dizziness.

She felt a frown furrow her brow as Niko lifted his left arm which was tied with the same purple scarf. "So, you didn't remove the scarf from our wrists because?"

"It was late," he said, wiggling his wrist and causing the scarf to dance in the morning air, "and our drinks had been drugged and I wasn't too steady on my own feet."

"Ah," she said, relieved to discover the reason her head pounded like a blacksmith's hammer in a forge and her stomach rolled as if she sat in a boat tossed by a gale. "So, we did become members of Rikard's tribe last night," she said. As relief rushed through her, she bolted upright in the bed. With Rikard and the Elders in attendance, she felt sure that she had done nothing to feel guilty about other than pose as her sister.

"That too," Niko mumbled. She frowned as he slipped off the bed and gathered his boots. His diversionary tactic of answering in short sentences and revealing little indicated that there was more to last night than what he cared to reveal. So, what was he hiding?

Unwilling to let him go until she had the information she wanted, she grabbed at the purple scarf and tugged on it. As she did so, the counterpane dropped to her waist revealing her scooped-necked blouse had shifted, leaving her shoulders bare. Swiftly, she yanked the quilt up to her chin then inhaled sharply as she felt heat flush her face. Rattled by her inappropriate, impulsive action, she stammered. "A-anything else I need to know about what occurred last night after I drank the wine?"

She watched him shake his head. "Nothing that can't wait in the telling," he said, turning toward her. "Although, I do recommend that you stay abed until after the rebels leave camp," he added.

She gaped at him as he pulled a stool from beneath the small table. Did he really think he could just cast orders about without a discussion? She hardened her jaw. That was not the way Rita did things. Opening her mouth to quiz him, she paused as he slipped a knife from a sheath attached to the inside of his right boot. She gulped down her objection at the sight of the knife when he placed it under the purple scarf, turned his blade upward and began sawing through the material. While he might appear calm to most people, she knew he was hiding something. He had glanced at her too many times for her not to suspect him. But what reason could he have for keeping the truth from her?

"And will you also remain inside?" she challenged as a frisson of uncertainty rolled through her. What would happen to them if the rebels didn't leave? She knew, the longer the rebels stayed in the gypsy camp, the more real the possibility became that they would be discovered. And as a Colonel in the King's Forces, someone was bound to recognize Niko eventually. She held her breath, gulping down the air she held.

If they were discovered, then she wouldn't hazard a guess as to what would happen to them or to the members of Rikard's tribe who had harbored them.

"I suspect the reason the rebels have remained here is that they feel there is safety in numbers and they are waiting for others to join them," he said as he dipped his head to work at the purple material knotted to his wrist.

Belle inhaled deeply then paused. "Um-m," she mused, if he wouldn't answer her question, she would ask another. "How long do you think we'll have to stay hidden?"

"I'm hoping only until late morning," he said as he freed himself from the purple scarf. "If we are to get to Berat today, we will need to be heading out soon," he added as a light tap came at the back door. She slid out of bed, too antsy to remain there any longer. With at least one of them free, they could both move around unhampered. She watched as Niko unlatched the back door and pushed it open. Tass stood there holding a loaf of bread.

"Grams is bringing the porridge and Pop says you're to stay inside here and be quiet," the boy said in a low whisper as he entered the wagon.

"Here's the porridge," Etel said in a loud voice as she hurried in after him. "And, young man, you're eating this meal right now before you decide to take off and go fishing in the stream," she scolded as she closed the door behind her. Pivoting, she placed her bony finger over her lips. "Best you both stay hidden in here," she added in a whisper then cleared her throat. "Grandson, hand me those bowls," she said loudly as she waved her hand toward the small stack sitting on the shelf above the bed.

Lifting the four bowls down, Belle handed them over to Etel without a sound. She bit her lower lip as Etel stopped beside the bed to stare down at the rumpled bedding. She felt her face warm as the old woman arched her brow. Pointing to the pristine bunk across the aisle, Etel waved her hand at the messy bunk as if to ask Belle is she'd lost her mind in allowing Niko to share a bed with her.

As profuse heat swept through Belle, she realized that this hadn't been the first time she and the Colonel had shared the same sleeping space. It had happened before...in the cave.

Belle stole a quick glance at Niko as she realized that sleeping near him wasn't such a terrible sin. Her heart jumped into her throat at the thought. She felt as giddy as a school girl as she realized that spending this time alone with Niko not only felt entirely right to her but that she might use it to free herself from her brother's machinations.

She paused as an incendiary idea began to take hold. If it became known to the Duke of Umberford that she had traveled unchaperoned with a man and had spent overnight with him, would he end their engagement? Surely, the pompous Duke would shout the information to all of society. A heaviness settled in her chest as a chill swept over her. Was she brave enough to defy her brother and suffer the loss of her reputation? She felt her breath hitch in her chest. Although she would be free of the Duke, what would the ramifications be to Rita if their ruse was discovered and it was learned that she had been traveling through the countryside disguised as her sister, the future Queen of Barovia?

She shook her head as a chill shivered through her. Nothing could take precedence over her obligation to her sister. She couldn't allow her own selfish motives to govern her actions. And to honor that commitment, she had to maintain a safe distance from Niko in order to carefully guard their ruse. If anyone discovered she wasn't their future Queen then her greatest fear would materialize.

She felt her blood freeze in her veins. Accepting the bowl of oats and barley from Etel, she settled herself on the rumpled bed covers and dipped her spoon into the bowl. As she took a bite, she wondered why Niko had refused to tell her what had happened last night.

Had she inadvertently let slip something she shouldn't have? A sinking sensation settled in her stomach as she swallowed her porridge. Sticking her spoon back into her bowl, she paused. But surely, she wasn't foolish enough to think that she could hide the truth forever. Lifting the spoon to her mouth, she took a bite. But wouldn't she be better off when the truth came out? After all, by then she would have regained her own identity and resumed her own life. She narrowed her gaze on her bowl and paused. She knew when perpetrating a lie, consequences always followed. Those duped in the process always felt like they had been betrayed when the truth was revealed. She bit her bottom lip as she realized that she and Rita would undoubtedly lose the trust of everyone close to them. No matter how noble her intention had been to give Rita the time and space to come to grips with the fact that she was marrying King Stephan, circumstances had snowballed out of control. By now, they should've been safely residing within the palace walls, each with their own identity intact. And her sister resigned to the fact that she was to be married and crowned Queen of Barovia.

She sighed. Dipping her spoon back into her bowl, she swirled it through the oats. Almost from the time they had concocted their ruse, things had gone wrong. First, they had suffered through a storm in the Ionian Sea and once on shore, they had been abandoned by their own government at the inn. Then their brother and King Stefan weren't there to greet them and she had discovered that Rebels had surrounded the inn. She was rushed out without given the opportunity to say farewell to her sister and thus hadn't been able to clue Rita in as to what was happening to them. And from there on, things had spiraled further out of control.

She frowned as she watched Niko settle on the three-legged stool she'd sat on the day before when Etel had driven the wagon through the forest. Dipping his spoon into his wooden bowl he began to eat. What was it about him that she found so fascinating?

Niko wondered at the frown he'd seen settle on Belle's porcelain features as he juggled his bowl in one hand and reached to accept the chunk of bread Etel was handing him with his other hand. Suddenly, the old woman snatched his bread away.

"Quiet," she snapped. "Great danger approaches," she added as she scrambled to her feet. Tossing the piece of bread and the loaf onto the small table, she grabbed the cooking kettle off the table. "Stay here," she ordered as she hurried toward the door. As she opened it, the sound of thundering hoofs and jingling harnesses filtered into the small space. Slipping down the steps, she turned back and pulled the door firmly closed.

Niko's stomach clenched at the sound. Great Cerberus! Had his men somehow divined where he had disappeared to and finally caught up with them?

No longer hungry, he shoved his half-empty bowl at Tass. "Here, take this," he ordered. No matter what, he needed to see who had ridden into the camp. Turning, he took a step past Belle.

"You can't" she whispered, latching onto his wrist. A bolt of heat zipped through him and he halted. "If Etel says there's danger then you can bet she's right." He felt her tighten her grip on his wrist. "She warned me just before we met the wounded rebels on the road yesterday. She was right then. So, I'm thinking she'll be right now." A frown settled between her brows. "How she knows such things is a mystery to me but if she says we need to stay safely concealed inside here, then that's what we need to do."

"Grams is always right," Tass said with a nod as he stooped and pulled out a wooden bucket from beneath the small table. "You'd best do as she says," he said straightening. Then collecting only two of the dirty bowls with their spoons, he stood. Placing the dirty dishes in the bucket, he sidled toward the door. "I'll go keep an eye on everything, then come back and tell you what's going on," he said.

"Be careful," Belle said as she slid off the bed and stood.

Caution warred with valor inside Niko. But caution gained the upper hand, only because his first duty was to ensure the safety of his future Queen.

He glanced over at her and watched her smooth the covers over the bed. Swiftly, he realized that he shouldn't be so surprised that his future Queen knew how to do something as domesticated as making a bed. Although at first, he'd considered her nothing but a fragile beauty, he'd found not only had he underestimated her but that she had a surprising amount of spunk and courage. And that she was a woman not only of rare intelligence but was kind and thoughtful as well. A lady any man would be proud to call his own. A woman...a partner most men would find not only attractive but easy to fall in love with.

He paused abruptly. A chill swept through him. Great Cerberus! Had he just included himself as one of her adoring fans? Was he nuts? He had no right to consider her anything but...beyond his touch. She was set to be his cousin's wife, his future Queen he reminded himself. He'd vowed he would get her safely to his cousin and that's what he would do...no matter what he might personally feel.

Shouts of welcome filtering through the front curtain had Niko twisting away from watching Belle and returning to the three-legged stool. Balancing one knee on the seat of the stool, he peered through the slit in the front curtain. His fist clutched the coarse, heavy material as he struggled to breathe. His breath stalled in dread. A few feet from where he knelt inside the wagon, his uncle, his father's younger brother, sat atop his ebony dancing stallion. Surrounded by the wounded, Prince Jorge raised his hand to halt the crowd of cheering rebels. Finally bringing his Arabian under control, he maneuvered his steed to the side and emitted a chilling laugh.

Niko gritted his teeth at the remembered sound.

"My fierce fighting friends," his uncle said addressing his men. Niko took a deep breath and realized a clean floral scent mixed with a touch of vanilla surrounded him. As he recognized the scent that belonged to Belle, he felt her presence hovering behind his left shoulder.

Leaning forward over his shoulder, she peered through the same small gap in the curtain, their cheeks almost touching. Disturbed by her nearness, he took a quick breath and shifted away from her as she asked. "Who is the man on the black horse?"

Niko shook his head, unable to understand why his uncle was the driving force behind all of the country's trouble. "Supposedly he is the rebel commander," he finally managed to get past the narrowing passageway of his throat. He could accept that his uncle might serve as the figurehead for whoever was the driving force behind the rebels but he was unable to accept that he was the brains working behind the scene.

"Do you know who he is?" he heard her ask through the dissipating haze of his doubt.

Why did he find it so hard to believe that his uncle was behind all of the trouble and unrest in the country? The proof sat right before him, spouting rhetoric that would surely inflame the rebels to further destroy the infrastructure of their country. It wasn't like they had ever been close.

He hesitated. What would be the most honest answer for him to give her yet still keep her safe?

"Victory will soon be ours," his uncle told his followers. Another wave of cheering erupted and Niko clenched his jaw as anger surged within him. There was no way he would ever allow this greedy, power-hungry tyrant to either grab control of the Kingdom or to sell their birth-right off to another country, no matter his kinship.

"Tell me his name," she demanded.

He paused, hesitant and reluctant to reveal his uncle. "It's...Prince Jorge," he finally muttered. "King Stefan's uncle."

He heard her breath hitch. "How...many uncles...does the King have?"

"Two," Niko said. Uncle Jorge and his father had forever been at odds with each other. His uncle had wanted to sell Greece and Hungary access to their country's mining rights while his father and Stefan's father, the King, had refused to sign the deal. Shortly after that debacle, his father had died. He shook his head. "The second uncle died about twenty years ago," he said, maintaining his ruse of only being a Colonel with the Royal Military Force. "Afterwards, a horde of Hungarian soldiers invaded our country seeking not only to strip us of our land but also our mineral wealth. That left the power struggle within the Kingdom between the eldest and the youngest son."

"And now this remaining younger brother seeks to wrestle control of the throne from his nephew, the rightful King?"

Arrested for a moment by the simplicity of her statement, Niko nodded slowly as he continued to study his uncle. The more he thought about the situation between his father and his uncle, the more he began to suspect that his father's death might not have been an accident. "I think you have succinctly summed up the situation."

"Is there anything we can do to stop him?" she asked as she leaned further over his shoulder to see through the small slit he had created in the curtain.

He took a slow, deep breath as he realized they were almost cheek to cheek. "Yes," he managed to whisper, "but we must wait."

"For what?"

The short puff of air from her words, feathered across his ear and he found his breath hitching in his chest as he said. "Until after they've left."

"And then what?" she asked. Her warm breath, light as a feather floated down the side of his neck.

Niko knew what he intended to do. But instead of informing her, he turned toward her. "What would you do if you had been left in charge?"

He watched her nibble on her bottom lip for a moment then straighten. "Realizing it's not safe for two people to be out traveling alone on the roads with such a large horde of rebels on the move, I would ask Rikard and his people to accompany us to Berat, post haste."

He nodded. "That's my exact plan." He grinned. Although he was surprised by her response, he was also extremely pleased to learn his future Queen had once again demonstrated her superior thinking skills. She had the makings of a true warrior Queen. He only hoped that Stefan would appreciate her strengths. He nodded in approval then noted her white clasped knuckles.

"How long then do you think Prince Jorge will be here stirring up his troops?"

"It usually doesn't take long to fire the furor of zealots," he said as he turned once more to study the individual faces of his uncle's men.

"Desperate men willing to snatch away a throne are intent on using greed and power to sway others in gaining their objective. Unfortunately, few in power ever consider the cost that each man might pay when supporting that cause. In fact, most leaders consider their soldiers fully expendable, as witnessed by the Prince's careless and bloody use of his men in his own search for glory."

"It's a shame that one can't appeal to the Prince's better nature," she said.

"He might not possess one," he mumbled as he watched the wounded men shift aside to allow a beggar to squeeze through their ranks.

"Do you?"

Niko took a deep breath and studied the erect stance of the man pushing his way toward his uncle. The prince must've spotted the man for he urged his horse forward. Niko clenched his jaw as he discovered his view of the man had been effectively blocked by his uncle's maneuver. Quickly swallowing his oath of disgust, he said. "I like to think that I do...have a better nature," he added. "Part of my task as a commander is to notify a family when their loved one has died or been wounded. As a commander, it's always in the back of my mind. And when I'm planning an assault, I try to use tactics that will not only gain my objective but will also yield few causalities. While that's not always possible, I do try."

"At least you make the attempt," she whispered as she straightened.

"In other words, half a loaf is better than none?" he asked, missing the scent of her feminine warmth as she pulled away. Refocusing his gaze on the beggar a sinking sensation dropped into the pit of his stomach. He had a sneaking suspicion that he ought to know the man. He closed his eyes attempting to visualize each of his officers as the beggar but then he popped his eyes open too afraid he would miss something crucial. But his uncle remained on his horse, continuing to block his view. "Darn," he breathed as he rubbed his bristly chin. If only he could hear their conversation then he might be able to determine the man's identity. Leaning forward, he balled his fists. Somehow, he needed to get closer to the action.

"Not only do I need to see but also to hear what they are discussing," Niko said as he craned his neck in the hopes of discovering some small thing to aid him in identifying the beggar man. "Any ideas on how I can accomplish that?"

"I could go in your stead," Belle began then paused as she swiped her tongue over her lower lip.

Lazily, Niko followed the movement. Quickly, he shook his head. "Don't even consider that," he grumbled wondering if his warning was for her or himself. "That's not going to happen."

"Oh-h?" Belle huffed as her minty breath swept across his cheek. "If you won't allow me to go then...you'll have to don a disguise."

He switched his gaze to note that her expressive eyes danced in merriment. "What kind of disguise were you thinking of?" he asked, deliberately keeping his tone light-hearted.

"Um-m," she said tapping her index finger on her chin. "One, your own mother wouldn't recognize you in," she whispered as her lips curved into a grin.

"As in?" he asked returning to stare at his uncle so he wouldn't be tempted to reach up and trace her lower lip with the pad of his finger.

"An elderly woman," she said, "and I'll help."

Niko shifted his gaze back to her and observed her devil-may-care smile. "You are actually enjoying this, aren't you?"

"About as much as you did earlier teasing me," she retorted then smiled. "Every once in a while, I like to...shock people," she added then chuckled softly.

"And the rest of the time?" he asked.

"I'm as predictable as the weather,"

"Should I warn the King?"

A pall fell over her as if he'd doused a light. "That won't be necessary," she whispered. Moving away, she lifted a piece of cloth. Spreading the small square out on the table she placed the loaf of bread in the center and securely wrapped it in a package.

Niko watched her for a few seconds more then switched his gaze back to his uncle.

Whatever the beggar had said must've not been to his uncle's liking. A deep frown plowed furrows in his uncle's forehead and one of his fists beat against his thigh. Niko watched as his uncle jerked at the reins and pivoted his horse. Then rising from his saddle, his uncle stood in his stirrups. "I've brought wagons and supplies for you," his uncle yelled. "Wounded go to the wagons at the front," he ordered. Then waving his arm toward the men who had remained on their horses and were beginning to form a column, he added. "Follow me."

Niko watched his uncle spur his stallion and canter toward the head of his caravan. Slowly, he released the air that he'd trapped in his lungs. Then once more leaning toward the narrow slit in the front curtain, he recounted the number of men, taking special notice of their ragged appearance. Not that their shabby garments were any indication that they lacked skill or accuracy he acknowledged as he scanned the men searching for the beggar amongst the departing soldiers. Unable to locate the man, Niko frowned and wondered about the man's identity. And how had his uncle procured the rations and armament for the rebels? Had he broken into the arsenals and stolen the ammunition and rifles intended for use by the Royal Army? If he had, the Crown could quickly find itself without means to protect the country.

He balled his fist as impatience forced him to his feet. He needed to get to Berat and warn Stefan that their uncle was leading the revolution to depose him. And that someone, quite possibly from within their own inner circle, had turned traitor and was passing their uncle vital information and granting him access to their supplies.

Niko waited anxiously as the rebels rode off, the sound of their jingling spurs and the cloud of dust finally dispersing into the distance. Leaning forward, he gave the front curtain a twitch as Rikard climbed up onto the front bench of the wagon.

"My friend," Rikard said, sitting on the bench and facing forward. "I assume you recognized the rebel commander?"

"Unfortunately, I did," Niko said as a cold, calculating determination filled him. "Therefore I need-"

"To allow this tribe of nomads to accompany you to Berat because you realize that it isn't safe for you and the lady to be traveling alone," Rikard finished for him as he held up his hand, halting any forthcoming objections.

Not about to question his good luck, Niko nodded. "What are we waiting for?"

Chapter Ten

"Berat," Belle mumbled. Who would've thought that she would gain entrance to the Royal Palace by going through a cave? Sidling into the opening of the dark, narrow entrance of the cave, Belle hesitated as a shiver of fear swept over her. She hated cold, dark and moldy smelling places. They reminded her too much of death...and the mausoleum where her parents lay. She took a quick breath to steady her nerves then wished she hadn't as the stink of rotting garbage permeated the air. She stared into the inky blackness and wished she could've remained with the gypsies as they set up their campsite across the river outside the capital of Barovia. She sighed as she followed Niko through the narrow passageway into the large cavern. She gaped in wonder as he lifted his lantern high and flashed it around the vast chamber. As the light struck the rugged rock walls, Belle counted three passageways leading off from the area.

"Remind me again why we are doing this?" she asked as she rubbed the chill from her arms.

"This is the only safe way to get inside," he said, his whisper echoing softly off the walls.

"And exactly where are we?" she asked, her voice a hushed whisper.

"In the vast underground system of tunnels," he said. "This entrance leads from the Lumii Osumit River up into the King's palace. Should we get separated, remember to always select the pathway to your right," he said as she moved closer behind him, not about to be left alone in the dark.

She shivered again as Niko flashed the lantern around, allowing the light to fall on the side walls covered in slime and lichen. She cringed at the sight. "A-and what happens if I veer off to the left?" she asked, testing his knowledge. "Where does that go?" she asked pointing at the tunnel she had spied that led off in the left-handed direction.

"You would find yourself in the dungeon."

"Oh-h." she gulped then started to move hurriedly after his dark silhouetted figure. As he stepped away from her, the flickering light of the lantern swung out ahead of him. "How far do we have to go in here?" she asked as she stumbled and her feet plunged into ankle-deep water that cascaded down over the slippery stoned walkway. She stiffened the muscles in her arms and extended them out on each side of her to keep from falling. Steadying herself, she thanked her lucky stars that before entering the tunnel, she'd hitched the train of her riding habit between her legs and tucked the material into her waistband. If she hadn't she would've found herself face first in the water. And she didn't want to speculate on either where the water came from or what might be floating in it.

"Not far," he said, pacing out ahead of her. "And it might be in our best interest to stay quiet."

She gritted her teeth as she slid her gloved hand along the moss lined wall to maintain her balance. She would like to hear what he would say if he was the one wading through the water seeping into his boots. She bit back her groan, not about to complain about her discomfort. Nor did she want to be snapped at for asking how a Colonel in His Majesty's Army knew of the location of a hidden entrance that she supposed only those closest to King would know about. And she most definitely wasn't about to ask him how he knew his way through the tunnel into the palace. "How much further?" She asked wishing they could pause and rest for a moment. Her legs were already stiff and achy from fighting her way up the slippery incline just to reach the entrance.

"Not much," he whispered in return.

"I do believe that's the same answer you gave me the last time I asked," she mumbled then bit her bottom lip to prevent complaining aloud. Tired and exhausted, she was so ready to be done with this adventure.

"And it's the same response you'll get every time you ask," he said, his tone sounding gruff to her ears.

Well, truly the man was about as aggravating as he could get, she decided as she hurried after him. Did he really think that had she been the real Queen, she would have continued to follow along so blindly? "Do you even know where you're going?" she asked, exasperated as he flashed the lantern into the darkness ahead of them. The light bounced off the lichen covered stones lining the seeping walls in front of them as he gave a short grunt.

Cold and miserable, all Belle wanted was a hot bath, a well-cooked meal and her life back. And preferably in the reverse order she had named them. Her sister was more than welcome to her life as Queen Rita of Barovia. All Belle wanted was the return of her own identity. She sighed in despair.

This sneaking through the tunnel in the cold and dark was it. If nothing else, this experience had taught her never to switch places with her twin again. No matter how much Rita might beg...stomp...kick or squeal, she would simply refuse to do it again. From now on, Rita was on her own. Having reached that conclusion, Belle nodded in resolution as she trudged along behind Niko.

"You're mighty quiet all of a sudden," Niko whispered as he flashed the lantern back at her.

Momentarily blinded by the light, she raised her hand to shield her eyes from the brightness. "I thought I was supposed to be," she mumbled. As Niko moved the light away, he lifted the lantern above their heads. As her eyes re-adjusted to the darkness, she caught a glimpse of a white rope running along the side of the wall a few feet above them. "Why is there a rope overhead?"

"It's so that no one gets lost down here," Niko said.

"How does it work?" she asked as she reached for the rope.

"Don't touch it," Niko ordered, his sharp command causing her to drop her hand. "It's only to be used in an emergency," he added, his tone more modulated than before. Then clearing his throat, he added. "And this isn't one."

Well, maybe he didn't think it was an emergency...but she definitely did. "So, is there some sort of system rigged to ring a bell somewhere in the Butler's Pantry?" she asked.

"No, it rings into the guard's room," he said as he slowed and flashed the lantern ahead of them. "It's there to alert the guards of possible intruders invading the palace through the tunnel system or if someone becomes lost down here when attempting to find the wine cellar," he added as he veered to the right as the passage they were traversing ended and they turned right into another tunnel. "And since we don't know if the palace has fallen to the rebels, it behooves us to keep quiet and keep our hands off the rope. We'll use it strictly to guide us to the door that opens up inside the corridor leading to the throne room."

"Then what?" she asked as she hobbled after him, her toes cold and wet from wading through the water.

"I will determine if it is safe to enter the hall near the throne room. If it is, I will escort you to your chamber and then I will go find the King. And-"

"And if the rebels have taken over the palace?" she inserted. "Then what?"

"We will turn around and go back to the river," he replied. "My mission is to keep you safe no matter the personal cost to me. You are the mother of the future of this nation."

Belle gulped at the enormity of the thought. She understood that if the rebels overthrew the country, Barovia would become a battleground between three nations vying for control. Each using more drastic tactics, hoping to defeat the other. What she didn't understand was how the single act of Rita marrying the King would save the nation from this fate. She swallowed back a groan, hoping the country of Barovia wasn't depending upon England to come to its aid. Her sister was only one, insignificant entity. Why did the welfare of the nation rest on the slender shoulders of such an irresponsible woman who only ever held her own self-interests in her heart? Hadn't Rita always maintained that no one person could make a difference? That no one could alter the course of history and prevent bloodshed? She straightened as she realized that Rita was wrong in her thinking.

History had already presented numerous examples of how one person could make a difference. A niggling sense of honor crept its way into her consciousness and Belle swallowed back her groan of dismay. No, she had already decided never to assist her twin again. She hesitated as a twisting sense of loyalty and obligation slithered through her.

But what if Rita refused to marry King Stefan? Could she then for the safety and well-being of people like Rikard, Etel, and Tass, make the ultimate sacrifice? Could she surrender one last time to her twin's demand and become the King's bride?

She clutched at her stomach as a cold chill settled over her. Duty... the single most frightening word her brother had used to hammer home his point and force both she and Rita into agreeing with his far-fetched plan of rescuing the fortunes of their family. And now, as soon as she and Niko made their way into the palace, she would have to face her self-serving ruthless brother. With Rita wavering about marrying the King, Edward wouldn't care which sister he forced to marry the man as long as one of them did. She bit her bottom lip knowing the odds-on favorite was that her brother would side with Rita. It would be two against one and she would be coerced into marrying the King.

She gulped back her groan of despair knowing she could no longer avoid the inevitable. She needed to decide what she was going to do and plan how she was going to handle the consequences of her actions after she switched places with her sister. Although the switch had originally been Rita's idea, she had gone along with the ruse feeling she had to complete one last action to feel she had done everything she could to make up to Rita for causing the death of their parents. "H-how long before we g-get to the door?" she stammered, attempting to focus her mind on anything other than how angry her brother would be when he discovered their ruse. She felt her breath hitch in her chest. Edward had always sided with Rita. And like her sister, he had blamed her for the deaths of their parents. She shook her head at the uncertainty of it all.

"Here, take this," Niko said, holding the lantern out to her. "Best dip your head," he added as she took the light. Slapping the lintel with the flat of his hand, he tapped once on the waist-high flat stone to the right of the door then paused.

Thinking she had heard someone behind them, she twisted her shoulders and held the lantern high over her head. Although she saw nothing moving in the darkness behind them, she frowned as she heard a clicking sound. She turned. "What are you doing?" she asked, peering over his shoulder as Niko slapped the stone again.

"If you listen for the click, it means, the door will open after I've tapped in a code," he said as she heard another distinctive click.

"How is it that you know all of this?" she asked beginning to wonder what else the Colonel was privy too. After all, he'd been extremely closed-lipped about revealing anything regarding his background. Realizing the significance of that thought, she felt her frown deepen. What did she really know about this man, other than what he had told her? She bit her bottom lip. Had he told her the truth or merely a series of well-planned lies?

She felt her breath catch in her throat. She hated being so wishy-washy. But if what she did know was a lie, then did that mean that he was part of a conspiracy to depose the King? Fear coursed through her as the door opened. She gulped down her hesitation as she followed Niko inside. She realized that if Niko was indeed in cahoots with the rebels then she needed to quickly get inside the palace and warn King Stefan.

She nodded in resolution. First though, she would find the King and alert him to the danger he was in. Only then could she find her sister and aunt and lead them out to safety. Daunting though the task seemed, she would not rest until she knew she'd done everything necessary.

As the door slid open, she handed the lantern back to Niko then studied him as he lifted the light above his head. "Now, don't get all squeamish on me," he said, flashing the light upward to reveal a long, narrow stairway leading almost straight upwards. "It's not as difficult as it looks," he said. "I'm going to have you go first. That way, I'll shine the light over your shoulder for you to see every step. Just go slow. Be sure you have a firm stance on each step. And you will be fine."

"But there's no railing," she said as panic began to rise within her. She couldn't climb steps that steep without something to hang onto. Did he think she was part mountain goat? "The treads are so narrow that without a railing, I'm sure to fall."

"Not if you go slow and hold onto my hand," he said extending the hand which was not holding the lantern out to her palm up.

Relieved to accept Niko's assistance, she turned and placed her hand in his. Immediately, her hand warmed from his touch. Buoyed by the current racing up her arm, she took a deep breath and whispered back over her shoulder. "Are you ready?"

"Whenever you are," he replied lifting the lantern above her left shoulder and lighting the four steps directly in from of them.

She nodded. "Then we'd best tackle this mountain like we're sure-footed goats," she said. "That light can't last forever," she added as she began to climb.

"B-a-a-a," he bleated then added, "and don't even think about our light. If this candle goes out, you will have to stand perched on these narrow steps until I can replace it."

"Is that likely to happen before we get to the top?" she asked as she tried to focus on placing her foot on the narrow tread in front of her.

"I'm not taking any chances, stay right where you are," he said, then released his hold on her hand. "I'm going to tuck the extra candle and strike sticks into my pocket. It never hurts to be prepared for the unexpected."

She gave a slight squeak then decided she's best not move an inch. "So, when we get to the top of these steps," she said hearing the quiver of uncertainty in her own voice. "Is there another door like we just came through where you need to tap out another code?"

"There is but this time there will be a sizable landing on which we can both stand. At that point, I will pass the lantern to you like I did before. Then I will tap in the sequence. But when the door slides open revealing the corridor, we must be cautious. That hallway runs in front of the throne room. If the rebels have taken over the palace, they are sure to have men stationed outside that door."

She gulped back her trepidation at the thought. "How will we know if the men are rebels or guardsmen?"

"The Rebels will be as you remember them from Rikard's camp and the guardsmen wear a distinctive Dark blue and gold uniform," he said. "And before you ask, for their own safety the rebels won't be dressed as members of the King's Guard."

Belle thought about his reply for a moment then nodded. "What if you don't tap in the correct sequence?" she asked thinking it was better to tackle one problem at a time.

"I'll feel like a fool for disappointing my future Queen," he said, lifting her hand and holding onto it.

Belle squeezed her eyes closed for a moment then opened them to begin the climb again. She knew all about feeling foolish. She had made too many mistakes to ever rush to judge another person on short acquaintance. But did Niko ever look beyond 'what' a woman was and what she looked like and instead attempt to discern who the woman was inside? Or had all of this been only a 'duty' to him. Unable to arrive at a conclusion, she climbed the steep stairway toward the top.

Finally, the light illuminated a level platform located a few more steps above. Belle breathed out a sigh of relief. "I see the landing," she whispered as caution surged through her. Almost there, she reminded herself as she expelled a quick breath of relief that was followed by a hefty dose of wariness.

"I see it," Niko said, the relief she heard in his voice making her smile.

Heedful that haste makes waste, Belle stepped carefully on the landing and turned to accept the lantern from Niko. Joining her on the platform, he began to tap out the code and wait for the clicks. Finally, the door began to slide open. Quickly, Niko stepped in front of her.

As she peered over his shoulder, all Belle could see was a wall of black nothingness.

"Have we failed?" she whispered as a feeling of utter defeat swept over her. To have struggled and to have managed to come this far only to suffer a bitter defeat was a crushing blow. Her throat tightened in a wail of frustration.

"No," Niko murmured. "Just remain where you are. I need to lift a small portion of this tapestry away from the wall and scan the hallway to see if it's secure."

Belle shivered at the thought of falling backward off the landing. There was no way she would allow Niko to leave her behind. "Move over," she said nudging him. "I'm coming with you."

"Then for heaven's sakes douse the lantern before the old rug catches fire," he ordered.

Raising the glass lantern, Belle doused the candle then peered around the ornate tapestry. She felt her heart leap in surprise. At the top of a wide stairway, she spied her Aunt Ellie carrying her small dog, Muffy, accompanied by her twin. Both wore their outerwear as if they'd just come in from outdoors.

"That's my aunt," she said in a low voice as she slid out from behind the tapestry and rushed forward to greet her. As she hurried down the hall, Muffy jumped from her aunt's arms and rushed toward her barking ferociously. Then growling and snapping, the dog jumped around her attempting to trip her in the process. "Down boy," she ordered as she side-stepped the menace.

"Oh, my dear, we've been so worried," her aunt said hurrying toward her as Belle noticed her twin had hung back. "You'll never know how glad I am to see you are safe," her aunt said then stooped toward her dog as Belle spied Rita turning away and pulling the hood of her cape lower over her face. "You are such a bad boy, Muffy," her aunt scolded. "We do not treat Her Royal Highness like that."

Knowing there was no way she was going to calm the dancing bit of fluff, Belle ignored the yapping creature and focused on her aunt. "As I've told you before, Muffy is a canine with very discriminating taste. He's simply objecting to my tunnel rat smell."

"Now that I've delivered you safely to the palace, My Lady," Niko said recalling Belle's attention back to him. "And you have rejoined your entourage, I will bid you adieu."

Belle turned, feeling as if her heart had suddenly been ripped from her chest as she watched him bow. He was leaving. How could she have ever doubted his loyalty to the crown? Just because a man was reticent in divulging his background didn't make him a traitor. "Thank you for everything," she called, her heart plummeting inside her chest. "I deeply appreciate your dedication and your honor to your duty. Should you ever need a favor, know that I will grant it to you," she said, hoping that Rita would honor the commitment she had just pledged. Belle stared at Niko hoping to catch a glimmer of something indicating that she meant more to him than either duty or being his future Queen. But finding no sign, she dipped her head and told herself that some things were just not meant to be...and Niko was one of them.

Niko gave Belle another bow. "It was my pleasure," he said. Then executing a precise military about-face, he walked toward the throne room, his staccato steps echoing eerily through the silent corridor.

Halting a few feet before the large double doors, he turned and gazed down the hallway, hoping to catch a final glimpse of Belle. His future Queen, he reminded himself, the 'almost wife' of his cousin. Belle, who was strictly 'hands off'.

He froze at the thought. Great Cerberus! He needed to pull himself together if he was to get through the report he was to give his cousin. Reaching the door, he glanced one last time toward where Belle had met her aunt and the other woman who he supposed to be her personal secretary.

He knew without a shadow of a doubt that the next time he saw Belle, she would be gliding down the center aisle in the National Cathedral eager to marry his cousin. He stared at the empty corridor that felt as hollow as his heart.

Turning back to the doors, he nodded at the two guards. As they opened the door he realized that the inner reception area had been converted into a military planning room. Members of his elite staff were scattered around the room, pouring over open maps spread on tables while others of his inner sanctum stood at an easel arguing over strategy.

"Attention," his aide called then clicked his heels. "Stand for Prince Nikolai." The activity in the room ceased immediately as all stood at attention.

"As you were," Niko returned striding toward Cyrek who stood in the center of the action. As Niko scanned the setup he realized that Cyrek had done a superb job taking over his position while he had been gone.

"Am I ever glad to see you," Cyrek said as he grasped Niko's hand and shook it. "When you didn't make the rendezvous point I sent a squad of men out to scour the countryside. They brought word back that you were traveling with our friend, Rikard and his band of roving gypsies."

"With rebels amassing in the area, I thought it would be safer to travel with them," Niko said.

"And you managed to deliver Her Ladyship safe and sound?" Cyrek asked.

"As safe and as sound as I could keep her," Niko acknowledged. "While your men were out on patrol, did they encounter any resistance from the rebels?"

"There have been a few scrimmages," his friend replied then shook his head.

Niko knew something was wrong, for his normally loquacious friend was much too reticent. "Did they capture any of the rebels and bring them in for questioning?"

He watched Cyrek nod then noticed that his friend made a point of shifting his stance and turning his shoulders to peer around the room before he said, "About a dozen."

"Are they now housed in the dungeon?'

"Under heavy guard, why?" Cyrek asked as he shifted his attention back to him.

"Good," Niko nodded. "And is Stefan in the Throne Room?"

"Yes," Cyrek said with a frown. "He's meeting with the Elders. As soon as they are finished I am to present the latest information we've gathered on the rebels."

"Good," Niko said. "I want you to present those findings after I have given my report to the King."

"You've discovered something important about the rebels, haven't you?" Cyrek asked. "I can almost see the anticipation rolling off you, like water rolls off a duck. Can you at least give me a hint?"

Niko shook his head. "I'll deliver my findings to Stefan and let him make the decision of when to inform everyone else."

"Very well," Cyrek said. "I know better than to attempt to pry the information out of you until you are ready to give it."

"It looks as if you won't have long to wait. The doors are opening now," Niko said as the large black embossed double doors with a large gold-plated eagle carrying a small olive branch in its beak, opened slowly.

Niko swept his gaze around the Throne Room. At the far end on the raised dais, his cousin sat on the center chair. The Council of Elders, seated off the dais toward the front on each side of the aisle, began collecting their tablets and papers. Walking in a few steps, Niko halted and waited until the elderly men shuffled past him out of the room. Then as protocol dictated, he waited for his cousin to gesture him forward. Moving to the bottom step of the dais, he went down on one knee and took a deep breath. "Relieved to be reporting that your future bride is safe and sound within the palace, Your Majesty."

"Excellent," his cousin said. "Now that we've observed all the irritating bits of ritual, please join me up here," he said, patting the chair beside him. "And let me thank you for your willingness to sacrifice life and limb for me once more," his cousin added. "The rest of Her Ladyship's entourage arrived yesterday. We were all extremely worried," Stefan said. "Especially her aunt, who I had the honor of dining with last evening."

"We were unfortunately delayed," Niko said as he settled in the chair, "not only by a thunderstorm up in the mountains but also by the arrival of rebels in the gypsy camp."

"Did you learn anything of importance?" his cousin asked, steepling his fingers together.

Niko hesitated, knowing that Stefan would feel just as betrayed as he had when he'd seen their uncle in the gypsy camp. Then purposely leaning toward his cousin, he lowered his voice. "You mean other than to discover that dear Uncle Jorge is the Commander-in-Chief of the Revolutionary Forces and that there is a traitor somewhere in our own midst feeding him our troop movements?"

Surprise held his cousin frozen for a moment then anger flushed his face. "Jorge is a lily-livered rat!" Stefan hissed. "Why, doesn't he have the brains to realize that he is destroying this country? What can he possibly hope to achieve with this act of treason?

"He hopes to depose you, so he can become King," Niko said as he turned to face his cousin. "There is only one way to prevent that from happening and that is to strike him before he discovers we know he is the commander of the revolutionary forces."

"In other words, we catch him unaware with his pants down about his ankles," the King said tapping his fingers on the arm of his chair. "I like that," he added with a grin. "Do it."

"Only you, I and Rikard know our uncle is the rebellion's leader," Niko said quietly. "While Her Ladyship has seen him, I didn't inform her of his connection to our family."

"Then you need to meet with her and question her about what she's surmised," the King said. "If she's as intelligent as her aunt then she may have already gleaned the truth."

"I will as soon as I have ordered the necessary men and supplies to be gathered for our reconnaissance mission," Niko promised.

"Will that take long?"

"About an hour," he replied.

"Then you'll report back to me before you leave?"

"I will. And by that time, I will have already met with Her Ladyship and discovered what she knows or might suspect," he added.

"Excellent," his cousin said. "Now, about that traitor? Any ideas who it might be?"

"Since we have someone, somewhere in our midst, I'm going to turn that problem over to Cyrek," he said.

"Good idea," the King nodded. "How do you think Cyrek will ferret out the traitor?"

"By any and every means possible," Niko said. "And I'll definitely keep you informed," he added.

"I would appreciate that," Stefan nodded. "Now," he said rubbing his hands together. "When do we leave on our mission?"

"Sorry, but you don't," Niko said. "I'm leaving Cyrek with an elite force to guard you and your bride. The country needs you alive and ready to be married at noon in the cathedral, day after tomorrow," he said, hoping he sounded more upbeat than he felt. "And that won't happen if you are chasing all over the countryside looking for rebels.

"So by me staying-"

"The majority of people won't know I'm out capturing our uncle and rounding up the rebels," Niko said, hoping to appeal to his cousin's logic.

"You seem to have all the fun," his cousin said shaking his head.

"Talking about fun," Niko said. "I found your future wife a surprise. I hope you will also."

"If she's half as attractive as her aunt then we should rub along nicely."

Rub along nicely? Stunned for a moment, Niko stared at his cousin. What was Stefan thinking? Roughly, he cleared his throat. "Give her a chance," he said, "while she may be young, she's also a very sensible and astute woman."

"This from a man who considers women have few virtues?" the King asked then chuckled.

"I'll let you discover the reason for that, Your Majesty," Niko said then stood. "And now, with your royal permission, I'm off to prepare for my mission," he added with a bow. "I'll send Cyrek in to present you with the latest information regarding the rebels," he said then straightened. Receiving his cousin's flick of a wrist dismissal, he descended the dais, bowed once again and backed toward the door.

"Be sure you are at the cathedral," the King called to him, stopping him in his tracks. "I'm depending on you. You are my only attendant."

"That's not something I'm likely to forget," Niko returned as he heard the silent whoosh of the throne room doors opening behind him. Turning, he strode out. No, it wasn't something he'd likely forget. For it wasn't every day that the only woman he would ever want…married his cousin.

Chapter Eleven

Belle grabbed Rita's elbow and hurried her down the corridor away from the throne room. "What do you think you are doing parading around out here like this?"

"Oh, for heaven sakes," Rita snapped, coming to a halt. "What was I to do? You disappeared without a word. It wasn't until the next morning when Colonel Cyrek explained to us where you had gone and why that we knew what had happened to you. While I appreciate the sacrifice you made for me," she hissed, "I don't appreciate you leaving without first consulting me."

"I didn't have time," Belle retorted beginning to feel agitated by her twin's unjust accusations. As usual, everything had to be about Rita's comfort and convenience. She gritted her teeth then managed to add, "Niko insisted-"

"Niko?"

Annoyed by Rita's imperious tone, Belle cleared her throat. "Um-m," she said, "His full name is Colonel Nikolai Orsini-"

"My, aren't we chummy with the help," her sister said, her snippy tone warning Belle that her twin's quick-fire temper was on the rise. Then as if to emphasize her realization, Rita gave her a shove.

Belle grabbed for the railing that ran along the wall. "What are you doing?" she exclaimed as she latched onto it. She straightened and blood roared in her ears as she watched Rita cross her arms over her chest.

"I suppose the Colonel was that scruffy man dressed as a gypsy back there at the door in front of the throne room?" she asked, scorn resonating in her tone.

"So, what if he was?" Belle asked as a mist of belligerence rose up inside her at her sister's contemptuous tone. What did Rita think she would look like if she had traveled through the countryside dodging rebels and then had waded through ankle-deep water in a dark, smelly tunnel beneath the palace?

"I didn't realize that you went for the 'tall, dark and ragged," her twin said, her mocking distaste firing the tinder of Belle's own temper. "I thought you were more attracted to-"

"The fat, dull and aging braggarts you encouraged Edward to bring home with him?" Belle retorted.

"I didn't choose Umberford for you...Edward did," Rita snapped then began tapping the toe of her shoe against the marble floor.

The rat-a-tat-tat echoed the anger tightening the muscles in Belle's chest. Hastily, she looked around almost expecting her brother to spring from behind one of the large tapestries hanging in the corridor. "Speaking of Edward, where is our brother?" she asked.

"I have no idea," Rita snarled then pivoted. Quickly, she turned back, her face contorted in disgust. Belle knew it didn't bode well for her when her sister looked like that. She hesitated but before she could respond, her twin continued. "But according to what King Stefan told Aunt Ellie, Edward never presented himself to either the palace or the Council of Elders." Unexpectedly, her sister stamped her foot. "He is a vile and cruel man to have forced me into this marriage," she added shaking a clenched fist at her. "I hope his ship floundered in the storm and his bloated body has washed up in the bay."

Belle gaped at her sister. Stunned at the tirade she'd just witnessed, she glanced down the corridor. Thank goodness Aunt Ellie had stopped to talk with one of the guardsmen. Their aunt at least hadn't been present for Rita's frantically whispered outburst. Belle felt a frown furrow her brow. While she had heard her sister lash out at servants, wish ill on strangers and be rude to their friends, she had never heard her twin speak so contemptuously of their brother.

A frisson of wariness skated down her spine. She swept her gaze down corridor again and spotted their aunt studying a tapestry hanging on the opposite side of the wall. Arrested by the sight of the overturned coaches depicted in the wall hanging, Belle felt her breath hitch in her chest. Shards of ice flowed through her. If Rita could feel that callous about a brother who had always taken her part then what might she really think of her for having survived the accident that took their parents' lives?

Belle swallowed down the lump of inkling rising in her throat. "Let us not think...nor speak...such malicious thoughts," she said as she attempted to steer her sister away from her ruthlessness. "There's still plenty of time for you to confront Edward about your feelings when he arrives. And the next time I see Colonel Orsini, I'll inquire if he's heard anything," she added as she edged away from her vitriolic sister. "Now, where's my room?"

"Up that set of stairs," Rita said pointing to the grand stairway rising upward at the end of the corridor. "But we need to remain here until our aunt joins us," she added. "The last time I didn't, she ended up in the King's private chambers."

Belle rubbed at her forehead, hoping to ease the tension tightening her nerves. "With or without Muffy as a chaperone?" She managed to ask, wanting nothing more than to be gone from the vast domed gallery where at any moment their ruse might be discovered.

"Without," Rita said, waving her hand attempting to hurry their aunt along. Belle noted that their aunt paid not the slightest bit of attention to Rita but was instead rather intent on talking to her dog. "Daft woman," her twin muttered, "never pays attention to anything."

Belle felt her face flush. She hated it when Rita made snide remarks about Aunt Ellie. Not about to allow any further diatribe, she quickly asked. "Who found her?"

"King Stefan," Rita said then chortled.

Her sister's shrill laugh sent a quiver of dislike through Belle. Concerned for their aunt's tender sensibilities, Belle snapped. "Why didn't you go after her?"

"I wasn't about to enter the King's chamber, not when the forty-something-year-old man sat naked in his tub chewing on a cheroot," Rita replied, her jeering tone stretching Belle's nerves taut.

Belle halted as alarm flooded through her. "You don't find King Stefan attractive?"

"Well, he's certainly not like your Colonel," Rita said as she elbowed past her.

"He's not my Colonel," Belle mumbled then scurried to catch up with her sister. "But, how can you tell what the Colonel is like?" She asked as she latched onto her twin's forearm and brought her to a halt. "Near as I've observed, you've kept your face turned away, hidden by the hood of your cape."

"It's your cape," Rita corrected, "and I've noticed plenty."

Belle took a slow breath, hoping to calm her rising irritation at Rita's taunting. "But you're wearing my spectacles," she said. "How can you see anything in the distance when my specs are for close up reading?'

'It doesn't take a pair of specs to notice a powerful set of shoulders or the way a man's trousers hug his posterior. But," Rita said, waving her hands toward the throne room, "what I couldn't see was if he had large hands. And I do so love men with manly hands," she added holding her palms out as if to emphasize her point.

"Then you had best hope King Stefan has hands the size of ham hocks," Belle countered in disgust. She knew that whatever Rita wanted, by hook or crook, Rita got. Removing the sapphire brooch from her lapel, she dropped it onto Rita's outstretched palm. "Take that. It's yours. I never want to wear it or ever pretend to be you again."

"How dare you disrespect me," her sister exclaimed attempting to shove the brooch back into her hand. "Take it back."

"No," Belle hissed, "I won't." Whirling away, she scampered down the hallway. When she reached the stairway at the end of the hall and glanced over her shoulder. She stopped to watch Rita stamp her foot. A bubble of joy burst within her chest and she smiled as she waited to see what her sister would do next. Finally, she'd found the courage to say 'no'.

"I will not tolerate your insolence," Rita growled. Then shaking the costly brooch at her, her sister stalked down the corridor toward her. "I am not ready to change back. Therefore, you will continue to be me," she ordered as she stopped to stamp her foot again. "From now on, in my presence, you will wait...until I have granted you the permission to breathe."

Belle felt her mouth drop open. She gawked at her sister in disbelief. The...Rita becoming a Queen thing...must've really gone to her sister's head if Rita thought she would ever ask permission for something as essential as a breath.

"I'm not likely to ever request that," Belle snapped as she glared at her twin. Then like the sun rising in the east, a dawning awareness crept over her. This wasn't the sister she remembered from their childhood. And while Rita had always been unpredictable, the more Belle thought about it, the more she realized that her sister's behavior over the years had become more demanding and disruptive. No matter if her actions were because she was to be Queen, Rita had become an out-of-control stranger.

She felt her breath hitch in her chest at the recognition. She stared at her sister. As the realization that she had been so short-sighted that she had given Rita free reign to use her as the scape-goat for all of her shortcomings settled over her.

The icy breath of betrayal swept over her. That feeling was soon followed by the intense heat of humiliation. She had allowed that behavior to go unchecked for years because she had thought that she owed her sister for surviving the coach accident when their parents hadn't. How could she have allowed her guilt to take over common sense and how had she missed Rita's manipulations and not discerned the truth before now?

Belle shook her head. She felt her eyes widen as she peered at the woman she'd called sister. A haughty, grasping woman stood before her. Concerned with her own welfare, Rita basked in the glory of being Queen. Queen or not, she no longer deserved either her respect or her help. Clenching her teeth tightly, Belle vowed never to become a victim of her own making again. Nor would she subject herself to being her siblings' scape-goat. "Then it's a good thing that I've finally discovered how truly selfish and self-centered you are," she retorted.

"If you think I will allow-"

"Give me back my specs," Belle demanded, holding out her palm. Waiting for her belligerent twin to comply, she continued. "And don't try any tricks. I've learned a few things while we've been apart," she added. "And I guaranteed you won't like what I've learned." Then realizing that Rita had no intention of handing over her glasses, she snatched her specs from her sister's nose. Tucking the earpiece inside the bodice of her shirt, she placed her hand over her specs. "Now, we are officially finished here. I leave it to you to deal with the aftermath of what you've instigated in any way you want."

"Oh, my dear," their aunt said as she hurried toward them carrying Muffy in her arms. "I do hope you two are not fighting again," she said looking first at Rita then switching her gaze to Belle.

Belle swallowed back her hasty retort.

There was a momentary silence as a stunned expression flitted across their aunt's face and then she emitted a gasp, "Oh, no!" she moaned. "What have the two of you done?"

"Something we shouldn't have," Belle mumbled as she felt her cheeks burn. Unable to look at their aunt's horrified countenance another second, she dipped her head. As she took a step to the side she realized that Muffy hadn't given away their ruse after all. It had been Queen Rita and her power-hungry insidious demands. She didn't know whether to laugh or cry as relief flooded her.

A feeling of lightness lifted Belle's spirit as if she'd been released from the shackles chaining her to her twin. "All is back to normal," she added, attempting to reassure their aunt. "Once again, Rita is safe. That is all that matters now. She will be the future Queen of this country. From this moment onward, her fate rests solely in her hands," she said then gently patted their aunt's arm. "You need not fear that I will switch places with her again," she vowed

"That is what you promised me the last time you did this," their aunt protested as she snatched her arm away. Belle inhaled sharply at the reminder then hunched her shoulders as she remembered the morning she had inadvertently answered a question posed by Queen Victoria's wardrobe mistress as herself and not as Rita. Hearing her response and realizing the two had switched places, Aunt Ellie had whisked her away from the palace in shame. Surfacing from the memory, she glanced at their aunt and was jerked out of the past as Aunt Ellie asked. "Now, how am I to explain all of this to Edward?"

Belle gulped at the question. "When...he shows up, you may tell him... whatever you think is best," Belle said, doubling her effort to soothe her distraught aunt. She realized the shame and humiliation for the entire ruse rested on her shoulders, no matter how innocent her intent had been in the beginning. She fully accepted the blame. Against her better judgment, she had allowed Rita to sway her from her own convictions. Out of guilt, she had agreed to participate in the ruse. And she now realized that like so many others caught in Rita's web of deceit, she had been duped by her twin. But unlike the others, she had no one to blame but herself. She felt a hot flash of anger roll through her as she considered her own stupidity.

"I will not condone this irresponsible behavior," her aunt said, shaking her index finger at her. "Your behavior is disgraceful. When this ruse becomes known, it will humiliate our family beyond anything that has ever happened before. When your actions come to light, we won't be able to show our faces anywhere in society."

While Belle wouldn't mind being excluded from society, she knew how much the good name and reputation of their family meant to their aunt. She hated the fact that she had brought such anguish and misery to her. She gulped down the knot rising in her throat. "Then what can I do to make amends? How can I make this better?"

"Nothing will ever make this better," their aunt snapped. Then suddenly, she splayed her fingers on her breastbone. "Oh, my" she moaned. "What are we to tell King Stefan?"

A cold ball of fear slammed into Belle's chest. There was only one way to handle this and that was to take ownership of what she'd done. "The truth," she said as she squared her shoulders. "He deserves to know the truth. But whatever he is told," she said, "know that I'm forever done here."

"Wait, you can't leave me to face all of the consequences!" Rita exclaimed. Latching onto Belle's wrist, she tightened her hold as a look of horror settled on her face.

"That's not my intention," Belle said, prying herself away from her twin. "I will do one last thing for you," she said as she moved away from her sister. "I will tell the King."

"You owe me more than that," her sister hissed. "Why if it hadn't been for you-"

"I owe nothing more to you," Belle said firmly then paused. "But, for all of the years you've heaped the guilt upon my head, you do owe me. And for payment of that debt, you will go with me when I talk to the King."

"Why should I do anything for you?" her sister said her lip curling in a sneer.

"I figure you're going to need this new experience of being held accountable for your actions," Belle said. "It will stand you in good stead as Queen. After all, it was your idea to switch places," she said then shook her head. "I only helped you out of guilt. I even had the mistaken idea that you might finally appreciate all I've done for you. But obviously, I was mistaken" she said as she shrugged. "Now, if you will excuse me, I'm going to clean up. I will meet you in Aunt Ellie's chamber to figure out when we're going to confront the King."

"Thank you," their Aunt mumbled. "The quicker that is done, the better I will feel," she said. "At the top of the stairs, you will find your room is four doors down on the right. I'm in the suite directly across the hall," she said waving her hand in dismissal.

Belle nodded then hurried up the steps. Walking down the long corridor, she opened the fourth door down and entered a sitting room.

To the left of the room, an open door led into a formal gathering area, to the right of the sitting room a door remained partially opened and she heard her maid's off-key humming. Relieved she would have help, she followed the sound. Entering the bedchamber, she closed the door. Turning back, she grinned as her maid gasped in fright.

"Oh, My Lady, is that really you?"

"That it is," Belle said with a smile.

"I was so afraid when no one could find you," the maid said, wringing her hands. "It was as if the kelpies had suddenly spirited you away."

"Wasn't a kelpie," she said not wanting to talk about either her experience or explain the ruse she and her twin had perpetrated. "But, never mind," she said as she hastily began removing her shoes. "If you wouldn't mind helping, I need a bath, clean clothes, and food. And not necessarily in that order."

"I'll start the water then go to the kitchen," the maid said hurrying off toward what Belle soon discovered was a bathing room.

It didn't take long for Belle to bathe and wash her hair. It took longer for her to dry her hair and dress. And while her hair was being arranged by her maid, she ate the cold luncheon of cheese, assorted meats, bread and strawberries the palace had supplied for her. Then checking her appearance in the mirror, she opened the door for the maid, who left to return her lunch tray to the kitchen. Sticking her head out the partially opened door, Belle checked to see if the sitting room she shared with Rita was clear of her presence. Finding it so, she stepped through the doorway. But suddenly, she heard her sister bid their aunt "good luck" from the other room.

Still angry with herself and not about to become embroiled in any more of Rita's schemes, Belle scurried back into her bedchamber. Peeking through the narrowly opened door, she spotted her sister leading Niko toward the formal gathering room.

Belle's heart hammered in her chest as she realized she had a major problem. It wouldn't surprise her in the least if Rita decided to continue their ruse on Niko by pretending to be her. A hot blanket of shame enveloped her as she considered how their deception would be viewed by others. But seeing him in their suite, brought home the fact that she owed him a personal explanation and an apology. But would a man as honorable and upright as him understand? She bit her bottom lip, knowing he was more apt to condemn than condone. The one thing she'd learned about men from her brother Edward was that a man's pride was sacrosanct. And while she may have found her courage to defy Rita, she had yet to think she was brave enough to face Niko and the King.

But what if, knowing her planned confession, Rita ruined everything by continuing their ruse and posed as her with Niko?

Widening the opening of the door, Belle clenched her fists as anger coursed through her. Although there were no guarantees when dealing with Rita, she felt confident that Niko could fend for himself. Rita might play her coy games with Niko but he was smart and could take care of himself.

But what if Rita...believing she had the right to enact her own revenge disappeared before the wedding and left her to clean up the mess? Belle froze at the thought. Then as she began to unthaw she realized there was only one way to guarantee that Rita behaved ... and resumed her own identity...and became Queen.

Belle shivered at the reality as the simple solution came to her. She had to leave. Plain and simple, if she wasn't there, Rita would have no other choice but to accept her responsibility. With her gone, her twin could no longer use her as a pawn. Rita would be forced into compliance.

A burden seemed to lift off her shoulders. After the utter shame and humiliation she'd brought upon her family, she knew they would be relieved to find her gone. Belle gulped down the burning knot rising in her throat. Stepping back, she quietly closed her chamber door. Her heart pounded in her chest as she realized the ramifications of what she was about to do. Leaving would mean that Aunt Ellie would have to talk to the King. And for a lady who maintained the belief that one never aired the family's faults in public, that meeting would be humiliating. Belle pressed a fist to her lips. The fact that she was running away would make it harder for her aunt to face what others were sure to call a cowardly action. No matter what, society's perception of the reputation of the family had always been Aunt Ellie's first consideration. But Belle realized with her gone, there would be the initial humiliation, but it would pass quickly and then the family could begin to rebuild their reputation and the honor of their good name.

Suiting action to her decision, Belle rushed to her traveling trunk and flung open the lid. If she was to leave the palace and make her way back to the gypsy encampment, she would dress like a Barovian. To travel unaccompanied, she'd need to be disguised as a boy. She dug through the contents until she found the pirate costume she'd planned on wearing to Rita's Masquerade Ball scheduled as an evening celebration after the Royal Wedding. Lifting portions of the garment out, she donned the stockings and trousers then wrapped her chest and slipped on the blousy shirt. Tying the neck, she added a weskit, coat, and boots. Then tucking her hair up into the tricorn hat, she sorted through her trunk until she found her own black gloves, a muffler, and a cape. Next, she pulled a drawstring bag from beneath two ball gowns and looped it around her neck. Then finding her reticule, she transferred her pin money from it into the drawstring pouch and tucked it inside her shirt to rest between her bound breasts. Finally, she hurried to the window that opened onto the veranda that ran the entire length of the wing. She opened the window then glanced back. A burning knot formed in her throat as she realized that she could never return. Not only couldn't she return...but she would never see her loved ones again. Hot tears coursed down her face at the thought and she swiped at them using the sleeve of her coat. She scolded herself sternly. There would be no more tears. Her family's welfare had to come first.

Squaring her shoulders, she climbed out the window. A pressing sense of urgency had her sprinting to the end of the veranda. Spotting a set of steps, she hurried down them. Pausing to survey the area, relief rushed through her as she spied several buildings off in the distance surrounded by green pastures. Hoping she might be able to catch a ride, she headed toward the stables.

As her feet pounded the gravel, she decided once she was settled some place she would contact Aunt Ellie, Niko and the King and offer her apologies. As for her siblings, by leaving, she was granting them the biggest favor of all. With her gone, when their ruse became known it would be easier for Edward and Rita to blame everything on her. She felt her breath hitch in her chest. Right, wrong or indifferent it was what it was. She would not blame anyone but her own weak-willed self.

***

Niko frowned at the over-friendly woman who edged closer to him as he sat on the sofa. While she might look like Belle, she neither acted nor smelled like his Belle. Belle smelled like warm vanilla sunshine while this woman smelled of heavy musk. And she was much bolder than the woman he had come to know as Belle.

"I am so-o very grateful," the woman said, her gushing tone grating on Niko's nerves as he observed her closely for any clue that might help him determine why she was impersonating Belle. He felt his eyes widen as he noticed the milky white skin of the woman's hand. He knew for certain that this wasn't his Belle for when they were in the gypsy encampment Belle had used a herbal mixture that had darkened her creamy skin with the brush of sunlight.

"You are welcome," he returned as he edged away to sit at the very end of the sofa, wondering what game the woman played if she thought she could get away with impersonating his future Queen. "But, I didn't come to receive more thanks from you," he said as the woman closed the gap separating them.

Determined to waste no further time on the woman or her charade, Niko sprang to his feet and backed away. "I don't know what hoax you're perpetrating
but-"

"You are clearly mistaken," the woman interjected as she smoothly stood and stepped toward him.

As she neared, he bit back his hasty retort. Caution flared within him. Feeling more like the hunted than the hunter, he knew if he did what he wanted to do and turned tail and ran then he would find no answers. He raised his palms to halt her movement as her cloying scent sucked all the air from his lungs. A sour taste filled his mouth as he took a slow breath. Hoping to rattle her composure, he said, "I came here to inquire what you observed about the rebel commander," he began. "Yet-"

"And now you have questions?" she asked. Although she slowed, she continued sidling toward him until they stood toe-to-toe. "He's a man like any other. What do you want me to say? That I found him handsome?" she asked tapping her index finger on his chest. Surprise held him captive for a moment before he caught her hand and held it away from his body. "Do you want to know that I found him exciting and felt drawn by the power he exuded?" she asked as she lifted her chin.

"That's not the impression I gained from you as we stood and watched him," he said, briskly. Releasing his hold on her, he stepped away, waiting to see what effect his terse comment had on her.

"Why would I think that when you are so much more?" she purred. Then suddenly, she rushed forward, threw her arms around his neck and mashed her lips against his.

Seized by disgust, Niko grabbed the woman's wrists and pushed her away. "Stop," he ordered, backing away from the grasping woman. "This isn't honorable," he managed to say as fear trickled through him and he wondered what this imposter had done with Belle. "Who are you and where is Belle?" he demanded.

"I am whoever you want me to be," the woman said flipping her long chestnut hair over her exposed right shoulder. "Now, if you were to be King then I would gladly be your Queen," she said as a coy smile settled on her lying lips.

"While I have no intention of ever being King," he stated. "I do demand that you tell me what you've done with Belle."

"Ah, my twin," she said, moving toward him once more. "She is next door," she said then turning, she entered and walked across the private sitting room to open the door that led into a bedchamber. "Belle," she called. "You can come out now." When no one answered, she turned back to him and shrugged. "Um-m, seems my sister must be hiding from you. Or perhaps she went to the kitchen to get something to eat," she said as she arched one of her eyebrows. Then sashaying back toward him, she twirled a lock of her hair around her index finger. "But why would you want her...when you can have me?"

Her answer rocked him back on his heels. But determined to not allow her to know that she had knocked him off his stride, he squared his shoulders. "You would never be my choice of a consort," he said taking a menacing step toward her.

"Now, wait just a minute," she began then quickly lifted her hands as if in surrender. "I swear, I've done nothing to harm my sister. This was all her idea. She readily agreed with me that I needed time to adjust to the idea of being the Queen of Barovia. Belle willingly changed places with me and agreed to be me for a few days. I see no harm in that, do you?"

"You wouldn't," Niko aid as indignation surged through him. Belle had placed herself in grave danger by acting as a decoy for her twin. With his uncle commanding the Revolutionary Forces and a civil war threatening to break out in the country, had Belle been recognized, she would've been captured and used as a pawn by his uncle. He studied the haughty woman standing before him as his hands clenched and unclenched at his sides. The callous female cared only for herself and certainly nothing for Belle's safety or welfare.

Goaded by the enormity of the woman's indifference toward Belle, a guttural roar began to form a knot in the back of his throat. Taking a deep breath, he paused. But what of Belle? Had she not cared about her own safety? He thought they had established a mutual trust between them but obviously, he had been mistaken because she had not told him the truth about who she was. The knot burning in his throat slid downward to become a hot churning mass in his chest at the realization. He balled his fists as a streak of angry determination seized him. He would not rest until he came face to face with Belle. Turning away, he straightened. "And what name do you go by?" he asked, refusing to face the duplicitous woman.

"I am Marguerita Isabelle," she said, pride evident in her tone. "I am the oldest twin and I will soon be crowned Queen of Barovia."

Niko hardened his jaw at the bold statement. Not if he had any say in the matter he almost retorted then tempered down that response by clearing his throat. He wasn't about to tip the hand that he'd been dealt. "And your sister, what name is she known by?"

"She's Belle or sometimes Isabelle Marguerita," she said. "Our father thought it a great joke to name us with the same names but in reverse order."

At least Belle hadn't lied to him about her name he thought as he turned to face the woman. "I find nothing humorous about any of this," he said appalled that anyone would actually encourage such behavior.

"We meant no harm," she said, her pleading tone ratcheting up his dislike of her.

"Perhaps you didn't," he said, "but your actions when revealed, will bring this nation to its knees and effectively destroy all hope the people of Barovia have placed in the honor of this monarchy."

"Oh, don't get your trews in such a twist," she said beginning to tap rapidly with one of her toes. "I was just making sport of you," she added then rolled her eyes and flashed him a grin. "Your valet puts way too much starch in your cravats."

A pounding sounded in his ears as he shifted his stance and planted his feet wide apart. "Do you think this is some huge joke? Or...perhaps you think you can blackmail me into not telling His Majesty about what has happened?"

"Oh, do what you like," she said, waving her hand in dismissal. "I could care less what you say or do. I didn't want to marry the King to begin with."

"What?" Niko asked not sure he had heard her correctly.

"I mean that-"

"Rita, my dear. Have you seen Belle?" A slender middle-aged woman asked as she hurried into the sitting room, her arms full of a frothy blue gown. "I don't think it's appropriate that she wear a pirate's costume to the masquerade. I found this delightful shepherd's costume," she said then stopped as if she'd just noticed him. "Oh dear," she said. "I didn't realize we had company."

"Colonel Nikolai Orsini, at your service," he said clicking his heels together. "Would you like me to explain to you what is going on here?" he asked flashing a frown at Rita.

"I suppose that dear sweet King Stefan sent you," she said as a frown wrinkled her brow.

"As a matter of fact, he did," Niko replied. "I'm his cousin."

"Oh, my," the aunt exclaimed. "And I thought the palace servants were closed-mouthed. Stefan never mentioned you at all."

Thank goodness, Niko wanted to say but instead, he muttered, "I'm seldom here." He frowned, not about to get side-tracked. "But tell me about Belle."

"Oh dear," the aunt said dabbing at her eyes with a kerchief. "I had so hoped that the girls might've been able to keep their switch a secret."

"It's way too late for that," he said rubbing at his forehead. "Now, tell me about this ruse."

"Well, as to that, I'm their Aunt Ellie. And there are days when even I can't tell them apart," she said shifting the costume from one arm to the other. "And my precious Muffy is no help," she said, her tone exasperated. "Had it not been for Belle's specs dangling from her...oh, my never mind," the aunt said, her face flushing a bright red. "It was her...darkened skin tone...yes, that was the clue," she said, nodding her head. "Had it not been for that bronzed color I still would not have a clue as to what they had done. Why I can't-"

"Belle has been jealous of me all her life," Rita interjected as Niko watched her wave the aunt in a shooting motion to a chair near the fireplace. "Since I was born first, it has always been my right to be first in everything. That was something Belle just never understood," she said, leaning toward him. Niko took a quick step back and watched as she straightened. Lowering her brows, she gave an audible huff and continued. "So when I was chosen to marry King Stefan, Belle threw a royal fit. Her jealousy became so intense...and terrible that I simply couldn't help but...feel sorry for her. After all, it was my fault she is to wed the fat Duke of Umberford and become mother to his five motherless children. What was I to do," she asked then shrugged, "but let her be me for a day? I had no idea that...one day would become two, now did I?"

"Obviously not," Niko mumbled disgusted at the picture Belle's twin was painting of her. He knew for a fact that the Belle he'd met and spent the last two days with was nothing like the petulant shrew that her sister, Rita, had described to him. "And so," he prompted as he wondered what other lies the woman would tell.

"When we got to the Black Swan Inn, I surrendered my beloved betrothal pin to her, so she would know what it felt like to be the King's intended. How was I to know that she aimed to steal it and run off without a word?"

Niko knew that wasn't what had happened, but he also knew the woman who was slated to be his future Queen and cousin-by-marriage left a foul taste in his mouth. Knowing he couldn't stay a second longer without correcting the deceitful woman, he clicked his heels together. "Then by your leave, ladies," he said and gave a bow. Straightening, he frowned. "Please tell Belle the King needs her to answer a few questions." Then executing a precise military about-face, he opened the door and got the heck out of there.

What was he to tell Stefan? He gritted his teeth as he strode down the corridor away from the guest wing. Did he confess they had both been duped? What then did that say about the character and the integrity of the two women? Which twin was really the weak-willed one that had allowed her stronger, more dominant twin to rule her? He took a deep breath. Whatever he decided, it had better be quick because it was imperative he inform Stefan about the problem they now had with his bride-to-be. Then he needed leave. With his mission to defeat and capture their uncle his first priority, as far as he was concerned, the dilemma of Belle and her sister would have to wait for his cousin's decision.

***

"Hey, you, there...boy. Give me a hand," a portly gentleman said as he mounted his horse using a mounting block at the Royal Stables.

"Yes, sir," Belle said after dipping her head and lowering her voice.

"What do you need me to do?"

"Hand me that basket there," he said pointing to a wicker basket setting near the mounting blocked he'd just used.

"Aye, Sir," she replied. Bending, she tugged her hat down and lifted the wicker basket. Then careful not to allow the man to glimpse her face, she straightened and offered it up to him.

"That's a good lad," he said taking the basket from her. She sneaked a quick look at the man as he settled the basket on his lap. Stepping back, she watched as he pivoted his horse. Her chest lifted in relief, grateful he hadn't seen through her disguise. "Here you go," he said flipping a coin toward her.

Surprise held her captive for a moment then reaching up, she snatched it out of the air before it hit the ground. Her mouth dropped open as she opened her fist and stared at the gold Florian. "Many thanks, Sir," she called as he cantered toward the road that fronted the palace.

Her worry eased as she stared at the coin. If nothing else, she would not have to remove any of her pin money from the bag secured around her neck. With this one coin, she would have more than enough to carry her through until she found Rikard and his tribe. She nodded in relief as she followed the man toward the road that led away from the palace.

* * *

Niko entered the busy command center that had been set up in the waiting area of the Throne Room and found that his cadre had stacked their personal belongs to the side beyond the door. His men had gathered around the easel and were discussing the plan of attack on the board. He waved away the announcement of his entry as he quickly strode through the room. Snapping to attention, the Royal Guards opened the Throne Room doors and announced, "His Royal Highness, Prince Nikolai."

Niko waited inside until Stefan rose from the desk he worked at and motioned him forward then met him half-way. "Walk with me toward the balcony," his cousin said. "I need your opinion on how to deal with our uncle and this situation he has created."

"Plain and simple," Niko said hardening his jaw. "His actions demonstrate that he will allow nothing to get in his way. His goal is a coup d'état which will throw this nation into chaos."

"I agree." The King nodded though a frown furrowed his brow. "What would you do if you were King?"

"In this case, I would give no quarter," Niko replied without remorse.

"I would declare him a traitor and hold him to the strictest penalty under our laws."

"Which is death by a firing squad," Stefan said.

Niko felt his breath hitch in his chest. Although he had never been close to his uncle, the man was still his father's brother. And not only was Uncle Jorge a family member but he was also third in line to the throne. So, while others might act cavalier about the King's decision, Niko wondered if he would be able to carry out the order. He stared down at his hands then clasped them loosely behind his back. Taught to always put the good of the country first, he knew he would do what was best for Barovia. Unclasping his hands, he squared his shoulders. "Uncle Jorge witnessed the public execution of the six men caught colluding with the Hungarians a few years ago when they attempted to usurp your father. He knows the consequences he will face when he is brought to justice. Yet he persists in this mad pursuit," he said shaking his head. "What he fails to understand is that at some point we all must come to the realization that excuses for bad behavior are offensive...that those excuses will no longer be tolerated by others. And that we will be held accountable for all of our actions, past and present." He took a quick breath then finished, "For our uncle, that day is swiftly approaching."

"Good, we are in agreement," Stefan said giving a crisp nod. "Do what must be done. If you can take him alive...then do so and bring him here to face justice. But let me emphasize," his cousin said leaning toward him. "Not at the peril to your own life. If you must kill Jorge to save yourself or others, then do so," he said then straightened. "Are we clear?"

Niko nodded, relief flowing through him. "Yes," he said then paused. "There is a problem I've just become aware of," he said, slowly. "I don't know of any way to address this but to simply state it and let you decide how you want to resolve it."

"That is one of the many things I've always admired about you Nikolai," his cousin said. "Your honesty."

"Then you will be just as surprised as I was to learn that our future Queen has a twin," Niko said.

"A twin?" Stefan asked, his pitch lifting an octave. "And we are just finding out about this now?" Niko watched Stefan's eyes widen. "What else do you think we don't we know about her?"

"Good question," Niko said running his hand through his hair.

"And to complicate matters, the twins are identical and they switched identities," he said then hardened his jaw. "That means the woman, Belle, whom I thought was our future Queen and I protected with my life...is, in reality, the second sister and not our future Queen at all."

"Adikia!" his cousin exclaimed. "That means Lady Rita is actually... my intended?" Stefan groaned, his hands grasping his head. "This is a disaster."

"I agree," Niko said. "And the solution on how to handle this is solely in your hands."

"And to think I thought the only danger we faced was from our uncle," his cousin muttered then gripped the sill of the window overlooking the gardens at the back of the palace. "From what I've observed of the Lady Rita, she is a self-serving, spoiled shrew. One that I do not want to marry."

"I'm sorry, I apologize for having to dump this in your lap right now but I didn't want to leave without first alerting you that we were duped. What with your wedding planned for the day after tomorrow -"

"Which in light of everything going on will have to be delayed," the King finished for him.

"I'll leave that decision best to you," Niko said thankful that was a decision he didn't have to make. "Now, if you will excuse me," Niko said with a bow. "I have a mission to compete."

"Stay safe," Stefan said giving him a distracted wave.

"You also," Niko said as he backed toward the door. Pivoting, he strode into the Command Center and halted beside Cyrek to study the attack plans formulated to subdue the rebels. Satisfied by what he saw, he turned to scan the room. Locating two of his Field Operations Officers, Majors Kelso and Bjorni along with two of his Line Officers, Captains Elser and Metzer, Niko realized he was missing a Field Officer. "Has anyone seen Major Hondros?" he asked.

The men looked at each other and either frowned, shrugged or registered a surprised expression on their faces.

"I saw him yesterday morning cantering away from the palace," Major Bjorni said. "He was out of uniform. When I checked the off-duty roster later in the day, he was listed on it. But I never gave it another thought after Colonel Domokos arrived and we began constructing Abatist and Cheval-de-frise defensive positions in the forest around the palace."

"Will you check to see if he's signed back in and let me know?" Niko asked Major Bjorni as a sinking sensation settled in the pit of his stomach. The trouble with men like Hondros who worked as double agents was they could become caught between their duty and their personal loyalties. When that happened, they often lost touch with reality and inadvertently exposed their duplicity. But if Hondros had turned traitor at least he had left before construction of the defensive positions had begun.

"If the Major hasn't signed in, report back to me then notify Captain Richter that he will be leading the Major's unit," Niko said.

"Aye, that I will," Major Bjorni said then saluted.

Niko returned the salute then glanced at his men. "If there are no further questions," he said then paused a moment to note there were none. "Then we're off," he added as he strode out of the Command Center with his cadre following him.

Chapter Twelve

Riding at the head of the column, Niko led his men along the road running adjacent to the palace walls. They would soon be away from the city and then he could increase their pace. He raised his arm then dropped it as he spotted his forward scout galloping pell-mell down the road toward him.

"Your Highness," Weiss shouted. "Rebels ferrying across the river near High Bluff," the young man yelled. Pulling back on his reins, his horse reared. Bringing his steed under control, Weiss gasped out. "Cannons being rolled into position on the bluff."

"Into the trees," Niko shouted to his troops. "Ride to the palace," he ordered Weiss. "Warn Colonel Domokos. Inform him we'll take out the cannons, assault, and flank then feign retreat to lure the rebels into the range of his guns. Now hurry," he said as a ka-thume-m-m whistled through the air overhead of them.

Cursing, Niko wheeled his horse. He watched Weiss disappear safely down the narrow road toward the stables as the cannonball hit the base of the palace wall and exploded. A fierce shower of rock and debris, along with a plume of dust lifted high into the air then fell to land in the wide section of cleared ground separating the castle walls from the forest his men called 'a cleared field for killing'.

Heading into the trees behind his soldiers, Niko knew there wasn't anything to be gained by returning to the palace. With the Rebels attacking the palace, he needed to lead the counter charge and halt the assault once and for all if Stefan was to rule the country. Pulling his spyglass from where it rested in a pouch looped to his saddle, he guided his horse to the small knoll and aimed his glass at the High Bluff. "Adakis," he exclaimed as the smoke drifted off to the south. Not only had he found Major Hondros but his uncle as well.

"Scoundrels!" Major Kelso exclaimed. "That hit the palace," he added as he waved his riflemen into the forest. Just then another cannonball whistled overhead and hit near where the first ball had exploded. "Who do you suppose is directing such accuracy?"

"Take a look," Niko said passing his spyglass to the Major. "That is if you can see anything through the smoke."

"I count three heavy pounders," the Major said, handing the glass back to him.

"As did I," Niko confirmed.

"Let me take a squad of men and destroy those guns," Kelso said. "Eliminating them will prevent the rebels from doing any more damage to the palace structure."

"Then do it," Niko commanded. "After you've destroyed the cannons, burn the boats they used to sneak across the river. They will have no means of escaping through the back door. Have the rest of your unit join you as you are destroying the cannons. Establish a line. Hold it by killing all those trying to retreat," Niko said. "I'll send a squad of Captain Vogel's best marksmen to assist you. They will take out the cannoneers," he added. "Also pass the word to all of your men that I saw Major Hondros standing with Prince Jorge and the rebels atop the bluff. If possible, I want him alive," he said as a sour taste filled his mouth. The Major either hadn't been able to slip away and report to Cyrek or he had turned traitor.

Kelso stared at him for a moment. "I will," he said then saluted. Approaching his men, he picked ten men then turned his unit over to Captain Anzodus. Waving his squad forward, he led his men, single file, amongst the trees toward the river. Once at the river, Niko knew Kelso would flank the bank using the rugged terrain to cover their movement toward the bluff.

Turning, Niko spurred his horse toward Captain Vogel and his marksmen and Major Bjorni waiting with his cavalry. "Captain Vogel," he called as he approached the two officers. "Send a squad of your best shots to join Major Kelso. They're to pick off the cannoneers while Kelso is getting into place to destroy the cannons. We don't want any of the artillerymen to pick up rifles and join their fighting comrades. Then take your men and right flank the ridge above that valley," he said pointing toward the rugged ridge lined with boulders. He turned toward Major Bjorni. "Major take your cavalry and left flank the ridge. When both you and Captain Vogel's units are in place, move the rebels toward us, pushing and pressing them toward my men who will be dug in. We will hold the line allowing your units to attack and retreat pressing them ever closer into the range of the palace guns. Caution your men to never go beyond the boulders rimming the ridge." The men nodded and turned to leave. "And pass the word to all of your men," he said as the two turned back toward him, "that before the first cannonball flew, I saw Major Hondros standing with Prince Jorge and the rebels atop the bluff. If possible, I want him to remain alive."

The two men looked at each other. Nodding, they saluted. "Aye, Colonel," they said in unison.

"Captain Elser," Niko called. "Station three of your ceremonial archers in the trees behind my men who are dug in behind the downed logs. And pass the word to all of your men that before the first cannonball flew, I saw Major Hondros standing with Prince Jorge. If possible, he's to remain alive."

"Aye, Colonel," the Captain saluted.

Approaching his Infantry Captains Metzer and Richter, Niko motioned them forward then bent to draw a line in the dirt with the tip of his riding crop. "Both of you will spread your men out in the forest beyond where my men are stationed here in the trenches," he said pointing to the line he had drawn. "Have your men advance to the barrier of the downed trees," he said drawing another line beyond the first one he had made. "Caution your men not to stray beyond this line of defense," he said tapping the line. "If they do, they will be gunned down by our own cannons." Straightening, he paused as he glanced at the two Captains. "If you need to retreat, fall back beyond my men and join forces. They are stationed there to hold that position and have been ordered to stand down until your men have cleared the field of combat before they commence firing Captain Elser's archers will be stationed in the trees above my men and will notify us if there are stragglers." He tightened his grip on his crop and frowned. "And pass the word to all of your men that I saw Major Hondros standing with Prince Jorge and the rebels atop the bluff. Try not to harm him."

With his men positioning themselves, Niko raised is glass and watch the rebels begin their noisy downward descent from the top of High Bluff. As the rebels came within the palace's cannon range, a volley of cannons began firing from the palace behind them.

Niko turned as another rebel ball whistled overhead and hit near where the other two cannon balls had exploded. Debris and smoke plumed in the air then fell to the earth. He realized that a few more hits like that one and the rebels would breach the palace wall. Swinging his glass back to the High Bluff he watched Captain Vogel's marksmen shoot a soldier swabbing the bore of the cannon to put out any residual sparks remaining in the hot barrel of the cannon. As the soldier fell to the ground, another bullet plowed into the chest of an artilleryman grasping the device used to elevate the bore. Niko swung his glass from the center cannon to the far right. There, all six men lay unmoving around the caisson. Moving his glass to the far left, he watched as a gunner make a valiant attempt to light the fuse on the cannon but a bullet to the chest ended his effort. Niko nodded. With the cannons now silenced, the battle would soon become fierce.

Suddenly, another volley of shells from the palace cannons whistled overhead, exploding amongst the clusters of the rebels running en masse down the steep hill. Those surviving kept running although more cannonballs plowed furrows into the terrain and lifted the earth as plumes of dirt and debris reigned down over the rebels. Those that made it into the lush green valley, fanned out, their boisterous battle cry alerting his men that they would soon meet their enemy.

Niko watched as Vogel and Bjorni's men stealthily appeared on the ridgeline above the forest floor. Waiting until the palace guns had silenced, Vogel and Bjorni's men began moving silently down into the valley closing in behind the rebels as they ran deeper into the forest.

Niko handed his spyglass to his aide. "Remain here," he directed the young man. "But if you see the rebels coming, take my horse and ride to the stables. Alert Colonel Domokos. He knows what to do."

"Aye, Your Highness," his aide saluted. "Good luck," the lad called as Niko ran into the forest to stand and fight with his men.

***

Belle moved through the densely, crowded marketplace hoping she had correctly remembered where the wharf was located. Raising her head in anticipation that she would catch a whiff of fish and brine, she swallowed back her disappointment when the smells of sweat and unwashed bodies assaulted her. But no matter how disgusting the smells might be, she knew she had to find the wharf. Once there, she would discover a way across the river where she could seek out Rikard's camp.

Only then would she be safe. Finding her way to the camp might be the easy part she decided as she noticed banners of her twin's portrait hung from second story windows. Fluttering in the light breeze, the pennants proclaimed Rita to be their next Queen. Good luck with that she thought just as a whistle and an explosion erupted somewhere in the distance.

A clamor arose from the marketplace and people began pushing and shoving their neighbors through the narrow street. Belle pivoted. Suddenly she was thrust against a stone pillar. She gasped as she grabbed her hat to keep it from tumbling off her head. Sidling around the pillar she peeked out at the undulating mass of pushing, shrieking people. She hugged the pillar, her heart thundering in her chest. She realized that she had been lucky to have escaped the unruly horde. Slowly straightening, she surveyed the chaotic street and observed that many of the shopkeepers along the avenue rushed in and out of their establishments, gathering up their goods from the tables positioned in front of their stores and depositing them safely inside, away from the stampeding throng of bellowing citizens as another whistle followed by a second explosion erupted in the distance.

Mercy, she thought as she gripped the pillar. Either the palace was under attack from the rebels or the Colonel's artillery had set up a practice session.

As the elderly leather goods merchant swiped up more of his merchandise, Belle loosened her grip on the pillar and leaned away from it. "Please sir," she called in Italian, "can you tell me why everyone is running?"

"Go away! Get out of here," the old man yelled. "I don't deal with vagrants like you," he added as he dumped his goods in the doorway of his shop. Lifting a riding crop from a container nearby, he brandished it at her.

Stunned by his action, she stood motionless for a moment then as the whip flicked toward her, she scampered away from the sudden violence of the unwarranted attack. Her heart hammered in her ears as a mighty ka-thume hissed in the distance. She sucked in air to fill her lungs as the earth suddenly shook from an explosion.

"Merciful Heavens," she gasped fighting to catch her breath. The palace must be under attack by the rebels. The only safe place for her was with Rikard and his people. Reaching the public square, she veered to the left to avoid the swelling crowd of people flooding into the public square. She paused to gain control over her rioting emotions. Glancing over her shoulder, she sighed as relief rushed through her and she realized that the herd of people hadn't sought the safety of the narrow alleyway. Shifting her gaze forward, she scurried down the alley, hoping she looked like any ordinary citizen fleeing the trouble happening in the distance behind her.

She halted as she came to a wide cobblestone lane. Across the road lay a slow moving river and beyond that river, she knew Rikard and his tribe had set up their camp. She swallowed back her yelp of joy and stared at the beach that lay directly in front of where she stood. Knowing not the depth of the water, she looked to the right and spied a long pier jutting out into the water about two blocks away. Trusting she might persuade someone to ferry her across, she darted along the quayside, moving in and out of the men and women hurrying along the walk. As she passed, fishmongers called to her, hawking the last of their wares while noisy gulls added to the clamor by circling overhead. A boat carrying people docked and the fishermen rushed to gather their nets as the smell of sulfur settled over the city. As a savage yell lifted in the distance, the old men shouted at each other then dropped their gear and hurried away.

Rushing down the wharf, Belle noted that the docked boat was now tied to the pier and its passengers had scurried off. No help there, she decided as she became aware that the sun was beginning to set. She had to get across the river and locate Rikard's camp before they packed up and left. Or was it already too late? Had they packed up and left when the first cannonball had hit? Afraid the fighting would filter into the city, she turned to survey the horizon then spied the royal flag hanging among the gray smoke hovering above the palace ramparts.

Continuing to hurry north toward the bend in the river, she slowed as she remembered seeing the same royal flag as she'd stood with Niko on the river bank waiting for a skiff to come across for them that morning. She brightened as she realized that if she used the flag as a landmark, she would be able to find the gypsy camp. Swallowing back her yelp of joy, a more ominous thought crossed her consciousness. What was she to do if the gypsies had left the area? She chewed on her bottom lip for a moment then decided that she would simply find them. But first, her main focus had to be finding a way across the river.

Dashing along the quay, she slowed to climb a rickety set of wooden stairs. As a sudden gust of wind caught her cape, she hunched her shoulders and held onto her hat with both hands, not about to allow the frivolous wind to destroy her disguise. Then spying a young girl selling meat pies down the street, she crossed the narrow ribbon of cobblestones. Digging into her pocket, she pulled out a coin and placed it on her open palm. "Is this enough for one of those?" she asked speaking in Italian.

The girl nodded and quickly offered her a steaming pie. Handing the coin over, Belle heard her stomach growl as she accepted the pie. The smells of roasted meat, sage and garlic teased her nose. "Have you heard what's happening?" she asked before taking a bite of her savory spiced pie.

The girl only shook her head then shrugged her bony shoulders.

She realized that either the young girl knew nothing about the situation or the child didn't understand the Italian being spoken to her.

Hastily finishing her pie, Belle licked her greasy fingers. "Well then, thank you," she said then paused as concern for the young girl warred with her need to leave. "Best go home now," she said as she glanced around wondering what had happened to the rebels. Finding the street quiet, she noticed a posting inn midway down the block where she could purchase an ale to quench her thirst. "Take care," she said as she turned to find the girl had taken her basket of pies and disappeared down an alleyway. She sighed as tension eased out of her.

As she started toward the inn, a black coach pulled by four matching gray horses rolled by her and stopped in front of the establishment a few feet away. As she neared, two men climbed out, one, a middle-aged, well-dressed man with a hooked nose and the other, a much younger but scruffy looking man with a black beard. The men turned back toward the conveyance as an elderly woman stuck her head out the window. "I don't care what you have to promise. Get the directions and do it now," the old woman croaked in an unusually deep voice for a female.

Belle sidled past the coach and rushed toward the inn as a fisherman exited. Before the door could close, she scooted inside then halted to survey the dark, smoky tap room that smelled of spilled hops and unwashed bodies. Apparently, the people inside weren't concerned with what was happening with the bombardment because the inn appeared to be doing a brisk business. As the outer door opened and the last rays of light drifted inside, she quickly stepped out of the way as the two men from the coach brushed past her and hightailed it toward the bar set off to the side.

Realizing the two men were familiar with the establishment and that if she wanted something to drink she'd best follow them, she suited action to thought

"The sun has fallen on the bluff," the younger man said as he leaned toward the barkeep.

Belle slowed, unsure she had translated the Italian being spoken correctly. Stopping a few steps behind the men, she frowned as she concentrated on their conversation.

"Best flee into the night," the barkeep said as he accepted the small bag the older man slid across the marred surface of the bar to him. "Out front, go to your right," the barkeep added as he lifted a tankard and began filling it. "He's wait'n."

Belle moved out of the way as the men turned and hurried toward the entrance to disappear out the door.

"You there, boy," the barkeep called as Belle turned back to note that the man was wiggling his index finger at her. "Quick, take this out to the coach," he said as he slid the tankard toward her.

Not about to look a gift horse in the mouth and forgo the coin she might receive for completing the errand, Belle nodded. Lifting the mug, she hastened out the door. But outside, the coach had disappeared and the street was deserted. She frowned then stared down at the mug she held in her hand. It looked as if she'd found something to wash the pie down after all. Stepping around the corner, she took a sip of the tasty brew then drank part of it before she noted the setting sun. Dropping a coin into the mug, she set the unfinished drink off to the side of the inn steps then dashed down the street. As she came to a crossroads, she veered to the left and found the quay again. Searching for a means of transportation across the river, she caught sight of the old woman and her two minions being rowed by a big strapping giant who seemed to be struggling against the current as he rowed. Belle bit her lip in disappointment. If the muscular man was finding it difficult to cross the river then there was no way she could hire a skiff and safely row across on her own.

A shrill whistle pierced the air. Turning, she noticed a belching barge was loading on goods several piers away. She brightened and wondered if it would ferry her across the river. Rushing down the wharf, she panted as she joined the queue waiting to board. Before she could inquire about the particulars, she heard a silver-whiskered man call. "Last trip across. All aboard now."

In front of her stood a young woman holding a small child in one arm and a basket filled with produce on the other. Leaning forward, Belle softly asked in Italian, "Excuse me, do I need to buy a ticket?"

"No," the young woman replied in the same language. "They collect your money on board. But if you don't pay, they will throw you off."

Belle felt her jaw drop open then she snapped it closed. Her stomach clenched as she realized she was indeed living in a ruthless world. Her knees began to wobble at the realization. She was alone. The power of her name meant nothing because she had not the resources to go with it. Her decision to separate herself from her family would have resounding implications for the rest of her life. She had no one to depend upon but herself.

The dark breath of loneliness whispered through her. Swallowing back her groan of regret, she inhaled sharply. If she was to make her way in this rough and foreign world then she needed to grow a backbone and assume a strong sense of fortitude...and do it quick. She squared her shoulders at the thought and followed the rest of the passengers on board the barge.

After helping the young woman she'd stood behind find a place to sit, Belle moved away to stand at the stern of the barge. Watching the shoreline disappear, she took a deep breath. Relief tinged with sadness filled her. She had escaped the rebels but sadness lodged in her throat at leaving Aunt Ellie behind. But with Niko in command, Aunt Ellie was bound to be safe. She shook her head. There was nothing to be gained by remaining in Berat nor was there any use second-guessing her decision. She'd done the right thing in holding Rita accountable.

She knew that if she'd stayed, she wouldn't have been able to remain silent as her sister deviously destroyed the Colonel's good name. But perhaps she worried about him for naught. Niko was a strong-minded man and men like him...she paused as she remembered that even Samson, the strongest and most fierce warrior of his time had succumbed and been destroyed by the wiles of a powerful woman. She bit her bottom lip as she stared at the palace for another minute. She'd done the right thing. By leaving, she had forced Rita to finally be accountable for her actions.

As she turned away from the palace, a renewed conviction flowed through her. No matter what happened to her, where ever she ended up had to be a better place than where she'd come from. Surreptitiously, clearing her throat, she lifted a coin from the drawstring pouch she'd looped around her neck and closed her fist over it. While she had more than enough money to pay for her passage across the river and the necessities of daily life, she wasn't sure she had enough to get to Bari, Italy then find passage home to England. She took a deep breath and reminded herself that while she needed to learn how to plan ahead, she also needed to calmly take each day as it came.

Seized by determination, she scanned the various men and women standing huddled in groups or sitting on benches shielded from the wind by the boathouse. If she could learn to blend in and live as one of them then she would count herself successful. A group of three lads caught her attention as they playfully jostled and slapped each other on the shoulder. As the tall, ebony-haired boy turned to the side, she inhaled sharply. There on the bow of the barge stood Rikard's son, Tass, laughing and poking his finger at the other two boys. A bubble of joy burst within her as she sauntered toward where he stood.

Stopping to pay her fare, she inched up to stand behind Tass. Then she gently tapped him on the shoulder and waited for him to turn.

Breaking off his conversation with the lad, he turned as he said, "I think-"

"Remember me?" She asked quickly, hoping she could stop him from revealing her disguise. "We met a few days ago and I rode with your Grams."

She chuckled as his eyes widened in surprise. "I-I never thought to see you again," he stammered. "What's happened?"

Belle gulped back the lump forming in her throat at his friendly concern. Not about to succumb to a public display of emotion, especially not when she was dressed as a lad, she dug her nails into her fisted palms. "Things aren't always as they appear," she said then quickly cleared her throat, hoping to diffuse its wobbly timbre. "And now I find I'm in need of a bit of help."

"Then you will find that with me and Grams," he said. "No matter what's happened to you."

"Thanks," Belle muttered. "You have no idea how relieved I am to be among friends again."

"We're also family," Tass reminded her then flashed her a mischievous grin. "You became one of us when you joined the tribe."

"Ah, that I did," Belle nodded then frowned. "Although I don't remember much about anything after I drank that Ouzo," she added as she noted that the barge had slowed to pull into the dock on the other side of the river.

"That will do it to you every time," he laughed. Then gathering up the stuffed burlap bag sitting at his feet, he straightened. "Ready to go?"

"Lead the way," she said. After disembarking from the barge, she followed him through the woods in the dusky twilight. Reaching the outskirts of the gypsy camp lit by several campfires, Belle grabbed his wrist to stop him. "I suppose there's a perfectly good reason why we came through the woods instead of taking the shorter, easier route by the road?'

Tass must have flashed her another mischievous grin for all she saw was his teeth gleaning in the gathering gloom. "You know, you're as curious as a cat Grams once had."

"So?" She asked then released her hold on him as she spied Etel's wagon sitting a few feet ahead of them amid the trees. "I know you're dying to tell me, so, what happened to the cat?"

"It died," he said then added in a low voice. "Naturally."

Belle released a whoosh of air at the obnoxious youth then pulled on his sleeve to halt him. "Are you trying to tell me that curiosity killed that cat?" she whispered.

"Yup!"

"In other words," she said, tapping him on his forearm. "You are warning me not to ask too many questions or I might suffer the same fate as the cat?" she asked as she made a slicing motion across her throat.

"You're family," he said as he began gathering sticks for the cooking fire. "The cat wasn't," he added then straightened. "While I might put a spider in your shoe or dump sugar in the stew you're making, I would never really harm you...only embarrass you."

"That's reassuring," Belle said then paused. "Why are you gathering sticks at night?"

"Cause Grams has a rule I'm not supposed to come back into camp without something for the fire," he said.

"I see," she observed. "Now, tell me why you were in Berat," she said as she began looking for sticks to add to his collection.

"Not happen'n," he said, "and I'm depend'n on you not to say a word."

"I'll not tell an outright lie," she warned then straightened unable to see much of anything in the dark.

"If you follow my lead, you won't have too," he said then began to walk toward his grandmother's wagon carrying a handful of sticks with his burlap bag strung over his shoulder.

"I'll try but I won't make any promises," she said, following him. As they reached the side of the wagon, he dropped the sticks he'd gathered into the wood box affixed to the side. As the lid banged shut, Etel hobbled around the side of the wagon.

Hoping to gain a measure of composure before she confronted the elderly woman, Belle dipped her head.

"Lands-a-sakes!" Etel gasped. "Where have you been, child?" She asked as she grabbed a hold of her grandson's sleeve and gave it a shake.

Belle peeked over at her as Etel released Tass and turned toward her. "And who's this urchin you've brought back with you?'

"Found her wandering around," Tass said then knocked Belle's hat off her head.

Belle jumped away grabbing for her hat. As she tugged it away from him, her topknot came loose and her hair tumbled down her back. "Um-m-m," she said clearing her throat as she gazed at the woman who had treated her with nothing but kindness. "Hello, Etel," she finally said then realized for the first time in her life she was truly embarrassed to ask for assistance.

"Mercy, child! We need to get you out of that get-up and back into look'n like a female. Up you go," she said grabbing Belle's wrist and pulling her toward the back door. "I don't want anyone to see you look'n like this," she said as she pushed Belle up the back steps. "Put on the skirt and blouse you wore when you were here before," she said as she closed the door with a bang. "Mercy, what is this world com'n too with a married woman runn'n around wear'n a man's get-up!"

Belle's mind slowed. Had she translated Etel's mumblings correctly?
Had Etel really said married?

She shook her head. What was Etel talking about she wondered as she reached for the peasant blouse and skirt folded neatly atop the shelf above the bed? How had the woman come up with such a crazy idea? Her married? Not in this lifetime...or at least...well, maybe...it wouldn't be too bad if she liked him, she thought as she began to disrobe.

"When you're done chang'n, come on out," Etel called. "We need to talk."

"About what?" Belle returned as she stepped into the blue, yellow and red flounced skirt and pulled it up to her waist.

"Your husband?" Etel yelled. "Where is he?"

"Husband?" Belle froze for a moment, knowing this time she had interpreted Etel's Italian correctly. "I don't have one," she fired back then paused as she slowly slipped the white blouse over her head. A chill swept over her as she wondered if the initiation ceremony she and Niko had participated in might've been more than them joining the tribe. Her arms felt like lead as she pulled the blouse down over her torso and moved down the center aisle wondering if Niko had realized there was more going on.

"You certainly do," Etel hooted as she rapped loudly on the door.

"Then who is he?" Belle demanded even though she was afraid she already knew the answer. She yanked the door open.

"The Colonel," Etel said quietly as she backed down the steps.

Belle grabbed the door frame to keep herself upright. She hated it when she surmised correctly. She stared at Etel for a moment, knowing she looked like a beached fish gasping for its last breath. "N-no-o-o," she squeaked as Etel nodded. "I don't want a husband," she managed to say as panic squeezed all the air from her lungs. Releasing her hold on the door, she slowly backed away to sit on one of the beds. "This can't be possible."

"It is by Barovian Gypsy Law," Etel said, firmly.

Belle bit her bottom lip then paused as she recalled that she and Niko had spent the entire night tied together in the back of this very wagon. Ice crusted her veins at the realization. According to the morals of society that meant no matter if she was in England or Barovia, they were as good as married. She shook her head. This was insane. Niko would think it just as crazy as she did and would laugh if he was ever confronted with the insanity. Nothing had happened between them that night. There was no need to think anyone had been caught in the parson's mousetrap, regardless of what people thought. She wouldn't be foisted on a groom who would be just as unwilling to be married as she. She respected Niko too much to force him into a marriage of convenience with her.

Slipping her feet into the comfortable pair of shoes she'd borrowed before, Belle hurried to the open door and inhaled sharply as she realized they had gained an audience. Outside beyond the steps in the flickering firelight, not only stood Etel and Tass but also Rikard and the three tribal elders. Her face heated as she gaped at them. "When did I become subjected to Barovian Gypsy Laws?" she asked, hoping she wouldn't hear what she dreaded most.

"The moment you agreed to travel with us, you came under the jurisdiction of our laws," Rikard said, inching up the steps. Although he stopped short of entering the wagon, his body formed an effective barrier, blocking her exit. "And by becoming a member of this tribe, you also married the Colonel and both of you became subjected to our laws."

Shock quickly yielded to fury as she stared at him. She was so angry she could hardly speak. "Then you can just 'un' marry us," she countered, hotly. There was no way she would stay married to someone who had been forced into marriage with her.

"N-n-not possible," the first elder stuttered as his bulbous nostrils twitched like a rabbit in the firelight.

"It's like this," the gravel-voiced second elder said. "Once you are married...you are married for life."

"That's right...for...life," the oldest member nodded his silver-haired head. "And that's a very...long...time." Belle noticed the man grimace, which only added more creases to his already wrinkled face.

"I don't care," she said, not about to be bullied into accepting something she would never agree to. She stiffened her resolve. "I-I won't be married to someone who allows another woman to...embrace him. I simply won't," she added as she swallowed hard, hoping she'd come up with an ironclad excuse to negate the marriage.

"How do you know he did that?" the first elder asked rubbing his balding head.

"Well, um-m," she said then gave an anxious cough. "I saw him with my sister," she added as her words tumbled over each other.

"Oh dear," the eldest member said, his ancient voice drifting into a higher octave. "That's not good."

"Is the man blind?" the second elder interjected waving his arms about as his angry retort hardened the furrows between his eyes. "Look at her, she's a beauty."

She flinched, knowing that wasn't true. She'd looked too many years into the mirror at her ordinary features to ever believe that drivel. But she had to be honest with herself and admit how much his words truly cheered her.

"Who is to say?" the oldest elder shrugged. "Maybe the sister is more-" he paused waving his palms creating an hourglass figure.

Heat scalded her cheeks. Thank goodness the shadows from the tree branches hid her flushed face.

'Um-m," the second elder said clearing his throat. He swept his hand through his ebony graying hair. "You might be right."

A protest hovered on the tip of her tongue. Merciful heavens, was this embarrassment to never end?

"So, what's to be done?" the first elder asked, resting his bony fists on his hips.

"Nothing," Belle inserted into the sudden silence. Then she forced her lips to part in a stiff smile. "I'll be traveling to Bari, Italy then onto England. That effectively ends the problem. That is," she began then hesitated, "if you will help me get to the shipping docks in Durres."

"We'll be leaving in the morning," Rikard said. "We're headed north to KaCave to trade horses at the fair." Her breath hitched in her chest as she observed his narrow-eyed glint. "You're welcome to stay with us...as long as you honor our laws," he added.

She knew it wasn't so much his words but his underlying tone that mattered the most. And in this case, it was the uncertainty his words aroused in her that made her decide. "As long as you don't try to marry me off again, then I'll have no problem obeying your rules," she said as a frisson of warning swirled through her. She realized that the warning wasn't so much meant against the tribe but against herself. She needed to carefully monitor and be aware of what was going on around her and not depend on others to do it for her. It was time for her to assume responsibility for her own life and not leave all the decisions of it in the hands of others. But for now, she had a day or two to bide her time then she would find a boat to take her to Italy and she would be free of Barovia and its laws forever.

Chapter Thirteen

Niko strode into the Command Center, his uniform streaked with dirt and blood. "Someone please tell me that Prince Jorge and Major Hondros have been captured," he demanded as he searched the faces of his cadre who were just as dirty and as tired and hungry as he.

Receiving no affirmative answer, Niko slammed his palm down on the map table that he stood beside. Although he wanted to shout out an obscenity he needed to calm down and think rationally. Taking a deep breath, he straightened. "We need a breather," he said. "Meet me back here in two hours. We will then plan how we are to find Prince Jorge and end this revolution." He glanced at his officers then nodded. "Dismissed."

He waited until his cadre had departed the room before he turned to Cyrek. He knew frustration had been clearly evident not only in his voice but also in his manner. He plowed his fingers through his hair to give himself a moment. "Major Kelso saw to it that we closed all conceivable avenues of escape. So, I don't know how Uncle Jorge slipped through the trap we set for him."

"And you trust the Major?" his best friend asked as he began folding and stacking the maps together on the table.

Niko paused. "Don't you?" he asked as he realized a tense silence throbbed between them.

"I do," Cyrek said. His resolute answer not only melted some of the tension but also left Niko in no doubt about the man's sincerity. "When did you last see Prince Jorge and Major Hondros?" his Second in Command asked.

"Just before the rebels fired the first volley," Niko replied, knowing by his friend's terse tone that he was about to play the devil's advocate.

"And you never saw them again?" Cyrek asked as he paused in sorting through the maps.

Niko shook his head. "The smoke was so dense, it was difficult to see much of anything after that."

His best friend nodded. "Maybe Prince Jorge thinking he was springing a surprise attack on us realized he was so out-gunned, out-manned and out-maneuvered to the extent that he turned tail and ran before Major Kelso and his detachment arrived to secure the area?"

"That is a distinct possibility," he agreed then moved over to the strategy board which had a map of the palace and the city pinned on it. "That means he either crossed back over the river well before the Major set fire to the boats," he said pointing to that position, "or he fled into the city. And if that's the case, he could be holed up somewhere in there," he said tapping the area along the river.

"Do you want to do a house-to-house search?" Cyrek asked as he leaned toward the board.

"First, let me send the trackers with their dogs out along the bank," Niko said. "Depending on what they find, we can send the men and dogs through the streets to do a door-to-door. This will free up our troops for locating my uncle's base camp. It has to be somewhere he can easily defend."

"Like his estate?" Cyrek asked.

"Or his hunting lodge hidden deep within the KaCave forest. We need to be onsite to check both places early tomorrow morning," he added.

"Although I know this is like hunting that proverbial needle in a haystack," Cyrek said, "he will be found," he promised, a note of sincerity in his tone.

"I'm surprised he didn't try to use the tunnels beneath the palace," Niko said turning away from the map to face Cyrek.

"I was afraid he would do just that," Cyrek said. "So, I stationed guardsmen down there. Since there's been no report of anyone either approaching or attempting to enter, I feel the palace is relatively safe."

"I would feel safer if no tunnels existed at all," Niko said. "No matter how many twists and turns the engineer created, their very existence leaves the palace vulnerable."

"One thing for sure," Cyrek said. "No one in their right mind would want to be lost down there."

"I agree," Niko said running his finger around the inside of his scruffy uniform collar. "You and your men continue to man your posts and remain on alert, I'll send word to the kitchen and have meals brought up here for you."

"We will," Cyrek said. "And as soon as I organize the trackers, I'll send them out."

"I'll be back in about an hour or so," Niko replied. The quicker his uncle was found and arrested, the safer their country would be. As the throne room doors opened, he turned to watch his cousin, King Stefan, stroll into the Command Center.

"Nikolai," his cousin, Stefan said. "Will you be joining us for dinner?"

"I hope so, but first I need to clean up and change. I wouldn't want to upset the ladies with my dirt and grime," he added then swept his hand in the direction of the corridor indicating for Stefan to proceed him.

"Horror of horrors," Stefan gasped then smiled as he stepped into the wide hallway. "We couldn't have that now...could we?"

"You are a devil," Niko grinned as they began to walk down the corridor toward the stairs leading to their private quarters. "Are the twins really that bad together?"

"I wouldn't know," Stefan said with a dismissive wave of his hand. "I haven't seen them."

Niko slowed then frowned. "Not even when the palace was under bombardment?" he asked as he began to wonder where they had gone to seek safety.

"Not so much as a hide nor a hair was seen of them," his cousin said then shrugged.

"Wonder where they went?" Niko mused as they mounted the stairs leading to their chambers.

"Perhaps you ought to ask them that question during dinner," his cousin said as Niko arrived at the door to his sitting room.

"And get told it was none of my business? No thanks," Niko grinned. "The Lady Rita considers me obnoxious enough. As for Belle, she'll just narrow her gaze at me and tell me that she can take care of herself."

"Sounds like you got to know the lady very well," his cousin observed.

"Well enough to allow her a measure of freedom," Niko confessed.

"Quite demanding is she?" Stefan asked, a curious expression settling on his face.

"Not at all," Niko said with a shake of his head. "For the most part, I found her boldly impetuous but gentle in her manner, kind in her words but firm in her convictions. And that's what doesn't add up."

"What doesn't?" His cousin asked.

"Her twin, Lady Rita, claims that the Lady Belle is a demeaning, jealous shrew. Never satisfied, always demanding she be given what she can't have," Niko said then hesitated.

"Sounds to me that you have described the Lady Rita to a 'T'," Stefan said. "How Ellie puts up with her bad manners and tantrums is beyond my understanding.'

"At her age, she has actual tantrums?" Niko asked in stunned disbelief.

"Oh, yes," Stefan said. "And it is very disconcerting to witness. But I digress," he said. "I need to let you go or you will be late for dinner and I know how much you hate eating a cold meal.'

"Like your mother used to make me do if I was as much as a half-a-minute late to the table?" he asked.

"Ah, those were the days," Stefan chuckled. "But you need not worry, I will always have the staff keep your food warm for you if you are late."

"I appreciate that," Niko said placing his hand on the doorknob leading into his chamber. Bowing to his cousin, he waited for him to proceed toward his regal chambers at the end of the hall. Opening the door, he strode inside and found his valet, Briggs, laying out his evening clothes. "Just a clean uniform," he said as he shifted out of his coat. "I'm afraid this one will need to be replaced," he added handing it to his man.

"Your water has been drawn and a shot of whiskey has been set beside the tub," briggs said as he held the soiled uniform away from his well-groomed self.

"Thank you," Niko said as he disrobed dropping his clothing as he hurried toward the bathing chamber. "I'll need you to pack a larger grip this time. Once it's ready, please take it down to the Command Center," he requested.

"Will you be gone long, Your Highness?" his valet asked.

"Only as long as it takes to complete my mission," Niko replied as he stepped into the tub then quickly sank beneath the water and just as quickly, sat up. He didn't have time to linger. The first thing he needed to do after he finished changing was to inform Belle how long he would be gone.

"Do you need me to accompany you?" Briggs asked as he stepped into the doorway.

"Not this time," Niko replied, scrubbing an arm with soap and a cloth. "I'm only going fishing," he said then chuckled. Trolling for a wily old carp known as Uncle Jorge wasn't something he was about to tell anyone other than Stefan and Cyrek.

***

Later as he entered the Royal Dining Room, he paused as he looked at the two women seated on each side of his cousin at the small intimate table set for five. Recognizing the aunt, he wondered if it was Lady Belle or the Lady Rita that sat on the far side of his cousin. Selecting the chair nearest the aunt, he took his seat. "I see we are eating as a family this evening," he said as he stared at the only twin in the room. As he leaned closer to her, he caught a whiff of an exotic eastern fragrance, a heavy musk blended with a touch of patchouli. The same scent he had smelled on the Lady Rita earlier that day.

"So, what has happened to Lady Belle?" he asked, removing his white linen napkin from its solid gold napkin ring. "Is she not feeling well enough to join us this evening?"

He watched the Lady Rita's mouth drop open and then he wanted to smile as she snapped her jaw closed. "How do you know that I am not she?" she asked, her petulant tone grating on his nerves.

Niko took a slow sip of his white wine as the first course, a lobster bisque soup was served. He supposed he could tell her the truth but decided that if the twins changed places once, they could do it again. And he wasn't about to be duped a second time.

"I am sufficiently familiar with Lady Belle to know that she possesses certain traits," he said as he stared at the Lady Rita dipping her gold spoon into her soup with her right hand.

The spoon halted, midway between the bowl and her mouth. "You sound very sure of yourself this evening," she said then lifted the spoon to her mouth and sipped. Then waving the empty utensil at him, she narrowed her eyes. "You didn't seem quite so sure of me...or yourself earlier today. Why was that?"

Niko returned her stare and hardened his jaw. "While I do acknowledge that I am somewhat familiar with Lady Belle," he said. "I have yet to fully understand her. I know she loves to sail but doesn't like to ride a horse. She loves to read but doesn't like to sew."

"That's not knowing her," Rita scoffed, a sneer curling her lips. "Understanding Belle...is knowing she's mean-spirited...arrogant...and demands-"

"That's enough!" her aunt suddenly interjected, her chair scraping the marble floor as she scooted it away from the table. "You've carried things too far this time. Running your sister's character into the mud is not acceptable. This is the dinner table and I insist you put away your animosity."

"Well, I-" Rita said, popping up from her chair and tossing her napkin down into her soup bowl. As the linen landed in the soup bowl, it began absorbing the liquid.

"Sit. Down." Stefan said as he slapped his palm flat on the table causing the silverware and stemmed glassware to dance and jiggle. "You will not behave in this manner in my presence. As long as you are a guest in my country, you will be courteous to all. Especially to your aunt and your sister. I will suffer no more of your antics. Have I made myself clear?" he asked, his eyes narrowed into slits.

Niko wanted to cheer as he watched Rita gape at his cousin for a moment. He suddenly realized that no one had probably ever called her to task or held her accountable for her actions before.

"I am still waiting for my answer," his cousin said, his gaze hardening as he leaned toward her.

"Y-yes, Your Majesty," Lady Rita replied then rapidly fluttered her lashes and flashed an insouciant smile at his cousin.

"Good," the King retorted as he straightened. "Now, tell us what you've done with the Lady Belle?"

Niko bit the inside of his cheek to keep from smiling. This was better than attending the theater.

"I-I don't know," she stammered as Niko noticed tears pooling in her eyes. 'I-I'm not her keeper," she gasped out as if she were the wounded party.

Although annoyed by Lady Rita's vacillating act, Niko surmised the spoiled twin was not only a consummate actress but she was desperate to regain her favored status.

"Why don't you know?" the King asked. "While Nikolai may be out of my sight, I still know where he is and generally what he is doing because we are family. Why then, don't you know about your sister?"

"I just don't," she said as Niko heard a definite snap in her tone. "She's supposed to take care of me. After all, I am the firstborn. It's her duty to serve me. Not the other way around."

Niko stared at her, astounded by the further proof of her arrogance.

"Why?" he asked, hoping to goad her into further revelations of her true self. "Why must Belle serve you? She isn't your slave."

"She owes me," Rita said, anger lashing her words like a volley of fire shot from a cannon.

"What does she owe you?" her aunt demanded. "That is the one thing I've never understood."

"She killed our parents," Rita cried out. "They died because of her selfishness."

Niko highly suspected the tears rolling down Rita's face were fake. She was the type of female who would stop only after she had everyone's sympathy.

"Why would you think that?" her aunt asked, her face a mask of horror.

"She insisted they had to go to the winter fair," Rita wailed. "And she was granted her wish while I was forced to stay at home. Then she-"

"Rita," her aunt gasped. "Stop right this minute. That isn't true. I know for a fact that your parents were bringing Belle to stay with me. You had come down with a contagion. They were deadly afraid that if she stayed, she too would contact it. People from the village were dying. It had been touch and go with you. In fact, the morning they left to bring her to me, the physician insisted Belle be removed from the house. So you see, my dear, your sister had nothing to do with your parents' deaths at all."

"But Edward said-"

"What does he know?" her aunt huffed, waving her hand in dismissal. "He wasn't there. He was away at school. Whatever story you and your brother have concocted is wrong." She paused then clasped her hands together. "And I ask that you stop holding your sister accountable for something she didn't do," she added as she took a noisy breath. "Can you at least do that for me?"

"I...suppose," Rita mumbled, as she dipped her head. Although she looked thoroughly chastised, Niko doubted her sudden act of humility.

"So where is Belle?" he asked again.

"I truly don't know," she said. Lifting her head, she glared at him.

"Then it's about time we find out," he said motioning the Majordomo to come to his side. As Andres bent forward, Niko whispered. "Please send someone up to Lady Belle's chamber and inquire if she's joining us for dinner?"

"As you wish," Andres said then went to the door to relay the request to a palace sentry

Niko knew Belle had been fine when he'd left her. But with Rita as a sister, he figured anything could've happened to set her off. He frowned as the next course, asparagus spears served with a hollandaise sauce arrived. He glanced around the table wondering if the other three were as concerned about Belle as he was. His jaw tightened as he watched Lady Rita stab one of her asparagus spears and slash it into bits, her knife grating across her plate. Turning away, he not only noticed his cousin's hand laid atop Lady Ellie's but Stefan had placed his other arm across the Lady's shoulders as if to comfort her. He lifted his brows in surprise at the unexpected intimacy their body language suggested. Curious, he leaned toward them but their low whispered words made it impossible for him to hear over the screeching of Rita's knife skidding across the surface of her china plate. A tap came at the dining room door. Niko shifted his gaze to watch Andres close the door and come to stand beside him. "Well?" he asked.

The Major Domo cleared his throat as if he had something lodged inside it. "It appears, Your Highness that she's not in her chamber."

Niko stared at the man for a moment as he wondered where she could be. "Then we need to find her," he said, finally.

"I'll send the guards to check the palace now, sir," Andres said. Then clicking his heels together, he straightened. "Anything else, Your Highness?"

"Have the guards conduct a thorough check," Niko said and then frowned as concern raced through him. This didn't seem like something the Belle he'd come to know would do unless she'd been provoked beyond all reason by her twin.

"Yes, Your Highness," Andres said then bowed.

"When was the last time anyone saw her?" the King asked as he set his wine glass on the table.

"The last time I saw Belle was when she disappeared down the corridor in front of the throne room with Lady Rita and her aunt," Niko said, suddenly noticing his appetite had fled.

"Don't look at me," Rita shrugged. "I didn't do away with her. She went into her bedchamber all on her own."

"Excuse me, but the Lady Belle appears to be no place in the palace," the Major Domo announced as he stopped beside Niko's chair.

"Did you ever see her come out of her bed chamber?" Niko asked, waving his fork at the Lady Rita.

"As I've said before," Rita said with a definite clip in her tone. "It wasn't my day to watch her. She's a grown woman. She can take care of her herself far better than I can."

"Then I suggest it becomes your 'day'," Niko said shoving away from the table. "Now, if you will excuse me, I'm off to the Command Room to organize a search of the rest of the grounds."

"And I will find her maid and bring her to you for questioning," Aunt Ellie said as she stood. "Please excuse me, I will return shortly," she said as she hurried from the room.

"And what will you do?" Niko asked Rita as he pushed his chair into the table.

"Not a single thing," she retorted, her chin angled haughtily to the side. "She has enough people running around looking for her. Maybe she should consider others needs before her own."

Niko shook his head in disgust. He glanced at his cousin who was shaking his head. If Stefan married the Lady Rita, his cousin's life would be a living nightmare. And he didn't want that to happen. Stefan deserved to find peace and contentment after the turmoil he'd suffered with the death of his father and their uncle instigating a revolution. Thinking of the chaos their uncle had created, Niko wondered if Belle had become a victim of his uncle's machinations. Fear stabbed through him at the thought. He'd best get to the Command Center and issue the order that those searching the city also needed to quietly include the Lady Belle in that search.

Chapter Fourteen

Niko leaned forward and studied the outline of the boot prints in the waning light. Scanning a few feet more, he noticed that the prints suddenly ended in the trampled grass beside the muddy road wedged beneath the High Bluff and the river. He straightened in surprise. His uncle was either desperate or he had underestimated his Uncle Jorge. It appeared that his uncle had planned a second avenue of escape in case he couldn't safely flee back across the river.

"Over here, Colonel," Captain Zeno, his chief tracker called. "Appears a coach came by way of Berat and turned around here," he said pointing downward, "then it headed back in that direction."

No longer surprised by what had been found, he crossed the muddy road to join the men. He clenched his jaw realizing there wasn't much he could say other than he wouldn't make the mistake of underestimating his uncle again.

"Over here's where the heavy coach drawn by four horses turned," Major Bjorni said, drawing Niko's attention to the rutted furrows.

"Undoubtedly made by my uncle's heavy traveling coach," Niko replied then straightened. "Major Kelso, send two men to scout along the south road leading out of Berat. They are to ask about sighting a shiny black traveling coach pulled either by a team of four matching ebony or gray horses. They are two of my uncle's favorite teams," Niko said. "Also have them inquire if a man of my uncle's description was traveling with a young woman," he added then turned toward Major Bjorni. "Send two men to check all the coaching inns north of the city using the same descriptions and inquires. And tell your men, to meet us at the crossroads to Duress late this evening. We have a bit of traveling to do."

"Aye, Sir," the Major said then saluted and moved off to carry out the orders.

"Any word on the progress of the house-to-house search from Colonel Domokos," Niko asked Captain Takis although what he really wanted to know was if Belle had been found.

"None," the Captain replied.

"Then assign two of your men to act as liaison between me and the Colonel. We need to keep in touch when we discover our quarry."

"Aye, sir," Captain Takis said with a salute. Turning, he hurried away.

* * *

Niko squared his shoulders. After what had been a long and relentless night of searching, finally, word had reached them that a shiny black coach pulled by four matching gray horses had been spotted going north of Berat. A woman dressed all in black and two men were reportedly traveling inside. There had been no sign of Belle. He took a deep breath and noticed that he breathed easier. Wherever Belle was, at least she hadn't been kidnapped by his uncle. At this point, all he could do was hope she remained safe until he could find her.

Turning, he nodded to the barrel-chested Captain Takis, pleased to have been proven right in placing the deep-voiced man in charge of all the scouts. He had definitely lived up to his reputation of having a blood-hound nose. After they had received definitive word from Captain Takis's men that a shiny black traveling coach with matching horses had been spotted on the northbound road, Niko had sent two companies of men to surround his uncle's country estate while he led his men toward his uncle's hunting lodge.

Now just before sunrise, Niko moved furtively up the steep, rocky terrain to pause at the top of the hill over-looking his uncle's hunting lodge. He raised his glass to survey the isolated lodge, really a small palace setting on a knoll in the center of the compound. Numerous buildings hugged the walled outer perimeter, reminding Niko of more prosperous times long ago. Perhaps that was why this was his uncle's favorite place. The ghosts of his uncle's misdeeds flitted away to be replaced with his memories of wine and wild parties. Moving his glass, he scanned the forest that surrounded the compound on three sides and spotted his men furtively positioning themselves. In the small picturesque meadow facing the River Reba, his scouts lay waiting for his signal. On the bluff above the narrow ribbon of grazing land adjacent to the river waited not only a battery of his artillery but hidden beneath the trees was a contingency of his cavalry. He checked the sentries briskly walking their posts in his uncle's courtyard then lowered his glass, pleased by not only what he'd seen but by the relief lifting his chest. Judging by the snap in the sentries' walk, he had found his uncle. He smiled as he turned to Major Bjorni.

"Well done," he whispered, afraid his voice would carry in the silent pre-dawn and alert the sentries guarding the royal hunting lodge that they were about to be attacked. "Any report that the black traveling coach has been spotted in one of those buildings in the compound?" he asked as he raised his glass to survey the outbuildings.

"None," the Major said. "But we will keep you updated."

"Excellent," he said then motioned Major Gianakis who was in charge of his infantry to come forward. The middle-aged man had seen many campaigns not only under his own father's command but also with King Rinaldo. Niko surmised that the prematurely gray-haired man had never visualized that he would be hunting down a traitorous member of the royal family. "Are we ready?" he asked.

Major Gianakis seemed to harden his square jaw. "Both Captain Vogel's and my men are in position," he said. "Captain Cuno has his artillery batteries positioned on the bluff over there," he said pointing across the river just above the tree line. "Below to our right and further toward the east overlooking the lodge, we have spread the rests of our sharpshooters."

"Good," Niko nodded. "Let's hold our positions until the Calvary are ready," he said. "Then Captain Elser and his archers will take out the sentries. Major Bjorni will lead the Calvary charge from the north, Captain Vogel and his infantry will converge from the south and the sharpshooters in the meadow will take care of anyone fleeing," he said then nodded to Major Gianakis. "You'll come in with your infantry from the east along with Captain Metzer and his Calvary. I will lead the charge and assault the entrance," he said, pointing his riding crop at the main entrance. "Once inside, we will root out the rebels. If they refuse to lay down their arms and surrender, then we will fight."

He paused then lowered his crop. "Once we have secured the lodge we will need to search every inch of it, making sure all walls, fireplaces and niches are checked for hiding spaces. As for the staff, try not to harm them," he added. "With their safety ensured, they might become allies and help us ferret out our enemy."

"Aye Commander," Major Gianakis replied then saluted.

Returning the salute, Niko turned back to survey the hunting lodge. Now all they needed to do was capture his uncle and the rebels.

***

Belle stared at the shiny black traveling coach with the four matching gray horses sitting off the side of the road. Right away, she spotted the elderly lady that she remembered seeing in Berat. The deep-voiced old woman was striding back and forth ahead while her younger companion directed her two coachmen on how to remove the Coach's broken wheel. She wondered briefly what had happened to the throaty-voiced hook-nosed man that had been with them in Berat but shrugged her shoulders as Rikard raised his arm signifying a halt.

"My son," Etel called as the caravan rolled to a stop. "Come here," she said, waving her hand summoning him to them. Belle frowned as Rikard waved off his mother as he dismounted.

"May I be of assistance?" he asked, walking toward the disabled coach.

"Hit a bad spot in the road and cracked two spokes," one of the coachmen called as he straightened from his task.

"Oscuro disturbo," Etel muttered, her knuckles whitening on the reins she held.

Dark trouble? Belle's breath hitched in her chest as she realized the translation of the words. Curious, she stood from the stool she'd been sitting on behind Etel.

"One of these days that son of mine is gonna learn its best if he lis'ns to me," Etel muttered. "I sure hope it won't be too late for us all."

"Why do you say that?" Belle whispered as she leaned over Etel's shoulder to better see what was happening off the road.

"Danger," Etel said, her low voice cracking in warning.

Knowing from past experience that one didn't always understand certain things but that didn't mean you discounted the importance of their warning, Belle took a deep breath. "Where's the danger coming from?" she asked. "From the men...the coach...the wheel?"

"The woman," Etel said, her low voice trembling.

"The old woman?" Belle asked, hearing the note of surprise in her own words. "She looks harmless to me."

"Just because one looks or acts old...does not make it so," Etel retorted.

Belle frowned. "I don't understand." Although her first impression of the woman leaning from her coach window hadn't been favorable, she wondered what Etel sensed that she didn't?

"Age causes one's movements to slow. We don't stand as tall, move as quick or think as fast," Etel said. "So, what do you see regard'n the old woman?"

"I see," Belle said squinting into the glaring sun, "an old woman pacing back and forth."

"And?" Etel prompted.

Belle sat up straighter. "She's walking very fast, her shoulders and upper body reminds me of the military," she added, proud to have observed that much through the sun reflecting off the surface of the shiny coach.

"Ah ha!" Etel crowed. "What else?"

"I...see," Belle said beginning to enjoy the game that was relieving her boredom, "I feel...a tremendous amount of impatience rolling off her."

"Do you also see as she turns, she's wearing hessians?" Etel asked.

Belle felt her jaw drop open. She had been so intent on the over-all impression she hadn't considered the individual things. "No, I-"

"Then watch," Etel instructed.

"Oh-h, my heavens!" Belle gasped as she watched the woman pivot. As the black skirt of her widow's weeds flared outward, a pair of men's boots came into view. "That i-isn't a woman at all," Belle stammered then clapped her hand over her mouth, hoping no one had heard her lowered voice but Etel.

No wonder Belle had heard such a deep voice from the old woman in Berat. It made perfect sense. But why would a man disguise himself as a woman? Unless-"It's a very effective disguise," she said climbing over the bench and settling beside Etel. "But what do we do now?"

"We watch," Etel replied, looping the reins around the wagon brake.

"And?" Belle prodded unable to decide if waiting was the best answer.

"We whistle," Etel said, a grin lifting her wrinkled cheeks.

"What?" she exclaimed turning to face the older woman.

"We pull our lips together and-"

"I know how to whistle," Belle said placing her hand over Etel's bony fingers. "My questions is, do I whistle a particular tune? Or-"

"Don't make this so difficult, child," Etel said as Belle heard her swift intake of air.

"Just a straight...whoosh?" Belle asked still unclear as to what Etel wanted her to do.

"Well, of course, you will need to put some power behind it," Etel chuckled.

"I will make it as loud as I can," Belle promised with a nod.

"You might want to practice," Etel said then grabbed Belle's wrist. "But not now," she whispered. "Looks like we're about to have company."

Belle shifted to watch the man posing as the old woman approach their wagon.

"You there," the deep-voiced person said. "I need something to drink. What do you have?"

"Water," Etel said pointing to the water barrel she carried attached to the driver's side of her wagon. "Help yourself," she said. "The ladle is clipped to the inside of the lid."

Briefly, Belle wondered how she had failed to recognize the man's ruse. Then she decided she had been so preoccupied finding a way across the river, locating Rikard's camp and worrying about her reception that she'd had little time to consider anything else. A frisson of fear coursed through her as she remembered all the banners with her likeness hanging from the second story windows welcoming their future Queen to Berat. She hoped the man had been so caught up in his own ruse that he hadn't noticed a thing.

Taking several long thirsty gulps, the man returned the ladle inside the lid and closed it. Prickles of trepidation danced over her skin as the man crossed back to the front and stopped beside where she sat. Peering down at him, Belle shivered as his quick-silver eyes welded her to the bench.

"Have we met?" he asked, his deep, menacing tone flooding her with a current of ice.

She shivered. "I don't believe so," she said hesitantly then lowered her uncomfortable gaze to stare at the toes of the man's boots peeking out from beneath the black taffeta skirt he wore.

"You look very familiar," he persisted as he placed his black-gloved hand on the edge of the bench near where she sat.

"I...get that a lot," Belle said, leaning toward Etel. Her mind twisted and turned for an idea to prevent the man's further inquiries, but nothing seemed to stick.

"As we were leaving Berat, we were told a major battle had taken place north of the city. Have you encountered any soldiers or rebels while you've been on the road?" he asked dragging a fan from the reticle hanging from his wrist and deftly flipping it open.

Clenching her jaw, Belle inhaled slowly then schooled her features to remain non-committal. Either the man was lying or he was hoping to manipulate them into doing something for him. She glanced over at Etel. "I've been in the back, working," she said. "Have you seen anyone on the road like what's been described while we've been traveling?"

Etel shook her head. "Other than you and your men," she said nodding at the man. "I haven't seen a soul."

"You know, of course," the man said, "that could be the result of inattention on your part."

"Possibly," Etel replied although her mild tone was at odds with her furrowed frown. "That happens when one gets old," she added then cackled.

Belle held her breath as the man frowned then walked away without further comment. Relief rushed through her and she released the breath she held as he rejoined his companion who was directing the repair of the wheel.

She scanned the forest once more wondering about the grizzle-haired, middle-aged man who had been with the other two yesterday in Berat. Seeing no sign of him, she shrugged. Perhaps he'd remained behind in the city. With nothing more to occupy her time, she sighed.

"How long does it usually take to fix a coach wheel?" she asked, hoping they didn't have to wait too long as she batted away a flying insect.

"Um-m," Etel said then scratched her ear. "If parts must be made...a day or two," she said waving her hand in the direction of her son crossing in front of their wagon. "Usually, Rikard carries spares but it doesn't look like that today."

"We'll be stuck here for two days?" Belle squeaked in dismay.

"Calm down!" Etel said reaching over and patting her hand. "Rikard won't let that happen. We'll be in KaCave tomorrow and in two more days we'll be aboard'n a ship in Durres and go'n to Italy."

"We?" Belle gasped as she stared at Etel thinking she hadn't translated the elderly lady's Italian correctly.

"You're one of us now," Etel said, patting her hand again. "We don't let no tribe member travel alone, 'especially no female," Etel added. "T'aint safe."

"Oh, thank you," Belle said with a grateful sigh. Then she hesitated as she realized this trip involved more than just herself. If others were traveling with her, then she needed to tell them she had no intention of returning to England. She bit her bottom lip and peeked at Etel, knowing there were bound to be objections to her remaining in Italy, teaching English and working as an interpreter. But she had to support herself somehow, didn't she? And if she returned to England she would be forced to marry Umberford. She inhaled sharply at the thought, not about to let that happen. But no matter what, she knew that she couldn't have stayed to witness the mockery of her sister and the King's marriage ceremony. And there was no way she could've remained and watched her sister manipulate and destroy the Colonel. Belle scrubbed at the pain forking through her chest. Hopefully, the Colonel would be vigilant and safe from all harm.

"Excuse me, Ma'am." the young man who had accompanied the disguised man said. "My aunt isn't feeling well. And since there are no spare parts, we must abandon our coach here. If she could ride in the back of your wagon to the Red Feather Inn in KaCave, we would be happy to pay you for any inconvenience," he added as if that bit of information would sway them.

"I've no room for her to stay with us tonight," Etel said. "But we do have a tent you can pitch."

"We thank you for that," he said with a bow. Then turning, he strode off toward the disabled coach.

Belle leaned toward Etel and whispered, "So, who do you think they are?" She watched the coachmen pull numerous trunks form the boot of the coach and set them on the ground. "And why do you suppose that disguise is necessary?"

"Whoever they are, that disguise means they're up to no good," Etel said gathering the horses' reins. "And as soon as they're settled inside Rikard's wagon, we're moving. Best you start practicing your whistle."

Belle nodded. There were too many things that didn't make sense not to take Etel's warning to heart.

Chapter Fifteen

Niko paused as he entered the lavishly furnished great room of his uncle's hunting lodge. It wasn't as he remembered it. The once comfortable room had been painted white and now was accented with gold leaf. Rich royal blue velvet hung from the windows and had been used for chair covers. The tables draped in pristine white linen had been set with gold plates, silverware and goblets ready for a large banquet. He shook his head. The room appeared to be decorated in anticipation of his uncle being crowned King, a ceremony he was determined wouldn't happen.

"Colonel," Captain Vogel said, interrupting his thoughts. "The rebels are secured and the staff have been assembled for your convenience."

"Well done," Niko said turning toward the Captain. "Have the men mounted and ready to move out shortly," he added as he noticed Major Gianakis waiting a few feet away.

"Aye, Colonel," the Captain said then saluted.

Returning the salute, Niko waved Major Gianakis forward. "Now, let's see what my uncle's staff knows," he said as he spied the men and women who served his uncle assembled in the hallway. Nearly all had their heads bowed and were staring at the parquet floor. As he came closer he felt their fear roll toward him as he stopped a few feet away from them.

"Good afternoon," he said, tempering his tone to cordial. "I am Colonel Orsini," he began then paused as he noted several of the older men and women had raised their heads, a stunned look of recognition crossing their faces. "I am here to reassure you that no harm shall come to you or your families. You are safe with me," he said then paused as more heads were raised and it appeared that most were now looking at him, including the small boy peeking at him from behind a woman who Niko supposed were his mother. "I do need to ask a few questions regarding my uncle," he said as he noted the youngster sidle out from behind his mother and dash toward him.

"No. Keiv," the mother scolded as she attempted to grab the child.

But escaping her arms, the boy wrapped his arms around both of Niko's knees. "Please, sir," the boy begged, "can you save my papa?"

Stunned for a moment, Niko dropped to his haunches to stare at the child in front of him. "And where is your papa?"

"Down," the boy said pointing to the floor.

Puzzled, Niko raised his gaze to notice the people had moved closer to him.

"Does anyone know what the boy is talking about?" he asked as he stood.

"Sir," the boy's mother said as she grabbed her son's wrist. "The rebel Captain threw my husband, who is the house steward, in with the rest of the prisoners for refusing to give him the keys to the treasury."

"There are prisoners here?" he asked. Outraged streaked through him at the information.

"Aye, sir," a white-haired old man said hobbling forward. "They be in the root cellar. Has bars in it. Aye, sir, it does," he added with a nod.

"You use your root cellar as a dungeon here?" Niko asked then realized that this piece of property was much more sinister than what he'd supposed.

"Always has been," the old man said. "And woe be to ye if'n you cross Prince Jorge," he said making a rapid sign of the cross.

"I see," Niko said wondering what he might discover about his uncle's proclivities. He turned to the Major. "Take a detail down and free the prisoners," he said. "But be careful that no rebels are hidden amongst them."

"Aye, sir," the Major replied.

"Now, who will show the Major the way?" he asked, studying the group.

"I will," a man dressed as a cook said.

"Good, let him lead the way," he cautioned quietly before turning back to the old man. "Tell me, how many are housed down there?"

"Eight," an adolescent boy said shouldering his way to the front of the group.

"How do you know?" he asked, eyeing the boy.

"I counted them. Had too," the boy said. "It's my job to see they returned all the bowls and spoons."

"Does anyone know what they did?" he asked.

"Four of 'em be foreign'rs," the old man said. "One's a dook. Imagine that," the old man chuckled.

Niko frowned. "And the others?"

"Two be servants, the other says he's a Brit Off'cer."

"Great Cerberus!" Niko exclaimed. "What are they doing in my uncle's cellar?"

"The gam'keep'r claims they be snar'n rabbits," the old man said shaking his head. "Don't think they know how tah do it."

"Why not?" Niko asked, encouraged by the elderly man's candor.

"That Duke' so uppity, he claims his cot's gotta be wiped clean afore he sits," the adolescent boy pipped up to say.

"And the other, the officer?" Niko asked.

"He's always harp'n on the rules an reg'lations," the adolescent boy said, "It all hurts my ears."

"Don't think he'd know how tah rig a trap," the elderly man said.

Niko wasn't so sure. "Why did my uncle incarcerate them?'

"Well, as to that," the white-haired old man said, scratching his whiskered chin. "You'd have to ask 'em."

"I will," Niko nodded. "Anything else?" he asked then fielded a few questions about their jobs. He offered his assurance by saying, "You will all remain in your present positions for the time being." When it seemed he had reassured them, he dismissed all except the old man, the Steward's wife, and their son.

Lowering himself to one knee, Niko smiled at the boy. "Thank you for being so brave and letting me know about your papa. Someday I hope to have a son who is just as brave as you." He stood as he heard the clatter of boots and loud talking. The boy made a yelp as the dirty, bedraggled prisoners scurried into the hall. Not only did they look as if they hadn't eaten or bathed in weeks, they looked as if they had been beaten and tortured while held.

"Papa," the little boy cried as he started to run toward the freed men.

"Oh," the woman gasped as Niko watched her rush forward to where a tall man stood propped between two of his officers. He noted that the severe bruising on the man's face and arms indicated he'd been repeatedly beaten. He bit the inside of his cheek to keep the oath rolling on the tip of his tongue quiet.

"I demand to see whoever is in charge," a querulous voice said. Niko shifted his gaze to the group where he noted a man of medium height, assisted by the British uniformed officer, had pushed his way through to the front of the men.

"I bet that's the Duke," Niko said in an aside to the old man.

"Tis not a bet me be tak'n cuz me no lik'n to lose," the old man replied.

"Let's get these men cleaned up and fed," Niko said to the officers that had freed the prisoners.

He turned to Major Gianakis. "In the meantime, I'll be in my uncle's chamber, sifting through his things trying to figure out our next move."

"And the Duke?" the Major asked.

"Assure him that Prince Nikolai Orsini will grant him a private audience after his leg's been seen to and he's had a bite to eat. Then bring him to my uncle's sitting room."

"Very good, your Highness."

"Alert the men there's been a delay and they might as well eat and clean their weapons."

"Aye, sir," the Major said. "I'll also have them scrounge a wagon to carry the prisoners in."

"Excellent," Niko nodded. That was one of the things he liked most about having such good and able-minded men around him. They weren't afraid to add their thoughts and concerns to what he'd ordered.

After being directed to his uncle's chamber, Niko searched desk drawers, footstools, under cushions and mattresses, atop bureaus and the inside and outside of his uncle's clothes press. After methodically examining the bathing chamber, bedchamber and a sitting room, he discovered a room his uncle must have used as an audience chamber. It contained a desk off to the side of the room and a large intimidating throne which sat in the center of the room. A long, narrow blue carpet ran from the doorway to the bottom of the dais. No longer surprised by what he was finding, he wondered if his uncle's vanity and arrogance would prove to be his final defeat. He clenched his fists as he realized he'd found nothing to incriminate his uncle. He would have to catch his uncle in a traitorous act to prove his guilt.

Removing his timepiece from the inside of his vest, he frowned at the lateness of the day then strode to the window to check the afternoon sun. Turning, he hurried from his uncle's chamber to find Major Gianakis. They needed to meet up with the rest of his battalion at the crossroad between Duress and Berat before nightfall. The audience with the Duke would just have to wait.

***

Niko scanned the dense forest bordering the road ahead. He unsnapped his holster, knowing he couldn't afford to relax his guard until they had reached the main road and were traveling back toward Berat. As a child when he had traveled this road to and from his uncle's, he'd imagined gnomes hiding behind every tree. Now he knew the forest likely housed rebels who would be waiting to ambush them. Turning, he scanned his troops and noticed that many of them studied the surrounding terrain. Satisfied, he shifted his gaze to the eight men riding in the purloined wagon he'd taken from his uncle's stable and filled with quilts.

Thank goodness, his men had been alerted by his Uncle's cook to move the stacked barrels in the storage room. Finding the trap door, they had opened it and discovered the nine men stuffed inside the small root cellar located beneath the storage room floor. His officers had found not only the young boy's father but the British Duke, the Major in the British Army and their two servants along with a Hungarian fishing boat Captain and his crew of three.

A bitter taste filled his mouth as he stared at the men his uncle had held prisoner. The Duke suffered from a severe fever due to his infected wound, the two servants had cuts and abrasions while the Major had a broken wrist. The fishing boat Captain complained of dysentery and his entire crew had rashes due to miscellaneous bites. The steward had been so angry with his incarceration that he'd complained loud and long about the injustice of everything.

Clearly, this was an indication that his uncle's reasoning had slipped beyond sanity. To think a Duke and a Major in Her Majesty's Army could disappear and no inquiries would ever be made, demonstrated his uncle's reasoning had become extremely unbalanced.

Wheeling his horse around, he rode to the wagon to make sure the eight men had their weapons ready to defend themselves in case of an attack. "Bradford," Niko said addressing the Duke then glanced at the other seven. "Did all of you check the weapons you were issued before we left the lodge?"

"They did, after I insisted," the Major said. "Told them we couldn't take any chances and if we got into a fight, while I could handle a pistol they would have to use the rifles."

"Good job," Niko said. "I find I live longer when I expect the unexpected." He watched the men nod then having done his duty, he switched his gaze to check his men at the front of the cavalcade. More comfortable riding in the lead position, he tightened his knees and lifted his reins urging his horse toward the front.

"Prince Nikolai," the Duke called as Niko began to turn his horse to the side. "Do you now have time to answer a few questions," he asked, disdain ringing in his tone.

Niko clamped down on the retort hovering on his tongue and eased his horse back to travel alongside the wagon. Obviously, the Duke knew nothing about the responsibilities a Commander carried. He paused then bit the inside of his cheeks to prevent a smile from lifting the corners of his mouth as he decided diversion was his best policy. "I suppose no one has informed you that your twin sisters and your Aunt Ellie arrived safely in Berat a few days ago?"

"Did they?" The Duke's cold response to the welfare of his family was enough to make Niko want to lean forward and slap the man. "So, how did you find them?" he asked as Niko noticed the man's attention was focused on twirling his signet ring around his little finger.

He frowned unsure he'd caught the Duke's meaning. "Find them? What do you mean?"

"You know," the Major interjected as he nudged the Duke with his elbow. "Haughty...kind, rude...nice? That kind of thing."

"I find that depends upon which twin you are referring to," Niko said. "And...if they are 'who' they claim to be at the moment," he added.

"Oh-ho," the Major chortled then cuffed the Duke on his shoulder. The Duke groaned but the Major just grinned. "Told you they would get up to mischief," he said before turning away from the Duke to face Niko again. "What did they do this time, switch places?" the Major asked as a huge smile split his haggard and dirty face.

"Do they do that often?" Niko asked, hoping to gain more insight into Belle.

"Not since Rita convinced Belle to take her place and spend the summer at Brighton with the Queen," the Duke said. "I could've cheerfully killed them both when I discovered what they had done," the Duke added as his eyes narrowed to slits. "They promised me they would never do it again but it seems they had no intention of honoring that promise."

"Who instigated the switch?" Niko asked as he leaned forward eager to discover whether Belle had been the victim or the instigator.

"Belle did it to make my life a living torture," the Duke muttered. "And to embarrass me before Queen Victoria's Court when their perfidy was discovered."

"That's not exactly true," the Major said shifting toward Niko. "Belle only agreed to it in order to save the family from embarrassment. As I remember it, Rita had absolutely refused to be at the beck and call of all the royal princesses for the summer."

"I supposed Belle told you that?" the Duke asked as a sneer twisted his mouth. "If so, you ought to know by now that she has always been jealous of Rita being the firstborn."

"That's utter rot," the Major fired back. "Belle hasn't a jealous bone in her body. She is kind and generous to a fault. A fault, I might add that Rita capitalizes on all the time."

"And yet you sought my permission to marry Rita?" the Duke scoffed.

"I did," the Major replied, "because I love her and I know she loves me," he added, turning his back to the Duke.

"What has love to do with anything?" the Duke snorted. "She's marrying King Stefan and that's final."

Niko felt his lips curl into a satisfied smile. "Maybe not," he said. "I think the Lady Rita might've overplayed her hand with the King. He is not inclined to allow any female to ride rough-shod over him," he said leaning toward the Duke. "And as near as I have observed, Lady Rita is not only rude and obnoxious but also demanding and throws temper tantrums," he added as he straightened to deliver the coup d'etat. "Not exactly qualities one wants in their future Queen."

"That's my gal," the Major said turning back with a grin. "When Rita's pushed into a corner, she comes out swinging. Necessary traits for a military wife."

Niko stared at the Major for a moment then shook his head. Thank goodness, Belle wasn't like that. He wanted a helpmate, a wife, not someone he would have to constantly monitor and correct.

"While that may be true," the Duke said. "I know Queen Victoria ordered the Captain of the HMS Sea Hawk to marry Rita to King Stefan by proxy before she ever stepped foot on Barovian soil. So I do believe the King is stuck with her as his wife." A smug grin settled across the Duke's thin lips.

Niko clenched his jaw and swallowed back a variety of oaths. He highly doubted his cousin had been informed about the proxy. Therefore, it was imperative he get word to the palace that his cousin delay the cathedral ceremony with the Lady Rita. Once those vows had been solemnized by the church, only the Pope could grant a divorce or annulment decree.

"What?" The Major exclaimed. "You slithering asp!"

Niko nodded in agreement. In his missive, he would caution his cousin not to be found alone in the same room with Lady Rita. If discovered, they would be forced to marry, no matter Stefan's objections. He paused in his concern for his cousin. "So, what happens to Lady Belle?" he asked.

"As soon as Rita is officially married to King Stefan and crowned Queen, Belle will be sent packing back to England. She will be marrying my good friend, the Duke of Umberford where she will become the mother of his five obnoxious brats and live out the rest of her life in the wilds of northern England," the Duke said as a feral grin flashed across his face.

"All nicely tied up with a bow," the Major said then paused. "Except, you seemed to have forgotten that both Rita and Belle consider themselves modern women. And that means they think for themselves. I wouldn't be surprised if you find those plans stuffed down your throat."

"Now see here," the Duke sputtered.

"Gentlemen," Niko said. "Let's not get your smalls in a twist. Once we get back to Berat, we can sort this all out," he said hoping that by the time they arrived, his men would've located Belle. And as far as he was concerned, she would be going nowhere but into his bedchamber where they had much to discuss.

"Colonel," Weiss, his scout called as he rode toward him. "I think you'll want to see what I've found."

Niko rocked slightly in his saddle as hope filled him. Had signs of Belle or his uncle been discovered? Eager to leave, he straightened as he nodded to Weiss. "Excuse me, gentlemen," he said. Wheeling his horse away, he cantered after the scout until they lost sight of the column.

Slowing, the scout waited for him to join him. "Pardon me, Colonel," Weiss said. "But I thought that you would want to see this first," he said. Veering off the road, he halted a few feet from a large oak tree.

Niko pulled on his reins as a pair of hessian boots dangling a few feet above the ground came into view. An icy chill swept over him. His breath hitched in his chest as a wave of dread crept through the corridors of his mind. He realized what he would find but all he wanted to do was to shout his denial.

Forcing his steed forward, they rounded a clump of hawthorn bushes and discovered Major Guri Hondros hanging from a branch by a rope tied around his neck. Niko's stomach tightened into a hard knot. From the color of his face, the Major had been dead for several hours. He swallowed rapidly, his throat burning from the sour taste filling his mouth. "Cut him down," he finally managed to say.

Although he had learned to admit that his agents daily courted death, he would never be able to accept their merciless deaths. "After the column passes, I'll request that Major Gianakis have two of his men wrap Guri's body in a blanket and return it to the palace."

"Aye, Colonel," Weiss said with a salute. "Then it's back to...business as usual?"

"Yes, and wait for us at the northbound road to KaCave," Niko said then spurred his horse to rejoin the column as vengeance coursed through him. Finding Major Hondros dead had left more questions than answers. Since there had been no horse grazing nearby, the motive for killing the Major could've been for personal gain. But the method used in his death suggested the Major had been hung as either a traitor or a spy. The motive and person behind the murder could be anyone. His uncle...the rebels...or co-conspirators afraid their identities had been compromised. But although he suspected his uncle was responsible, whoever ordered or committed the Major's murder, he would leave no stone unturned until he found the culprits. He paused at the thought.

Uncle Jorge had been neither hiding at his lodge or at his estate. He hadn't been found in the door to door search his men had conducted in Berat. And recently, his uncle...or some of his uncle's men...or someone out for personal gain had been in this forest because someone had killed the Major.

So, where was his Uncle Jorge?

Chapter Sixteen

As the gypsy encampment settled into the task of preparing the evening meal, the ground rumbled and the sounds of jingling harness were heard. Belle straightened from where she stood on the lake shore washing clothes. Fearing the rebels had returned, she quickly scampered to hide behind the trunk of a large tree. Waiting for a moment, she peeked around the tree trunk then gasped as she spotted Niko riding at the head of a column of soldiers. Her breath hitched in her throat as she drank in the sight of him. Her heart thundered in her chest as she slapped a hand over her mouth to contain her shout of welcome. Overwhelmed at the joy flooding through her, she took several deep gulps and then hurried back to the lake shore.

Hoping to regain her composure before she greeted Niko, she lifted a soiled skirt from the basket of dirty clothes. She plunged it into the lake as her arms began to tremble. Biting her lip to contain her excitement that she would soon see Niko, she raised the dripping garment and spread it out on the large flat rock. Then scooping a handful of homemade soap from a jar, she began to hum as she smeared the soap over the material and rubbed it in.

Turning aside, she plunged the skirt into the water. Lifting it, she checked to see if she had rinsed the garment clean. She grinned, satisfied with the results. Twisting the skirt, she wrung out the excess water and hurried to the bush she'd selected nearby to drape it over to dry. As she approached the bush, she froze as she spied Niko leaning lazily against the trunk of a nearby tree.

Excitement thumped in her chest and although she knew she must look a fright, she slowed her steps as she neared the bush. From the beginning, she'd been both attracted and repelled by him. At first, she had considered him pompous but soon she'd discovered that a forthright, intelligent and caring man existed beneath his uptight military façade. And as they had shared the journey to Berat, she'd come to not only respect Niko but to trust him as well.

That wasn't easy for her to admit. She'd had a fractious relationship with her brother, Edward for years. She knew they would never be friends, not like she'd been with Major Tony who had treated her like a younger sister. Because of the turbulent relationship with her brother, she didn't know much about men. But what she had observed had forced her to distrust the majority of them. So the warm and fuzzy feelings she was experiencing at the sight of Niko created a maelstrom of mixed emotions within her.

Belle bit her bottom lip as she watched him straighten and saunter toward her. Her face heated and she gulped as she noted that his gaze seemed to deepen to a smoldering caress.

"Had you remained at the palace you wouldn't find yourself doing your own laundry," he said with a grin as he stepped closer.

Puzzled that his words ran counter to his expression, Belle swallowed back her pithy retort. Overwhelmed by the joy flowing through her, she was much too grateful for his presence to allow animosity to gain the upper hand. "True, but I-"

"Why did you do it?" he asked as he stopped in front of her.

Assuming he was referring to the switch of their identities, she swept her eyes over his granite-like jaw and knew it was time to confess. No matter the consequences, she needed to tell Niko the truth. "I assumed my twin's identity because I owed her a debt."

"Is this in reference to the death of your parents?" he asked as thunder rumbled nearby.

Stunned, Belle felt her jaw drop open. Air seemed to have become trapped in her lungs because she was having difficulty breathing. "H-how did you know?"

"I had dinner with your aunt," he said lifting her hand to cradle it in his.

"And?" she managed to gasp unable to wrap her mind around the fact that the death of her parents had been a topic of dinner-time discussion.

"It's interesting what is revealed in the heat of a moment," he said as he side-stepped her question.

"I'm not following you," she said confused by his evasiveness.

"From what I can gather, your twin Rita remained at home the day they died because she was extremely ill. Your parents had bundled you up and set off for your aunt's."

"No," she said. "We were going to the winter fair," she added as a crushing weight settled over her chest.

"That's what your sister and brother have cruelly led you to believe all these years," he said. "In reality, you were going to stay with your aunt."

"You're wrong," she inserted then paused as a staggering thought invaded her consciousness. What if he was right? What if her parents had been taking her to Aunt Ellie's? She pressed her hand against her chest. Then that would mean for all of these years Rita and Edward had forced her into living a lie. She had been swamped with guilt so intense that the mere thought of what she had done had nearly crushed her spirit. Ice seemed to trickle through her veins. But why would they punish her?

She inhaled sharply as anger rolled through her. There was only one thing to do. She had to return to Berat and talk to Aunt Ellie. And if Niko was correct, she also needed to confront Rita and discover the reason why she rather than Rita had been blamed for her parents' deaths for all of these years.

"If you don't believe me," Niko said as he stopped beside her. "Return to the palace and talk to your aunt."

"I will," she began then paused as a flash of guilt struck her. Carefully snapping the wrinkles out of the skirt, she meticulously spread it over the bush. "That is just as soon as I get back to Berat. But first," she said as she raised her gaze to meet his. "I need to confess that while I did switch places with Rita...and she is the one who will be your Queen and not I...I'm deeply sorry for leading you to think otherwise. Had it not been that we were traveling by boat again, I would have never gone with you."

Niko frowned. "Why is that important?"

Belle gulped at his question and raised her chin, knowing she had to continue. "Rita was ill the entire time we were on the HMS Sea Hawk. Once we arrived at the inn, she began to feel better. I couldn't subject her to another round of mal-de-mer, not when she needed to be at her best when meeting King Stefan."

"And what about your welfare?" he asked. "Did you ever once consider the danger you had placed yourself in?'

Belle shook her head. "I love the water," she admitted. "But as you have probably guessed, my twin and I are the exact opposites. While I love water, she hates it. She loves horses and I'm a disaster just getting near one. I'm left-handed and she uses her right. I'm-"

"Calm, quiet and a thinker," he said, his lips curving upward.

A ripple of elation coursed through her at his description of her personality. She forced herself to glance up and honestly admit, "Rita is bubbly, fun and a ray of sunshine that brightens the grayest of days."

A grin took over his features as Niko gave a low chuckle. "Yet I find your sister, opinionated, stubborn and spoiled," he said. A bolt of heat zipped through her as he captured her hand. "It is you who brings light and warmth to the dreary days. Your twin is nothing like you at all," he added as she wondered if he'd felt that hot jolt of awareness as they had touched.

"Are you telling me that I did a lousy job of portraying my sister in the switch?" she asked, flashing him a sassy smile as she scanned his face hoping to discover if he had been affected by their touch.

"You are much too honest to be anyone but yourself," he said leaning toward her.

"Really?" Belle whispered as she gazed up at him, her heart hammering in her chest. "You think I'm honest after the way I pretended to be Rita?"

As he moved his large hand to cup her chin, a warm shiver coursed through her. "Thank goodness, it was you I was traveling with and not your sister," he said, his breath whispering across her cheek like a soft caress. "For I find her much too demanding and spoiled for my taste."

Her stomach muscles tightened as jealousy slashed at her innards. "And yet realizing all of this," she said planting her palm in the center of his chest. "Why did I witness the two of you kissing in our sitting room?" Although she intended on giving him a small shove, instead she found herself held firmly. So close she could feel the heat of his body and the wild thump of his heart. Staring up at him, she found it difficult to tear her gaze away from him. Now instead of finding answers, all she sought was the warmth and security she'd found within his arms. Then of their own volition, her eyes seemed to focus on his lips. Lips made for kissing. She gulped at the thought and realized that she could no longer deny the truth. She wanted Niko to kiss her.

"Ah, my dear," he whispered. "That wasn't any kind of kiss...but this is," he said, lowering his lips to hers.

At the touch of his lips, a thrilling swirl coursed through her. Lacing her arms around his neck, she raised to her tiptoes. She closed her eyes, both wanting and needing more. Then suddenly, embarrassed by her own eagerness, she pulled back. Opening her eyes, she gazed at him. His eyes had filled with an unbelievable tenderness. "I need more than this," she found herself whispering.

"As you command," he said, reclaiming her lips

His kiss sent spirals of ecstasy racing through her as she returned his kiss with a reckless abandonment. Never had she felt such joy, such all-consuming passion. It was as if she had at last found her way home.

But then a throat cleared, loudly, nearby.

They sprang apart at the sound and Belle placed her hand over her thundering heart. Heat flushed her face and she turned away from the intruder.

"Pardon me Colonel but your assistance is needed in the camp," a young voice said.

"Of course," Niko said as he dropped his arms. "I'll be back," he whispered.

Nodding, she turned and watched Niko stride away with a young soldier. Then just before he disappeared up the pathway toward the camp, she heard him ask, "What is it this time?"

She turned away as the heat of embarrassment burned at her cheeks. Surely Niko must think her desperate for throwing herself at him like that. Merciful heavens! What was wrong with her? She wasn't Rita. She didn't go around kissing men willy-nilly. That was Rita's forte...or so she claimed. Belle shook her head then spied the basket of unfinished laundry waiting for her.

She shivered as a cold breeze rippled across the water lapping at the sandy shore. Kneeling, she dunked the last piece, a skirt, up and down in the water then she scrubbed, rinsed and twisted the excess water from it. Rising, she nodded as a sense of accomplishment at finishing the mundane task rushed through her.

Lifting her gaze, she discovered dark, churning clouds had gathered over the top of the mountains on the other side of the lake. She shivered as she watched lightning flash across the threatening sky and heard the thunder rumble and echo across the mountains. Hurriedly pulling herself together, she gathered the wet garments she'd spread over the bushes and dropped the wet items into her basket. Nothing ever dried in the rain.

As she dropped the last piece into the basket, a streak of lightning forked through the roiling clouds. Quickly, she began to count the seconds until she heard the clap of thunder. "Five," she muttered then divided that number by five. She realized that by using the scientific formula from the article she'd read, that the storm was one mile away. That also meant that if the time difference between seeing the lightning and then hearing the thunder was less than thirty seconds, she immediately needed to seek safety.

Thunder boomed and she swiftly lifted the basket. It hadn't taken reading the scientific journal to convince her that one stayed away from both water and tall trees during a thunderstorm. She understood the importance of safety being her first consideration. Turning, she spied the man dressed as the old woman moving along the shoreline toward her. "M-may I help you?" she asked. Although she didn't want either to be caught out in the storm or alone with the man, she felt obligated to warn him about the perils inherent in the oncoming storm. Quickly, she swallowed back her hesitation as he planted his boots a few feet away from her.

"Uncanny!" he said in a deep male voice. Belle inhaled sharply as she wondered why the man no longer feigned his assumed gender. "My men were right. The resemblance is amazing!"

Knowing that if she took so much as another step back she would end up in the lake, she gritted her teeth and held her position, not about to concede defeat. "To what do you refer?" she asked hoping to throw the man a red herring.

"You," he said, pointing his index finger at her.

She hardened her jaw. "Me?" she asked knowing if she delayed too much longer that the storm gathering nearby would catch her in its grips. "I have no idea what you are talking about," she hedged. Darting a glance sideways, she scanned the area to see if she had a get-away path. Finding none, she glanced back at him. "I really should get back to camp and help Etel," she said. "It's not safe for us to be standing near water or under tall trees during a thunderstorm."

The man waved his hand dismissively. "Just when I think I'm all done in, something always crops up to help me out," he said as his obsidian eyes hardened to coal. "And you my little gypsy are my ticket to redemption," he said grabbing her by the upper arm and pulling her toward him.

"Let her go."

Niko's command had her nerves jumping as she turned to watch him step onto the path. "Ouch, you're hurting me," she gasped as the man tightened his hold painfully on her upper arms.

"Say nothing more," the man warned, "or he won't live to see tomorrow." Smothered by the smells of the man's stale wine and sweat, she felt her throat close as the man yanked her in front of him and anchored her back to his chest. As the man's arm tightened across her waist, she froze, afraid Niko would be harmed. Then she gasped as the man flashed a knife before her face and laid the tip of the cold blade at the base of her throat. Disorientated, a numbing fear invaded her, leaving her almost too afraid to take a breath.

"Well, nephew," the man said. "How did you get into camp without my men alerting me?"

Nephew? Belle felt the air stall in her throat. Was Niko really related to this man who held her at knifepoint? She stared, trying to find a resemblance between the man and Niko.

Niko took a slow step back from where his uncle held Belle, knowing he had to remain calm. "That's easy to answer, Uncle Jorge," he said, feigning nonchalance. "You no longer have any men. There is just... us," he added. "Now, let her go."

"And I suppose you think this confrontation is going to remain a private affair between us," his uncle said, disdain coating his every word. "And that you will save the country for Stefan?"

"I can only hope," he said then paused as thunder cracked and rolled overhead. "We really shouldn't be standing out here in the open," he said as he began inching toward his uncle.

"Stop," his uncle called. "Any further and I'll gut this little gypsy like a fish."

Niko halted. "Do that and I'll give no quarter," he warned although he had no intention of placing Belle in further jeopardy.

"Let me remind you that I have nothing to lose," his uncle growled as a clap of thunder sounded close by.

He balled his fists as he watched Belle's face blanch. Hoping he could convince his uncle to release Belle, he said. "Ah, but what you don't know is that I've been given the power to save your life." Knowing if his uncle accepted the half-truth, he might persuade him to release Belle unharmed, he added. "There is only one condition you must meet," he said as the afternoon darkened with the coming storm, "and that is to release Belle."

His uncle chucked, the low-toned sound sent a chill skittering through him as lightning flashed in the darkening sky. "You disappoint me Nephew. Did you really think I would fall for that claptrap?"

Niko took a deep breath and relaxed his hands. So be it, he reasoned. If his uncle wanted directness then he would lob the first volley. "Lately, I've had the distinct feeling you were hunting me," he said then frowned as thunder crashed and the clouds rolled above the trees. "Why do you suppose that is?"

"You've been as slippery as an eel," his uncle said removing the knife from Belle's throat and tilting the point it at him.

The air seemed to sizzle as Niko noticed that Belle had tucked her lower lip between her teeth. "And you would know something about that strategy wouldn't you?" he said as his uncle returned the knife to Belle's throat. His breath hitched in his chest as he watched the color drain from Belle's face. Afraid she would crumble into a faint, he added quickly, "but, you always did seem to be a step ahead of all of us."

His uncle's low-pitched cackle ratcheted up his alarm as a cold wind swept over them. "It's my touch of magic. With a slight of my hand and a poof of smoke, I've managed for years to fool you all," he said, his boastful words slicing through the veil of mystery covering the past. "And I aim to do it again," his uncle challenged as he ran the back of his blade along Belle's jawbone and up to rest it beneath her ear.

Niko gritted his teeth as he watched Belle's nostrils flare. Hoping to turn his uncle's focus back to him, he took a wild gamble. "My mother always suspected my father's death wasn't an accident. Did you have a hand in it?"

Like a cannons' volley atop a ridge, thunder roared above them. "I not only planned it, I pulled the trigger," his uncle said, his face alight with unholy glee. "He was standing in my way. So, what are you going to do about it? It's not like it was the first or the last time I killed someone."

Niko's breath stalled in his throat as anger and grief flashed through him. He clasped his hands behind his back, not about to let his uncle know how devastated he truly felt upon learning his father had been murdered because of a brother's quest for power and greed. "I'll tell you what I plan to do," he ground out. "But first tell me, did you poison Uncle Rinaldo?"

"Why rehash the past?" his uncle shrugged as lightning lit up the darkening area. "Everyone knew my brother wasn't to be served mushrooms but he was."

"No one in the kitchen prepared them," Niko said as he realized his Uncle Jorge had also murdered Stefan's father. A cold chill settled in his chest. "Clearly you had a hand in it."

"I killed both of my brothers," his uncle said, his boastful tone setting Niko's teeth on edge. "What are you going to do about it?"

Niko's mind raced, searching for an answer as he contemplated how he was going to save the woman he loved. Whatever he decided he knew the one thing his uncle desired above all else was to hold the power of the throne forever in his clutched fists. Killing Belle would gain his uncle nothing. But if his uncle used her as a bargaining chip, it would force him to negotiate a settlement with his uncle. While Belle would be returned safe and sound, the only possible term his uncle would sue for was his freedom. And that was the one thing he wouldn't grant him. He chewed on the inside of his cheek then paused. Unless...he could provoke his uncle into accepting a duel.

"Only the scum of the earth hides behind a woman's skirt," he taunted. "For once in your life Uncle, be a man. Face me in a duel to the death." He heard Belle's gasp as he watched his uncle lower the knife from her neck. Unexpectedly, his uncle gave her a mighty shove. As she stumbled forward, Niko rushed toward her and caught her in his arms. Holding her safe, he tucked her close to his chest. "Are you-," he began. A tremendous boom sounded directly overhead. It was louder than any cannon he'd ever heard. The earth shook as if it were about to split in half.

Aware of their danger, Niko tightened his hold on Belle. "Drop," he ordered, pushing her to the ground. A brilliant flash of light sizzled through the air and he dropped, shielding her with his body and waiting for the jolt. When nothing happened, he raised his head and scanned the area where his uncle had stood a few seconds ago. Nearby, a tree had been split in half. Tiny spirals of smoke rose into the air. Slowly, he surveyed the area near the tree. Finding no trace of his uncle, he realized that once again he'd allowed his uncle to slip out of his clutches. He opened his mouth to let loose his frustration but then he spied his uncle escaping across the open beach, running toward a copse of trees.

Struggling to his knees, Niko was forming the word, 'stop' when another earsplitting crash sounded overhead. A swift bolt of lightning entered his uncle's body and it lifted his Uncle Jorge off the ground. Fire shot from his uncle's fingertips as his body contracted and contorted into spasms reminding him of the gyrating movements of a marionette lifted into the air.

A sense of the unreal assaulted Niko as the stench of scorched flesh and burning hair filtered through the vibrating air. Surrounded by white light, his uncle stood as if riveted in place then the paralyzing glow faded and his uncle fell backward onto the sand.

He stood for a moment, frozen in place then gazed down at Belle who seemed equally as stunned. "Belle," he said, his voice sounding hoarse to his own ears. Reaching to assist her to her feet, he managed to ask as the rain began to pelt them. "Are you hurt?"

"No," she said, her voice wobbling as she raised her hands to shield her head. "Shouldn't we go and check on your uncle?"

"Come here," he said, opening his cape to her. "We'll check on him after the storm has cleared the area," he added as he wrapped his cape around her.

"How long do you suppose that will be?" she asked as she clasped her arms around his middle.

Feeling her shiver, he tugged her closer to his chest as sheets of rain hammered them. "According to the latest issue of the Scientific Journal," he said, dipping his head to shield her from the onslaught, "the lightning threat may last for more than thirty minutes."

"That long?" she asked as he felt her tighten her hold on his waist. "I think I would really like to read this article."

"I'll loan you my copy when we get to Berat," he said, hoping to get a definitive answer that she would indeed be returning to Berat with him. He tilted his head back as he realized that while the wind still blew, the intensity of the rain had lessened.

"What are you looking for?" she asked.

Disappointed by the change in topic, he gazed down at her. "When thunderstorms are in the area but not overhead," he began. "The threat of lightning can still exist even if it's not raining," he said, wiping his face with his hand, "and even if it's a clear, sunny sky."

"So, we could be here for a while yet?" she asked.

"As long as there is a possibility of another strike, yes," he said, scanning the sky as the rain tapered to a drizzle. "The odds of another strike are probably not high but I'm not willing to chance it."

"I-I did try to tell your Uncle to stay away from water during a thunderstorm but he ignored me as if I was an ignoramus."

He rested his chin on her head. He knew the only way he could help Belle was by being honest. "Uncle Jorge was like that. He was always only for himself."

"How can people be so callous? It's as if-" She stopped and lifted her head.

He watched her eyes cloud with worry as the drizzle became a mist. "You're thinking of your own brother and twin, aren't you?" He watched her nod. "Then don't. They both have proved to me that they, like my uncle, care only for themselves.

"I know," she whispered. "But how do we live with the ramifications?"

He looked through the mist to where his uncle lay sprawled on the sand. "I'm not sure," he admitted as he gathered her closer to his chest. His mind raced as shame warred with anger. How had he missed all the signs pointing to his uncle murdering the male members ahead of him in the line of succession?

As she snuggled closer to him, he realized the feelings he had for Belle would come to naught. No woman wanted to become embroiled with a family whose uncle had not only committed murder but had betrayed and nearly destroyed their country. His breath hitched in his chest. No family, let alone a fledgling monarchy could survive the scandal about to rock the country when it was revealed what his uncle had done.

His stomach tightened. He glanced down at Belle then wondered how he was to break things off with her. Her coolness under fire, her quick wit, her gentle, caring attitude had all been amazing. And although she must've been terrified at being held at knifepoint, she had exhibited such grace and poise. He doubted even he would've been able to remain that quiet and contained. He paused as he wondered when his simple caring for her welfare had grown to such an extent that she had become the single most important person in his life. He paused and swallowed back his anguish at the thought that he would soon have to let her go. He released his hold on her and opened his cape.

"I think it's safe to go to your uncle," she said, withdrawing her arms from around his waist and stepping back. "But be careful. He may still be dangerous," she said as he took note of her warning. "He has a very sharp knife."

"I don't think we need worry about the knife," he said, having difficulty processing that he would soon lose Belle. He took a step away, attempting to focus on the issue at hand. There was no way his uncle could still be alive, not after being struck by that bolt of lightning. "If he was wearing his metal chest armor, he's dead," he said as he unfastened his cape and placed it over Belle's.

"Nevertheless, be careful," she said as she pulled his cape under her chin. "And thank you," she added, "I'll remain here but if you need help-"

"I'll call," he said, relief rushing through him that he wouldn't have to worry about what she was about to see. Then hurrying toward the shoreline, he slowed as he neared where his uncle lay. Although he knew it was callous, he gently nudged the toe of his uncle's boot with his own. Receiving no response, but taking no chances, he removed his pistol from his holster and cocked the hammer. Settling on his haunches, he checked for a pulse on his uncle's out-flung wrist. Finding none, he placed his hand on his uncle's chest and felt the ridge of the metal plate his uncle had been wearing beneath his disguise.

Snatching his hand back, he swallowed in disgust. If his uncle been held accountable for his actions his entire life then his father might not have been murdered over greed and blind ambition. Dropping his uncle's hand over his chest plate, Niko stood. Releasing the hammer on his pistol, he tucked his weapon away. There was nothing more to be done. The Revolution was over.

His chest heaved in relief and he lifted his gaze to check on Belle. Spying her walking toward him, a tremendous sadness flooded through him. Waiting until she neared, he said. "He's dead. The chest plate he wore didn't save him this time." Then unable to stop himself, he reached for her hand.

"Come," Niko said, holding out his hand to her. "Let's get you back to camp and have Etel take a look at you. I'll send Tass back for your laundry basket," he added as she slipped her hand into his. Then bringing her closer, he placed his arm across her shoulders and guided her back across the sand to the path leading toward the Gypsy Camp.

"Is there anything I can help you with?" Belle asked. He noted that her voice was as unsteady as her trembling hands.

"I appreciate your offer," he said, amazed she'd managed to find the stamina to remain on her feet. "But Uncle Jorge had you in a fierce grip and I want Etel to take a look at you. I'll take care of him," he said waving his hand in the direction of the lake and his uncle, "in a few minutes. But, what about you? Is there anything I can do for you?" He watched her bite her bottom lip then shake her head.

His throat thickened as a lightness rushed through him. Belle was safe and no one else would be harmed in his uncle's relentless search for power and glory. His chest swelled with gratitude. Stefan could now find the ways and means to regrow their flagging economy and he could seek trade agreements between their country and the rest of the region. And best of all, they no longer needed to feel beholding to England solely on the basis that Stefan needed the expeditious marriage between Rita and himself. He smiled at the thought.

Chapter Seventeen

Belle slipped down the back steps of Etel's wagon, still shaken from her near-death ordeal. She truly hoped she would never experience such terror again. Rounding the wagon, she stepped to the water barrel attached to the side of the wagon. Dipping the ladle in, she filled it with water and took a sip. Hoping to locate Niko, she scanned the camp through the early evening light. But instead, she noticed that wounded rebel soldiers were receiving treatment for their wounds. Quickly finishing her drink, she affixed the dipper back on the lid and strode forward, ready to offer her help.

"Belle, over here," Etel called, waving to her.

Altering her course, she hurried over to where Etel stood beside an old hay wagon. Peering over the side, she inhaled sharply as she met the angry gaze of her brother. Nearby, she heard a gasp. Shifting her gaze, she found her good friend Tony sitting behind a stack of luggage. "What happened to you?" she exclaimed, happy to see Tony but not so happy to discover her brother there.

"Long story," Tony chuckled. "Just thought I would take a short detour from sailing to India to plead my case to your brother. I had hoped to convince him to allow your sister and me to marry. But we found ourselves blown off course, seized by a madman and thrown into his oubliette."

"Is all of that true?" she asked turning to her brother.

"That does rather sum it up," Edward said as he scooted himself toward the wagon's tailgate.

"What have you done to your leg?" she asked as she observed that her brother's left leg had remained in a stiff, straightened position as he'd scooted himself toward the back gate. Pausing in his endeavor, he wiped his bearded face with the sleeve of his dirty coat.

"That's what happens when one falls afoul of a gamekeeper," Tony said. "If we'd stuck to the road like I wanted," he began.

"Leave off," Edward said, his tone sharp as Etel opened the back tailgate and placed her hand on the tattered dirty bandage binding his leg.

Belle took a good look at the crusted, filthy neckcloth used as a bandage and bit her bottom lip. She knew it didn't bode well for her brother if his leg had been left to fester. She frowned. "I'll bring hot water, cloths, and whiskey," she said, hoping to get away from the sickly sight and smell of what she imagined her brother's leg looked like. Although she knew she shouldn't care, she did and she truly hoped it wasn't too late to save her brother's life.

"Lay out a blade on the fire," Etel said, placing her hand over Belle's wrist. "This way it will be ready if I need it."

She nodded. Taking a sharp breath at the mention of a knife, Belle shivered. She hoped the knife wouldn't be needed as she left to get Etel's supplies. After gathering the items requested, she placed the knife blade in the fire then stirred their evening meal, a pot of rabbit stew cooking over the flames. Then knowing she couldn't delay any longer, she returned to help Etel with her brother.

Dipping a clean cloth into warmed water, she wrung it out and placed it over the crusted neckcloth until the make-shift bandage became saturated enough to loosen it. Peeling it way, she winced at the sight of the raw and angry wound. "How long has this been left untended?" she asked, attempting to keep her voice steady but hearing a distinct wobble in it.

"At least a sennight," her brother said.

Tony leaned toward her brother to inspect the wound and shook his head. "Yup, looks bad."

"You do realize that you could possibly lose-" she began.

"Now, let's not jump to any rash conclusions," Tony inserted as he frowned at her and shook his head.

Belle swallowed the rest of her warning. If Edward didn't want to hear that he was likely to need his leg amputated, then so be it. She shivered at the prospect. A 'whole' Edward was cantankerous enough, she didn't want to consider what her brother would be like if he lost the lower half of one of his legs.

"Are we ready?" Etel said bending toward the wound Belle had uncovered.

Belle gave a resigned sigh. "Yes," she muttered although she dreaded what was to come.

"Any sign of fever?" Etel asked in a whisper as she leaned toward her. She shook her head. "Not that I can feel."

"Then hand me the whiskey," Etel said holding out her hands.

As she lifted the jug and handed it to Etel she heard Tony's grunt of disapproval. "It's used for cleaning wounds," she said to reassure him.

Just then her brother gave an agonized howl, "Ah-h-h."

As her gaze shifted to where Etel was pouring the whiskey over his open wound, he bolted upright into a sitting position. "The whiskey aids the healing process along with honey and comfrey leaves packed atop the wound," she said hoping to instill confidence that Etel knew what she was doing.

"Sounds as if you've learned a thing or two," Tony said, his brows arched in surprise.

"Not only did I learn the intricacies of running a royal household while at Brighton," Belle said, as Etel leaned over her brother's wound. "But also about herbs and how to prepare tinctures, salves, and rubs. The rest, I've picked up from my time with Etel."

Watching Etel tip jug in preparation for dousing the wound a second time, Belle quickly asked her brother. "Do you need something to bite down on?"

"Ah-h-h," he yelled as whiskey splashed over his leg. "Stupid chit, it's much too late now."

Spots flashed in Belle's vision as she took the jug from Etel and slid back to the time she'd cowered in her hidey-hole in the library while Edward lashed the room with his riding crop, calling her all kinds of names. She had decided then that she would never accept that degradation from anyone again.

She lifted her chin at the memory of her vow. "Enough is enough," she snapped. "J-just because you are f-family, doesn't give you the right to c-call me names," she said, struggling to find the right words as she hugged the whiskey jug to her chest. "So, if you can't be p-polite and treat me with respect, then don't speak to me at all," she said as Etel picked away at the dead skin and debris embedded in his wound.

Straightening, Etel paused and flashed her a grin. "Would you care for a strap to bite on, Your Grace?" she asked removing the whiskey jug from Belle's grasp.

"No," her brother growled. "Just get it done."

As Etel doused the wound again, Edward yowled out in pain. Taking the jug from Etel, Belle tightened her grip on the container. "Will you need the knife?"

"Let's see if the whiskey and herbal pack will do the trick," Etel said then shook her head. "If not, I suggest that when you get back to Berat, you have a doctor remove his leg."

Belle nodded, hoping their measures would be enough to save Edward's limb.

"Will you serve the men the stew?" Etel asked inspecting the wound then beginning to smear it with a mixture of honey and crushed comfrey leaves.

"My pleasure," Belle said, relieved at the excuse to slip away from the lingering sickly-sweet odor of her brother's wound. While she might have learned about herbal concoctions, her stomach still lurched whenever she tended oozing wounds.

Rushing to Etel's wagon, she gathered the bowls and utensils needed for the meal. Then crossing to the kettle of stew, she ladled out two bowls and hurried back to the men. Handing one bowl to her brother and the other to Tony, she realized something more was needed. "Let me get some cups and bread," she offered, turning to retrieve the items.

As she scurried away, she heard her brother call. "Ah, Prince Nikolai, will you join us?"

Belle slowed and spun around. Prince Nikolai? Surprise held her hostage for a moment as she gaped at the man she'd come to know as Niko. How had she failed to realize that if Niko had been called 'nephew' by Prince Jorge then he would also be called 'Prince'?

Frozen in place, she watched Niko nonchalantly wave away her brother's offer as he continued to walk across the camp.

"Yes, Your Royal Highness," Tony called. "Please join us and accept my bowl of stew."

Royal Highness? Belle felt her tongue stick to the roof of her mouth as Niko altered his course and sauntered toward the hay cart.

A large knot began to burn in the center of her chest as she returned to Etel's wagon. She was such a fool. When would she realize she couldn't take things at face value? Grabbing another spoon, a bowl and the loaf of bread off the table, she rushed outside. Then darting to the cook pot, she ladled the stew into the bowl and marched over to where the three men were sitting on the tailgate. "Your spoon," she said as she dropped Niko a curtsey. She felt a smile curl her lips as she plopped the spoon into the bowl he was holding. Shoving the bowl of stew in Tony's hands, she lobbed the loaf of bread at her brother. "Enjoy," she called as she pivoted and headed off to retrieve her basket of laundry.

As she rushed toward the lake she wondered when Niko had planned on telling her that he was more than the Commander of the King's Army. When they arrived back at in Berat...or never?

Chapter Eighteen

Early evening settled over the campsite as Belle dumped the pan of sudsy water she'd used for washing the dishes. Drying the pan, she turned and found Niko...His Royal Highness...Prince Nikolai...sitting on the back step of Etel's wagon watching her.

She clenched her jaw to keep herself from saying something she shouldn't. Striding toward him, she tightened her grip on the pan. Stopping a few feet away, she relaxed her jaw. "Did you ever plan on telling me who you really were?" she asked as she waved the pan at him. She watched him quickly get to his feet and step off the stoop. "Or were you hoping I would never find out?"

"Now, My Lady," he began, a teasing tone trickling through his words. "Surely, you can now understand how I felt when I discovered you had switched places with your twin."

"And how was that?" she challenged too upset to give him any leeway.

His eyebrows squeezed together. "First, I was angry," he said, slowly. Belle felt her breath hitch in her chest as a pained look swept across his face. "Then I felt betrayed." Pausing, he cleared his throat. "Then confusion set in and after considerable thought, I finally felt relieved," he added and grinned.

"Relieved?" she asked, gaping at him

"Deeply relieved," he said, reaching out and cradling her hand in his. At his touch, Belle's heart leaped in her chest and she gazed up at him. "Because it meant that I hadn't developed lasting feelings for a woman I could never ask to be my wife," he said, squeezing her hand.

Belle stared up at him, stunned by his declaration. She bit her bottom lip fighting to control her joy. But then a disturbing thought raced through her consciousness. Surely Niko didn't think she would just fall at his feet because he was a prince? Pulling her hand away from him, she frowned. This time she was going to take a leaf from Rita's book on how to control a man. Prince or not, Niko needed to understand trust was a two-way street.

"It's good," Rikard chuckled as he joined them, "that the two of you are already married. Otherwise, you would have to wear a pole for separation."

Belle gaped at him for a moment as her mind began to whirl. A pole?

"What do you mean by married?" Niko asked, his words sounding terse to her ears.

"I mean, in order for you to stay with us that first evening, you had to be married," Rikard said with a wave of his hand.

Not about to be dismissed, Belle stared at Niko as words of protest tripped across her tongue. Finally, she managed to ask, "But how can a marriage between us be legal when-"

Niko moved closer to her. "To make it legal," he said quickly, "we both had to give our consent. Which we did," he added, softening his tone. He watched Belle's face tighten in disbelief.

"But we didn't say vows or...exchange a ring, or even have a blessing-"

"Instead of a ring, we had a scarf," he inserted. "Instead of vows, we shared a glass of Ouzo. As for the blessing," he said then shrugged. "That part is a bit fuzzy."

Her frown deepened. "So you knew?" she asked, her brow arching.

Niko knew he'd best be honest. "I wasn't certain," he said, "but I... did wonder."

"But surely, we had to have signed a piece of paper with our signatures on it to make it legal?" she asked, her voice rising a full octave.

"No," Rikard said, shaking his head. "Whenever I get to Berat, I visit the Archbishop and give him the information and he records the particulars."

Niko paused as he watched Belle rub her upper arms as if she was cold. "Have you visited the archbishop?"

"That was my first stop after I left you off near the palace," Rikard said with a nod.

A chill flowed through Niko. While all he felt was immense relief that he'd secured Belle as his wife, apparently she didn't feel the same way.

"Then...we are truly m-married?" she asked as a dazed look settled across her features.

"It appears so," he said but he knew from the way Belle was frowning that she was unhappy with the situation.

"But," she said, brightening. "How could the ceremony be legal if I was posing as Rita?"

"You called yourself, Belle. So, that was the name I registered with the Archbishop," Rikard said as if explaining the situation to a child.

"Oh-h," she sighed as Niko watched her squeeze her eyes shut.

Realizing he was digging himself into a deeper hole with her, he said. "I suggest we sleep on this tonight and when we return to Berat tomorrow we can straighten everything out." Peering down at her, he waited for her answer.

Belle opened her eyes and nodded, relieved to shelve the subject of their marriage until after they arrived in Berat. "I hope you won't mind if I straighten things out with Rita and Aunt Ellie first?"

"Not at all," he said. "I will need to report to Cousin Stefan."

"Ah-h, yes, the King," she said knowing that trust wasn't just something Niko needed to learn but her as well. "How early do you plan on leaving tomorrow?"

"First light," he said, beginning to turn away.

"Then I will be ready to ride alongside you," she said. She watched him swing back, a grin lighting his face as he nodded.

"I look forward to that," he said. Turning, he took a few steps then called over his shoulder, "Have a good evening."

"You also," she said. Taking a deep breath, she faced Rikard. Right, wrong or indifferent, she had an obligation. "I would like to thank you for your hospitality and for your generous offer of escorting me to Durres," she said then she straightened. "I...however would like your promise that before you perform another tribal initiation ceremony with a...non-tribal couple...that you inform them that what you are really doing is marrying them. Do I have your word that you will tell them that?"

"My Lady," Rikard said with a bow, "Are you so certain your marriage is unwanted?" he asked as he straightened.

Rattled by his unexpected question, Belle opened her mouth but decided she needed to seriously consider her answer. "I need to wish you a good evening," she said. Pivoting, she began threading her way around Niko's soldiers standing guard around the perimeter of the captured rebels sitting in the center of the camp.

"My Lady?" an elderly soldier called to her as she maneuvered her way past the area used as triage for the wounded. Thinking the man needed assistance, she altered her course and stopped next to him.

"How may I help you?" she asked as she noted some of the wounded who were able had moved nearer. Although she felt no threat, she did glance up to find her closest guard gripping his weapon. Warily, she asked, "What can I do for you?"

"We understand that Prince Jorge is dead," a middle-aged man leaning on a make-shift crutch said. "He promised that he would take care of us and our families if we fought for him, but now we find-" the soldier paused to shake his wooly head.

"We're branded as traitors to a country we love," a gray-bearded soldier called out a few paces behind the man.

"We're wanted men," another man added from nearby.

Belle's chest tightened as she scanned the faces of the troubled and forsaken men.

"Our families will suffer," a young soldier resting on a mat near her said, "for what we believed was the right thing to do."

"Please, My Lady, as our future Queen," the elderly soldier said. "We-"

Belle's breath hitched as a terrible weight settled in her chest. Future Queen? Dear heavens, was this one of the results of their ruse? Quickly, she held up a trembling hand to stop the words tumbling from the man. She had to make this right. "Please, I am only the twin sister of your future Queen," she said. "I do sympathize with your plight and understand you need help." She paused as she glanced around at all the prisoners. There were close to fifty men. Many of whom might not make it home alive because of the seriousness of their injuries. She gulped back the hot ball rising in her throat. She knew how helpless and defeated these men must feel. The same way she'd felt when Rita and Edward had treated her as an evildoer. She didn't want anyone to suffer the rest of their lives with the untenable humiliation and rejection she had.

She bit her bottom lip as a fierce urge to help them flooded her. But how was she to do that when what the men needed was a miracle? She had no magic wand or...she paused as a gem of an idea came to her. Although she couldn't guarantee the King would grant them amnesty, yet the compulsion to help them was flailing her.

Unsure how the King would respond to her overstepping the boundary of hospitality, she proceeded with caution. "What we must do is...present an amnesty plea to the King," she said, brightening as the idea took hold. "If this country is ever to be whole again," she said feeling her way through her jumbled thoughts. "Then you must sign a pledge to His Majesty...King Stefan that you will lay down your arms and never participate in a revolt against him again," she finished slowly, hoping the King wasn't the vengeful sort.

Several voices lifted in agreement and she raised her hand for silence. She worried her bottom lip as she peered at the men, wondering if the majority would accept or reject her idea. As the men quieted, she spied Niko standing with his cadre nearby. "Please," she called. "I am sure the King wants peace. To have peace...there must be forgiveness." As she paused to gather her thoughts she realized that forgiveness was a virtue she also must practice. She squared her shoulders. "The only avenue you have to save yourself and your families is...to sign this pledge. Although there is no guarantee the King will accept this proclamation, are you willing to sign it?" she asked as she spun around to look at the men sitting on the ground beyond her.

A roar of agreement arose from the men. She lifted her hand to quiet them once again then noticed Niko was threading his way through the rebels carrying a lap writing desk. A huge wave of relief swept through her at the sight of him coming to her aid.

"I believe this is what you require, my lady," he said opening the lap desk for her.

"T-thank you," she stammered, accepting the small portable surface from him.

"One of the many things I like most about you...is that what you start, you bravely see through to the finish. This is no different," he said softly so that only she could hear. Bending the flaps back to create the writing surface for her as she held it balanced on her inner forearms. 'This document need not be fancy," he added, lifting the top off the small bottle of ink. "Just keep it simple and use the men's own words," he added quietly.

Swallowing back her hesitation, she nodded as he took the desk to hold it for her as she wrote. She stared a moment at the sheet of parchment affixed to the writing surface. Dipping the pen into the ink, she began to write as silence filled the camp.

Seeking amnesty for participating in the Rebellion led by Prince Jorge, we the undersigned do hereby pledge to immediately lay down all weapons and we do individually vow never to participate in a revolt against the King again.

This is my solemn pledge given on this day of June 30, 1859.

Finishing up, she sprinkled it with sand from the small bottle attached to the lap desk. Clearing her throat, she looked out at the men.

"It's ready for you to read," Niko said as he presented the desk to her and took a step back.

She nodded then dropping her gaze, she read the proclamation aloud. As she finished reading, her hands trembled as she realized the only thing she heard was the breeze rustling through the leaves. She raised her gaze and stared at the men, hoping she had effectively expressed their sentiment. But their very silence seemed to indicate condemnation. She felt her heart shrivel in her chest. Once again she'd failed. She turned, ready to sprint away but a warm hand landed on her shoulder, and she heard Niko whisper, "Stay."

Suddenly a boisterous shout of "I'll sign it," rang through the rebels. She watched in humble gratitude as men struggled to their feet to form a line in front of her. Her vision seemed to blur as the elderly soldier placed his callused hand over hers. "My Lady," he said, "Let me hold this for you while all the men sign their names."

Releasing her grip on the lap desk as the elderly soldier took it from her, Belle trembled at the overwhelming relief coursing through her, knowing that this simple act was about to make a huge difference in so many lives.

"Well done," she heard Niko whisper from behind her. "I would like to see you carry that petition and present it to my cousin."

Belle nodded as a tight knot formed in her throat. She knew that no matter what happened in the future, she would forever remember this moment. "I would be honored," she managed to say. For the first time in eight years, she'd done something right. And it hadn't been done out of guilt or obligation but because it was truly the right thing to do. A light, floating-in-the-air feeling bubbled inside of her. Lifting her gaze to Niko, she smiled as she realized what if felt like to be truly happy. The last time she remembered feeling so secure and loved had been...she froze as her heart hammered in her chest as she stared at Niko. From the first moment they had met he had kept her safe. And as they had traveled through the countryside, he had become more than her safety net. She had come to trust his judgment, admire his courage, honor his commitment to his cousin and love his-

Love?

She gulped back her shout of surprise. She loved Niko.

She froze at the realization. Heavens!

Her pulse leaped with excitement. But she cleared her throat, denying her reaction, unsure of what Niko might feel about her.

"What are you not telling me?" he asked, a frown furrowing his brow.

Belle swallowed back her quick denial. There were things she hadn't told him. Like...she'd just realized she loved him and she couldn't decide what she should do about it...that her sister had already married his cousin by proxy aboard the Sea Hawk and personally, she could see no rationalization for a national ceremony. She inhaled, sharply as she realized the second secret was the one that could be the death knell to any feelings Niko might have for her. As protective as he was of his cousin, her failure to tell him about the proxy might cause him to never want to have anything further to do with her. And suddenly, she knew she didn't want that to happen. All she needed was more time. Time to discover if Niko loved her as she loved him. She took a quick breath as she realized that she was no longer her sister's keeper. The secret of the proxy marriage was Rita's to reveal. She drew in a deep breath and answered his question the best she could. "Mainly, something that isn't mine to tell."

"I can honor that," he replied, "as long as you remember we are married. And by Barovian Law that means we will remain so."

Her breath caught as caution warred with hope. She bit her bottom lip. She had to probe further to discover the extent to which he would go to keep her near. "In England, m-many couples live separately."

"We will reside in one domicile," he said, in the firmest voice she'd ever heard him use. "Together...as husband and wife."

Afraid to allow the joy surging within her to gain a foothold, she froze. Then knowing she had to be absolutely sure of his motives, she gazed up at him. "I don't understand why you are so insistent we honor this marriage," she said. "Unless...is it to save face?"

"Why do you find it difficult to believe that I admire you?" he asked as he cradled her hand in his. "I admire your courage. How you put yourself out there to protect those you care for. I would like...if you would let me...to do the same for you."

His gentle words filled her with hope, making it difficult to doubt him but she had to be sure. She'd lived the past eight years in a world filled with sibling rancor and discourse. She wouldn't live the rest of her life in dissension. She felt guilty enough that Niko's right to choose a proper spouse had been ripped away from him but now she worried that he was only saying kind things because he had no other option. "Why aren't you angry that your freedom of choice has been taken away? Wouldn't you rather be married to someone else?"

"Would you?" he asked, bringing her hand to his chest. "Is that what this is about? You prefer someone else?"

"No," she whispered as her palm warmed in answer to the thumping beat of his heart. "I don't," she said then quickly added, "so many things have happened since I've left England that I'm unsure about-"

"If time is what you need, time is what you shall have," he said as he lifted her hand away from his chest. Turning it palm up, he placed a kiss in the center of it. She stared in wonder as he gently folded her fingers over his kiss. "In the meantime, if you need anything, please promise me that you'll notify me," he added as he released it gently.

She stared at her rapidly cooling hand. "I-I will," she stammered as she noticed he took a step back. Disappointment smothered her hope. She couldn't let him leave without some token of her true feelings. Standing on tip-toes, she gave an impulsive peck to Niko's cheek.

Surprise held Niko immobile for a moment, then he asked, "What was that for?"

"To thank you for your thoughtful words," she said then turned and tossed a quick, "Good night," as she hurried toward Etel's wagon.

Niko rubbed at the boulder-sized lump settling in his chest. Did she mean that she needed more time to figure out whether she loved him...or she needed more time to fall in love with him? Either way, he wanted her to realize that she loved him. He hoped he'd made it clear that no matter how their marriage had come about, married they would stay. He took a deep breath daunted by their uncertain future and went to get his sleeping blanket.

Sometimes doing the right thing wasn't the easiest route to walk. But he loved her enough to give her time to grow accustomed to the idea of them living together as husband and wife. Spreading out his gear next to where his men were bedded down, he decided that only time would tell if he had chosen the wisest path to follow.

Chapter Nineteen

Belle placed her hands on Niko's shoulders as he lifted her off the horse in front of the wide palace steps. Although it had been a long morning, she noted his devilish smile as he lowered her slowly to the ground. Heat flushed her cheeks as their bodies brushed against each other causing a warmth to pool in her lower abdomen. Her breath hitched in her chest. Just because they were married didn't mean she was ready to act on it. They had a few things to iron out before that.

"It appears I'll make a horsewoman out of you yet," he said as he set her on her feet.

"Appearances can be deceptive," she said then inhaled sharply as she realized her faux pas. "I am so sorry," she whispered. "I didn't mean to make light of the ruse we perpetrated against you."

"It is all right," he said, offering his arm to her. "You are absolutely correct. While it's a lesson I won't forget...I have already forgiven you," he said as they entered the palace foyer. "Remember, I also didn't reveal the total truth to you." His forehead furrowed for a moment then relaxed as she heard his deep sigh. "I know you must be exhausted but will I see you at the mid-day meal?"

"I will be there," she said. "But first, I need to present the Amnesty Petition to the King."

"I advise we present that to my cousin after we eat," he said as they began to ascend the grand staircase to the next floor.

"Then I'd best find Aunt Ellie and have that serious discussion I'd planned to have with her," she said.

He nodded. "While you are with your aunt, I'm going to introduce your brother and the Major to Stefan, that is as soon as they find their way inside," he added as he turned to look behind them.

"Good luck with that," she whispered, relieved she wouldn't be there to witness it. "My brother has this nasty habit of lobbing long-winded paragraphs at one so rapidly that it leaves your head spinning," she warned then hesitated as she realized she didn't want to part from him. But needing to set things straight, she gave a small wave as they parted company in the corridor in front of the throne room.

Belle hurried up the stairs to the next level then crept toward the sitting room that she had shared with Rita a few days ago. Slowly opening the door, she stood quietly inside the room for a moment. Her sister sat at a small desk scratching away while their aunt paced in front of the long windows overlooking the back garden. She cleared her throat, softly. "Hello," she said brightly.

Their aunt turned then gasped. "Belle, where have you been?" she asked as she rushed toward her. "I've been worried sick about you." She enfolded Belle in a fierce hug. "Why did you disappear?"

A burning sense of regret swept through Belle as she returned the hug. Although she hadn't purposely sought to worry her aunt, Belle knew the past two days had irrevocably changed her. And given the results, if the exact set of circumstances presented itself again, she would repeat her actions. "It matters not where I've been," she said, releasing her aunt and stepping away. "But what I've come to discover."

"And what would that be?" Her sister asked, her tone as tart as a fresh cut lemon.

"The truth," Belle replied removing her borrowed cape and placing it on a chair near the door. Turning, she lifted her chin, her chest muscles tightening in readiness.

"And I suppose you think the truth will set you free?" Rita asked, fiddling with the feather pen she held in her hand.

"Whether it does or doesn't remains to be seen." Clenching her fists, Belle strolled toward her twin.

"Then precisely what are you wanting to know?" Rita asked, setting her pen aside.

Belle pivoted toward their Aunt Ellie standing near the long windows with a worried frown marring her middle-aged face. "The day our parents died, was I coming to stay with you?"

"Oh, my dear, child," their aunt gushed as if in relief. Rushing forward, Aunt Ellie enfolded her in another hug. "Yes, you were."

Returning the warming hug, Belle leaned back and briefly studied her aunt's face. "Was it because Rita had contracted the measles?" she asked, watching for any tell-tale signs their aunt lied.

"That," their aunt nodded, innocently, "and your staff who had families living in the village were also ill," Aunt Ellie added before she released her hold and took a step back. "The circumstances were dire. There just wasn't enough help to take care of everyone," she said as she extracted her lace handkerchief from her cuff and dabbed at her eyes.

"I see," Belle muttered. She frowned as heat singed the back of her throat. Swirling around, she leveled her index finger at her sister. "Then why did you punish me for our parents' deaths all of these years?" She waited as her outburst fractured the silence in the room. She heard their aunt gasp as her sister stood slowly, her mouth opening and closing like a fish gasping for its last breath.

Finally, her sister said, "Well...Edward said that-"

"Edward was covering his own short-comings," Aunt Ellie inserted as she rushed forward to stand between the two.

"What?" Belle wheezed as shock held her immobile for a moment.

"With Edward being his heir, my brother thought his son could do no wrong," Aunt Ellie said, balling her kerchief in her hand. "My husband could never understand why they died on that particular day... and on that particular stretch of road. So, he investigated it," she said, her hands no longer moving. "Though he could never find any witnesses or evidence, he often felt it had something to do with your brother's gambling...and other proclivities," she said, using her kerchief to blot her flushed cheeks. "That's why we secured your dowries so that Edward couldn't touch them."

"So, you think Edward is the one behind the death of our parents?" Rita asked. A dazed look settled on her face.

"I do think so," Aunt Ellie said then shook her head. "But being still at university, who was going to come forward and press charges against a boy who had just inherited the Dukedom?" she asked. "You must realize no concrete evidence was ever found," she said twisting her hanky this way and that. "But my husband and I always felt there were too many coincidences that pointed to Edward."

Ice seemed to have settled in her veins for Belle felt frozen to the spot. "Why haven't you said something before now?"

"I had no idea something needed to be said," their aunt said in a broken whisper. "A-and even if I had, I have no proof...only suppositions."

Belle nodded, knowing she had been just as at fault. She should've questioned their aunt about what she knew about the accident long before now. But their parents' deaths had been so traumatic she'd never wanted to remember, let alone talk about it. She swallowed back the bile rising in her throat. All of these years she had needlessly suffered barbed accusations and been the brunt of meanness from both her sister and her brother. Was she now expected to blithely sluff that animosity off? She clenched her jaw as she raised her gaze to stare at her twin. One thing for certain, if she was ever to find peace of mind, there were a few basic rules Rita needed to understand.

Briefly, Belle scanned the room's interior, deciding her next move. Aunt Ellie had returned to her embroidery hoop. She sat stabbing the needle into the cloth and pulling the needle quickly through the material. As for Rita, she had returned to the desk. Belle squared her shoulders and stepped toward her twin. "Just so you know, I meant every word I said to you the other day. Don't ever ask me to take your place again... or demand that I fetch for you...or ask me to be you emissary or go-between. I will not do it. Do you understand?"

"Like a brass bell," Rita said as she paused in sanding her letter.

"Good," Belle said as she strolled forward to stand beside the desk her twin sat behind. Pressing her palms flat on the surface, she leaned forward. "And if you ever lay your lips on Nikolai...or so much as bat an eyelash at him...I'll gut you like a fish. Are we also clear about that?"

Belle watched her twin visibly swallow and vigorously nod.

"Good," she said, straightening. Pulling off her gloves she turned toward their Aunt. "Edward and Tony are meeting with King Stefan as we speak. Shall we go to join them?"

"What?" Rita squealed. "Tony is here!" Belle shifted her gaze to watch her twin pop out of the chair and rush toward the door.

"He's in the throne room," she called as her sister disappeared into the corridor.

"Wait for us," their aunt called. "I didn't get a chance to tell you–"

"I'm afraid your news will have to wait," Belle said threading her arm through her aunt's. Then she also realized that she had a bit of news to relate as well.

Chapter Twenty

Niko strolled into the throne room then stepped aside to wait for the Duke and Tony to join him. As he glanced at his cousin sitting at his desk off to the side of the room, he felt his own eyes widen. Stefan wasn't dressed for the marriage ceremony that was to begin in less than two hours. He took a deep breath, hoping his prayers had been answered and the ceremony had been canceled...permanently.

"Good," Stefan called, motioning him forward. "Nikolai, come here," he said waving off the Duke and the Major. As Niko walked toward his cousin, Stefan grabbed a rolled scroll and shook it out. "I just can't do this," his cousin said, dangling the scroll in front of him. "I've changed my mind," he added as he took a small knife from the top of his desk. "I cannot and will not marry the Lady Rita."

"Really?" Niko said, relief holding him captive for a moment.

A shout of "No," came from behind him. Recognizing the Duke's voice and the sound of footsteps rushing up behind him, Niko feared the Duke was about to attack his cousin. He turned and without regard to the Duke's previous injuries, rammed his elbow into the man, knocking him out of the way. He had pledged to keep his cousin safe, no matter what he had to do. Stepping protectively in front of Stefan, he watched as the Duke groaned and picked himself up off the floor.

"You can't renege on our agreement," Edward wheezed, rubbing at his chest. "You get Rita and I get grandfather's estate," he added, shaking his fist at the King. "That was the bargain."

As Stefan came to stand beside him, Rita followed by Belle and their aunt rushed into the throne room.

"Tony," Rita screeched as she bolted toward him. The guards stepped forward, denying the women further access into the room.

Swiftly, his cousin called out. "Guards, allow them to pass." As the men released the women, Stefan made a shooing motion with his hands. "Now leave but remain close at hand outside," he ordered.

As the sentries left the room, Rita rushed forward. Throwing her arms around the Major's neck, she pulled his lips to hers. As the Major wrapped his arms around Rita, he turned, shielding their moment of intimacy.

"I am not marrying the Lady Rita," Stefan shouted as he strode forward and extended his hand to their aunt. "But I am marrying the Lady Ellie who consented to be my wife early this morning," he added in a modulated tone.

Niko felt a smile curl his lips at the welcome news his cousin was marrying Lady Edgecombe instead of Belle's sister. All he wanted to do was shout in relief.

"But how can Aunt Ellie become your wife when you are already married to Rita?" Belle asked as his attention snapped back to what was happening in the room.

"No, he's not married to me," Rita said peeking over Tony's shoulder.

"But I was there," Belle said, turning to face her sister. "I witnessed the whole thing as the Admiral married you to the King by proxy."

"While you did witness a marriage, it was your name I signed on the bottom of the certificate, not my own," Rita said.

Niko inhaled sharply as an icy deluge cascaded through him. "What?" he heard everyone shout as if from afar. He shook his head to clear his senses. As Belle seemed to wilt before his eyes, he moved to stand beside her, ready to catch her if she fainted.

"I told you that I would not marry anyone sight unseen," Rita said folding her arms over her chest and beginning to tap the toe of her shoe against the marble floor.

"So, instead you not only disobeyed me but Queen Victoria as well," Edward said, his face flushed red.

"I told you that I wouldn't marry anyone but Tony," she said. She rested her cheek against the Major's gaunt chest.

He glanced down at Belle to see how she was fairing.

A hot core of anger swept through Belle. "Well, at least one of us will be happy," Belle mumbled then hardened her jaw. Although Rita might think she would have the last word and blithely skip away without being held accountable for the mess she'd created, Belle wasn't about to let that happen. Her future with Niko demanded she stay strong.

She glanced up at Niko and noticed his worried frown. She threaded her arm through his and watched his face relax. She would fight with tooth and nail to free herself from her sister's deception. Her breath hitched as he laid his warm hand over hers. She smiled as her heart trilled in her chest.

"I will not release you," he whispered, dipping his head toward her.

"Nor will I you," she said as she heard a throat clear nearby.

"I believe there might be a way to solve this quagmire," the King said. "Fetch me that proxy."

Belle squeezed Niko's hand as hope bubbled inside her.

"Right away, Your Majesty," Rita said pulling Tony from the room with her.

"Hurry," Stefan called after them then stepped forward to lift Aunt Ellie's hand upward. "We have about an hour. We might still have time to make it to the altar in time, my love."

"Then we shall," her aunt said, dipping her head.

Belle found herself studying her blushing aunt. Then as happy tears welled in her eyes, her gaze turned to Niko and regret swept through her. She had missed her opportunity to be with Niko.

"Why not just decree the proxy invalid," Niko said. "As one of the principal parties, you were never notified of it happening," he added. "It shouldn't take but a few minutes to have the scribes work it up for your signature."

"Good idea, Nikolai," his cousin said. "You have always been more astute than I."

"Here it is, Your Majesty," Rita said as she rushed into the room waving the proxy in the air. Handing it to the King, she curtsied. "And now if you will excuse me, Tony needs my care." Backing away, she turned and disappeared from the room.

Fear warred with hope as Belle stared at the proxy the King held. Rita was doing what she always did...leaving it to others to sort out her messes but was there a way to clean up her mess this time?

As the King read the proxy an uncomfortable silence stretched over the room. When finished, he seemed distracted as he drummed his fingers on his desk.

Belle felt her stomach plummet. "Well?" She asked unable to stand the suspense any longer.

"Just a moment," the King said. "I have a question for you, Prince

Nikolai," he said then cleared his throat. "Are you not first in line to inherit the title of King if anything should happen to me?"

Belle watched Niko frown. "I am," he said then rubbed the back of his neck. "But the rebels have surrendered and our uncle and the traitor Hondros are dead. Why are you asking me this when you are no longer in harm's way?"

"There are other forces to consider," Stefan said then scratched his chin as he turned to Aunt Ellie. "Dearest, would you be terribly disappointed if you weren't...crowned Queen?"

"Not at all," her aunt said, a serene smile stretching her lips wide. "Do whatever you wish. I will be just as happy being your wife and living away from the palace."

"That settles it," the King said slapping his hands on his desk as the Archbishop of the Cathedral hurried into the room wearing his impressive regalia.

"Your Majesty," the Archbishop said with a bow. "You will be late for your wedding if you do not hurry," he added as he straightened. He paused as his jaw dropped open. "B-but, what seems to be the delay?"

"It seems the Queen of England had me marry this young woman by proxy without informing either of us of the deed," the King said as he waved the proxy at the Archbishop.

"England had no right to do that," the Archbishop huffed. "Barovian law clearly states in a proxy, all parties must be notified. If not, the contract is null and void."

"Excellent," the King said as he grabbed a pen off his desk. Dipping it into the ink, he slashed a diagonal line across the paper and wrote the words, 'null and void' in bold letters on it. Then dipping his ring into melted wax, he affixed his symbol to the document and gave a hearty laugh.

Belle felt joy bubble inside her. She raised her gaze to meet Niko's. They smiled at each other. "We are free," she whispered.

"To be with each other," Niko said as a grin curved his lips upward.

"Does this mean the wedding is canceled?" the Archbishop asked, disappointment coloring his tone.

"Not yet," Stefan said. "Now that I'm no longer married to the Lady Belle, I am free to marry Lady Edgecombe. Shall we do it today, my dear?"

"Yes," she whispered then leaned in to receive his kiss.

"Excellent," the King said after giving her a peck on the lips. Straightening, he waved Belle and Niko forward. "Now that I am free to marry the woman I love, I am going to step down as King and pass my crown and scepter to a much younger and more qualified man than I. To you, my first cousin, Prince Nikolai."

Surprise followed quickly by wariness rushed through Niko. "Why are you doing this?"

"Because I realize it's not enough to be a kind ruler," his cousin said. "One needs knowledge and leadership skills. You have those. You know when to strike and when to pull back. When to advance an agenda and when to hold your ground. And you balance the scales with honor and integrity. You have the welfare of this country always in the foreground and are the man this country needs to forge ahead and bring it into recovery. Will you do this for me and the people of this nation?"

Niko gaped at his cousin for a moment then switched his gaze to Belle who stood nodding, a smile on her face. Slowly, he turned back to face his cousin. "I will but only if you will remain at my side as my main advisor and assist me with the Council of Elders."

"I will," Stefan said then chuckled. "And my first duty will be to find you a Queen." He grinned down at his intended. "What about Lady Belle? She looks to be up for another adventure," he said. "Besides, she's smart, sweet and lovely, and would be an asset to this country."

"She has already brokered a fair and balanced amnesty agreement between us and the rebels," Niko said as he lifted her hand and kissed the back of it. "I would say, she will be a phenomenal Queen. What say you, Lady Belle?"

As Belle gazed up at him, a calmness flowed through her. "I believe we might be able to negotiate a deal," she said then paused to study his face. "But first I need to tell you...that I love you."

"You are the Queen of my heart," Niko said, dipping his head. "I will love you for now and always."

"As will I," she promised as she stood on her tip-toes. "But shouldn't we tell them that we're already married?" she whispered.

"Later my love," he said near her ear. "Let's not spoil their fun," he added then lowered his lips to meet hers.

The End

About the author

L.J. Dare has always loved reading, especially a romance that is based on history and includes a dash of mystery. She is a retired teacher who has wandered the world with her military spouse. Currently, she lives in Western Arizona with her husband. When she isn't writing, reading or researching, she can be found out in the garden or in her kitchen creating new flavors of fudge that she donates to various charities for fundraising events.

Also by L.J. Dare

The King's Blade

After surviving a massacre, Lady Megan MacKelloch intends on seeking sanctuary with the Poor Claires for herself and her young sisters. That is until Lord John Lindsay, known as The King's Blade, is ordered to find her.
As the Crown's chief criminal investigator, Lindsay metes out justice as he deals with murder, betrayal and intrigue but never has he encountered such female resistance. Life has taught John and Megan not to believe in love. So, when forced into marriage by a Royal Decree, can they set aside their differences and learn to trust their hearts?

More of our titles

Their Lady Gloriana by Starla Kaye
Cowboys in Charge by Starla Kaye
Her Cowboy's Way by Starla Kaye
Punished by Richard Savage, Nadia Nautalia & Starla Kaye
Accidental Affair by Leslie McKelvey
Right Place, Right Time by Leslie McKelvey
Her Sister's Keeper by Leslie McKelvey
Playing for Keeps by Glenda Horsfall
Playing By His Rules by Glenda Horsfall
The Stir of Echo by Susan Gabriel
Rally Fever by Crea Jones
Behind The Clouds by Jan Selbourne
Trusting Love Again by Starla Kaye
Runaway Heart by Leslie McKelvey
The Otherling by Heather M. Walker
First Submission - Anthology
These Eyes So Green by Deborah Kelsey
Dark Awakening by Karlene Cameron
The Reclaiming of Charlotte Moss by Heather M. Walker
Ryann's Revenge by Rai Karr & Breanna Hayse
The Postman's Daughter by Sally Anne Palmer
Final Kill by Leslie McKelvey
Killer Secrets by Zia Westfield
Crossover, Texas by Freia Hooper-Bradford
The King's Blade by L.J. Dare
Uniform Desire - Anthology
Safe by Keren Hughes
Finishing the Game by M.K. Smith
Out of the Shadows by Gabriella Hewitt
A Woman's Secret by C.L. Koch
Her Lover's Face by Patricia Elliott
Love Times Infinity by K.L. Ramsey
Naval Maneuvers by Dee S. Knight
Perilous Love by Jan Selbourne
Love's Patient Journey by K.L. Ramsey
Patrick by Callie Carmen
Love's Design by K.L. Ramsey

www.ingramcontent.com/pod-product-compliance
Lightning Source LLC
Chambersburg PA
CBHW030138180626
46812CB00002B/743